"What do you wear to sleep in?"

"T-shirt and cotton shorts usually," Anna said, crawling into bed next to him. "Or a cami if it's hot."

"No fancy nighties made of silk and lace?" Duke asked.

"No. Why?"

"I don't know—guess I just thought you seemed like that kind of girl."

"I actually have a lot of that kind of stuff. Just haven't worn it in a while. Are you disappointed I don't wear lacy stuff every night?"

"Nah. I bet you're cute as hell in your t-shirt and shorts. And hot as hell in your lace when you decide to wear it. Hell—guess I don't much care what you wear 'cause you'd make anything look good."

A soft grin stole over her, "Then why'd you ask?"

"Guess I just wanted to be able to picture you here, what you'd look like going to bed at night."

"And what do you wear to sleep in, Mr. Dawson?"

"Sometimes underwear. And sometimes nothin' at all."

When her cheeks pinkened, but her expression appeared more aroused than embarrassed, he gave a small laugh and said, "You gonna picture that in your head when you lay down to sleep tomorrow night?"

By Toni Blake

TONI BLAKE

HALF MOON HILL

A DESTINY NOVEL

AVON
An Imprint of HarperCollinsPublishers

This is a work of fiction. Names, characters, places, and incidents are products of the author's imagination or are used fictitiously and are not to be construed as real. Any resemblance to actual events, locales, organizations, or persons, living or dead, is entirely coincidental.

AVON BOOKS
An Imprint of HarperCollins*Publishers*
10 East 53rd Street
New York, New York 10022-5299

First Avon Books mass market printing: May 2013

Avon Trademark Reg. U.S. Pat. Off. and in Other Countries, Marca Registrada, Hecho en U.S.A.
HarperCollins® is a registered trademark of HarperCollins Publishers.

Printed in the U.S.A.

10 9 8 7 6 5 4 3 2 1

To Lindsey Faber
for being by my side through thick and thin,
and for being the most patient, caring,
considerate friend a girl could ever have.
I don't know what I'd do without you!

Acknowledgments

My sincere appreciation goes to:

Lindsey Faber, for early brainstorming, note-taking, plot-problem-solving, and being an amazingly supportive friend and cheerleader as I wrote this book.

Renee Norris, for lightning-fast feedback as my official "first reader" and for, as always, finding the problem spots and figuring out how to fix them. You help me make every book better than it was when I gave it to you.

Michael Perry, for answering my questions about home repair and renovation, and for giving me a couple of ideas that made their way into the story.

My agents, Meg Ruley and Christina Hogrebe, for their fantastic support in so many ways over the last eight years.

My editor, May Chen, for her incredible patience when I ran late, and for always being super fun and easy to work with.

Pam Spengler-Jaffee, Shawn Nicholls, and everyone else at Avon who does such a great job getting the word out about my books!

" . . . one can get used to everything . . . if one wishes . . . "

Gaston Leroux, *The Phantom of the Opera*

One

*A*nna Romo had actually begun to like the peace and quiet. Maybe a little too much. As she stepped off the porch of the old Victorian house she'd bought last summer on Half Moon Hill, soaking up the solitude and delighting in birdsong coming from the trees that surrounded the place, she stopped in her tracks and cringed. *Who am I? When did this happen?* She'd never delighted in birdsong in her life. And she'd never consciously used the word *birdsong*, out loud or in her thoughts, either. Clearly, the town of Destiny was getting to her.

Oh God, I'm becoming one of them.

Not that she was sure why that sounded so unpleasant to her. She liked the people here. She even loved some of them—in particular, her brothers, and she'd grown quite attached to their wives, too. And the rest of Destiny's residents—well, they were just good, kind people, no two ways about it. She'd begun to make real friends here. And she'd come to appreciate the small town welcome she'd received—even if it had overwhelmed her a little at first.

But no matter how much she loved or liked them all, she really *wasn't* one of them. She'd grown up in the city. And her life had been . . . well, all things considered, words like *bizarre* and *challenging* didn't even begin to scratch the surface.

Then, just over a year ago, her mother had died. Well, her "other mother." And that had come with money—an unexpected and ample amount that had been passed down through the family and saved just for her. Yet an inheritance had done little to make up for the shocking truths that had been revealed on her mother's deathbed. That was when *bizarre* and *challenging* had taken on whole new meanings.

And somehow it had all led her *here*, to a hometown she didn't remember, to a whole family she didn't remember, and to this house she was refurbishing with plans of opening a bed-and-breakfast—if she ever got the renovations done.

She'd come out to check the mail, but now stopped and turned to face the house. Parts of the awning that covered the wraparound porch sagged as if being pulled down by invisible anchors, and most of the gutters were rusted, some sections having disintegrated altogether. The roof desperately needed replacing, several shutters hung at a tilt, and parts of the porch had begun to rot, the decorative gingerbread trim suffering most of all. And the whole once-white house, along with the detached garage, was sorely in need of paint.

She'd spent the entire winter and most of spring working on the inside, room by room, and she was proud of her progress. But now that she'd flipped the calendar page over to May and warm weather was here, she couldn't avoid starting on the outside any longer. The only problem being that the project made her feel the same way the town of Destiny, Ohio once had: overwhelmed.

"Meow."

Flinching, she glanced over at the fluffy black cat who was always sneaking up on her. One minute she was alone—the next the cat appeared out of nowhere. She eyed him warily. "Why don't you go catch a mouse or something?"

"Meow." He looked at her like he wanted something, but she had no idea what. She'd fed him already today—twice. That was always what she did when he came meowing around—because she had no idea what else he could be asking for.

"Look, I don't know what you want from me. And I'm beginning to think this was a bad idea."

A bed-and-breakfast needs a cat, Amy had said. *People will think it's quaint. He'll curl up in the front window, or in a rocking chair on the porch, and he'll give the place a feeling of warmth.* Okay, that much she had bought. *And besides*, Amy had gone on, *you'll love having a cat. And he'll love having a real home.* Those parts, though, weren't quite happening.

Amy Bright owned the bookstore on the town square, Under the Covers, and as Destiny's resident cat lover, she was always taking in strays at the shop, letting them live there until she could find someone to adopt them. And the truth was, Anna had only adopted Erik—as Amy had named the cat, after the "Opera Ghost," upon once finding him asleep on a shelf next to the original *Phantom of the Opera* novel—because she and Amy had gotten off to a rocky start when she'd first come to town. She'd felt it might help cement their growing friendship—and besides, she'd seen Erik as a bit of an outsider, just like her.

But so far, she hadn't fallen in love with having a cat. Amy had apparently succeeded in making everyone *else* in Destiny fall in love with cats—both of Anna's brothers and their wives had adopted a bookstore cat, as well as her real estate agent, Sue Ann. So she'd taken the cat on faith. But this just provided more proof that, deep down, she'd never really be like everyone else here. She'd never really fit in the way the rest of them did.

Which maybe explains why you spend all your time alone in this big, empty house.

In the beginning, the idea had made perfect sense. Buying the old home that had been on the market for nearly ten years had been about starting over, finding her place here, finding a way to take her background in the hotel industry in Indianapolis and integrate it with life in Destiny. And the fact that the home was in a relatively isolated area outside town, on the tall bluff overlooking Blue Valley Lake far below, had been convenient for putting a little much-needed distance between herself and her brothers—especially the oldest, overprotective one, Mike.

It had seemed like the ideal solution to numerous problems. And maybe it still would be. She remained excited and energized by looking forward to the day when the Half Moon Bed & Breakfast opened its doors for business. But somehow or other, without quite planning it, she'd become a hermit at the tender age of thirty-one. And as someone who had been a very confident, outgoing woman when she'd first arrived here, she wasn't sure how that had happened.

The slightly twisted, gray metal mailbox that had seen better days was empty. Big surprise. She didn't get a lot of mail. And some days she wondered why she bothered to check it at all.

So what now?

You could drive into town. Go to the bookstore. Stop by the police station and see if Mike's there—God knew it would make her overprotective brother's day if she purposely paid him a visit.

Or . . . she could do something that sounded easier.

Berries. You can pick berries. She'd seen some blackberries on a walk in the woods recently, but they hadn't yet been ripe. Maybe they would be now. *Maybe you can make a pie from them.* Not that she'd ever made a pie in her life. But it seemed like something an innkeeper should be able to do. And if she picked berries today instead of going into town, she wouldn't have to try to fit in and pretend she had life completely under control.

Heading into the large detached garage, which held her 1965 cherry red Mustang and also served as storage space for now, she retrieved one of several brown wicker baskets that had hung from nails on the wall since before her arrival.

A moment later, the scent of freshly blooming honeysuckle met her nose as she stepped from the bright sunlight at the yard's edge into the shaded isolation of the woods. At first, going for walks here had made her uncomfortable—it was one more new experience that had taken a little getting used to. But she'd soon discovered there was nothing to fear, and while the house and her yard were both peaceful, there was something different about being surrounded by the lush green of the woods. The forest was a distinct world of its own, one that couldn't be easily tamed or controlled, and maybe she liked that a little.

She moved past tall, thick, old trees and stepped her way carefully through low shrubbery and brush. A glimpse of yellow wildflowers in the distance made her smile—though they were hidden deep in the woods, seeing them meant their beauty wasn't wasted.

Oh God, this place really is *getting to you.* She'd never thought such deep thoughts, let alone about something as pure as nature, before coming to Destiny.

But if you're changing in ways, it must be because you want to.

She'd just caught the scent of more honeysuckle when something moved up ahead. She didn't see anything—but she'd just entered a particularly dark, shady part of the woods. So she just kept walking. Where were those berries anyway? Hadn't they been right around here? She returned to scanning the low greenery around her looking for ripened blackberries.

Aha—there they were! And they looked nice and plump

and dark, ready for picking, just like the pictures she'd Googled to make sure.

She'd just started dropping the big, healthy-looking berries into her basket, though, when the brush moved again, much closer to her this time—and she looked up to find . . . oh dear Lord, a wildman. The sight paralyzed her, fear numbing every limb.

Over six feet in height and bulging with muscles that gave her the impression he could tear her limb from limb, he emerged through a patch of tall shrubbery, flashing crazy, piercing blue-gray eyes. Unkempt brown hair hung to his shoulders and a scraggly beard covered the bottom half of his face, not quite obscuring the angry scar that slashed its way down one cheek.

Anna lost her breath, let the basket drop to the ground, then began to take instinctive steps backward—promptly stumbling over a large tree root. Her butt collided with the packed earth as she tried to break the fall with her hands. Pain shot through her ankle and she heard a cry of anguish escape her throat, all the while sensing the rapid approach of the brute who had somehow materialized out of nowhere in her woods.

Get up. Get away. That was what her brain was telling her, but her body wasn't quite obeying. She struggled to get to her feet, but her ankle gave out as she rose, and she landed on her rear again, even harder this time.

She raised her eyes to the hairy beast now stalking her. Oh God, his eyes were still just as crazed! Where on earth had he come from? Her heart beat like a drum in her chest as she flew into defensive mode—*flight* had failed, so that left only *fight* to fall back on. "Who the hell are you and where did you come from?"

Despite the question, she hadn't quite anticipated him replying with "For God's sake, Daisy Duke, relax," in a deep, raspy voice that actually sounded . . . well, surprisingly confident for a wildman. She'd imagined him communicating more by . . . grunting or something.

But wait a minute. He thought she was Daisy Duke? Like from the old *Dukes of Hazzard* TV show? Clearly, this meant he really *was* crazy, or at least not in his right mind.

Her reaction? Another desperate attempt to get to her feet and get the hell out of here before he attacked her—but it turned out to be just as futile and she ended up plopping painfully to her ass again with an "*Oomph.*"

"Jesus, woman, stay down already," he told her. "Doesn't seem like walking's your strong suit."

She flinched. Whoa. The wildman was actually insulting her now? She huffed out a breath. "I'm injured, you Neanderthal."

"Well, it's no fucking wonder the way you keep falling down. Sit still, for the love of God."

She just blinked, doubly stunned now. "Who the hell *are* you?" she asked again. "And what are you doing in my woods?"

His eyes still looked just as menacing, but his answer came with a bit less bite. "I didn't know they were *your* woods. I'm just . . . staying in the cabin awhile."

The cabin? What cabin could he mean? She didn't know of any—

But then she stopped mid-thought, her jaw dropping. Because maybe she did know the structure he was referring to—but if so, she thought *cabin* a generous description.

She supposed it had been a cabin once upon a time, but it had long since decayed into an old shack that tilted to one side, its decrepit walls covered with ivy. She'd assumed the only creatures inhabiting the place were more along the lines of rodents. Of course, she still thought this guy looked more like beast than man, so maybe that didn't bother him. But . . . why the hell would someone live in that place? Was he just some wandering homeless dude? And what was she going to do about him?

When she didn't reply, he narrowed those gray eyes of his to say, "You really don't know who I am, do you?"

Huh. She was supposed to? The fleeting idea that he was

some famous rock star who'd decided to run away from it all flitted through her mind as she replied, "No. That's why I keep asking who you are."

"I'm Duke," he finally told her. "Duke Dawson."

Even while seated on the ground, Anna drew back slightly. She couldn't have been more surprised if he *had* turned out to be a rock star. "Lucky's friend?" she asked, utterly bewildered. Because she'd met her youngest brother's best friend, Duke, several times, but . . . well, he hadn't looked like *this*.

"Yep."

"So . . . you don't really think I'm Daisy Duke," she felt the need to clarify.

And he sighed as if *she* were the one making this a difficult conversation. "Of course not—Anna," he said pointedly as his gaze dropped to her denim shorts.

Oh—they were what people called Daisy Dukes. Sort of.

But even if a few things were starting to become clear, some definitely were not. "What are you doing out here? I mean . . ." And then everything she knew about Duke Dawson's situation, gleaned from Lucky, came rushing through her head. Some months back, Duke had witnessed a bad accident. He'd gotten injured. A friend had died. And as a result, he'd sold his business—a biker bar called Gravediggers— and moved to Indiana where he had family.

But apparently that last part wasn't exactly true.

"Let's just say I'm not into being around people right now." *Or into engaging in common hygiene, either, apparently*— but she kept that part to herself.

Rather than respond to what he'd said—because things were awkward enough here and she barely knew him—she replied, "Surely you can understand why I didn't recognize you. Unless you haven't seen a mirror lately."

"I haven't," he said. "Not real concerned with what I look like right now." And his tone warned her not to explore that topic further, which left her flailing about for what to say next—when he solved the problem for her by going on. "You got a problem with me using the cabin?"

Did she? And if she did, was she brave enough to tell him so? "Um, not really, I guess. I just . . . well, it's not exactly the Ritz."

"I don't need the Ritz. Don't need much right now at all except to be left alone."

Everything about him continued to unnerve her. "Okay," she said, still more due to feeling intimidated than because it was really okay with her.

"And you can't tell Lucky or anyone else I'm here."

Once more, she found herself balking from her spot on the ground. Because agreeing to let him stay was one thing—but keeping a secret from her brother, who loved Duke enough that he'd asked him to be the best man in his wedding? That seemed like a lot more to ask. "You want me to lie to Lucky? Why?"

"It's not about Lucky. It's like I said—just don't wanna be around people right now. Wanna be left alone. And that was going pretty well until today."

She let her gaze widen at his curt tone. The nerve of him. "Yes, it was terrible of me to think I could pick berries on my own property."

At this, his slate gray eyes shifted to the fallen basket and the berries scattered around it. "You never struck me as the berry-picking type, Daisy Duke."

"I'm not. Usually," she admitted. "But maybe I'm trying to be . . . more like everyone else here."

"Also never struck me as the type to go changing just to please other people."

"I'm not trying to please anyone but me," she informed him—but still felt judged by a guy she thought in no position to be doing that. "And on that note, I'll just leave you to your skulking about in the woods—or whatever you were doing before I got here."

After which she pulled her feet up under her and started to stand—only to have her ankle give out once more. "Damn it," she snapped as her butt connected painfully with the ground yet again.

"I *told* ya to give it up and stay down."

She flashed Duke Dawson a light sneer. "Well, I can't just sit here forever, can I?"

The excess hair on Duke's face didn't hide his annoyed expression. "Guess I'm gonna have to help you."

Oh hell. As much as she wanted to end this bizarre encounter, it did indeed look that way. "Sorry to put you out," she said, her voice thick with sarcasm.

And then Duke Dawson—who still didn't look a bit like Duke Dawson to her—reached a hand down to her. "Don't put weight on the bad one," he reminded her, and between following that advice and taking his hand, she finally managed to stand—albeit only on one foot.

And as if things weren't awkward enough already, he then bent to smoothly curve one arm around her back and the other beneath her thighs, hoisting her easily into his arms, same as a bride about to be carried across a threshold. She tried to hold in her gasp of surprise but didn't succeed. She'd thought he was going to support her while she limped—not pick her up.

"Put your arm around my neck," he instructed, and such close contact instantly made her feel . . . too warm. She suffered the urge to wriggle free somehow, though she wasn't sure exactly why. Was it because he looked so different to her now, like a stranger, making this seem way too personal? Because being in his grasp brought her eyes so close to the scar on his cheek? Because he was grubby and smelly from living in the woods? But no, it wasn't the last one—since he smelled more . . . musky and masculine than dirty. His scent filled her senses as he started toward the shack just a stone's throw away, so blanketed with ivy that it almost blended completely into the forest.

"Wait," she said, remaining startlingly aware of just how close they were. "We're going the wrong way. My house is in the other direction." She pointed over his shoulder.

"Didn't realize it was you who lived there 'til now," he

said in his usual detached tone. "But I'm not taking you to your house. We're going to the cabin."

Anna flinched yet one more time, just before she glared into his eyes. Except—yikes, that might not have been the best move. They were looking at each other, their eyes uncomfortably close given that they barely knew each other, and she was struck by the depth of their color. It made her think of storm clouds, gunmetal—there was something harsh yet stunning there.

But she refused to let that daunt her as she prepared to protest.

"I don't *want* to go to the cabin," she told him in her most commanding voice—the one she generally saved for Mike and had failed to use successfully so far today. But this time it came out with all the authority intended. "I want to go to my house." Which suddenly sounded like the safest place in the universe compared to that ramshackle lean-to.

Because it had been bad enough to have the wits scared out of her by some beastly guy in the woods. And it seemed even worse that he was actually carrying her in his arms now. And despite Lucky's affinity for Duke, he could very well be dangerous. Clearly the guy wasn't exactly in a good place in life, after all. Living in the woods? Looking like a wolfman? Acting like she was the one trespassing here? It was one thing to let him help her—but that didn't mean she trusted him. And it sure as hell didn't mean she felt safe letting him take her inside that secluded little shack.

She waited for him to turn around and head the other way, back toward her house. Which was also fairly isolated but at least it sat along a road, where cars occasionally passed by. And where there was a phone.

Yet that was when Duke Dawson surprised her yet one more time, brusquely informing her, "Well, that's too damn bad, Daisy Duke. Since you don't seem to be the one calling the shots here, do ya?"

"Ah, I frighten you, do I?"

Gaston Leroux, *The Phantom of the Opera*

Two

*A*nna started feeling panicky all over again. Finding out the wildman was Duke and not some crazed derelict had calmed her fears—well, in some ways—but now her skin prickled with fresh worry. "Why? Why would you take me to the cabin?"

His look suggested she was an overreacting idiot. "Because it's a hell of a lot closer and I've got ice for the swelling."

Oh.

A glance down revealed to Anna that—dear Lord—her ankle was indeed fat and swollen. With all the excitement over running into a wild wolfman in the woods, and then figuring out he was actually her brother's best friend, she hadn't noticed. So maybe she *was* an overreacting idiot. But . . . "You have ice?"

Again, his expression implied that she was being thickheaded to assume he was living like a caveman. "I have a propane fridge."

"Oh." This time she said it out loud. And maybe the news made her feel a little better, since maybe his answers actually made some sense. But she still wished they were headed back to her place and not deeper into woods that suddenly felt darker and more forbidding by the second.

As they approached the fallen down shack, she noticed the old wooden door was missing a handle, sporting only small holes and indentions where it had once been—just about the time Duke lifted one foot to kick it open. She flinched anew at the loud *bang* and he gave her another look of irritation. "Relax, Daisy. I don't bite."

"I know that," she said firmly—but did she? Something about him certainly unnerved her. Part of it was the way he looked. And maybe now she was starting to remember more of what she knew about his past—like that years ago he'd been in an outlaw biker gang with Lucky. Somehow that had been forgivable when it was her reformed brother they were talking about, but right now the word *outlaw* suddenly sounded a lot scarier than it ever had before.

Inside, the cabin was a little more domesticated than she'd expected, but it looked far from comfortable—like the kind of place only a homeless person would appreciate.

An ancient Formica table with rounded silver edges sat in the middle of the floor, and on two adjacent sides stood old kitchen chairs with brown vinyl padding, one of them sporting a rip on the seat. The propane refrigerator he'd mentioned stood near another fridge that probably dated from the forties. And given the lack of running water, the old porcelain sink lined with rust stains appeared to serve more as storage for a few dishes than anything else. Other remnants of someone's past life here—tattered white curtains, a faded picture in a frame that hung tilted on a wall—sprinkled the place, but the only other signs of current life were a blow-up camping mattress and the dark green sleeping bag on top, and next to it on the floor a small battery-operated camping lamp.

As Duke lowered her gently into the untorn chair, she tried not to be too freaked out by thinking about him living here, by wondering what that meant and witnessing what most people would think of as squalor. And it was easy enough to focus on Duke himself instead. Because she still hadn't quite gotten used to how he looked now. And because she wondered if the scar bothered him and if, despite his attitude, he might secretly be embarrassed to have anyone see him this way. Another thing to focus on: He'd just returned from the fridge carrying a washcloth full of ice to sit down in the opposite chair and carefully lift her foot onto his knee.

His blue jeans were faded and worn, his knee sturdy. His hands were more gentle than they looked as he cupped her ankle in one and held the makeshift ice pack in place with the other.

She hissed as the freezing sensation made its way through the cloth and onto her bare flesh.

"Toughen up," he said in response—and she quickly decided any gentleness she'd just seen in him must have been a figment of her imagination.

"It's cold, damn it," she protested, sick of his attitude.

"Ice usually is," he groused. "If you're gonna go traipsing around in the woods, ya gotta get a little tougher, Daisy Duke."

"I wish you'd quit calling me that."

For the first time in a while, he raised his gaze to hers, unnerving her all the more. "Why? It suits you. Your shorts anyway. They show off those long, tan legs damn nice."

Anna just sat there. Normally she liked compliments as much as any girl. And usually she knew how to accept them, whether graciously or flirtatiously, given the particular situation. But she wasn't sure how to respond to this, now, from Duke Dawson—not only because he still frightened her a little, but because with one warm palm still cupping her ankle, she felt the sentiment ripple its way straight up her thigh. Which caught her completely off guard. She'd quit noticing the ice quite as much as she was noticing his touch.

When she didn't reply, Duke just let out a laugh, the hardiest sound she'd heard from him. And she didn't ask why because she wasn't sure she wanted to know.

"Is the swelling going down?" she asked instead, eager to change the subject.

"Give it a few minutes, Daisy. Don't be in such a rush."

Easy for him to say. With each passing second she became more anxious to leave, to be back in her homey, friendly house—which now seemed in her mind much homier and friendlier than ever before.

Even if the way he held her ankle felt good.

Maybe that was part of the problem here. He looked like a monster. And his behavior didn't exactly qualify as gentlemanly. So how could she possibly like the warmth of his hand on her ankle? Why was she so freaking *aware* of it, for that matter?

They stayed quiet after that, giving Anna time to vaguely wish the picture on the wall weren't so faded and that she could see it better from where she sat. She looked at the tattoo of a motorcycle on Duke's biceps, realizing that if she'd noticed it sooner, peeking from beneath the dingy sleeve of the snug white T-shirt he wore, she'd have known it was him.

"This should be above your heart," he said out of the blue.

She had no idea what he was talking about. "What?"

"When you're at home later, lie down and prop your ankle on pillows, so it's higher than your heart. Better for the swelling. But looks like it's going down some," he said, pulling the icy, wet cloth away to glance underneath.

She took the opportunity to carefully but swiftly lower her foot to the floor. His knee had become far too comfortable of a pillow for it. "Then I'll just head on home."

"Like hell you will," he grumbled.

And once more, she recoiled. "What's the problem *now*?"

"You're still not gonna be able to walk on that thing," he informed her.

"You don't think so?" she asked, feeling a little desperate at this point. "Because I—"

"Save it, Daisy. I'm carrying you."

Life had taught Anna how to handle weird or uncomfortable situations and she generally pulled it off without a hitch. She could usually convince herself she had things under control—even at times when, deep down, she didn't. Coping mechanisms—she had tons of them. So why were they all failing her now?

On the entire walk back through the woods, she stayed alarmingly aware of the places their bodies connected—which, under the circumstances, were quite a few. She continued to drink in his mannish, musky scent. And she tried not to look up at his face, but sometimes she did anyway—and it always came as a shock.

Of course, at first, what she noticed was mostly the beard, and all that scraggly, uncombed hair. Would it really be so much trouble to pick up a brush? But as the disquieting journey continued, and as she got a little more accustomed to studying him—surreptitiously, of course—she began to narrow in on other things. His eyes, which had drawn her attention earlier, too. Now they appeared sad and resolute, and maybe just a bit empty. And the little crinkles at their edges seemed to punctuate what she saw in them, marking him as a man who'd walked a tougher road than she—which, in her opinion, was saying something. She also lowered her stealthy gaze to that scar on his cheek. It was easier to see on closer inspection that it was fresh. There was something raw about it—the pink flesh looked tender, not quite healed, even though it had been a while since the accident. Maybe some wounds *never* healed.

They didn't speak as he carried her, which was a relief. In addition to the scent of Duke himself, the smell of honeysuckle and a hint of wild roses wafted past. And despite all her discomfort, a strange part of her was almost sorry when they emerged into her yard, back into what suddenly felt like real life.

After heading across the gravel driveway, then up the sagging front steps onto the porch, he asked, "Can you get the door? My hands are kinda full."

She looked to see if he was smiling, since it had sounded almost like he was making a joke—but he appeared as serious as he had most of the time so far. In response, she reached down for the screen door handle, opening it wide.

A few seconds later, he was lowering her to the couch in the front room.

"Don't happen to have any crutches, do ya?" he asked.

Normally, the answer would be no. But . . . "Actually, I think I've seen an old wooden pair in the attic, but I'm sure I don't need them."

He just gave her a look through those gray eyes that had turned steely again since leaving the shade of the forest. "Nah, somebody who can't walk wouldn't need crutches for anything," he said dryly, then turned to start glancing around the room—before peering down the hall. "How do you get to the attic?"

She rolled her eyes—which felt safe mostly because his back was to her. "Folding steps drop down from the second floor hallway, but . . ."

He was already headed toward the stairs like he owned the place, so she just saved her breath on the rest. And maybe he even had a point. She just didn't enjoy feeling like an invalid with him any more than she already did.

A few minutes later, she heard his footsteps on the staircase just before he reappeared, the old crutches in one hand. He wordlessly leaned them against one arm of the overstuffed couch. "I'm sure you're a smart enough girl to use these," he said—and then, just like that, he started back toward the foyer.

She was contemplating if she should say something when he glanced over his shoulder. "You're not gonna tell anybody I'm here, right?"

And Anna hesitated. She really didn't like the idea of keeping a secret from Lucky—God knew there'd been enough secrets in their family.

But she also understood wanting to distance yourself from people, and seeking a little solitude. So even if she still didn't understand why Duke Dawson was living in a horrible little shack in the woods, she finally said, "No, I won't."

In reply, he simply gave her a short nod and turned to go.

"Duke."

With his hand on the screen door, about to push it open, he stopped, looked back again.

"Why'd you take me to the cabin if you were only going to carry me back here anyway?" The question had occurred to her while he was in the attic.

In response, his expression darkened. "Why? Were you afraid? Think I had some evil plan I changed my mind about in the end?"

Lord—way to make an awkward situation much worse, Anna. Even if something in his tone *had* sounded a little ominous. "No," she said, unsure if it was the truth or a lie. "I just wondered."

"It was a judgment call," he told her. "Swelling went down some, but not enough, that's all. If it had gone down more, woulda saved me a hell of a walk with my arms full."

And despite herself, she resumed feeling a little weird to let him just leave like that. He'd been a jerk in ways, but he *had* helped her. Even when she'd been too stubborn to admit she *needed* help. So when he turned to depart again, she stopped him once more. This time with "Thank you. For taking care of me." But—oh God, she immediately wanted the words back. The way she'd phrased it, mostly. She didn't need a man to take care of her. She didn't need *anyone* to take care of her.

Yet he only said, "No problem, Daisy. But use the damn crutches 'til it feels better."

And then he was gone, the screen door slamming softly behind him.

Duke followed the same path down to the stream that he'd taken every day for the past month or two since he'd gotten here. He carried the old metal bucket he'd found in one corner of the cabin, thankful that someone, a long time ago, had seen fit to put it inside rather than leave it out to rust in the elements. Sometimes it was the little things that made all the difference in life.

Reaching the clear-running creek that provided his drinking water these days—as well as what he used to wash his few dishes, and a few times some clothes—he looked in the direction of the small lake it emptied into in the distance. Not nearly the size of Blue Valley Lake down below Half Moon Hill, it was more like a long, narrow pond—but seeing the sun sparkle on the surface lifted his soul a little. Not much, but he'd take what he could get these days. He drew in a deep breath, drinking in the peacefulness he'd found here.

Though the area had felt a lot more peaceful before he'd run into Anna Romo in the woods yesterday. Damn, he couldn't believe, of all the people who could be living in that big old Victorian, it was Lucky's sister. What shitty luck.

But then, his luck hadn't exactly been great lately—or ever, really—so maybe this shouldn't surprise him. Until now, he'd seen so little movement at the place that he'd just assumed some little old lady, or couple, lived there. It looked like that kind of house. Especially since it was so run down. He knew after taking her home yesterday that it was only run down on the outside—but still, the place's appearance had given him an entirely wrong impression. What on earth did one girl need with a house that big?

Whatever the case, now he just had to hope she'd keep her

word. Not that she had any reason to—she barely knew him
and owed him no loyalty.

Just the same, though, he was going about his business
today like normal, assuming nothing would change about
the quiet existence he'd made for himself out here. And if
she did tell anyone, like Lucky, or her other brother, Mike—
well, he wasn't breaking any laws, besides a little trespassing. Yet it would mean he'd have to explain himself and find
someplace else to go—neither of which appealed.

He had no idea how long he planned to stay here. Or
where he'd go when the time came to move on. He hadn't
thought that far ahead. In fact, he was making an effort not
to think about much of anything. And that was what made
it easy to be here. He didn't have to think. He didn't have to
answer any questions, or deal with other people, period. And
he didn't have to feel like some kind of pathetic charity case
because his face had gotten fucked up.

*Surely you can understand why I didn't recognize you.
Unless you haven't seen a mirror lately.*

It stung to hear her words again, even just in his mind.
But he shook it off. Because he had to. Because wallowing
in the situation wouldn't change it. Women wouldn't want
him anymore—so be it. That was a tough pill to swallow,
but . . . well, one more reason why the isolation of the woods
suited him.

Of course, even if she didn't tell anybody, things would
be different after this. He officially had a neighbor now. *But
don't over worry it. Maybe it'll be fine.*

No matter what he told himself, though, the encounter yesterday stayed on his mind, in more ways than one. It hadn't
exactly been pleasant, but it had definitely felt different—
more personal—than the couple of times he'd ridden his
motorcycle over to Crestview for a few groceries. And she
was probably the nicest sight his eyes had seen in months,
but hell—that brought his thoughts right back to what he
could no longer have: gorgeous women like Anna Romo.

Why couldn't she have just stayed in her damn house, or at least in her damn yard, and let him be?

Stop. Thinking. As he trudged back up the slight grade, bucket still in hand, he tried to clear his mind and get back to the solitude he'd found here. God knew that a ramshackle cabin in the woods wasn't where he'd expected to be at this point in his life, but it was—oddly—where he felt best now. Not that best equaled great or even good—but it was the better end of misery, he supposed. For a man of thirty-six, he felt far too tired inside.

He'd camped a lot as a kid, and now he realized that he'd likely come here—out into the near-wilderness—because it took him back *there*, to the time when he'd been eight, or maybe ten. Back to a time when life had seemed pretty damn simple compared to all the shit that had happened later. There was something honest and real in hauling your own water, eating simple foods, sinking into nature and letting it absorb you. It had made him realize that most of the things people worried about on a day-to-day basis were crap, not worth their time or attention, let alone their emotion. And the rest of the stuff people worried about—the stuff that did matter—well, that was mostly out of anyone's control, and in the end, it just wore you down. All of which was why blending into the woods for a while had ended up being the easiest choice.

Just then, Denny Bodkins' face flashed in his mind. Damn. *Stop. Don't see it. He knew. He knew there was nothing you could do.*

And then he pulled his focus back in, close and tight, on the things he really *could* see right now. The thick foliage around him on the trail back to the cabin. His work boots as he put one foot in front of the other, step after step. The click of an insect somewhere nearby, and then the tweet of a bird. All simpler, better things to concentrate on.

And it was because he was keeping his eyes close to the ground, on the path directly ahead of him, that he spotted

Anna Romo's basket in the distance, still lying where she'd dropped it in the clearing near the blackberries. It struck him funny that for all his focus on these woods, he hadn't even realized until yesterday that there were blackberry bushes thirty yards from the cabin.

Approaching, he saw that most looked good and ripe. Lowering his bucket to the ground, he stooped to set her wicker basket upright, then gathered the handful of scattered berries that had fallen from it.

He wasn't sure why. It wouldn't hurt anything if he'd just left them lie.

But maybe there was something just a little bit heartening in the notion that after all that had been ruined in his life lately—some parts by him, some by fate—there were still a few small things he had the power to clean up, a few things he could actually fix or repair. Even if it was just a basket of spilled blackberries—somehow the mere act of picking them up restored a tiny bit of order to Duke Dawson's world.

Two days after her bizarre meeting with her brother's best friend in the woods, Anna's ankle felt back to normal. She'd mostly stayed off it, and when lying down, she'd done as Duke had suggested, propping it on pillows to keep it elevated above the level of her heart. When necessary to get around, she'd used the crutches. But now she was bored to death, so it was a relief to wake up and discover that it felt enormously better. She wouldn't be running any marathons just yet, but she could resume normal life.

Which meant getting back to work on the house.

Of course, that meant the outside of the house, a notion which, unfortunately, still intimidated her. Sue Ann Simpkins, her real estate agent and now friend, had redone the inside of her own Victorian, so she'd given Anna some help over the winter. And Lucky's wife, Tessa, an interior designer, had assisted with selecting furniture, rugs, and curtains. But when it came to the outside of the place, Anna didn't know where to begin—or how she'd handle the heavy lifting that would surely be involved.

And yes, she could ask Mike and Lucky—and they would be more than happy to help—but she couldn't bear the idea. Mike would hover, and probably try to completely take over the project without even realizing it. She'd bought the house, after all, to put a little distance between herself and her new family. And if she hired someone from town to work with her, her brothers would find out and insist she let them help instead.

"So you're on your own, baby," she told herself, trying to gear up for the challenge.

And at that precise moment, she tripped over the crutches where she'd leaned them in the wide doorway that led to the foyer. "Crap," she muttered, steadying herself. Her ankle remained fine, but this inspired her to go ahead and put the crutches back in the attic where they belonged. She could climb the fold-down steps with them if she was careful, and getting them out of her way seemed like a good idea. Even if it might also equal five more minutes of procrastination.

She soon stepped into the warm, musty, woody scent of the attic, a place she'd found more friendly than foreboding, as attics went. Even now, bright sunlight spilled through the windows, lighting the thick gable beams that met overhead.

"Meow."

She glanced down, slightly startled but somehow not surprised to see her cat. "What are *you* doing up here?" she asked. And though he didn't reply, she knew the answer. *Following you. Because I'm sneaky that way.*

She'd barely seen the black cat while she'd been injured, but now, here he was, creeping up behind her. "Where were you when I was in pain?" she scolded him. "Isn't that what cats are for? Weren't you supposed to be cuddling with me and comforting me? But no—you only show up when I don't need you."

"Meow," he said again, as if in defense.

She just rolled her eyes. "Whatever."

She'd just propped the crutches between two of the exposed wall beams, then turned to head back down, when she caught sight of Erik sniffing around the bottom of an old oak trunk she'd noticed before. The attic was filled with things left behind by the previous owner, and she'd already decided that someday she'd refinish this particular item and use it as a coffee table, or maybe to store blankets at the foot of a bed in one of the guest rooms.

And it was then that she noticed a book, lying facedown on the floor between the trunk and an ancient bicycle—what appeared to be an old tree swing was propped at an angle that mostly obscured the book from view. Moving back toward the trunk, she stooped down and gingerly drew the book to her—though, yuck, it was covered with the same thick dust of years as everything else up here.

By the time she rose back up, her cat stood atop the trunk in a messy circle of dusty paw prints. "If you track that dust downstairs, mister, I'll . . ." Well, she didn't know what she'd do to him exactly, but . . . "You'll be in big trouble, I promise," she finished, pointing a finger at him as threateningly as possible.

Then she shifted her attention back to the book, turning it over in her hands to find—to her shock—an old edition of *The Phantom of the Opera*, written by Gaston Leroux, about the cat's namesake, long before anyone ever thought about performing it on a stage. She glanced down at Erik. "You planned this, right?"

"Meow."

Thinking Amy would probably love this and that it might make a good gift for her, Anna opened the front cover to see how old it was. But she was stopped in her mental tracks by the ink inscription there. *To my sweet Cathy. Thank you for taking care of me when I was sick. Love, Robert.*

Something inside Anna lit with excitement and curiosity. It was so easy to forget that every person who'd ever lived before her had their own story, their own pains and passions and emotions, the same as anyone now. Could Cathy be the woman Sue Ann had told her last lived here when Anna was deciding to buy the place? Did the book's inscription hold romance, or just simple thanks? She thought romance—definitely. And suddenly the idea of being taken care of by someone didn't sound so weak—Robert somehow almost made it sound . . . well, actually kind of sexy.

Of course, maybe she was reading too much into one simple message written in a book. But it suddenly made her want to know what hid inside the trunk. She'd always absently wondered but never opened it. And now the urge to investigate further burned inside her.

So after shooing Erik off the top and watching him pounce to the floor, she set down the book and used both hands to lift the heavy lid.

And inside she found . . . oh, another whole wonderful world. She spied a stack of record albums, what looked like a scrapbook, two old leather-bound diaries, and three stacks of letters, each tied with faded pink ribbons. It was just like the world of the forest, except that this was a world of history, and of someone's life, and of a story that she immediately wanted to uncover.

Were the letters to Cathy? From Robert? Another little thrill shot through her when she spotted *Catherine Worth* on the outside of the first envelope in small script. Were the diaries hers, as well, and what romantic tales might they tell? She suddenly wanted nothing more than to plop down on the attic floor and spend the entire day reading.

Except . . . "That would be more procrastination." She looked at the cat, who now stood near her feet. "And I've just lost two days to a sprained ankle."

"Meow."

"And if I don't start using my days wisely, the whole summer will pass in a flash and I'll never get my business open. And then I'll just be a crazy lady—and with you here,

I guess I would even qualify as a crazy cat lady—who lives out in the country alone for no good reason."

So, with a sigh, she closed the lid on the trunk—but if she started making some measurable progress on the outside of the house, maybe she could reward herself with some of Cathy's letters or a diary.

"Come on, time to head back down," she told Erik, then followed the cat to the folding stairs, a little jealous of the agility he exhibited scampering down them so neatly, and a little sorry to be leaving the rich smell and feel of the attic behind.

"Let's go outside," she said. "Let's go outside with enthusiasm and optimism and find a place to start. Let's find one project on the outside of the house we think we can accomplish, and then that will lead to another one, and then another one."

Only . . . dear God, since when did she talk to cats? She really *would* become a crazy cat lady at this rate. Lifting her gaze from the feline to the front door as they descended the stairs to the foyer, she repeated, "Just one project." It wasn't talking to the cat if she didn't look at him. It was just . . . talking to herself, which, in her mind, actually sounded healthier.

Ready to finally dive into a brave new world of exterior renovation, motivated by the promise of someone's old romantic letters and diaries, Anna opened the door to step out on the front porch—only to pull up short just before immersing her bare foot into the basket of blackberries sitting there.

"I was at first inclined to be suspicious . . ."

Gaston Leroux, *The Phantom of the Opera*

Three

Anna couldn't quite believe what she was seeing. Unless woodland elves had done this, Duke Dawson had picked her blackberries for her and brought them here.

Stepping around the basket and out onto the porch, she looked around, but didn't find any sign of him. Not that she really expected to. Given that he'd been living in the woods next to her house undetected for who knew how long, she suspected he might be as skilled at sneaking around as the cat.

Why had he done this? To get on her good side? To help ensure she'd keep his secret?

She couldn't say—she only knew it was the last thing she'd expected.

And it came to mind to wonder what he ate. And if perhaps the very question made it extra nice of him to have picked the berries for her when maybe he could have used them himself.

But stop. A few berries didn't turn him into Mother Teresa. In fact, she'd do well to remember the word *outlaw* had once been attached to him. And that even if Lucky loved the guy, she'd still seldom run into anyone more frightening-looking in her life. She'd do well to stay a little afraid of him.

And besides, it wasn't her problem to worry about whether Duke Dawson had enough to eat. No, her problem, among others, was trying to forget there was a wildman living in her woods. She didn't need to go having a soft spot for Duke, of all scary people.

Stooping to scoop up the basket, she carried it in to the kitchen counter, then thought—now what?

Well, you wanted berries to make a pie; you should probably make a pie.

Not that she had the first idea how to do that.

So even though the idea had originally been about *not* going into town, now it looked like a trip to Under the Covers was in order—for a cookbook—and maybe while she was there she could ask Amy why the dumb cat followed her around meowing all the time.

Of course, that meant another day would likely pass without starting on the outside of the house—but it wouldn't seem right to let the berries go to waste after all the drama that had been involved in getting them. So it was pretty easy to talk herself into believing she just wasn't meant to dive in on it today, after all.

No, apparently today she was meant to bake a pie.

"Getting ready to do a little cooking?" Amy asked as she keyed the price of the cookbook into the old-fashioned cash register on the bookstore counter.

"I'm going to bake a pie. My first ever," Anna admitted.

"Yum," Amy said, cheerful as always. "What kind?"

"Blackberry. From berries in the woods by my house." She left out that she hadn't picked them herself, and further didn't mention that they *had* been picked by the extra hairy outlaw biker living in her woods, whom Amy had, in fact, walked with in Lucky and Tessa's wedding back before he was quite so hairy.

Amy appeared to be thinking something over as she pushed a strawberry blond curl back behind one ear. "Hmm. Since you have blackberries, a cobbler would be easier starting out. Unless your heart is set on pie."

Anna shook her head, glad for the tip. "No, my heart's not set on anything in particular, and a cobbler sounds just as much like something a bed-and-breakfast owner should be able to make as a pie." Then she glanced down at the book she'd just bought. "But I'd better make sure there's a recipe for that in here. I already checked it for pie."

"Or I can call my mom," Amy offered. "Or Logan's. They both make great cobblers. Or Edna probably has a recipe, too." Edna Farris was Mike's wife's grandmother, known far and wide for her baking skills, especially her apple pie.

And for heaven's sake, why on earth had Anna even bothered buying a cookbook anyway? She should have known every person in Destiny would have an award-winning recipe for any and all baked goods known to man. She smiled her appreciation. "That would be great."

"I'll start with my mom," Amy announced, then picked up the phone. Anna smiled her appreciation as she waited, truly grateful for Amy's kindness. Last summer, they'd both pursued the same guy—fireman Logan Whitaker—but now Anna could see that her attraction to Logan had been more about seeking a port in a storm than anything else. Logan and Amy were clearly meant for each other, and were happily engaged now, and Anna was only glad she and Amy had moved past that and into real friendship.

When the little bell above the bookshop's door jingled, Anna looked up to see Sue Ann and her friend Jenny Brody walk in.

"Hey Anna—what's up?" Sue Ann greeted her with a smile. "How's the house?"

Anna shifted her own smile in Sue Ann's direction. "Coming along," she replied. "I'm about to start on the exterior." Maybe saying it with confidence would give her some.

Anna greeted Jenny, as well, who explained that they were having lunch with Amy. Then Jenny checked her watch, glancing to Amy, who was now busy writing, the phone tucked beneath her ear.

"In a hurry?" Sue Ann asked. Both wore pretty, feminine dresses, making Anna feel the differences in them all the more as she glanced down at her cutoff shorts. "I thought *I* was the busy one with the lunch hour ticking away fast. You're on summer break." Jenny was a teacher at Destiny High School.

"Just want to get to the café so I can take a few minutes in the restroom," Jenny said, then held up a plastic bag from the drugstore around the corner. The look on her face told Anna that Sue Ann must know what was inside.

And in response, Sue Ann rolled her eyes. "Seriously? You're going to take a pregnancy test *there*? You want to find out you're pregnant at Dolly's Main Street Café?"

At first, Anna wondered if maybe they'd forgotten she was there—but maybe everyone in Destiny was so chummy that they just didn't care.

"Don't worry, I won't be," Jenny replied glumly. "Since I never am. So I'd just as soon get the disappointment over with rather than spend the day building up any hope, you know?"

Now Sue Ann glanced at Anna. "She and Mick have been trying for a while without any luck and it's starting to get to her."

Okay, she'd been right—apparently this was just how open the ladies of Destiny were about personal things. And since Anna *wasn't* that open with people she didn't know well, she felt uncomfortable and simply murmured, "Oh. Wow. I'm sorry to hear that."

Jenny shrugged and attempted a smile that came off more like a grimace. "Thanks. I just keep hoping it will suddenly happen."

"Well, maybe today's your lucky day," Sue Ann said, clearly trying to be more supportive now. "Maybe Dolly's will actually turn out to be the magic spot. Or . . . you can just go here while we're waiting on Amy."

But just then, Amy hung up the phone. "Hi girls," she said, casting her usual friendly grin their way. Then she looked to Anna, holding out a sheet of pink notepaper. "My mom swears by this recipe."

Anna took it, expressing her thanks, and then felt obligated to tell Sue Ann and Jenny that she was embarking on her first real baking project, on which they both wished her luck.

"Are we ready?" Jenny asked then. "Not that I mean to be impatient, but—"

"But you've got a pregnancy test burning a hole in your pocket," Sue Ann finished for her in a matter-of-fact way.

"Well, what about Tessa and Rachel?" Amy asked, looking confused.

Sue Ann replied. "Tessa's meeting us there. And Rachel had to cancel—sick with some kind of stomach bug."

"Ugh," Amy said, wrinkling her nose. "She wasn't feeling well when I talked to her a few days ago, either." Then she looked back to Anna once more, her eyebrows lifting hopefully. "Anna, why don't you join us?"

"Yes!" Sue Ann said, so enthusiastically that Anna couldn't help being flattered. "That would be great. Come with us."

Even so, though, she hesitated. It was sweet of them, and she knew the invitation was sincere. But they all knew each other so well—they'd known each other since they were little. And though Anna *had* been born here, she still felt acquainted with them in only a casual way. She wasn't sure she felt at ease enough with them to be hearing about personal things like trouble getting pregnant or . . . who knew what else they might bring up.

So even despite knowing it was the perfect way to start

feeling less hermit-like, she heard herself saying, "Thanks for asking, but I'll have to make it another time. I really need to get to work on this cobbler." She held up the recipe as if it provided proof.

Yet Sue Ann tilted her head to one side. "Lunch is only an hour—you'll have plenty of the day left for baking."

And Amy gave her head a persuasive tilt. "Come on, it'll be fun."

But, perhaps sadly, Anna wasn't even tempted. She truly liked Amy and all her friends, yet at the same time, she just preferred to be alone these days—with her blackberries and her dumb cat. *Maybe you really* are *becoming a hermit.*

"Thanks," she said, "but I have so much to get done on the house, I need to get back to work as soon as I get this cobbler in the oven. We'll do it another time—promise."

Anna stood back and looked at the disaster area her kitchen had become. Stray berries sprinkled the new countertop she'd installed over the winter, and purple blobs stained every surface. The whole space appeared lightly coated in flour, with bits of sugar mixed in for good measure. Given the mess, she thought it was a wonder that enough of the ingredients had made it into the baking dish to actually create a cobbler.

"Meow."

She peered down at the cat who currently traipsed about in the flour at her feet. "Darn it, I forgot to ask Amy about you. And don't let me find flour paw prints in the hallway . . . or else."

"Meow." He didn't sound the least bit nervous.

While her creation baked, she cleaned up the kitchen, and herself, and her cat's paws. She thought about moving forward on repairs, determined to find a project to start on before the day was out. She knew she could do this—it was just a matter of getting started, easing into it.

And maybe that was how life in Destiny would be, too—

maybe it was a matter of easing into it, bit by bit. Maybe the next time someone asked her to lunch, she'd go. Maybe it would be easier if it was only one other person—just Amy, or just Sue Ann. And it wasn't that she lacked confidence or social skills—it was still simply the innate knowledge that she was so different from them and always would be. She didn't like cats. She didn't know how to bake. She remained slightly turned on by the memory of the wildman in the woods touching her feet.

Whoa—where had that last one come from? And sheesh, it was still hard to believe. But this sealed the deal—because truly, no self-respecting Destiny lady would respond that way.

Oh well, it's over now. You might not even see him again. And probably the only reason she'd suffered that strange reaction was lack of sex. It had been a while. And really, a lack of men in her life in general, other than her brothers. In ways, it had been an awfully long winter. *And that's what you get for becoming a hermit—bizarre sexual responses to the first masculine dude you run into, even if he needs a haircut worse than anyone you've ever met.*

She gave a little shiver, trying to shake the whole thing off—but again the fleeting thought passed through her mind: *What does Duke eat out there?*

When the inviting aroma of warm cobbler wafted past, she glanced at the clock and—oh God, it was past time to take it out! Rushing to grab up a couple of the gingham potholders Amy had given her as a housewarming gift last fall, she yanked open the oven door, pulled out the casserole dish, and . . . wow, it was pretty beautiful! Berry juice bubbled through the top of the golden brown crust like little bits of hot purple lava—and it smelled even more delicious now.

"Meow."

She looked down to find Erik still at her feet, staring up.

"I know," she said, nodding happily. "It looks pretty amazing, doesn't it? I might just be a good innkeeper, after all."

And now that she felt like a successful baker and her confidence was high, she set the dish on a trivet to cool and walked outside. *Find a project on the outside of this house. Pick one. And then figure out how to get started. You're clearly a born baker—so you're probably a born carpenter, too.*

But as she stood in the front yard, looking at the grand-but-now-shabby old Victorian, her attention was for some reason drawn to the woods to her left—to the old path that led into the trees next to the honeysuckle bushes. The path she'd followed to pick berries. And the path on which Duke had carried her out.

What *did* he eat? And what was he doing right now? How on earth did he spend his days? And sure, she got that he didn't want to be around people right now, but what exactly was his plan? To just live alone like an animal in the woods for the rest of his life? How much sense did that make?

But these aren't your questions to ask; they aren't your problems. You have enough problems—even if, admittedly, Duke's made her own seem much more manageable. It was one thing to become a hermit in the way *she* had, but another altogether to do it in the way *he'd* chosen to.

And was he hungry? When was the last time he'd had anything delicious, or even good?

Sighing, she glanced toward the front door of her house and thought of the cobbler in her kitchen. God knew she didn't need to sit around devouring a whole cobbler that she'd baked as an experiment. The truth was—she'd gotten the bright idea to bake it, but she hadn't thought about who would eat it.

Maybe Duke would like it.

And maybe that was a crazy thought in ways—after all, he'd made it clear he wanted to be left alone and he'd acted perfectly self-sufficient with his propane refrigerator. For all she knew, he was having gourmet meals every night.

But she didn't think so.

And *somebody* needed to eat the cobbler.

And he *had* been nice enough to pick the berries and bring them right to her door.

So maybe she'd just return the favor by taking him the cobbler. In the same way his bringing her the blackberries had felt like a peace offering of sorts, taking him the cobbler would be her gesture of peace in return. And then she'd somehow feel like they were even—and like it was saying they were both okay with the situation.

All in all, she couldn't help thinking it was a good idea.

Of course, ten minutes later as she trudged with her cobbler dish between her hands through the woods—even darker now than they'd been the last time due to clouds that had moved in this afternoon—it began to seem like a slightly more *stupid* idea. She started remembering that he scared her a little. And that he had a mysterious—dangerous—past. And that even if he'd seemed completely in his right mind the more she'd talked to him, a guy living out in a fallen-down shack in the forest by choice couldn't really have it all together. Suddenly, the word *Unabomber* came to mind. Shit—what was she doing? When had she become the Hermit Welcome Wagon?

Still, she felt she'd come too far to turn back, especially when the old cabin suddenly appeared in the distance. Like before, the ivy and other vines covering it served as camouflage, making it so she didn't quite see it until it was right before her eyes, like something materializing out of nowhere. *Poof!*

Was he in there? Well, regardless, maybe she should just leave the casserole outside and be on her way, the same as he had with the berries. Yes, that sounded like *another* good plan.

Fortunately, a small window next to the door stood open, creating a wide enough sill on which to set it safely. She'd covered it with a gingham cloth—another gift from Amy, who seemed almost as fond of gingham as she was of cats—so it would be less likely to draw bugs or animals before Duke found it.

Stepping slowly up to the window, she paused, listening for any movement inside, and when she heard nothing but the faint tweet of a bird somewhere, she edged closer to the old dilapidated sill and carefully lowered the cobbler dish. For good measure, she straightened the blue and white cloth, making sure it covered all four corners.

There, a nice treat for Duke when he came back from wherever he was.

That was when a fist clamped down on her wrist.

The shock of it shot up her arm and into her heart as she let out a yelp. Her gaze locked on the masculine hand that held her, and a second later, Duke Dawson's hairy face and gray eyes appeared above it through the open window. "If you're gonna go sneaking around, Daisy," he said, "you gotta be a little quieter."

She blinked, flinched. "I was *perfectly* quiet." She was trying to get used to being touched by him again. And wondering why he hadn't yet let go.

He chose that exact moment to release her arm from his grasp, leaving her in a weird state between relief and slight disappointment. A few seconds later, the door opened a few feet away and her wolfman stepped out. "About as quiet as a freight train. Heard you tromping through the weeds twenty yards away."

She knew he was exaggerating, but thought he looked more amused than he had during their first encounter, like he was actually teasing her this time.

Not quite sure how to respond to teasing from Duke, she went barreling full steam ahead with "Thank you for picking the berries."

He gave a short, simple nod in reply. "Thank you for . . ." He looked toward the windowsill. "Whatever that is."

"A cobbler. Made from the blackberries. I . . . didn't know what you were eating out here, so . . ."

"Don't worry about me, Daisy, I'm getting along just fine,"

he informed her, and she was just about to regret trying to do something nice for him when he added, "But thanks. Haven't had anything like that in a while and it'll be a nice change."

"You're welcome. I . . . hope it's edible." She hadn't exactly planned the last part—she'd just been thinking aloud.

Still seeming more lighthearted than she could have anticipated, now he even let out a quick laugh. "Should I be scared?"

For some reason, she moved right past the irony of the question and found herself feeling unusually sheepish. Maybe even a little vulnerable. In the past, she'd mostly stuck to doing things she was naturally good at—maybe life had held enough challenges without her having to challenge *herself* on top of it. So she wasn't used to being in the position of having no idea if her efforts were a success or not, and she'd only remembered a minute ago that she didn't actually have a clue how the cobbler would taste. Plus—hell—something about him just kept her feeling a lot more tense than usual, whether or not there was a cobbler involved.

"It's . . . the first thing I've really baked," she admitted. "Sort of an experiment. I'm planning to open my house as an inn once I finish all the repairs, and . . . I thought it would be nice if I could serve homemade baked goods. I also got a cat. For the inn. Because it seemed like something people would like." *Oh God, shut up. He's a motorcycle gang member with a jugged scar on his face living in the woods—he doesn't care about your Mary Poppins aspirations as an innkeeper. Or your cat. Unless maybe he needs something to focus on during target practice.* She cringed slightly, suddenly worried for Erik, no matter how irritating she found the four-legged meowing machine.

"Makes sense," he said simply.

"It does?" Her eyebrows shot up.

"Wondered what you needed that great big house for. Now I know."

"You don't have to worry, though," she heard herself

adding, even if she wasn't sure why she cared about reassuring him. "I have a lot of work to do on the outside, so I won't be opening for a while yet. So, I mean, there won't suddenly be guests around—you'll still have . . . privacy. For now."

He narrowed those dark eyes on her, and his pointed stare pinned her in place. She was generally good with men—confident, comfortable—so why did she find it hard to make eye contact with this one? *Maybe it's the scar and scraggly hair. Maybe it's because there are so many question marks surrounding him, some of them pretty ominous.* "Does this mean you're willing to keep my secret?" he asked.

"I told you I would."

"Figured you might've changed your mind by now."

She just shook her head. "Nope. I can be a good neighbor if you can."

One corner of his mouth quirked into not-quite-a-smile. "Yep, I can be a good neighbor, Daisy Duke."

Her spine stiffened slightly. "I might think you were a *better* neighbor if you'd quit calling me that."

"Why? I like the shorts. They suit you." And when he glanced down at her hips, she did, too. Today's particular jean shorts were cutoff Levi's she'd torn badly while installing a new bathroom sink a few months back. She tended to wear a lot of denim these days because it was both comfortable and sturdy. And she wasn't about to ask exactly how they suited her, God forbid—but her cheeks heated slightly anyway, and she only hoped the shadiness of the woods hid her reaction.

"Ankle's all better, looks like," he said then, dropping his gaze lower and saving her from coming up with a reply.

She nodded. "Yes. Good as new, thanks."

"Use the crutches?"

"I did," she assured him.

"Good girl."

Her eyes darted up to his and their gazes locked. The small liberties he took with her unnerved her a little—how did a guy in his position have the guts to be so bold?—and yet somehow she was beginning, bit by bit, to grow less wary of him.

This time her lack of reply created one more slightly awkward moment until she pointed vaguely in the direction of her house. "Well, I should go."

He offered a quick nod. "Thanks again for the dessert."

"No problem," she said softly as she started backing away, suddenly eager for escape. But this wasn't about fear—not this time. It was about the way he kept her on edge and was so full of mystery. And that the angry scar on his face provided a constant reminder of some darkness inside him, dark enough to send him here, retreating into the woods as if maybe he was hoping to just fade away.

"Be careful walking back, Daisy," he told her, still not quite smiling.

"Sure," she said easily, now putting still more distance between them—and then she stumbled backward over a tree root and lost her balance. Oh Lord.

Reaching out a hand—maybe it was more like flailing, actually—she made contact with a tree trunk and steadied herself before falling. Thank God. Then she lifted her gaze to find Duke watching. "I'm fine," she assured him.

He spoke low, under his breath, but she still heard it when he murmured in a deep, provocative tone, "Yes, you are."

And then, finally, for the first time, Duke Dawson cracked a grin—just before she turned around and rushed away through the trees.

"You are afraid of me! And yet I am not really wicked."

Gaston Leroux, *The Phantom of the Opera*

Four

*S*am Cooke's smooth voice echoed out the window as Anna toted a heavy ladder from the garage. Although she could have turned on the radio or listened to her iPod, she'd felt the urge to play some of the albums she'd found upstairs last night in Cathy's trunk. When she'd come across an old record player in the attic, too, it had seemed like kismet.

She had a plan. Or at least the start of a plan. And that was definitely better than no plan at all. First, she would remove the rusted old falling-down gutters that weren't even serving a purpose anymore. Then she'd replace a few loose boards and take off the shutters. Then she would paint the house. Not that she'd ever done any of those things before. But she'd bought books covering all phases of home repair—from Under the Covers, of course—and she figured it was just a matter of diving in and following instructions.

That would still leave a lot—the porch and trim repairs, adding new gutters, painting and reattaching the shutters, and the roof. And who knew what else she'd come across by that time—or how long any of this would take. But at least she was getting started. And that was why she now found herself climbing the ladder she'd just leaned against one side of the house, wearing a tool belt she'd found in the garage. Whether or not she knew what she was doing, at least she looked the part. And something about the old music motivated her—maybe she liked the idea of restoring the house to what it might have looked like when the records had originally been played here. Maybe they reminded her that real lives had taken place here, real people had lived here. Which she'd known all along, of course, but the things in the trunk had made the house begin to come alive for her in a whole new way. And if that gave her the oomph she needed to get going, she'd take it.

As she hooked the pronged end of a hammer around the first rusty nail she came to in the decrepit gutter, her mind drifted to what she'd brought down from the attic yesterday evening—the two old diaries she'd spotted when investigating the trunk, complete with worn spines and yellowing pages.

To her delight, she'd quickly figured out that both had belonged to Cathy, and they'd been written in 1959 when Cathy had been sixteen years old. The first page of the earliest diary began:

> *Today is my sixteenth birthday. My cousins came, and the rest of the family, and we had a grand party. Mother thinks I have an aptitude for expressing myself, so she bought me this diary. I'm not sure what I'll write about—so far nothing has happened to me that feels worth writing down—but I'll give it a try. The weather has been unseasonably warm for March, so we held my party on the summer porch.*

Anna was pretty sure the summer porch Cathy referred to was the large screened porch on the back of the house, and she'd found it fun to imagine a young girl blowing out candles on a cake there, and opening gifts, party streamers wafting in the breeze.

Though as Anna had read on, she'd found that not every page was captivating—some days Cathy had nothing more on her mind than the list of chores she'd finished that afternoon or the school assignments she'd completed. Yet even when skimming those entries, Anna had felt she was holding history in her hands. And it fascinated her to hear what life was like in her house that long ago, in a time when Destiny was a much younger, more isolated little town and Half Moon Hill must have seemed even farther away from civilization.

Since, while remodeling inside, she'd seen hints that her home had once been a much fancier place, she wasn't surprised to learn from the diary that Cathy's family had been well-off. They'd owned more than one car—which Anna could tell had been a big deal—and Cathy had often felt ostracized at school since most of the kids were poor. Cathy's dad, Otto Worth, had been the president of the Bank of Destiny from its inception—the bank still operated on the town square today, and Anna had noticed the year 1944 carved into the building's cornerstone.

And then, finally, after over an hour of reading, she reached the part she'd been waiting for. The part about Robert, who'd given Cathy the novel.

> *The boy's name is Robert and he's living in the cabin in the woods that Daddy says was here before our house. He's eighteen and has a dangerous look about him, and Daddy says I should stay clear and not talk to him when he's working in the yard or inside. Daddy doesn't know where his parents are but thinks he ran away from an orphanage.*

*When Mother asked why we should have some-
one around who he doesn't even want me talk
ing to, he said that's why the boy is living in the
cabin and not in the house with us—that it was
far enough away not to be a worry—but he never
really answered her. If you ask me, Daddy wants
somebody who will work cheap because even
though we have plenty, he doesn't like giving any
of it away. He says too many folks have too little
and will rob us blind if we let them, so we need to
hold on tight to what we've got.*

After that, the diary had resumed talking about things
like the mean girls at school, a shopping trip that resulted
in a new blue dress, and the butterflies Cathy watched in the
yard and was attempting to sketch with colored pencils. And
she'd also mentioned sitting in the swing that hung from the
big maple tree in the front yard, leaving Anna to wonder if
it could possibly be the same swing she'd seen in the attic.

She'd been just about to turn in for the night, her eyes
drooping shut, when she'd come across the shortest but perhaps most alluring entry in the diary she'd seen by far:

*Robert is planting a garden in the little field
beyond the backyard. Daddy still forbids me to go
near him, but I watch him from the summer porch
sometimes. You'd think that would be boring, but
it's not. I'm not sure why.*

And something about that—those very simple words
from a young girl over fifty years ago—had helped Anna
fall asleep feeling strangely happier than she had in a very
long time.

Now, as she began on the house, thinking about Cathy and
her youthful fascination with Robert made Anna's work feel
easier, lighter. She used the hammer to extract the old nails,

one by one, some of which actually disintegrated into red dust as she pulled them out. A long stretch of rusty gutter now hung down loose behind the ladder, helping her feel she was actually making progress as she reached, leaning slightly, for the next nail, a short distance beyond where her ladder leaned.

Suddenly feeling productive and energetic, she looked forward to getting back to the diary. Of course, maybe she'd ultimately find out that nothing noteworthy or exciting had ever really happened to Cathy here. Maybe the giving of *The Phantom of the Opera* wouldn't hold the magic she hoped. Maybe she'd finish the diaries and realize they didn't make much of a story, after all.

But she just didn't think so.

Duke wasn't sure what led him on the path through the woods to the house. Boredom, maybe. He'd told her he was fine out here, that he had all he needed, and that was true. But maybe he was beginning to miss simple human contact. A little anyway. Which surprised him. But there it was. Maybe having those small bits of interaction with Lucky's sister had reminded him there was actually something valuable in connecting with other people.

For a lot of years, he'd blocked out that need. He'd convinced himself doing the lone wolf thing was best. But it had been a hard life, putting up that kind of wall, having no one. And then Lucky had come along and they'd hit it off, and somehow he'd known from the start that he could trust the guy, that they were coming from the same place.

"You were two lost souls," Lucky's wife, Tessa, had once told him when they were talking about his and Lucky's friendship. He didn't like getting all dramatic and philosophical about it like that, but he supposed she was right. Finding Lucky had changed his life. And he'd realized that having even one real friend in this world made him a fortunate man.

Though he and Lucky had gone through some hard times

together, afterward life had been pretty good for a while. He'd found . . . direction, purpose, for the first time. He'd worked hard—mostly doing construction—and saved up his money. He'd bought the bar in Crestview. He'd made a home for himself—at least as much of a home as he figured a guy like him could hope to have. And he'd been happy. Well . . . again, as happy as he expected he ever *could* be with the kind of baggage he dragged around.

And look at you now. Living in the woods like a fucking animal.

But that was your choice.

He just suddenly hadn't . . . known how to function among people anymore. Or maybe he just no longer had the energy. This was the closest he could come to disappearing, and he guessed that was what he'd wanted—to just disappear.

So he still wasn't sure why he was walking through the trees toward the big Victorian house.

It surprised him when he heard music. And not anything current, either—old stuff, like from the fifties.

He stepped up to the edge of the tree line, near the honeysuckle—to see the last thing he'd imagined. Anna Romo stood on a ladder, a hammer in her hand, a tool belt around her waist, her long, tan legs looking as fine as ever in another pair of those same shorts she always seemed to wear.

Maybe he shouldn't be surprised—she'd told him she was fixing the place up, and God knew it needed it—but he just hadn't envisioned her doing the actual work. She didn't look built for heavy labor.

She was full of surprises, Lucky's sister. Couldn't pick berries without twisting her ankle but was up there giving it her best to yank down an old gutter. For some reason the word *resilient* came to mind. He supposed it fit what he knew about her. She'd had a pretty weird, tragic past, too— but she seemed to make the best of it, and he couldn't help admiring that.

Maybe that was why she'd agreed to keep his secret. And

why she'd made him that cobbler—which had been pretty damn good. Maybe she'd realized they had something in common before *he* had—that they'd both seen some dark times. Maybe she was hiding out in the woods just as much as he was—just in a more civilized way.

And that was when he realized she actually *wasn't* built for heavy labor—or at least she didn't have the brains for it. Because . . . what the hell was she doing? She was reaching too damn far—stretching that hammer as she leaned to one side, rather than just backing down the ladder and moving it over like anyone with any sense would.

Just then, she reached a little farther, pulled a nail from the gutter, accidentally dropped the hammer to send it plunking to the grass below, and murmured, "Shit," right in the middle of "Twistin' the Night Away." Then the ladder tilted to the right, sliding along the roof a few inches, one of the two feet coming off the ground. Shit was right.

Duke moved rapidly across the yard, but by the time he reached her, the ladder was leaning, leaning, slowly falling away, out from under her, giving her just enough time to grab on to a couple of old wooden railings on a balcony over her head. The metal ladder clattered to the ground to leave her hanging there, about a dozen feet above him. Damn.

"Don't panic, Daisy, I'm here," he said, rushing forward to start maneuvering the ladder.

"Huh—what?" she yelled, clearly all the more startled by his presence. Then she glanced down and let out a yelp— whether at seeing how far up she was or just merely at the sight of him, which seemed to scare the hell out of her each time, he couldn't tell.

"Just keep holding tight, girl," he instructed her, work- ing to get the ladder upright again—a job that would have seemed easier if he wasn't trying to rescue some damsel in distress.

"Hurry," she was saying. "Hurry!"

A few seconds later, he finally got the ladder against the

roof next to her, then scooted it to where she could reach it. "There—put your foot over until you find a rung. And keep holding on."

"Like I'm gonna let go," she snapped. God, she was sassy. And he was too busy at the moment to know whether it pissed him off or if he liked it.

She swung her left foot onto the ladder, which he held firmly in place from the bottom. "There you go," he said. "Now the other one." But she was already doing that.

Though even once she was safe again, she still clung to those rails with a death grip, still looking panicked.

"It's all right," he said as soothingly as he could. Which probably wasn't particularly soothing—it wasn't a skill he'd ever much needed before. "Just relax—you're fine now. I'm holding the ladder—all you gotta do is back down, real slow."

He didn't pressure her after that, just waited until she finally moved her hands, one by one, to the ladder. He heard her pull in her breath before she began to take the first backward steps toward him.

"Just don't let go," she said.

"I won't. Promise."

And he didn't. Even as she neared the ground and ended up backing right into his chest.

Maybe it was awful, but having her up against him gave him the same sensation it had the last time—when he'd carried her home. A sexual tug. A reminder of passion.

But then came the bigger realization: No one would want him anymore, least of all this gorgeous, sassy girl with the killer legs.

So he moved forward in his thoughts to something more practical. And without weighing it, he said the first thing on his mind, speaking low, near her ear, since there was no reason to speak louder at the moment. "You worry me, Daisy."

She took a second to answer, and he spent that second

knowing he should probably be moving, letting go of the ladder, freeing her from having his arms on either side of her—but for some reason he still didn't.

Her voice came softer than when she'd been in panic mode. "I'm not usually as clumsy as I probably seem."

He wasn't sure if he believed that or not. "Either way, you still worry me."

Anna felt pleasantly imprisoned by him, but it was strange to know that if she turned her head and saw her wolfman so close, it would alarm her even now. So she just faced forward, her heart beating too fast from what had happened. Or maybe also due to where she now found herself, pressed softly up against Duke Dawson, a place that seemed nearly as perilous as dangling from the roof.

And she seemed to have lost the ability to calculate time— because she wasn't sure if it was five seconds or thirty before he finally released the ladder and backed away.

Only then could she gather the courage to turn and face him. And like always, she found the sight of him intimidating—though she began to wonder if it was still about the scar and scraggly beard . . . or if maybe now it was also the way his heated gaze penetrated hers. His eyes shone a little bluer in the sun.

"Guess I owe you another thank you," she managed.

He just shrugged. "Couldn't really let you fall."

It was hardly a heroic statement, yet it reminded her that he'd recently witnessed the death of a friend. Which somehow made her even more appreciative. "Well, actually, you could have. So thank you anyway." She dropped her glance briefly before lifting it back to his. "So . . . you were just passing by?"

Another noncommittal shrug. "Something like that."

Hmm. Had he been watching her from the woods? And if so, why? She didn't want to be scared of Duke anymore— but she also didn't want to be foolishly trusting of a guy in a bad place.

"Anybody ever tell you it's not real bright to lean when you're on a ladder, Daisy?"

Again, she found herself defending her intelligence and remembering life had been easier back when she'd stuck to what she knew. "Nope. Never talked to anyone before about *being* on a ladder. Or been on one before, either. I'm learning as I go—and now I know. Don't lean."

She couldn't quite interpret the slight smirk he cast within all that hair on and around his face. "If you've never been on a ladder before, what are you doing on one now?"

"Removing a gutter," she said, glancing toward the line of rusty metal now hanging almost to the ground, still barely attached at the top.

"That I can see," he informed her. "I just meant . . . if you don't know how to do this kinda stuff, might make more sense to hire somebody, or at least get some help. I'm sure your brothers would come lend a hand."

She drew in a long breath, let it back out. Though she knew he meant well, the very suggestion made her feel tired. "I'm sure they would, too. But . . . maybe I want to show them I'm capable of doing things on my own."

"That's fine—when it's something you *can* do on your own. But . . ." He leaned back, took a long look at the house. "Getting this place in shape is gonna be a big job. And a hell of a lot bigger for somebody without any carpentry experience."

"I did the inside mostly by myself with just a little help from Sue Ann Simpkins and Tessa," she explained proudly.

And for the effort got only another knowing shrug. "Not knockin' it," he said. "I know that's hard work, too. But inside work and outside work are two different things, Daisy."

Anna let out one more sigh. The truth was, she was beginning to see his point. She didn't like to give up on something—but just a few minutes with that gutter had shown her it was the tip of a very big home repair iceberg, and that even if she could muddle through it on her own, bit by bit, it would be a long, rough, project that she might not do an especially competent job on. And that she could end up growing old before she ever got her bed-and-breakfast open. Still . . . "The thing is, I love my brother Mike, but he has a bad habit of hovering over me and trying to do everything for me."

He nodded. "Yeah, guess I might have noticed that some last summer."

Anna wasn't surprised because she and Duke had crossed paths at more than one event last year, related to both Lucky's and Mike's weddings. "And if I get him involved, he'll just hover even more—which is a habit I'm trying to break and part of the reason I moved up here. To be close to my family, but not *too* close."

He nodded again, and she thought maybe he understood that since Lucky had once told her Duke lived in this area because it kept his family in Indiana within driving distance—but also far enough away that they didn't see each other often.

"And if I ask Lucky or even hire somebody from town, Mike will know and get involved whether I want him to or not. So it's just a situation I want to avoid." But now she found herself taking a long, disparaging look at the large house as well. "Even if it's beginning not to seem very practical."

The sun began to feel hotter to Anna than it had all day up to now as they stood there in silence, both seeming to weigh it. And just when she'd begun to wonder, for the first time ever, if she'd bitten off more than she could chew in buying this place, Duke quietly said, "I could help you."

As his words sifted slowly down through her, she dared to look at him once more. "You could?" She hadn't seen this coming from the hermit in the woods who had actually succeeded—wildly—in being an even bigger hermit than *she* had unwittingly become.

He gave another of his short, quick nods. "Not for free, though. You'd have to pay me."

She tilted her head, gave him a slightly critical look. "Or we could consider it rent."

He returned a glance just as challenging. "Then I'd be wanting a few improvements on the place, Miss Landlord."

She felt a conceding expression come over her face before she could stop it. Since the structure he inhabited was indeed a shit hole of the highest degree and his being there didn't cost her a dime. "Okay, point taken. And all right, I'm willing to pay you a fair enough wage. But . . ." She squinted slightly in his direction. "Why do you want to work on my house? I mean, I thought you were all 'I just want to keep to myself and live in the woods.' " She said the last part in a deep, gruff imitation of him.

"Maybe I could use some physical exertion," he replied without missing a beat. "Or maybe I need a way to pass the time."

She tilted her head first one way, then the other, still trying to size him up. Because there was clearly way more to Duke Dawson than she'd been able to figure out so far. "Fair enough," she finally said. "But . . . mind if I ask what you need money for? I mean, you just sold Gravediggers, and I'm guessing you got a lot more than you invested since, from what I hear, you built a good business. And your living expenses seem to be on the low side right now."

This time he hesitated, but only briefly, and his voice grew more wooden when he said, "Mind if I ask you to quit being so nosy and mind your own damn business."

She flinched—since she hadn't seen that coming, either. After all, it had seemed like an obvious question to her, and she seldom saw the point in beating around the bush. "Fine," she snipped. "Maybe it *is* none of my business. But . . . there's one more thing, and I'm *making* it my business."

"What's that, Daisy?" he asked, sounding annoyed.

"You need a haircut and a shave—bad."

He lowered his chin, offering up a bored, irritated expression—though she could barely see it beneath all that hair. "Told ya before—not real concerned with my looks right now."

"But I am. If you're going to be around the house, I don't want to think I've spotted Bigfoot in my yard every time I glance out the window." She didn't mean to be rude, but she felt strongly about this—if he was going to work for her, she didn't want to keep feeling frightened of him. If he looked a little more like he used to—the scar notwithstanding—maybe it would help.

Still, he balked. "Can't say I'm feeling much like a trip to the barber."

"Then I'll do it," she informed him.

His dark eyebrows shot up at the offer. "You know how to cut hair?"

Though she did have a little experience with it, she kept her expression dry. "What does it matter? It couldn't look any worse than it already does. Anything I do will be an improvement." If he could be belligerent, so could she. In fact, he seemed to bring it out in her.

When he hesitated a long moment, Anna thought maybe the whole deal might actually fall apart over this—until he surprised her by saying, "Okay." Just that.

"Fine," she said, offering up a pleased nod. "Come back tomorrow, around lunchtime, and I'll cut your hair. Then we can get to work."

Another quick flick of his head signaled his agreement, and he appeared ready to head back to the woods. Which suited her fine. As usual with him, she was feeling the need to escape, to process all this, but she couldn't really go running away from her own yard.

Though as he trudged toward the trees, crossing the driveway, she called, "One more thing."

He looked back, the tree line in the distance providing a fitting backdrop for the man who lived within.

She crossed her arms and tried to appear brave—even as she asked, "Do I have any reason to be afraid of you?"

He hesitated only a second before replying. "Don't worry, Daisy, you're safe with me." Then he added under his breath, "More or less." After which he turned and walked away, leaving those last three words to echo in her brain.

"Show me your face without fear."

Gaston Leroux, *The Phantom of the Opera*

Five

"*N*ice car," Duke said as Anna let him in the house. He pointed vaguely over his shoulder toward the Mustang in the driveway. And to her dismay, she still found it jarring to make eye contact with him in the first few moments they came face-to-face.

"Thanks," she said, shifting her glance in that general direction as well, even though she couldn't see the car from this angle—just because it was easier than looking at *him*. The classic Mustang got a lot of compliments, so given that he was a motorcycle guy and that it seemed like motorcycle guys were also often car guys, she was almost surprised it had taken him this long to comment.

As she turned to lead him to the kitchen, where she planned to cut his hair, she realized he'd paused behind her in the foyer and was looking back and forth between her and the car—slightly visible out a side window now. "Doesn't gel much, though," he said.

She blinked, confused. "What doesn't gel?"

"You and that car."

She flinched, feeling a little insulted. Since it was a great car—produced the first year Mustangs were ever made—and it was in mint condition right up to the black convertible top. She'd bought it right after she'd gotten her inheritance—an indulgence, a distraction, a reward for what she'd been going through at the time.

Duke narrowed his gaze on her. "Just seems like the wrong car for a girl hiding herself away up here on Half Moon Hill."

"You judge people by their cars?" she asked, letting her eyebrows lift.

He gave his typical shrug, "Party girls don't usually drive minivans. And librarians don't usually drive Corvettes. Or Mustangs."

"I'm not a librarian," she said dryly.

"Innkeeper," he reminded her. "Close enough."

She tilted her head, wondering if he was teasing her—or if he really thought she was boring. "Well, the innkeeper thing is new—and I've known a few librarians in my day who could party with the best of them. So just never you mind thinking my car is wasted on me. I promise it's not."

"Never you mind," he murmured, repeating her words as he followed her to the kitchen. "You learn that at innkeeper school?"

She let out a short laugh before she could stifle it. "No, I probably picked it up in Destiny—because believe me, a year ago, that phrase never would have come out of my mouth."

"So you're . . . going through some changes then," he acknowledged.

And that's when she realized she wasn't necessarily comfortable getting any more personal with Duke Dawson. Her

changes were *her* business. And he'd made it clear that whatever *he* was going through was none of hers, several times
now. So she simply answered with a noncommittal "Maybe,"
then pulled a chair out from the small table situated against
one wall, dragging it to the kitchen's more open area.

"Guess you do seem different—in ways—than when I met
you last summer," he said. "You didn't seem like an innkeeper then."

She could feel his eyes on her, could feel him picking a
bit, prying a little, hoping she'd explain herself. But that just
made her all the more stubborn about it. So she met his gaze
long enough to say, "And *you* didn't seem like a guy who
would hide out in a shack in the woods."

"Touché, Daisy," he replied.

And she said nothing more on the subject—but liked that
he'd used a word like *touché*. She hadn't seen that coming
from Duke Dawson. Talk about a man of mystery.

"I set out some shampoo," she said, motioning to the
kitchen sink. "You should wash your hair before I cut it."

He looked at the sink—then at her. "In the sink?" he asked.

Should she offer him her shower? But . . . no. Just no. Duke
Dawson naked in her house, for any reason whatsoever—
just . . . no. "Make do," she told him.

A few minutes later, he sat down in the chair, his hair
hanging in soft, wet, messy waves to his shoulders, some of
it falling down in his eyes, as well. As she draped a towel
around his shoulders, she tried to appear confident, as if she
were an expert cutter of hair—and as if being this close to
him again wasn't already making her uneasy. But it was.
It had been challenging enough just to talk to him in the
foyer—yet now she was touching him, sort of, as she secured
the towel. He smelled like the woods, but in a good way—
sort of piney, earthy. And why on earth had she thought this
seemed like a good idea?

She'd blurted out the suggestion before thinking
yesterday—it had seemed like the obvious solution and

she'd been under a lot of stress at the time. Now, though, she began to question *everything*. Cutting his hair. Letting him work for her. Even agreeing to keep his secret. Despite the moments he'd seemed normal, even bordering on friendly—and hell, he'd seriously come to her rescue yesterday—she still couldn't shake the idea that she was somehow being sucked into something a bit dangerous here.

"Meow." Anna looked down to see that Erik had arrived on the scene. Figured.

"Your cat," Duke said. Like maybe she wouldn't recognize him. As Erik padded about their feet and the chair legs, meowing a couple more times, Duke asked, "What does he want?"

"I don't know," Anna replied. "He's annoying that way."

"You feed him?"

"All the time. He's probably going to get fat. But it never shuts him up."

Ready to get down to business here—because she had to be—she reached for a comb. And then she paused. If she was cutting his hair, she had to comb it out—but even doing just that suddenly seemed . . . surprisingly intimate.

"Something wrong?"

Crap. He was looking up at her, those steel gray eyes pinning her in place as usual, even while peering through locks of damp hair.

"Nope," she said merrily. "Just . . . trying to figure out where to start with this mess."

"It's not *that* bad," he protested.

But she shrugged her disagreement. It was pretty bad. Yet she dove in with the comb anyway then, because she didn't want to appear too timid to touch his hair, for God's sake. After all, she was cutting it, not running her fingers through it in passion.

Yikes, where had *that* thought come from?

From your lack of sex. It's no biggie. Just cut the guy's hair and move on with your life.

She stood over him, carefully combing his hair back over his head, trying to be gentle. But *some* snarled tangles required actually working with the hair, holding locks of it in one hand while she combed with the other. She couldn't help noticing the texture of it between her fingers and thinking how odd it was that she'd ended up with her hands in Duke Dawson's hair.

"Ow!" he groused as she fought with one particularly tough tangle near his ear.

"You sure are sensitive for a big, tough biker guy," she said, still untangling.

"You sure are rough with a comb."

"Toughen up," she advised him. "I'm sure you've been through worse."

Though she kind of regretted the words as soon as they left her—she'd been teasing him, but maybe he wouldn't take it that way. Maybe it would be a reminder of bad things. Though . . . perhaps it heartened her a little to know Duke Dawson had weaknesses, just like everyone else.

Once his hair was combed out, hanging straight down now around his head, she reached for the scissors. She actually owned a pair of hair shears—one of her closest friends back in Indianapolis was a hairdresser, and when they were younger, Julie had given Anna a few lessons in trimming.

"Sure you know what you're doing with those things, Daisy?" he asked doubtfully, dark eyebrows knitting.

Rather than reply to the question, though, she simply warned him, "I'd be careful calling me that while I have scissors in my hand."

He just gave her a look and she didn't respond further. She couldn't help taking a little perverse thrill in still not putting his mind at ease about her skills. It seemed like a bit of payback for all the times she'd felt off-balance since meeting him in her woods nearly a week ago.

"So . . . what was with all the old music yesterday?"

She combed a section of his hair, pulling it neatly away from his head until she caught it between the fingers of her other hand and began to snip, cutting away a large chunk and letting it fall to the floor. "Albums and an old record player I found in the attic."

"Yeah?" was all he said, but his tone made her think he might actually find it interesting, the same way she did.

So she went on. "They belonged to a girl named Cathy who lived here in the fifties. Actually, I think she may have lived here all her life. The attic is filled with her stuff, and I've started going through it. Just out of curiosity."

This time his only reply was "Hmm," but again she thought he was more intrigued than bored. And it made him feel more . . . human to her or something. Unless she was just imagining it.

Don't read too much into this guy's personality. You still don't know him very well. Yes, he saved your butt yesterday—but that doesn't mean he's a saint. So don't go trying to make him into something he's not.

Stay wary.

It just seemed like good advice to give herself right now.

When things went silent, she said, "Can I ask you a question?"

"I'd rather you didn't."

She ignored the taut reply. "Why'd you sell your bar? And why, again, are you living the way you are? I mean, I can get wanting to be alone for a while, but . . . you're taking that to kind of an extreme, don't you think? And you don't seem to mind being around *me*."

"Don't jump to conclusions there," he said dryly.

And she let out a short huff. "Whatever. Are you going to answer my question?"

At this, he let out what she thought was a rather exaggerated and long-suffering sigh. "Look, I agreed to let you cut my hair, not interrogate me, Daisy. How about we just stick to business."

Standing behind him now, she sneered and stuck her tongue out at the back of his head. "Fine."

And then silence ensued, and Anna resumed concentrating solely on his hair. And that was probably good, because despite Julie's long-ago lessons, this wasn't exactly like riding a bike. Not that she figured she could really mess up or make it worse than it started out, but she wanted to do a decent job. Maybe she wanted him to think she was good at something. Better than she'd appeared to be at home improvement anyway.

As she gave him a simple, tidy haircut, she needed to check the layers she'd put in to make sure they were even. Which was why she found herself combing the fingers of one hand back through his now-short hair in the way Julie had once shown her.

Which suddenly made her stomach contract. And sent a tingly ribbon of awareness rushing up her arm when she least expected it. She held in her gasp, tried to act natural, tried to keep concentrating on her task.

But that meant running the same hand through his hair a couple more times, just in different places. So she did it—her fingertips grazing his scalp, her every nerve ending on red alert now, and more of that same sensation assaulting her.

Lord, why did this suddenly feel so intimate? She'd seen hairdressers do it to clients a million times. Why, when she did it to Duke, did it feel like something more than just checking her work? Why did it feel like . . . something she'd do if she were his lover?

Swallowing back the questions, she took a deep breath, let it back out. *Stick to business. Like Duke said.*

Though that was easier said than done, especially as she put the finishing touches on the cut, which required other little bits of skin-to-skin contact that suddenly felt . . . personal. She didn't want to run her fingertips over the top of his ear, but she had to, to remove a few snipped bits of dark brown hair that clung there. And she didn't particularly feel comfortable brushing the hair in front off his forehead, but it was necessary, to see if it was cut evenly.

She tried her damnedest to act unaffected, to keep any telling expressions off her face, but a desire she still couldn't quite understand echoed through her breasts and belly—and below, as well. As she moved around his chair, her inner thighs ached—and she wondered if she was the only one aware of all this, or if Duke could feel it, too.

And God—did she want him to?

No. No, of course not. Because she didn't *really* want anything to happen with him. He was so not her type. And not just because he was living like a caveman in the woods, either.

Even at his best, she and Duke were just . . . different. She went for the classically handsome, sporty type. Like Logan Whitaker, for instance. Or sometimes professional men, crisp suit-and-tie guys. But she *never* went for biker dudes with shady pasts. Bad boys were one thing, but *that* type of bad boy went beyond fun and into scary. And even if she'd accepted the idea of him working for her this summer, that didn't mean she *trusted* him.

When she had reason to touch his neck, she thought she'd never felt skin so soft. So much softer than she could have imagined any part of him being. Soft enough to kiss.

But stop it! Aren't lots of people's necks soft? There was nothing special about his, and thank God she'd suppressed the odd and sudden urge to lower a delicate kiss there.

All things considered, she'd never been so glad to finish a task in her life as when she set down her scissors, content that the haircut was finished.

"How is it?" he asked.

"It looks good," she replied, short and sweet.

"You didn't shear me like a sheep, did ya?"

She rolled her eyes. "Of course not. Relax."

Yet as she stood back before him, taking in her

handiwork—and still trying to look as if hair was the only
thing on her mind—she realized they still had that scraggly
beard to deal with.

So as she reached to the counter for the disposable razor
she'd brought down from her bathroom with the beard in
mind, she informed him, "But we're not done yet." She held
the razor out to him.

And he scowled at it. "It's pink."

She blinked. "So? It works the same way." And continued
offering it to him. "I'm guessing *you'll* want to do this part."

Though he surprised her by saying, "With that thing? Not
really." His voice dropped slightly as he added, "Besides,
I'm outta practice. Might cut myself. Especially without a
mirror." It was the first time she'd ever heard Duke Dawson
actually sound . . . a little embarrassed.

The fact was, Anna had never shaved anyone's skin but
her own. And she couldn't help thinking that a man's face
was probably somehow different than her legs or underarms.
And there was a lot of hair there to be removed. But something in his tone stopped her from questioning him further—
and it made her think something she'd never expected to:
that perhaps, just possibly, Duke needed somebody to take
care of him a little.

After using a different pair of scissors to trim off the bulk
of the beard, she grabbed up the pink can of shaving gel
she'd brought down as well. Squirting some into her palm,
she watched it expand into white foam, then began to smooth
it over his remaining beard.

Which was sort of like rubbing his face. Even if it *wasn't*
really. She could feel the warmth of his skin, even through
the hair and shaving cream; she could feel the shape of his
strong jaw. When her eyes darted to his mouth, she realized
how close their faces were—and purposely leaned back a
bit.

Her heart beat too fast as she moved to the sink to wash
the remnants of foam off her hand and she stayed there

longer than she needed to, trying to gird herself against what, again, felt like intimacy.

As she dried her hands on a dish towel, she found herself focusing on her every move, on her fingers, on the colors and texture of the towel itself—it felt weirdly as if time had slowed and everything before her had become more detailed and vivid. *Because you're nervous. You're nervous as hell.* Her movements now felt slow and wooden, too.

But just do this. Do this and then it will be done. And then the closeness will be over once and for all. There won't be any more haircuts or sprained ankles or near falls from ladders to bring your bodies back together again—and then you can just move on to fixing up the house, opening the B&B, and getting on with your new life in a good, healthy way.

With those thoughts in mind, she turned boldly back toward him and retrieved the razor from the counter where she'd set it.

Then she handed him a bowl for plopping the removed shaving cream into.

And after that, she began carefully shaving his chin.

She concentrated closely on her work, but also tried not to bring her face back too near to his. She tried to keep from looking into his eyes. She watched the dark, wiry hair come away and studied the bare skin the razor left behind. She made slow, smooth, steady downward swipes, one after another, revealing more and more of his face.

It was strange to see him changing so dramatically right before her. She wouldn't have believed it, but maybe she'd actually grown accustomed to him being all hairy and unkempt.

He'd always worn a goatee before, but she didn't know how to go about creating that, so she shaved all the hair away, bit by bit, her stomach tightening as she began to realize that . . . Duke Dawson was a much more handsome man than she'd ever realized.

Even with the scar.

When she got to that area of his face—which she left until last because it seemed like it would be harder to shave, easier to hurt him there—she found herself biting her lip, working ever so gently and carefully to remove the hair that partially covered it.

She wondered if the skin there was more tender, if it caused him any pain to have her working around it. She wondered if it embarrassed him to know she was so very aware of his scar in that moment and that she was exposing still more of it. In fact, the scar was longer than she'd realized, stretching down his right cheek almost all the way to his jawbone. It reminded her that he'd been through terrible things and made her feel too tender toward him.

That was when she lifted her hand to his other freshly shaven cheek, their eyes meeting. His skin was warm to her palm, his gaze paralyzing.

What are you doing, touching him? Despite her best intentions, she'd brought her face far too close again.

Lord. She wanted to kiss him.

Her mouth literally ached from the longing.

And—oh—from the look in his eyes, she thought he might want that, too.

But wait. You can't do that. You just can't.

So she sucked in her breath, dropped her hand, and stood upright next to him.

Turning away, she set down the razor, steadied herself. Her heart rose to her throat, but she tried to push down all the awkward emotion and desire currently throttling her.

You have to sound normal when you talk, not all breathy. "Okay, all done. Bathroom's down the hall if you want to check out a mirror."

He took slightly too long to answer, and when he did, his voice sounded shallow. "Okay. Thanks."

It was only after he stood, set aside the bowl he'd held, and walked away that Anna let out the breath she hadn't realized she was holding.

It's okay. You didn't do it, you didn't kiss him. And yes, this is crazy awkward. But it will pass. And he'll act normal. And you'll act normal. And everything will be . . . normal.

But then she bit her lip and faced the truth. Nothing between them had been normal so far, so what were the chances of it suddenly getting that way now?

" . . . by affecting excessive interest in outside matters, strove awkwardly to hide from each other the one thought of their hearts."

Gaston Leroux, *The Phantom of the Opera*

Six

Anna found herself back at Under the Covers. She'd told herself she wanted to pick up some classic and popular paperbacks for the inn—she hoped to grow one of the small sitting rooms on the east side of the house into a library of sorts, where her guests could come for reading material, and this seemed like the obvious way to start. Though she knew she was really just running away from Duke.

Well, not completely. Yet there was no denying that it was at least part of the reason she'd driven into town. She'd worked near him some yesterday afternoon after his haircut, and again this morning, but . . . damn it—the man was suddenly too good-looking. Scar or no scar. Somehow losing the beard, and the fact that she'd unintentionally given him a far shorter haircut than he'd had when she'd known him last summer, had turned him . . . shockingly gorgeous. Which made the not-kissing-him thing a little harder. And the working-with-him thing a little tougher. And so taking the rest of the day for a trip to town had seemed like a good idea.

She'd told him she needed to run some errands. So she'd figured she'd better come home with something in a bag in case he was still there when she got back. But hopefully she could kill enough time here that he'd have knocked off for the day by the time she made the return trip to Half Moon Hill.

"Are you ever going to plan that wedding, Amy? Tick tock and all that," she heard Sue Ann say from the front of the store. When she'd arrived, Amy and some of the girls had been congregated in the easy chairs near the entrance, big coffee cups in hand. They'd invited Anna to join them, of course, as they always did—and despite that even both her brothers' wives, Tessa and Rachel, were there, she'd politely declined, saying maybe after she selected some books. Secretly, she hoped the party would break up before then.

"I know, I know," Amy said. "Weird, isn't it? I've wanted to plan a wedding my whole life, but now that I have one to plan, I just can't decide what I want."

Rachel chimed in then, too. "Well, if you're still shooting for fall, Sue Ann's right—you need to get crackin'. So sayeth the maid of honor." As Anna understood it, Rachel, Amy, and Tessa had been best friends their whole lives, and they'd agreed to trade off maid of honor duties—Tessa had been Rachel's, Amy had been Tessa's, and now Rachel would be Amy's.

"Hope you're gonna be able to do your job," Amy said teasingly. "You've been so under the weather lately."

"I'm fine now," Rachel said emphatically, "so don't you worry about me doing my duties." Though Anna glanced up the aisle where she stood shopping in time to see blond, stylish Rachel make a face and press a hand to her belly. "Mostly fine. Stupid summer bug."

"Well, I'm glad you're finally getting well," Amy said, more sincere now. "I was starting to be concerned."

But as Rachel swiped a hand down through the air, confidently brushing off the worry, Tessa said, "And speaking of decisions . . ."

Everyone went quiet, clearly waiting for her to go on—and Anna waited, too, wondering exactly what decision her sister-in-law had made. Only that was when the door to the small bathroom in the rear of the store opened, and Anna looked down the aisle of bookshelves in the opposite direction to see Jenny Brody come out, her expression haggard, her posture tired. She shut the darkly stained wooden door, then turned around to lean back against it, shutting her eyes, and letting out a visibly sad sigh.

Anna felt like an accidental voyeur, witnessing a private moment not meant to be shared. Maybe she should ditch looking for books and join the other girls, after all.

Of course, Jenny chose that moment to open her eyes back up, making instant eye contact with Anna. Too late to run away and leave her be. Which left only one choice. Uncertainly, Anna took quiet steps toward her.

When she reached Jenny, she spoke low enough not to be heard at the front of the store where the other girls still chattered. "Um, I don't want to bother you, but . . . are you okay?"

Appearing a little shell-shocked, Jenny nodded—unconvincingly. But then immediately switched to shaking her head instead.

Anna felt uncomfortable, but plowed forward. After all, isn't that how any good Destiny-ite would proceed—let her concern override her fear of intruding? "Can I help?"

"That's nice of you, Anna, really—but . . . I don't think so. This can't be fixed." She still looked deeply pained, and Anna couldn't help thinking it would make much more sense for *any* of the other women in the store to be having this conversation with Jenny instead of her.

And then Anna remembered. "Is this about what you and Sue Ann were discussing the last time I saw you? About . . ." For some reason, she dropped her voice to a whisper, as if it were something forbidden. "Getting pregnant?"

Jenny swallowed visibly, then gave another nod, her expression switching to one of sheepishness. "I just get so emotional over it without warning. It's stupid."

Anna automatically reached out to touch her arm. "It's not stupid. It's natural." She'd never wanted to have a baby herself, not yet anyway, but she understood how deep that sort of yearning could run. Her deceased adoptive mother had once wanted a baby so badly that it had driven her to extremes.

"Is it?" Jenny asked. "You think so? Because I feel like a basket case."

She was clearly embarrassed, and it didn't help that she and Anna barely knew each other, so Anna wanted to put her at ease. "Of course. I mean, when you want something and aren't sure how to get it, it can be . . . hard to hold yourself together all the time."

Jenny's eyes softened as she said, "You sound like you know."

"Maybe," Anna said.

Then Jenny flinched, as if suddenly remembering something else. "Oh Anna—God, I'm so selfish. I mean, you've been through so much, and . . ."

But Anna shook her head. The two situations really couldn't be compared. "You're allowed to be upset, Jenny. I'm sure I would be, too, in your situation."

Jenny sighed, looked a little appreciative, a little awkward. Then she asked, "How do you do it, Anna? How do you stay so strong even when you're going through something hard?"

Anna drew in a breath, thought about the question. "Maybe some of it is just a good act," she admitted.

"And maybe some of it is finding other things to focus on. Maybe it's about . . . looking for new directions or something."

Jenny nodded, and appeared to be weighing the idea. "New directions. Like buying your house and turning it into a bed-and-breakfast."

Anna nodded. Though . . . maybe "new direction" was just a prettier way of saying "distraction." After all, even coming to Destiny—which had seemed so brave in ways—had probably at heart just been a distraction from her mother's death. And maybe it had only opened up new problems from which she'd then needed more distractions. And . . . now that she thought about it, even the house was now requiring still *more* distractions—or the guy helping her fix up the house was anyway. And it occurred to her that maybe seeking out distraction after distraction meant she wasn't really ever facing her issues—but at least it kept her moving forward in some way, kept her from crumbling.

"Well," Jenny said, "maybe I'll . . . try to think about that. Maybe find some way to apply it."

"I'm sure you'll find the answer," Anna encouraged her.

Jenny reached out, squeezed her hand, and made her feel like she'd actually said something worthwhile. "Thanks, Anna. And sorry to pull you into my troubles when I'm sure you have enough to deal with already."

Anna just shook her head. "I don't mind, really." And the truth was, just like with Duke, maybe it was comforting on some level to find out other people had problems, too. Even someone whose life looked as perfect from the outside as Jenny Brody's.

Jenny motioned to the front of the store. "I should get back to the girls." Then she offered a smile. "Come hang out with us."

And Anna took a deep breath. This should be easy. Easier than she'd let it be so far. So she said a quiet "Okay," then followed Jenny up the center aisle of bookshelves. She still felt every bit the outsider, but maybe it was time to start taking baby steps to change that.

As they emerged into the open area at the front of the shop, Tessa was saying to Amy, "Don't worry, I won't abandon you until you find somebody else. It's just that my business is finally doing so well that time has become an issue."

Amy sighed. "I knew this day was coming—I was just hoping I was wrong. I've so loved having you here the last few years."

"What's happening?" Jenny asked.

The other girls looked up, and Amy said, "Tessa's quitting." Tessa worked part-time at Under the Covers, but even Anna had tuned in to the fact that since Tessa's interior decorating business was picking up steam, she'd probably quit her bookstore job soon.

Though Tessa sneered, managing to look pretty even with her nose scrunched. "Quitting, blegh—that sounds so ugly. I've loved working here."

"Oh, I know," Amy said. "But I knew it couldn't last forever. I'll just need to find someone to take your place."

And then, very slowly, as the idea apparently began to blossom in Amy's head, she turned to peer up at Anna. "Um, any chance *you* want a job?" She raised her eyebrows hopefully. "It wouldn't have to be forever. And it's only part-time. And it's kind of fun—just ask Tessa."

Tessa smiled up at her. "It really is. And . . . if you don't mind my saying, Anna, I know you're eager to get the inn open, but it might do you some good to get out of that house more. It's made you . . . quieter than you used to be when you first moved here."

"And it would be a good way to get to know more people," Rachel suggested. "I mean, you're making your home here and starting a business, so getting to know the locals would be a good idea, don't you think?"

Hell. Anna couldn't argue with the logic, any of it, because it was all so true.

And there was a bigger reason staring her in the face right now, too, that no one knew about: Duke Dawson. If she started spending some afternoons or weekend days minding the shop for Amy, it would be that much less time she'd spend with *him*, that much less time she'd have to worry about how hard it was to look him in the eye—or about . . . wanting to kiss her outlaw biker neighbor-in-the-woods.

So even if a brand new job right in the heart of Destiny was, in one way, the last thing Anna wanted—in another, it seemed perfect. The perfect . . . new direction. Or distraction. Whatever. "Um, okay," she said. "I'll do it."

And as Amy clapped her hands and let out a happy little squeal, Anna took the opportunity to look at Jenny, standing next to her, and quietly say, "See? New directions. They're everywhere when you start looking."

Of course, that made her sound so much more together than if Jenny knew the whole truth behind her reason for so easily accepting Amy's job offer: *I need a distraction from the scary guy at my house who I keep wanting to kiss. Bad.*

Rachel Farris Romo stood in the living room of the old family farmhouse she shared with her husband, staring into the large mirror near the front door. Her skin looked pasty, and too pale for summer. And her stomach still wasn't right, no matter what she kept telling people. She supposed she'd been trying to will it away because she'd found at certain times in life that actually worked—she'd willed away a terrible virus in time for the prom back in high school. And—also in high school—she'd once willed away a hickey from Russell Jamison before her mother saw it. But this— whatever it was—didn't seem to be a matter of will.

Not much in life got Rachel down—she didn't let it. So the fact that this illness kept hanging on—and was starting to deplete her spirits—was more than a little troubling. She'd gotten married just last summer—to the man of her dreams, Mike Romo. She'd returned to her hometown and couldn't be happier. She and Mike helped her grandmother Edna run the family apple orchard which would one day be theirs. There'd been a time when she couldn't have imagined any of those things happening, and now that they had—now that she felt she'd found where she belonged in life . . . well, what if something was really wrong? What if this was something serious?

Don't think that way—it's crazy. Fate wouldn't do that to you.

But fate does that to good, happy people all the time.

Just then the front door opened and Mike walked in wearing his police uniform and looking grouchy after a long shift. But Rachel was used to her big, tough cop husband's gruffness—and she took pride in being one of the few people who could take it in stride. Dealing with a little gruffness was worth it for all she got in return.

But he'd caught her off guard and she knew she'd just looked up at him like someone caught committing a crime.

"What's wrong?" he asked.

"Nothing." But she sounded guilty even to her own ears.

He just tilted his head, gave her a look. Early in their relationship, trust had been a bit of an issue for them—like the time she'd snuck out to Duke Dawson's biker bar with Tessa so Tessa could "casually run into" Mike's brother, Lucky— and though her small deceptions were long in the past, she supposed suspicious behavior brought them back to mind. "What's going on here, Rachel?" he asked in a lecturing tone. "What aren't you telling me?"

She shook her head, then glanced back to her reflection in the mirror, downcast. Mike was the one person she could be the most open with, but she didn't want to tell him about this—she didn't want to make him worry. "It's nothing really. It's just . . ."

And then a wave of nausea came over her and she had to reach out to the sofa table beneath the mirror in order to keep her balance.

When she raised her gaze back to his, she knew he understood. "You're sick again."

"Or still," she admitted. "Depending upon how you look at it."

"I'm sorry you're still feeling bad, honey," he said, concern washing over his expression as he moved toward her.

Rachel sighed and knew she had no choice but to just come clean with him. "It's not so much being sick that bothers me as . . ." She'd dropped her gaze again but now lifted it back to his face. "I guess it's starting to worry me a little. It's been a few weeks. And a stomach bug shouldn't last that long."

Mike moved forward, drawing her into the strong embrace that always made her feel comforted, safe. It helped. "I'm sure it's nothing big," he murmured near her ear. "But maybe it's time we get you to the doctor."

Rachel *hated* going to the doctor, and in fact, she'd probably been there less than most people because she was usually very healthy. Maybe that was why this had her worried. And Mike was surely right—it was nothing. But she looked up and gave a small, acknowledging nod.

"Where's Shakespeare?" Mike asked then. Their big fat tabby cat, adopted from Amy's bookstore soon after they'd met.

"I don't know," she murmured. "Why?"

"Cuddling with him always makes you feel better when anything's wrong," he said. "Thought maybe you two could curl up on the couch while I make something light for dinner that won't bother your stomach. How's that sound?"

She managed a small smile for him, even through another light wave of nausea. "Perfect," she said. She'd never thought about it, but Shakespeare did usually take her mind off her troubles. Though when had she become such a cat person? Well, about the same time she'd become a small town person, and a person who loved Mike Romo.

Coming back to the little town where she'd grown up— and promptly abandoned after high school—had brought her so many blessings that it was hard to imagine still living the old life she'd left behind in the city. Now she just hoped she'd get to keep her new life in Destiny for lots of long, happy years to come.

Duke stood on the same ladder Anna had nearly fallen from a couple of days ago, hammering a nail into a piece of wood he was using to replace a worn one. This place needed a lot of work, but it had good bones, as his dad used to say when evaluating whether it was smarter to rebuild something or just tear it down and start over.

And the solid structure underneath all the disrepair made the work easier than it looked. He'd originally thought he might have to dismantle the whole wraparound porch and rebuild it from the ground up, but the underpinnings were sturdy, and that helped.

On one hand, it was a convenient time to dive in on the porch repairs—particularly the ones right outside the front door, and the steps that led to the yard, because Anna was gone and had been for hours. But on the other . . . Hell, he couldn't deny that something in being here, in the work itself, was a little less satisfying knowing she wasn't around.

Already, after working on the old Victorian with her for only a very short time, he realized that he looked forward to the parts of the day when they talked—even if Daisy got sassy with him. And he even missed times when she *wasn't* working directly with him. Just knowing that he might see her walk to the mailbox or pass by a window, just knowing she was somewhere nearby, kept the hours, minutes . . . more interesting.

You are fucking ridiculous, dude. He gave his head a short shake to try to clear it. He'd obviously been living in the woods too long if he got all worked up over just seeing a pretty girl check the mail.

Of course, he supposed things had escalated beyond the quiet, distant attraction he'd felt for her—during that haircut the other day. Damn. Every time she'd touched him, it had felt like an electric current shooting through his body. It hadn't made any sense to him because . . . well, he'd been close to her before, and yeah, he'd felt something those times, too—but these had been such small touches. Her hand in his hair. Her fingers on his neck. And each time, it left a trail of fire. It had been all he could do to sit there and act natural, especially since he'd been slowly getting an erection. It had been like no other haircut he'd ever gotten, that was for sure.

And he hadn't quite known it was a two-way street until a little later when he could have sworn she was going to kiss him. Even remembering that moment now sent a soft chill up his spine despite that it was eighty-five degrees outside and a hot May sun beat down on his newly shorn neck.

But he'd just sat there, hadn't made a move. Because she was his best friend's sister. And he knew she'd been through a lot herself. She'd been abducted at the age of five and had only found out about her real family last summer. He couldn't even imagine going through something like that. So . . . she had a lot of baggage. And since God knew he had a lot, too, it just didn't seem like a good combination—even just for some good, hot sex.

And turned out that had been a damn wise decision on his part, because that was when she'd backed away, ending it.

And he knew why, of course. The scar. She might have felt the same physical pull toward him that he'd been feeling toward her, but apparently when it came right down to it, when she'd seen how he really looked, even all tidied up—it wasn't enough. She'd figured out that she couldn't fix what was broken about his face, even with a haircut and a shave.

He'd known that all along, of course, so he wasn't surprised.

But it had still stung. Maybe more than he'd expected.

It had been one thing to see her freaked out by the way he'd looked *before*—but the way he looked *now* . . . well, that was real life, how he could expect women to react to him from here forward. And it had been one thing to know it would be that way, but another to experience it. To see the repulsion in someone's eyes. And especially someone as beautiful as Anna Romo. She'd looked as afraid of him as she had that first time in the woods.

Hammering the next board in place, Duke realized he was pounding at the nail too hard, leaving round dents in the wood. *Calm down. This doesn't matter. This doesn't change anything.*

It's not like he'd suggested working for her because he wanted to get in her pants, after all. He'd suggested it because the idea of some physical labor, of doing something solid and real that you could measure at the end of the day, appealed.

Before he'd left home and gone to California back in his early twenties, he'd spent most of his teens working with his dad and uncles constructing barns, docks, room additions—whatever anyone would pay them to build. And, of course, he'd done the same kind of work when he'd first come to this area, saving up the downpayment for Gravediggers.

He'd not realized he missed that kind of labor until he'd gotten a close look at her house and seen all that needed to be done. He'd simply felt the urge to do it, make it better than it was right now. And even though he'd asked her to pay him, it had nothing to do with money—he had plenty of money in a bank in Crestview. It just had to do with . . . needing to feel a little more alive than he did just hanging out in the woods all day. And that seemed . . . kind of healthy for a change—probably the healthiest feeling he'd had in a long time. And this was the perfect way to do that without having to dive right back into normal life, without having to deal with people. Well, except for Daisy Duke and her sexy little shorts.

Once he'd gotten used to the idea of her, those hot denim shorts had actually started seeming like a perk. But now it was a . . . perk gone wrong.

Doesn't matter, though. He'd just forget the perk part, the attraction part. He'd do what he'd told her—help her fix her house and consider it a decent way to spend his time. That was all.

And after that? After the house repairs are all done?

Well, he'd cross that bridge when he came to it. This was a big house and it would take some time. Most of the summer at least. And a lot could happen over the course of a summer.

When the project was over, maybe he'd be ready to somehow ease back into real life again. Or . . . maybe he'd just go back into the woods and do a better job of letting them swallow him up this time.

Duke had been working with Anna on the house for a few days now and she thought it was going well. Even if she hadn't liked accepting that there were some things she just didn't have the know-how or muscles to do, it was a relief to have someone who *could* do them. And despite the awkward moment she'd created after his haircut, things had been relatively normal since then. Especially since she'd spent part of the time gone—and since she knew she'd be spending even more of it gone now that she'd impulsively accepted Amy's job offer.

And when she was here, well, sometimes she discovered herself finding even more reasons to leave. While he'd removed the gutters yesterday, she'd driven to Crestview and ordered new ones—with information and measurements he'd given her. And today as he'd taken off the shutters, she'd worked on sanding the old, half-chipped-away green paint off them in the driveway, one by one. Which was still being here, but . . . also being away from him.

"I'm starting a part-time job at the bookstore in town," she'd told him earlier as he'd carried another shutter to the driveway for her. "So I'll be gone some afternoons. But I'm sure you can carry on without me." From the very first second he'd begun working on the house, after all, he'd pretty much started running the show.

He'd met her gaze briefly, but then shifted it away. "I'm sure I can, too."

Whereas he'd started joking with her a little before—now, ever since the near-kiss, he'd gone all straight-faced and gruff again. One more reason to regret that almost move. She'd kind of *liked* a jokey, teasing Duke—much better than this huffy and puffy one.

But as she'd watched him walk away, disappearing on the other side of the house, she'd decided maybe this was for the best. Maybe if *she* put distance between them physically, and *he* put distance between them emotionally, it would . . . just ensure they kept things all business. As they should have in the first place.

Now he stood out in the hot sun between two sawhorses in the backyard, measuring and sawing boards into various lengths and sizes to repair the wraparound porch and front steps. Anna, conversely, sat in the shade of the screened-in porch looking at paint colors. She was trying to decide if she wanted to go for a cheerful palette, or if an inn should focus more on being warm. She liked the happy, sunny feeling of a buttery shade of yellow, but she was also drawn to a paint chip just a bit darker than Wedgwood blue. Something about it felt solid. If, in fact, a color could *feel* solid.

She didn't need to make a firm decision yet, though, and she didn't want to rush it and regret her choice later, so for now she set the color chips aside on the wicker sofa where she sat—and indulged in the urge to pick up Cathy's diary again. She'd read more as time had permitted these last days, and though much of it had been dry recitations of schoolwork and a report on how much of what Cathy and her mother had canned one hot weekend in May, she still enjoyed getting a unique glimpse into this house she could have gotten in no other way—and she liked the idea that reading the diary was like bringing Cathy back alive in a sense, making her life matter all over again. More of Cathy's records played in the other room as she read.

Checking her watch, she saw that it was almost five. *So I'll read for a few minutes, then start dinner.* Not that she knew what dinner would be—while she'd dabbled with things like beef stew in the Crock-Pot, and meatloaf, back when it had been cold out, these days she tended to keep things light and simple, opting for hot or cold sandwiches. And she found herself glad her inn was going to be a bed-and-breakfast, because it meant she only had to perfect some dishes for one meal of the day—sadly, her meatloaf and stew hadn't been much to brag about.

She glanced out at Duke again in the yard, still sawing away. He looked down at his work and didn't see her watching, making her observation easier. God, he looked good. And not just his face now, either, but somehow cleaning him up had given his lean yet muscular body a whole new charm, too. She couldn't deny enjoying the way the muscles of his arms and shoulders moved beneath his T-shirt as he sawed.

But stop. Thinking. Of him. Like that.

She pulled in her breath, glanced away.

Yet as she opened Cathy's diary to the page where she'd last tucked the ribbon, she wondered if she should invite Duke to stay for dinner. Because she still didn't know what he ate out there in the shack. And she had plenty. And there was really no reason for both of them to eat alone when they could eat together.

Well, except for her decision to keep things all business.

Which she really, really had to do. It had been one thing to try to be neighborly before she'd almost kissed him, but if she kept being that way, now it just seemed like an accident waiting to happen.

So no dinner offer.

And maybe this attraction would blow over as time passed. Maybe as they worked together, and got more accustomed to spending time together, the urge would go away. It could happen.

But for now, play it safe. Keep your distance. Don't do anything stupid. Because getting any more involved with Duke Dawson would definitely be a mistake. And the longer she sat there watching him work . . . well, the more the urges inside her grew.

She'd just had no idea he was so handsome. Or that his jaw had that strong, chiseled look about it. Or that under that beard he'd possessed a tiny, sexy little dimple in his chin.

And as she'd recognized before, the mere act of being handsome seemed to amplify other appealing things about him. His broad shoulders. His muscular arms. His potent gaze, something she might now even sometimes describe as downright smoldering. Still watching, she continued to enjoy the way his muscles moved when he worked—hell, she liked the way he moved in general.

Okay, but stop watching him now. Read your diary. That seemed a much safer way to occupy her mind for the next few minutes.

> *Our beans are up in the backyard garden and*
> *Mother says this weekend would be a good one*
> *for canning them. I'm already so tired of early*
> *canning this year, though, that I could just die.*
> *And must we always do it when the weather's so*
> *hot?*
>
> *Robert is picking the beans now and tonight*
> *Mother and I will wash and break them. I*
> *offered to help with the picking, but Daddy said*
> *no—he still thinks Robert is some sort of danger*
> *to me.*
>
> *Though Robert smiled at me once last week.*
> *While talking with Mother about the day's*
> *chores, when she looked away he glanced*
> *toward me and gave me a friendly grin. And I*
> *don't think he's dangerous at all. Or if he is . . .*
> *well, it's somehow more . . . enticing than scary,*
> *if that makes any sense. And I'm not sure it does,*

since how could danger be enticing and appeal-
ing? All I know is that when he smiled my way,
it made something inside me sizzle like when
Mother is frying up chicken in a skillet, and I
wanted to know him better.

Ever since then, I've been hoping he might
smile at me again, but he hasn't. I keep watching
him, though, since, if I get the chance, I might say
hello to him, or if it's across a distance, maybe I'll
wave.

Anna smiled to herself, remembering that *enticing* had
been on a list of vocabulary words Cathy had written into
the diary a couple of weeks earlier. Then she lifted her gaze
back through the large screened window to where Duke
worked. Was this the same as Cathy's view of Robert when
he'd been picking beans? She suddenly wondered if, when
the home repairs were finished, she should perhaps ask Duke
to plant a garden for her. And then she laughed at herself, all
caught up in Cathy's first crush.

Looking back to the diary, she turned the page and found
entries about the end of the school year and attending the
graduation ceremony for the class above Cathy's. She'd
gotten another new dress for the occasion—white with
tiny pink rosebuds—and she liked it particularly because
the cut was more grown up than most of her dresses. And
while Cathy was glad school was over, the weather sounded
unseasonably hot even for the start of June, and the summer
seemed to be stretching endlessly before her without any
friends or fun nearby.

Then came an entire two page entry about a blue and
black butterfly that kept coming to the flower beds lining
the porch, and how Cathy came to think of it like a friend.
Which made Anna sad. *This is what happens to people who*
spend too much time alone in a big house. They start hang-
ing out with butterflies. And talking to cats.

She turned the page, pleased in a totally voyeuristic way
to see that *this* entry was about Robert. Because Anna liked
butterflies just fine, but Robert was a lot more exciting.

*This afternoon I was sitting on the summer porch
watching Robert hoe weeds from the cucumber
patch in the garden. The sun was beating down
hot—it was hot even in the shade—and I began
to think he looked thirsty. Daddy was still at
the bank and Mother was in her sewing room
upstairs, so I decided to take Robert a glass of
lemonade.*

*I thought maybe I'd be nervous doing it, but
instead, I walked right up to him, bold as you
please. Because the moment seemed to call for
that, you know—I think if you're going to do a
thing, you've got to just be brave and do it. Otherwise, what's the point? And so I held out the glass
I'd poured and I said, "Thought you might enjoy
this on such a hot day."*

*He looked up at me, looked right into my eyes.
His were so green, like a pine tree. I'd never
noticed that before, having only been close to
him a few brief times, but now I couldn't stop
noticing. When he took the glass, his hand
touched mine and it sent a wonderful tingle all
through me. He smiled and said, "Thank you,"
just that, but something in the way he said it
made me feel . . . special somehow. Like . . . if
Mother had given him the lemonade, he'd have
appreciated it and all, but not in the same way.*

*I stood and watched him drink it. I wasn't
sure if that was the thing to do, but I reasoned
he wouldn't want to be bothered with the glass
afterward, so I decided to wait. And I found
myself feeling oddly jealous of that cool, sweet*

lemonade sliding down his tan throat. And
seeing mysteries in him that I wanted to solve.
When he gave the glass back to me, he said,
"Appreciate it, Cathy." He knew my name!
"You're welcome, Robert," I told him. Because
I wanted him to know that I knew his, too.

Anna clapped the diary shut, sighing with satisfaction.
She didn't want to turn the page because nothing in the next
entry could match this—and she wanted to savor Cathy's
moment a little while, as if doing so somehow brought it
back and made it real again, not just a long ago occurrence
that no longer mattered in anyone's world.

Then her eyes fell back on Duke in the yard. He looked
hot. Figuratively and literally. He appeared absorbed in his
work, so she felt comfortable narrowing her gaze on him.
Had his T-shirts always fit him that way? And his jeans?
Something about the way those jeans hugged his butt—
not tight but not loose—was somehow just right. And—oh
Lord—there was a bulge. In front. She wanted to get closer
to it on sight.

Okay, stop this. Seriously. And don't let the experience
of a sixteen-year-old girl over fifty years ago let you get all
wistfully caught up in the idea of first passion. Maybe keeping Cathy's memories alive had a downside.

And stopping was easier commanded than done, since now
everything about her view of Duke in the yard was something
she felt as much as saw. Low in her belly. Lower, actually.
Raw desire stretched like long, feathery fingers down through
her pelvis, expanding wildly between her legs. Del Shannon's
"Runaway" came from the record player in the house.

Anna drew in a breath, let it back out. Then she bit her lip,
determined—and yet not quite able—to pull her eyes away.
She shut them in frustration and blew out a soft sigh.

Maybe I need to cool down with some lemonade. She
tended to drink a lot of lemonade in the summer and had

just mixed up a fresh pitcher this morning, so now seemed like a wise time to get up, go inside, and pour herself a glass.

As she did so, she consciously pushed down her feelings. She was an adult, after all, not an adolescent girl in the first blush of romance. And if she really wanted a guy, she could find one that would likely be a lot better for her—and safer, in lots of ways—than Duke Dawson. She could start hanging out with her brothers more, and meet their other friends. She could go with Rachel and the other girls to Mike's softball games, a place she'd learned last summer was absolutely teeming with sexy, sweaty, athletic men—just her type. And who knew—maybe working at Under the Covers really *would* push her out into "Destiny society" more and maybe she'd meet some eligible guys naturally. And then she wouldn't have to worry about getting all worked up over a very not-her-type guy just because he happened to be the only one in the vicinity right now.

But as she stepped back out onto the screened porch, she saw that—oh Lord—Duke had set down his saw in order to strip his sweaty T-shirt off over his head. She gasped slightly because it was a beautiful sight. She just hadn't imagined—couldn't have accurately envisioned—him looking this way. His skin was slick with sweat as another bead of it rolled down his well-muscled chest. And she couldn't help thinking that he looked . . . thirsty. Same as Robert had.

Would it really hurt to give him some lemonade? The man was working hard, after all, and it was hot. She couldn't have him getting dehydrated, could she? And sure, she'd told him to help himself to whatever he wanted in the fridge, and she'd seen him come in a time or two and leave with a bottle of water, one time a soda—but it couldn't hurt to save him the steps, right?

This is a very bad idea. He's way more dangerous than Cathy's Robert ever could have been—she knew that without doubt. She told herself again that if she wanted a sexy, sweaty man she could find plenty of them somewhere else.

And yet she found herself going into the house, pouring him a glass of the lemonade she'd mixed up this morning. She became aware that her fingertips, arms, actually tingled with the motions she made. Then she was walking back out, and over to the screen door, pushing it open. She heard it slam shut behind her, saw him look up. She wasn't even completely aware of making the decision—only felt herself moving toward him, almost as if gliding on the hot May air.

When his eyes locked on her, she couldn't read his serious expression and didn't even try. Yet her breasts ached beneath his gaze, and God knew she suffered the same heavy yearning below as well.

"Lemonade," she said. Though when had her voice gotten so husky?

Something in his hesitation, in the look in those blue-gray eyes, told her he was sizing up the move, trying to figure out if it meant something—if it was indeed about more than lemonade. But then he took the glass, their hands brushing—wetly, from the condensation on the outside— same as Cathy's and Robert's had. And like Cathy, she stood there and watched as Duke tipped the glass to his mouth and took a long, cool, somehow ultra sexy drink. She could almost feel it running down her throat as well, could almost taste the cold, lemony goodness at the same moment he did.

And then, just like walking out here, what happened next took place without her decision or consent.

Her hand rose, almost of its own volition, and reached out to touch his stomach.

She pressed her palm flat against his hard abs. She felt the sweat there, felt the heat. She knew her hand was cold from holding on to the glass.

Done drinking, that's when he lowered his gaze, his eyes locking back on hers.

And she realized what she'd done. Oh God.

Sucking in her breath, she pulled her hand away as emphatically as if she'd touched a hot stove. And her heart beat so hard that her chest hurt.

Go. Get out of here. Now. She could deal with the embarrassment of this later, but right now her instincts told her to run away. Just like when she'd first seen him in the woods.

But as she took the first step back, ready to turn and flee, Duke's free hand closed around her wrist. He drew her hand back toward him. He pressed it flat against his stomach the way it had been before, holding it there.

Anna could barely breathe. Her heartbeat pounded in her ears. And she felt the stark connection—her palm to his slick, warm skin—in her panties. "Um . . ." she began.

But Duke quieted her, saying, "Shhh . . ." And then he smoothly slid her hand downward, lower on his belly, over the waistband of his jeans, and then below—stopping it on the shockingly hard bulge behind his zipper.

She gasped just before he let the near empty glass fall to the grass and kissed her. And it was then that Anna understood what it was that had frightened her so much about Duke all along. It was this. It was the invisible thing about him that was as potent as it was powerful. And it was knowing, already, that she couldn't say no.

"You're trembling . . . you're quite excited . . ."

Gaston Leroux, *The Phantom of the Opera*

Seven

The kiss swallowed her, owned her. Anna had thought she'd been kissed passionately before, but this went beyond any kissing she'd ever experienced. There was no thought, no inner protest, no room for remembering what a bad idea this was. There was only his mouth on hers, his strong arms wrapped around her, his hard body pressed into her softer one.

And speaking of hard—oh Lord. She'd moved her hand from between them now, her arms twining naturally around his neck, but she could still feel—both in her mind and somehow still in her palm, too—how very hard he'd been. Her heart beat all the more violently for the knowledge—that he'd gotten that way for *her*, and that she'd touched him there already.

It had been perhaps the most starkly intimate moment

she'd ever shared with another human being—and it was someone she barely knew. And she thought that should have made it feel empty somehow, yet it didn't. It was as if she'd known him just barely well enough for that ever-so-personal touch to be shockingly powerful, to move up through her arm and out through her whole body like high voltage electricity. Maybe that was why she thought she could still feel it in her hand—the energy it had delivered had been left behind.

When Duke's tongue pressed into her mouth, she welcomed it and instantly let her own join his. The second their tongues touched, a fresh burst of arousal blossomed moistly between her thighs. As she became all the more lost to his kiss, she realized she clutched at his neck now, as if hanging on for dear life, her body gone weak. The sun blasted down, plastering their skin together with perspiration, but Anna felt nothing but heat.

As Duke shifted her body, his knee slid between her thighs, his leg pressing snug against the spot between, escalating her every physical response. The position drew their chests tighter together, their stomachs—and her hip met his erection, which she could have sworn was even bigger and harder than before, only that didn't seem possible.

She drew in her breath at the contact, the primal need for more coursing through her like wildfire, and it ended the kissing. Their faces remained close, though, their eyes meeting. In one way it broke the spell, the intoxication, the loss of control—but in another it heightened it. The locking of their gazes was like both of them acknowledging it. *This is real. We're right in the middle of it. We both feel it. We both want it.*

Just when Anna feared she would combust, Duke lowered another hot kiss to her mouth, somehow reckless and soft at the same time.

She'd known she was attracted to him; she'd known the pull was potent and increasing. But she hadn't known until now just how wild and untamed their connection would make her feel.

When Duke planted his hands on her ass, through her jean shorts, pulling her even more snugly against the column of stone behind his zipper, a small whimper erupted from her throat. And as he heaved her body upward, lifting her from the ground, her only response was to wrap her legs around his waist and hold on tight.

They resumed kissing yet again as he carried her through the yard, toward the house. Part of her didn't even want to bother—wanted him to just lay her down in the grass—but the idea of shade and coolness sounded nice, too; she liked the idea of him being in her bed, between her soft, flowered sheets. Because he contrasted with them so much, maybe. Because it would remind her all the more how dangerous he was, and right now, the particular danger he brought to her life sounded like a *good* thing.

She wasn't sure they'd make it all the way upstairs to the bed, though. Without planning it, she ground the juncture of her thighs against his erection, making him let out sexy little groans between kisses. And she wanted him inside her as she'd never wanted a man before.

She could tell herself over and over that this was just about not having had sex in a while, just that her body was missing it, but she could no longer deny that this was about more—a stark, heady chemistry that kept them gravitating toward one another, a hot, smoldering pull between them that had simmered and heated until finally now igniting into flames. She couldn't want just any man this badly—she couldn't. It was Duke Dawson she wanted; no one else.

They kissed more as he smoothly climbed the back steps with her in his arms and maneuvered the screen door open, carrying her inside. Crossing the screened porch, he got them through the inner door as well, and into the kitchen. Little Richard was belting out "The Girl Can't Help It" as Anna began to wonder exactly where they'd end up, figuring she must be getting heavy—when she felt him letting her slip from his grasp. So she untwined her legs, her feet finding the floor.

The cooler air inside the house wrapped invitingly around them as he pressed her back against the doorjamb between the kitchen and a small sitting room. They didn't stay there, though, both of them moving forward even as they touched each other, soon embracing again, making jagged, uneven steps toward the front of the house.

When they reached the front room, Duke stopped kissing her, pulled back, his hands planted on her upper arms. "This is as far as we go, Daisy," he rasped.

What? He was stopping? Anna nearly couldn't breathe. "Huh?" she murmured, dumbstruck.

His next words came between panting breaths. "No bed," he said "Sorry. Right here."

"Oh," she whispered, possibly more relieved than she'd ever been in her life. He wasn't stopping. In fact, he couldn't wait any longer. A realization which made her say, "Oh!" again, this time much more excitedly as fresh enthusiasm blossomed inside her and she threw her arms back around his neck, just wanting to kiss him some more.

Duke's hands clamped firmly onto her hips and he moved her a few steps backward, then pushed her down onto the same sofa where he'd lowered her that first day after she'd sprained her ankle. She lay there, propped on her elbows, eager and waiting, ready to be thoroughly ravished.

Within seconds, he was on his knees on the couch, between her thighs, reaching down to the hem of the embroidered tank top she wore, pushing it up over her breasts in one brisk move to reveal the hot pink bra underneath. Without hesitation, she lay back onto throw pillows, freeing up her arms to remove the top the rest of the way, over her head.

Her breasts ached and she knew the urge for him to see them so she kept going, reaching behind her to undo the hook and toss the bra aside. She felt like the wildest of sex kittens to have bared herself for him, to glance down and see her pointed nipples between them right there in the late afternoon light.

A low, sexy growl left him as he studied her, his gaze as potent as a touch and hardening the pink peaks further. But at the same time, he'd moved on, clearly as impatient as her—his fingers now worked at the button of her shorts.

She reached up to his waistband as well, a hot, heavy breath pushing past her lips as her touch brushed unavoidably across his erection once more.

They started pulling each other's pants down at the same time, and Anna lifted without reserve, letting him lower hers, her small panties coming down with them. Duke's jeans dropped to his thighs to reveal snug gray boxer briefs underneath—and, oh God, the tip of his erection peeked through the front opening.

Another tiny gasp escaped her at the sight, and her throat tightened with excitement, anticipation. Something about what had happened earlier in the yard made her bold now, bold enough to reach up, thread her fingers neatly into the slit in his underwear, extract his length, and wrap her hand firmly around it. It was hot to the touch.

Duke hissed in his breath in pleasure, and her chest heaved in unbidden response. She was so, so ready, and she knew he was, too.

Except—oh no—a terrible thought hit her. "Condom," she said, horrified. Because they didn't have one.

So it surprised her when he responded by reaching back, into the rear pocket of his lowered blue jeans, to pull out a wallet, then a familiar-looking foil square. She let out a sigh of relief—then asked, slightly stunned, "Even in the woods, you carry a wallet?"

He shrugged. "Habit, I guess."

"A good one," she murmured, and as he ripped into the condom, she relaxed back into her arousal and squeezed him in her hand again, beginning to rub and massage lightly.

His eyes fell half shut and his breath turned thready, and she released the hard column from her grasp only to let him roll the condom down over it. She parted her legs without thought or hesitation, looked up into his eyes, and waited—and then came the sweet, hot, filling entry she'd ached for.

She cried out as the pleasure spread through her, hard and deep. He hadn't been especially gentle—and she hadn't wanted him to. He'd made her feel it, really feel it. "God—yes," she breathed through clenched teeth.

Their labored breathing saturated the quiet air as Duke moved in her. Each hard stroke seemed to reach her very core, fill the need that had been running through her more and more ever since meeting him. Finally, he was inside her. It hadn't been terribly long since that first encounter, of course—but somehow it felt that way; somehow it felt like something she'd been waiting a very long time to experience.

She clutched at his shoulders, his arms. She loved the feel of his muscles beneath her fingers, the sight of his broad chest just above her, and his handsome face, eyes shut in passion now. She still didn't think about the right or wrong of it, the smart or dumb of it—because she still knew that it didn't matter now; she was in it, doing this, and she had no regrets. He felt too good. He filled her with more pleasure than she'd ever known, something thick and deep that went far beyond having an orgasm.

Even so, though, when he stopped moving after a while and began to shift, his hands on her ass, moving them both, she realized he was sitting them up, so that she'd end up on top—and that suited her fine. While the way he'd been pounding into her had delivered all the sensation she could handle, she liked the idea that he wanted to make her come and that he knew how. Even without his saying a word, she understood that.

Duke leaned against the sofa's backrest and Anna straddled his hips, feeling him even deeper that way. And mmm, yes—the mere position itself inspired her to move on him, ride him.

Just when she'd begun to think he might never touch her breasts, he lowered his eyes to them, then—almost tentatively, she thought—slid a work-roughened palm up onto one.

She sucked in her breath as he began to mold it in his hand. Letting her eyes fall shut, she covered his hand with hers, pressing his touch deeper, making sure he knew how much she liked it. Her nipple moved against his palm as *she* moved against *him* below, the rhythmic gyrations taking over her body now. There was something primal about sex with Duke, something that made her feel every bit of her womanhood while reveling in how very masculine he was.

She never made the decision to lean forward, to whisper, her mouth near his forehead, "Kiss them. Please."

But she heard his hot sigh, then drank in the joy as his mouth closed over the tip of her other breast.

"Unh." The sound left her as the sensation permeated her, spreading deep, filling up any crack or crevice of her being that the pleasure from below hadn't quite yet reached. Pure physical delight radiated all the way from her core out to the tips of her fingers and toes. She cradled his head against her breast, running her fingers through his hair—*this* time like a lover.

She peered through sheer white curtains behind the sofa out onto the yard and could have sworn the grass looked greener, the trees more billowy, the sky and white puffy clouds deeper, bigger. Heat filled her cheeks as, below, she knew she was getting closer, closer. She heard her own hot sighs, felt profoundly connected to him, and surrendered to it entirely.

"Oh God, oh God . . ." And then the orgasm broke over her in stunning waves of heat and pleasure that stole her sanity for a long blissful moment of pure abandon. A few short cries and whimpers left her as she rode out the climax, still hugging his head to her chest.

And when she was done, going still, thinking a bit of rest had come—Duke thrust up into her, hard, hard, hard, lifting them both from the couch, making her cry out. He groaned deeply with each upward drive, and Anna let her head drop back, eyes shutting again, just absorbing everything he wanted to give her.

"Aw—aw, now," Duke murmured deeply, then thrust even more roughly, again sending the powerful sensations the length of her body—before finally letting out a large sigh, all movement ceasing.

They slumped together in exhaustion. Anna whispered, "Wow." And then smiled to herself because when she'd bought the house on Half Moon Hill she never could have dreamed she'd find a wildman in her woods and end up having the best sex of her life with him.

"Um . . ." Anna said after a few minutes of silence.

Duke opened his eyes, which had fallen shut at some point in those post-sex moments when sleep came so easy. He found himself wishing they were in a bed, since falling asleep right now still sounded good, but being on the couch, sitting up, made that a little more awkward. He guessed her "um" meant she felt awkward, too.

And he probably should have let her off the hook, since he didn't really know what to say, either—but there was something about Daisy; he just liked messing with her, liked seeing how she handled it. Maybe because when he'd met her last summer, she'd seemed so cool and above it all. And she was so damn beautiful, too. Maybe it surprised him over and over to discover he could make her squirm a little. So he lifted his head from where he'd rested it on the back of the couch, expended the effort to raise sleepy eyebrows, and said, "Um what, Daisy?"

God, she looked even prettier as a deep, rosy color infused her cheeks. And the late day sun shining in the front window through the sheers shone on her eyes, making them a richer

shade of brown than he'd ever noticed before. "Um . . . that
was pretty great," she said quietly, almost tentatively.

He couldn't help it—it made him smile even as it warmed
something in his gut. "Yeah, it was."

It was hardly the first unplanned sex he'd ever had—
and it wasn't the first time he'd been in a situation where a
smoldering attraction had suddenly led to this kind of full-
blown heated encounter. But this . . . this meant more to him.
Because it changed things. It meant . . . maybe he wasn't as
hideous as he thought. Or that even if he was, she'd seen
something in him that had overpowered that. He'd honestly
never expected a woman to feel those things for him again.
Not in this kind of truly hot, feral way. He'd thought that part
of his life was over, and he'd even started accepting it—as
much as a man could accept that sort of thing. But Daisy
had just brought all that back in a heartbeat—the heartbeat
it had taken for her to press her hand to his stomach in the
backyard.

There were things he almost wished he could ask her.
*What made it happen, that hand on my stomach? What do
you see when you look at me? Am I some horrible, revolt-
ing beast—or not?* But maybe he didn't really want to
know, wasn't that brave. Maybe he just wanted to bask in
the moment, and the surprise of it. Maybe he just wanted
to keep holding her in his arms and know that feeling of
mutual desire. And hell—why would he bring that last part
up anyway? To anyone? Nah, it was easier to feel strong
if you just kept acting that way. That was something he'd
known all his life and it had never failed him.

*Then what the hell are you doing living in that cabin in
the damn woods?*

He let out a sigh, his eyes falling shut once more. This was
the one time when he'd finally lost it, that strength that kept
him going no matter what shit he was up against. The one
time he'd surrendered and just . . . run away. From everything. As much as he could.

But that didn't mean he had to give up the little bits of strength that might still be lingering inside him. If he'd finally found one—however unexpectedly—he wasn't about to throw it away. It was suddenly something to hang on to right now. And he already knew it would help him sleep a little more peacefully tonight.

"You, uh, wanna go upstairs? The bed might be more comfortable."

He opened his eyes and appreciated the uncertain look in hers. She was nervous inviting him.

"Are you asking me to snuggle, Daisy?"

The instant change in her expression told him she was trying to appear more aloof. "Or . . . take a nap. Whatever sounds good."

He met her gaze, wondered if she could see the affection in his eyes. "Sure—let's go upstairs."

She remained on top of him, with him still inside her, even now a few minutes after they'd both come. And as she eased up off him, the separation of their bodies was a raw, potent reminder of what they'd just shared. She let out a sigh at the disconnection as his length, partially erect even now, plopped against his belly.

And suddenly he wanted to stay close to her, just like they were—so as she started lifting her leg to unstraddle him, he said, "Nah—just wrap around me." And he didn't wait for her to respond before closing his arms snug about her waist.

After finally kicking off his pants, he got to his feet still holding her in his embrace—it was a lot like the way he'd carried her inside the house—and walked to the stairs. Turned out it wasn't the easiest way to climb steps, but when he nearly lost his balance and loosed one hand from her ass to grab on to the railing, saying, "Whoa," she clung to him tighter, all naked and sweet, and said, "Don't drop me!" and they ended up laughing.

"Left," she instructed him at the top, then pointed to the

last door in the open hallway that wound around the stair-case.

It was pretty much what he would have expected her bed-room to look like now that he was getting to know her a little better: cozy but full of light with the sun streaming through the front window, a quilt on the bed full of blues and purples and pinks. Pink roses that he assumed she'd cut from the large bush on the west side of the house protruded from an old-fashioned milky white glass pitcher, and their scent filled the room. He didn't know anyone still did that—cut flowers and brought them inside. It reminded him that his grandma had always done that when he was little, but he'd thought the world was just too busy for that kind of thing these days. And he'd have thought Anna Romo would be the last girl to do it—or he would have before recently. But he was learning there was more to her than met the eye.

He plopped her unceremoniously on the bed—then admired her body all over again. It was the first time he'd seen it from any sort of distance, and damn, the girl was amazing to look at. He'd always thought she *would* be—she generally dressed in a way he liked, showing she was proud of her curves—and he wasn't disappointed. She was a dark-haired, olive-skinned Barbie doll come to life.

He watched as she lifted her ass from the quilt, pulling it down and then scooting her way under. He might have thought it would be hot underneath but for the ceiling fan turning in gentle circles overhead, so he pulled back the covers on the side of the bed nearest him and got in with her.

Then he followed the urge to reach out, draw her to him, kiss her some more.

The truth was, depending on the woman and situation, he wasn't usually much of a cuddler. But he wouldn't have accepted the invitation to come up here if he didn't want to keep being close to her. If he'd ended up with this woman at some other time in his life, maybe it would have been strictly about the hot passion of the moment and then moving on from that—but right now, a little snuggling sounded good.

Maybe it all just amounted to . . . comfort. And hell, he couldn't deny that he could probably use some of that.

She lay on her back and he leaned over her, kissing her pretty berry-colored lips as he let his fingers flirt lazily, gently, with the outer curve of one full, round breast. He thought it might be the most perfect skin he'd ever touched, soft yet firm—so very feminine, and already tightening his groin again, just slightly.

When the kiss ended and he pulled back a bit, looking at her, she said, "I don't usually . . ."

"What?" he asked, amused. "Kiss on the first date?"

She smirked slightly, even while appearing a little sheepish. "I do kiss on the first date," she explained, "if I like a guy and feel the urge. But I don't usually do *this*."

He raised his eyebrows playfully. "No worries, Daisy—we're both grown-ups and I don't judge." Then he tilted his head, thinking back to last summer. "Even if what you just said surprised me some."

She didn't look insulted or even remotely taken aback. "Looks can be deceiving," she replied. And when he lowered his chin, a little caught off guard that she knew exactly what he was talking about, she added, "A girl can show a little skin without it meaning she gives it away to every guy she meets. But a lot of people don't realize that. A lot of people think it's advertising—when, for me, it's just being comfortable with who I am."

Duke didn't know what to say. Until he'd seen her here, at her house and in the woods, he supposed he *had* thought her sexy style sent a certain message. But now he felt stupid to have made that assumption. He was beginning to think Anna Romo was a lot more complex than most women he'd dealt with.

"Now that you mention it," he told her, "you seem . . . different. Than last year when I met you."

She bit her lip and appeared introspective, staring off in the distance. Then she shifted her gaze to his, asking, "How so?"

He chose his words carefully—because he didn't want to

say anything she'd take the wrong way. "Last summer, you just seemed . . . above it all. All cool and confident. Like nothing could touch you. And now, here, you seem more . . . well, I just wouldn't have pegged you to bake cobblers or have a country quilt on your bed. I wouldn't have picked you as a girl who'd be content living so far from town. You just seemed . . . too sophisticated for Destiny, and *way* too sophisticated for Half Moon Hill."

She lifted one side of her nose into a slight sneer. "I'm not sure whether that's a compliment or an insult."

"Neither," he said quickly, and it was true. "Just what I thought. But . . . maybe finding out I was wrong about that makes you a more interesting person."

She bit her lower lip, broke the gaze, let her eyes drift off in the distance again—toward the roses on the dresser across the room. "Last summer wasn't the easiest time of my life. And acting confident is how I get through stuff. So maybe I was laying it on a little thick then."

Duke knew good and well what she meant about last summer—but maybe he hadn't thought, until this very moment, about the fact that he'd been forming his opinions of her right when she'd been going through something so weird. And maybe he shouldn't ask, but . . . "Guess that was pretty damn strange, huh? Coming back to a place you hadn't been since you were little? Meeting your family for the first time since then?"

When she still didn't look at him, he decided maybe he shouldn't have brought it up, but it was too late now.

And he'd just decided that maybe she wasn't going to answer at all—when she did. "I can't even describe it. In some ways, it . . . fixed a lot of things. And it certainly made me feel a lot less alone in the world. But in others, it just complicated everything. I think maybe I should have waited longer after my mother—my other mother—died before coming back here. I'm not sure I was ready to be a part of a family as big as the Romo clan." She paused, scrunched up her nose. He thought she looked cute as hell. "But then again, I'm not sure I'll *ever* be completely ready for that. I thought I wanted to be part of a family—and I love them all, my mom and dad, Mike and Lucky—but to go from being an only child, who had to take care of her mother a lot and be the adult in the relationship far too early, to being part of a big, complicated family who still wants you to be a little girl . . . is hard."

Duke swallowed back the emotion he sensed welling for her inside him. Damn, he hadn't expected that. Because he hadn't expected Daisy to go soft on him. And maybe it was time to just shut up and quit talking—God knew the idea of kissing her some more, being inside her again, appealed. And it would probably be easier for both of them than discussing difficult things. And yet he found himself too curious to keep from asking . . . "Why'd you have to take care of your other mom?" He hesitated, almost afraid to pry. "Was she sick?"

Her eyes finally darted to his. "Lucky never told you?"

All he knew was that Lucky's little sister had been missing since the age of five, that it had torn their family apart in some ways, and that last summer she'd suddenly shown up in Destiny, explaining to the Romo family that she'd learned the woman she'd always thought was her mother had actually abducted her. "I knew your . . . other mom died, and that she told you right before then that she'd . . . taken you from that park." Another tidbit Lucky had shared—it had happened on a family camping trip to Bear Lake, about an hour away from Destiny. "But he never mentioned what was wrong with her, why she died so young."

"It was cervical cancer, but I had to take care of her long before that." She drew her eyes away again, and he could tell it pained her to talk about. Her discomfort, despite the brave way she tried to hide it, tightened his chest. "She wasn't well. In her mind. So there was just a lot of . . . taking care of. And making excuses for. And trying to act like everything was fine when it wasn't. So . . . I guess I was doing a lot of that last summer. Because nothing was very fine. But I didn't know any other way to deal with it besides just taking it day by day, and pretending it was all a breeze. And occasionally having a yelling match with Mike," she ended on a laugh.

Duke laughed along with her. Her brother Mike was an easy guy to misjudge—Duke had done that himself once upon a time, but then he'd found out what he was about to tell Anna. "Both your brothers are actually pretty damn good guys."

She shifted her head on the pillow to meet his gaze and appeared more relaxed. "Oh, I know. Mike just wants to be the big brother I never had. Or haven't had since I was five. Sometimes I think he wishes I was still a little girl because he missed so much of my life."

Duke narrowed his gaze on her, glad he'd managed to turn the conversation back to something at least a little less heavy than her abduction. And for some reason, what she'd just said reminded him how lucky he was right now, and that maybe he was wasting his good fortune by talking so much. Hell, when had he become such a talker anyway?

"You're definitely not a little girl, honey," he told her, easing his hand down her body beneath the covers. His palm drifted lazily across one breast, then over the flat plane of her belly and lower, until his fingers dipped between her legs. The moisture he found there seemed to ripple up his arm and down through him, settling in his lower pelvis and turning him rapidly hard again.

And once more it hit him—how he'd never expected to feel this mutual heat, this shared sexual electricity, again. He'd been flirting before, casting a seductive grin when he'd said she wasn't a little girl—but something caught fire inside him now that squelched any playfulness. It was need, thick and potent. Hunger. Urgency. And it instantly took him over.

In a flash, he was on her, towering over her, pinning her hands on either side of her head, their fingers interlocking. A short breath of passion escaped her as their eyes met and it was just like outside a little while ago—that perfect knowledge that they both felt exactly the same, that they were on fire for each other.

But then—aw hell. "Shit," he murmured. "Condom." His jeans were still downstairs.

She drew in her breath tightly at hearing the word.

And damn, he didn't want to stop—he wanted her so much he felt like he was about to explode.

"I'm always careful," he told her in a mere rasp, hoping to make her believe.

Her pretty brown eyes widened, searching his. "Always?"

"Always."

"Me too," she told him. But then she bit her lip, still looking wary, and he couldn't blame her. "Do you promise?"

He nodded, because it was the truth. "I'm a lot of things, Anna, but I'm not a liar. And I don't think I've ever wanted a woman as badly as I want you right now."

She said nothing then, continuing only to gaze into his eyes—until her reply finally came, silently, as she parted her legs beneath him.

"You are under a very dangerous spell."

Gaston Leroux, *The Phantom of the Opera*

Eight

*W*as she being stupid here? She didn't know for sure, but . . . she trusted him. A revelation which somehow made it that much more powerful when he thrust back inside her, flesh to flesh, nothing between them. She squeezed his hands tighter in hers at the impact and wondered again, ever so briefly, how on earth she'd gotten here—between the sheets of her bed with Duke Dawson.

But then she quit thinking and just basked in the pleasure as he filled her with it, over and over. She cried out at each deep plunge, letting the sensations echo outward from her core. She'd missed sex, but more than that, she'd missed this connection with a man. She'd missed the rawness of it, the honesty of it, the way it put their differences on display—hard and soft, masculine and feminine. And as she'd told him, she didn't usually have sex this quickly, so it had surprised her to discover how much she continued to feel that sense of connection with him, and how very right it seemed. Even if he was her brother's best friend. Even if he was the wildman in the woods. But now he felt wild in a whole different way.

She didn't know how long he moved in her, driving hard and fast, never stopping to rest—she only knew that soon thought ceased altogether and only sensation remained. She loved looking up into those piercing gray eyes, she loved the stubble on his jaw, she loved all the contours of his body against hers.

When finally his motions did slow, he released her hands from his to let his palms glide slowly, firmly down her body, over her curves in a way that echoed to her very soul. And then he kissed her, deeply. Her eyes closed and their tongues met.

And when the kiss ended a long moment later and she reopened her eyes to find his mere inches above her, meeting her gaze, she was almost shocked by the intimacy. It was something almost tangible, touchable. *How do you feel this with a guy you barely know?* And yet, there it was, nearly stealing her breath.

"Do you have any idea how damn beautiful you are?"

The words sizzled down through her. Lots of men had given her compliments—but something in Duke's tone, or maybe it was, again, in his eyes, made her really *feel* it in a way she never had before. So much so that she actually shook her head against the pillow. And whispered, "Not until right now."

He kissed her again and resumed those long, luscious strokes into her body. She met each one, surrendered completely to her desire for him, and soaked up all that he gave her—until a low groan left him and he bit off the words, "Aw . . . sorry, honey, can't stop."

And then he was coming in her, with four mighty thrusts that nailed her to the bed—and she didn't mind at all that she hadn't climaxed this time because she couldn't imagine feeling any more right now than she already did.

When he collapsed gently atop her, she drank in the musky scent of him, liked having his bristly cheek nestled against hers. His voice came soft and deep in her ear. "Sorry, Daisy."

She gave her head a short, exhausted shake. "Nothing to be sorry for," she told him. "That was . . . amazing."

"I like the way you think," he murmured, a hint of humor back in his voice, though she could tell he was about to drift off into sleep. And she didn't mind that, either, since she was, too, and she liked the idea of falling asleep together.

When Anna opened her eyes, Duke was gone. She felt that almost even before she looked beside her in the bed to see that his spot had been filled by the cat. "You're not who I was expecting," she said. "And don't take this the wrong way, but you're not nearly as hot."

Erik, curled up against the pillow next to her, let out a defensive-sounding meow.

Anna eyed the cat. "Maybe you need a girl kitty. Maybe *that's* your problem?" Then she let out a sigh. "But I'm not getting another one of you, so you'll just have to . . . suppress those urges. Better than I've managed to anyway." She rolled her eyes, realizing it was pretty nervy of her to scold the cat for possibly wanting what she'd just had—with great gusto.

It felt empty to be left alone. To be lying naked in her bed at the dinner hour, late day sun casting shadows across the room. She knew it was the way of the world—when people had impromptu, meaningless sex, one of them often left afterward without a word and that was supposed to be okay. The other person wasn't supposed to feel . . . deserted.

Maybe that was one reason she didn't usually have impromptu, meaningless sex.

And it almost embarrassed her to acknowledge the truth

she couldn't deny: For her, it hadn't been meaningless. She didn't know him well, but you didn't always *have* to know someone well to care about them. And now she cared about Duke Dawson. Because she'd shared something with him. Something so astonishingly intense that . . . oh no, was it possible he hadn't felt it, too? Could that part of it have been one-sided? Ugh.

But no, it hadn't. She knew it. Whether or not he'd felt anything emotional, he'd definitely felt the heat they shared—there was nothing one-sided about that.

And . . . when he'd said she was beautiful, well, it hadn't been just a line—she knew that as surely as she knew the sun would set soon.

But he left.

And that's okay.

You don't have to get all wrapped up in this just because he made you feel special for a few minutes. You can appreciate sex for sex's sake like all modern chicks are supposed to be able to do these days. You don't have to be all mushy and gooey and attached to him over it.

In fact, maybe this is a good reminder that you're getting too soft. Maybe Rachel's right and hiding yourself away up here in this big old house isn't healthy.

Because if this had happened to her a couple of years ago, sure, she'd still be a little bummed, feel a little deserted—but she'd be much cooler about it than she really felt right now.

Then again, maybe it was like she'd told him—maybe some of her confidence had always been an act, bravado. Even to herself—she'd pretended unerring confidence as a defense mechanism. And what was healthier—pretending to feel something you didn't and finding some strength in that, or just letting it all go and feeling what you really felt?

She wasn't sure.

About much of anything at the moment. But the one thing she knew for certain was that she didn't intend to just lie here wallowing in self-pity. Life with her mother had taught her that, no matter what, you keep going. So she intended to get up, get dressed, and make herself some dinner. Then tomorrow she would start her new job at Under the Covers. And it seemed like a better time than ever to put some distance between herself and her outlaw biker in the woods—only for different reasons now.

She'd agreed to make her first day at the bookstore a long one, arriving at ten to train with Tessa and Amy all day. And she'd hoped Duke wouldn't show up at the house before she left—or for all she knew he wasn't going to show up *at all* after yesterday's events. But it was not to be. She opened the front door to leave only to find him working on the porch steps.

Surprised to see him, she flinched.

"Morning," he said without glancing up from his work.

"Um . . . morning," she replied.

"The more I look at this porch, the more I can't believe you haven't fallen through it. I crawled underneath and propped it up with a bottle jack I found in the garage, but this front section is weak as hell."

"Ah," she said, still taken aback, now mainly by how normal he was acting—but she didn't think it was so normal under the circumstances.

Finally, he looked up at her, but focused on the black capri pants she wore with a pair of strappy wedge heels. He appeared slightly perplexed. "Where are your shorts, Daisy?"

"In my drawer, Duke."

When he cocked his head to one side, clearly perplexed, she explained, "I start my job today at Under the Covers. So I'll be gone all day."

He simply gave a short nod, then refocused on his work, pulling a tape measure from his tool belt—the same tool belt she'd been wearing the day she'd ended up hanging from the roof—and stretching it out alongside one of the steps.

Huh. That was it? He wasn't going to acknowledge anything that had taken place between them yesterday?

Well, if *he* wasn't, *she* was. "So . . . are we going to talk about what happened?"

He lifted his gaze to her again briefly, the glimpse she caught of his eyes reminding her of how close they'd been just over twelve hours earlier, and then he dropped it back to the steps again. "Is there something to talk about?"

"We had sex," she reminded him pointedly.

"Yep, we sure did," he agreed, then let the tape measure slide quickly shut with a *click* before looking back to her. "It was hot. And it was good. Is there any reason we can't just leave it at that?"

Anna barely knew what to say. Though she held in the few things that came to mind. *You said I was beautiful. You said you wanted me more than you'd ever wanted anyone else. You felt something more than you're pretending right now.*

But her chest tightened uncomfortably when she forced herself to realize some additional truths. They barely knew each other. They hadn't gone on a single date or shared a single kiss before falling into bed together—or onto the couch, as the case had been. And the fact that he was working on her house didn't make it any more than a one-night stand. No matter how he'd acted or what he'd said.

"No," she replied, trying to regain her usual cool confidence. Even if she'd told him it was fake sometimes. It hit her then what a huge confession that had been, what a personal thing to share. Why on earth had she done that? How did this man seem to draw out parts of her that she barely even knew existed? "I just thought maybe we should acknowledge it. Since we'll still be seeing each other every day. But no, I guess we can just leave it at that."

And with that she walked to the edge of the porch— thankful she didn't fall through now that she knew just how unstable it was—and moved down the steps and past him, feeling his presence even more than usual. It was at once a relief and a disappointment to get in her car and drive away.

Anna's day at Under the Covers went well—the work was easy and even pleasant, and spending the day with Tessa and Amy turned out to be fun. She decided that was another good outcome of taking the job—somehow *having* to be with them made her feel more relaxed and less like a third wheel who didn't fit in.

During a late lunch at Dolly's Main Street Café, which Anna had learned soon after arriving in town was one of Destiny's hot spots, Amy made a point of telling everyone they ran into that Anna was working at the bookstore now, and was soon opening a bed-and-breakfast, and how wonderful the place was going to be.

"That's great," Mary Ann Davis from the dress shop said, clasping Anna's hand warmly between hers. "My parents will finally have a nice place to stay when they visit."

And Betty Fisher's face lit up as she said, "Now that my daughter has a family of her own, I think she and her husband feel a bit crowded at our house when they come for holidays. I can't wait to tell her Destiny is going to have its very own inn soon!"

Since situations exactly like these had been the inspiration behind Anna's decision to convert the house into a B&B, their responses had thrilled her and, without quite meaning to, she'd fallen into cheerful, open conversations with both women. Then realized that Amy and the whole town really *were* rubbing off on her since, while she always tried to be polite, she wasn't that naturally chatty. Until now anyway.

"See? This job is getting you customers already, on your very first day," Amy said after Betty departed.

And Anna couldn't deny it. "You're right. Thanks for talking the place up."

"I can't wait to get the grand tour when it's all done!"

"Me too," Tessa added. "And Lucky said—again—to just

let him or Mike know if you need any help and they'll be glad to come up."

Anna just smiled. She really did appreciate her brothers' willingness to pitch in—maybe more now that she knew she wasn't going to have to take them up on it. "I will. But so far, so good."

"I don't see how you're managing the exterior yourself," Tessa added. "I mean, that's a lot of work."

And part of Anna wished she could tell the girls the truth about how the outside was getting done—but she'd promised Duke. Even if he *had* made her feel lonely and forsaken last night. "True, but . . . it's all coming together."

She smiled tightly as the words left her, since she wondered if she was talking about the restoration project or her and Duke's bodies. Since, try as she might, she was having trouble getting that off her mind. Even as she spent the day concentrating on shelving books and how the cash register worked, yesterday's amazing sex with Duke stayed with her.

But that's normal. You haven't been with anyone in a while. And you've been so strangely drawn to him since you met. Well, not since last summer, but since they'd met in the woods on that now-momentous day. She suddenly wondered—if she hadn't gone out picking berries, when would she have discovered Duke living in the shack? Or would she have discovered him at all? The questions suddenly made her desire to bake a blackberry dessert seem downright fated.

But even as she remembered how good things had been with Duke yesterday afternoon, the memories of his leaving were equally painful, too. So it would be best if she stopped remembering yesterday so longingly and lustfully. It would be best if she forgot all about the more tender moments and saw it the way he clearly did—as just good sex.

So upon returning from lunch, she tried much harder to concentrate on books and people and her new job. More than once, that led to thoughts of Cathy's copy of *The Phantom of the Opera,* and somehow that led back to Duke in her mind—but even so, she kept trying to push it all away, at least for right now.

At the end of the day, after Amy had taught her how to balance the register, Anna thanked her for making her training day so enjoyable. In fact, all things considered, she thought she was going to like working at Under the Covers—for far more reasons than she'd originally taken the job. "I already feel more . . . a part of things, a part of the town," she admitted, "than I did even this morning." Because yes, she'd been back in Destiny for a year now, but it had taken her this long to inch forward into truly *wanting* to be here, and wanting to be a part of the community. And now she knew this job was going to be a big help in continuing on that path.

"I've never lived anywhere but here," Amy said, "so I don't know what it's like to go someplace new. But I can only imagine what a culture shock this place has been to you, especially under the circumstances." Anna knew Amy meant coming home after being abducted so long ago.

Just then, Amy's cell phone made a meowing noise that caused Anna to flinch. "That's my text alert," Amy said with a smile. "Isn't it adorable?"

In truth, it creeped Anna out a little—sounded like a cat was trapped in Amy's phone—but she kept her *own* smile firmly in place. "Sure. Definitely."

Amy checked her phone, then called to Tessa, who was in the back of the store straightening books. "Logan says the game's been moved to six-thirty, so we'd better step on it."

A glance at her watch revealed to Anna that it was almost six-fifteen now. "What game?" she asked, mildly curious.

And when Amy looked up at Anna, her eyes brightened. "You should come with us. There's a softball game at Creekside Park against a big rival team from Crestview. I don't know why I didn't invite you sooner. Why don't you come?"

Anna thought she actually *did* know why Amy hadn't invited her sooner—because she usually turned down such invitations. Though she'd gone only once last summer, Mike and others had invited her many times.

As Tessa emerged from between two bookshelves, she raised her eyebrows in Anna's direction. "What do you say? I'm sure Lucky and Mike would both love to see you there." Lucky didn't play on the team, but Anna knew he often came to watch.

And she was actually tempted. Not only because she was suddenly warming a little to the idea of being more social, but also because of all the good-looking guys at the ball-park. After all, hadn't Duke let her know this morning that he didn't want anything more with her than the sex they'd had? And hadn't she been telling herself he wasn't her type anyway? And weren't the kind of guys who hung out at the ballpark—friends of Mike's and Logan's— a lot more likely to be her type?

But then she bit her lip, glancing down at her platform wedges. "Am I too overdressed?"

Though Amy instantly shook her head. "We're dressed for work, too, and you look great. And we can sit low on the bleachers so you don't have to climb in those things."

So Anna decided to cast any doubts aside. She needed to keep her mind off Duke; what better way than to find some new, and more compatible, guys to focus on. "Okay," she said, "I'll go."

Anna sat between Rachel and Sue Ann on the metal bleachers behind home plate, watching the game and listening to the other girls cheer on the team. Sue Ann's handsome, dark-haired boyfriend, Adam Becker, who ran a local landscaping business, guarded first base while Logan played shortstop. Mike was the pitcher, and though he claimed to enjoy this game, Anna thought he seemed even more on edge than usual. Behind her, Amy played patty-cake with Sue Ann's daughter, Sophie, and Tessa and Lucky sat a few rows higher up with Jenny and her husband, Mick.

As Amy had predicted, both Romo brothers had indeed been happily surprised to see Anna at the game—though even then she'd thought Mike's hug had felt stiff and he'd seemed quieter than usual when greeting her. Now he was the *opposite* of quiet—bellowing at his teammates for errors, and cussing at himself for throwing a wild pitch. And watching Lucky talk with Mick reminded Anna of his friendship with Duke, something she felt she was almost impeding in some way by keeping Duke's whereabouts from her brother.

After all, wouldn't Lucky want to help Duke weather whatever he was going through that had him living in that shack? At moments, the isolation of Half Moon Hill made it easy to believe she and Duke were the only two people that existed—but seeing Lucky reminded her that she wasn't the only person here who cared about Duke.

But stop. Caring. About. Duke. In that way anyway. It just seemed like a losing proposition, leaving her angry at herself for allowing the emotion to sneak up on her, and further, for letting herself be so open with him yesterday—both physically and emotionally—since she knew that was the reason she was feeling overly attached right now.

And besides, you're supposed to be here looking at guys.

And there were plenty to look at. A couple of other local firemen played on Mike and Logan's team who were none too shabby in the hot department, and more than one guy on the opposing team caught her eye, as well.

The only problem was that she kept thinking about Duke anyway. Watching them sweat made her remember watching *him* sweat. Watching their muscular arms as they swung bats and threw balls reminded her of the way Duke's arms and shoulders had looked when he'd been sawing that wood yesterday. Or, really, when he was doing about anything with them—and at this point she'd seen those arms do quite a lot of things. *I should have let myself enjoy it more when he was carrying me through the woods.*

Just then, Mike walked the other team's pitcher, creating a bases-loaded situation. He looked as tense as she'd ever seen him.

"Come on, Mike—get it together, dude," Logan called encouragingly from behind him.

And Mike spun to face him. "You wanna pitch the damn game, Whitaker?"

Logan just gave him a matter-of-fact look, relaxing his ready stance only slightly. "No, I just want you to calm down a little, that's all."

One of the things Anna had most admired about Logan when she'd had that crush on him last summer was his ability to remain unruffled by Mike's theatrics. In response, Mike just drew in a deep breath and looked like he was trying to do as Logan had advised.

"Does Mike get like this at every game?" Anna asked Rachel.

Rachel kept her eyes on him, though her expression struck Anna as being a bit distant. In fact, now that she thought about it, Rachel seemed quieter than normal tonight, too. "No, not usually."

"Maybe I picked the wrong game to come to," Anna remarked.

And Rachel merely replied, "Could be," her voice still sounding far away, and like her thoughts weren't entirely on the conversation at hand.

Anna hoped nothing was wrong, but decided not to ask. She'd endured a lot of prying questions herself upon her return to Destiny—even if they were well-meaning—and despite her sudden and inexplicable penchant for being all open and talkative the last twenty-four hours or so, that didn't mean *everyone* felt that way.

So go back to watching hot, sweaty guys.

She tried. She really did. And it was even enjoyable in certain moments. But it was hard to concentrate on them with Mike's grousing—especially when the next two batters hit home runs—and she just kept remembering being in bed with Duke anyway.

Rachel's body felt heavier than usual as she got out of Mike's truck and walked up to the Whippy Dip, the local dairy bar where the whole gang was meeting for post-game ice cream, despite the loss. Mike hadn't said a word on the ride from the ball field, and she hadn't tried to cheer him up. She'd never seen him play worse, and she couldn't think of anything cheerful to say anyway.

When they approached, everyone else already sat or stood around a large wooden picnic table, eating ice cream cones or scoops in a dish. A glimpse of Adam's hot fudge sundae almost made Rachel want to throw up, so she looked away.

"You want anything?" Mike asked her. Given the state of her stomach lately, he almost seemed to know she didn't.

"No," she said quietly, still almost stunned beyond comprehension by what she'd found out at her doctor's visit today.

"Me neither," Mike murmured. And Mike *never* passed up ice cream.

When they slid wordlessly into the open spots left on one side of the table, Rachel tried to tune in to what Logan was saying—something about he and Amy still not having picked a wedding date. But as more conversation about that ensued, her mind drifted elsewhere—to worry, and disbelief. She knew she should be thankful; she knew she could have gotten much worse news. And in that way she was relieved, and she knew Mike was, too. She just still couldn't believe the diagnosis they'd been given.

"Rachel? Are you in there? Hello?"

She flinched, snapping her gaze to Tessa's.

"You're not having anything?" her friend asked. "Stomach still bothering you?"

She just nodded, too preoccupied to muster words.

That's when Lucky spoke up. "Hey, wasn't today your

doctor's appointment? Did you find out anything?" She supposed some people might consider the question intrusive, but they were family, and really, their whole group of friends were close, so she didn't mind. Except that the answer was still so shocking to her.

"We did," she said. Just that.

"And?" Amy asked.

Rachel and Mike exchanged glances. They'd gotten the news just before heading to the park and had, in fact, almost been late for the game, so they'd had no time to digest it, or to discuss telling their friends.

Only now, unfortunately, she could immediately sense that her hesitation was making them worry. Their expressions grew grimmer with every passing second she made them wait. So she knew that even though she and Mike hadn't made any sort of decision about sharing, she had to tell them. Especially when Amy said, "Well?" sounding almost alarmed.

"Well," Rachel said, "I'm . . . pregnant."

"An agonizing silence now reigned . . ."

Gaston Leroux, *The Phantom of the Opera*

Nine

*A*nna watched Mike and Rachel's friends react. Cumulatively, their faces were painted with surprise, joy, and confusion. And she was pretty sure the confusion was because both Rachel and Mike appeared so downcast at what most happily married couples would consider good news.

And then there were Jenny and Mick. They sat at the far end of the table, on the other side from Mike and Rachel, their expressions wooden. Mick silently slid his arm around Jenny's shoulder, as if holding her up through this.

"What amazing news!" the ever-happy Amy said. She appeared to be the only person not tuned in to the fact that Rachel and Mike weren't beaming with joy. But when no one responded to her happy outburst, her expression changed. Her eyebrows knit as she bent her head slightly to ask, "Isn't it?"

"Look, we don't mean to be assholes," Mike said, "but . . . we just didn't see this coming. We never even talked about it. Except in a 'maybe someday' way."

"All we wanted was a cat," Rachel bemoaned, "and he's handful enough."

"*I* didn't even want the cat," Mike groused. "But I went along with it."

"And just like the cat, you'll love your baby," Sue Ann pointed out, often the voice of reason in the group.

"Of course we will," Rachel was quick to say. "We just . . ."

"You just what?" Tessa asked when she trailed off.

Rachel hesitated and sounded almost a little ashamed when she replied, "I don't know if I'll be a good mother. I mean, what do I know about babies? I know about clothes. I know about advertising." Anna knew Rachel had been an ad exec in Indy before coming home to Destiny. "But I don't know anything about babies."

"And seriously, me as a dad?" Mike asked the crowd at large. "Would any of you want me as a father?"

When they all stayed silent at the question, Anna, to her surprise, felt compelled to speak up. "You'll be a good dad, Mike," she said from the end of the table nearest him.

Their eyes met and his registered utter bewilderment, even though she suspected he was trying to hide it. "I will?"

She nodded. "Because you'll care. A lot." She knew that from firsthand experience.

And when still he and everyone else stayed speechless, she decided it was time to inject a little lightheartedness into the conversation. "Now, Aunt Anna might need to lecture you on not being too overbearing—especially if, God help you, it's a girl—but I know you'll be a good dad to your kid. Just like you keep trying to be to me." And she ended on a wink that made Mike's eyes soften a little, even if he didn't quite smile.

"And you'll be a great mom, too, Rachel," she went on. "With Sue Ann to give you pointers, and Amy to give you cat-themed baby stuff, and Edna to whip you into shape if you need it, how can you go wrong?"

And again, though a smile didn't quite make it to Rachel's face, Anna could see in her sister-in-law's eyes that her words were appreciated.

And that's when a huge revelation hit Anna square in the face. She'd known for a long time that she loved both her brothers, but maybe it had taken this long for her to . . . begin to let her defenses down. With them, with the girls, with the whole town. After the colossal lie her "other mother" had perpetrated her whole life, maybe she'd just had a hard time . . . letting herself depend on anyone, trust in anyone. But the small bit of kindness she'd just doled out to her big brother made her realize—*I trust him now. To take me as I am. To not bail on me. To be there for me. I'm starting to trust them all, bit by bit, step by step.* And every day it got a little easier.

"It'll all be fine," Tessa was saying reassuringly to Rachel when Anna came out of her reverie. And Anna heard it in a different way, almost like . . . a voice from above. *It'll all be fine.*

"Even if you guys are the two most ill-equipped people to have a baby that I've ever met," Logan added on a laugh that everyone joined in on—even Mike and Rachel a little.

Well, everyone except Jenny. And Anna's heart broke for her.

But at the same time, she was still basking in what she'd just figured out. Trusting in people was hard, especially after someone hurt you. Yet she thought life was a lot happier when you found the people who made you brave enough to believe in them.

A sweet evening breeze blew in through windows Anna had opened wide a few hours earlier, carrying the soft scent of honeysuckle. Temperatures were predicted to be cooler over the coming few days, and now that the sun had dipped behind the trees beyond the backyard, she could already feel more pleasant weather setting in.

Curled up in a loveseat in the small room she'd started calling the library, despite the modest number of books she'd amassed here so far, she sat reading Cathy's diary.

Before starting, though, she'd balanced several of the old record albums on the spindle in the center of the ancient record player, the kind that held a stack and let them drop one at a time. There was something in the simplicity of that, the old-fashioned mechanics of it, that appealed to her. Or maybe it was just the sense of being swept back to a simpler time.

As if to make the scene complete, on the trip to the attic to get more records, she'd also carried down the copy of *The Phantom of the Opera*, placing it on one of the room's built-in shelves. She wasn't sure she'd leave it there—mainly because she wasn't sure she would trust the average inn guest to realize how special a book it was and take care of it properly—but she'd also decided she probably wouldn't give it to Amy now. She wished she could, yet as she began to feel closer to Cathy—and to the house itself through Cathy's written memories—she now felt the book belonged here, within the walls where Cathy had held it in her hands and surely cherished it.

The day after she'd had sex with Duke, she'd worked at Under the Covers and then gone to the softball game, not returning until after dark, and other than that brief meeting on the porch, she hadn't seen him that day.

The next day, she'd worked a shift from ten to three at the bookstore, and when she'd gotten home, she'd heard a hammer banging on the far side of the house, but she'd made a point to just go inside and keep to herself. She'd done a little cleaning and paid some bills. She'd thought more about Rachel's news and Jenny's reaction to it. She sympathized with them both, just in different ways. It didn't seem fair that one person should get what another wanted so badly, especially when that person didn't want it at all, but Anna had come to understand better than most that we didn't always get to choose our fate, only how we reacted to it. And she hoped both Jenny and Rachel would be considerate of each other's position going forward.

Since then, she'd seen more of Duke, but not a lot. A couple more half day shifts at the bookshop had kept her away from home part of the time. And when she was here, she'd asked him if he needed her help with anything and he'd mostly declined.

But in those moments when their paths crossed, when they spoke to each other, Anna suffered a thick, almost desperate desire for him. The weather had gotten even hotter, and that didn't help. At times she'd been forced to ask herself: *Is it the heat making me feel so breathless or is it Duke?* And she wasn't sure of the answer. She only knew that in his presence, now her whole body felt heavy, needy. And with every second they were together she found herself remembering details of their sex: his powerful erection in her grip, her own cries of pleasure when he'd made her come, the way he'd licked and suckled her breasts so thoroughly, the way he'd pounded into her body with such relentless vigor. God, how could she *not* be breathless when being constantly barraged with such memories?

Did he feel any of that, too? She couldn't tell. Did he sense her thinking about it, feel the tension rolling off her in waves? She didn't know that, either. Was Duke just an expert at showing no emotion when he chose not to—or did he really feel as little about their sex as it seemed?

Since she was off from the bookstore today, she'd felt almost obligated to do some work on the house. Because yes, she was paying him, but she hadn't expected him to accomplish the entire job single-handed. So when she'd insisted on helping, he'd found jobs for her to do. He'd set her to sanding some pieces of wood he'd cut to repair some of the delicate gingerbread trim in the house's eaves. He'd shown her two different types of spindles he'd bought for the porch and asked her which one she wanted to use. He'd discussed with her the merits of covering the house with vinyl clapboard versus repainting it. The vinyl would be attractive, came in lots of colors, and would require little maintenance—while sticking with wood added value to a historic home and allowed for color changes down the road, but would require painting and other repairs every few years to stay looking good. She'd thanked him for the information, took a brochure of vinyl colors he'd picked up at the Home Depot in Crestview, and said she'd think about it and let him know.

And all the while, every second with him—for her anyway—had been fraught with sexual tension. That same need, that same hunger, that same sense of being incredibly drawn to him—and it multiplied at every small, incidental touch that came with something as simple as taking the bro-chure from his hand into hers. *Does he really not feel it? Is it only me?*

She still didn't know the answer and had simply been flip-flopping between wild need and trying her damnedest to be cool and let that go, between still feeling attached to him and reminding herself she couldn't be, that there just wasn't any future in letting herself feel that way for a man who'd openly told her what they'd shared was only sex.

Now he was gone—when it had suddenly grown quiet out-side, she'd stepped out the front door and taken a cautious stroll all the way around the house to find sawhorses empty and tools put away for the day; all was blessedly still and she was alone. Funny, just after they'd had sex, she hadn't wanted him to leave her alone, but now that she understood the situ-ation and had begun to accept it, she kind of did. At least right now, anyway. Maybe things would normalize in a few days, but for now she still felt awkward. And tense. And hurt. Which was perhaps stupid given that she had almost no his-tory with him, but it was how she felt. So for tonight, it was easier to be alone. And curling up with Cathy's thoughts and records felt like a sweet and romantic little escape from real life at the moment. More romantic than her real life anyway.

Unlike earlier reading sessions, now Cathy mentioned Robert almost every day, even if only in small ways.

I watched Robert hoe weeds from the garden again today. Just from that, my heart beats faster.

Today is Sunday, the one day of the week when Robert doesn't work for us. Even Daddy believes it's wrong to labor on the Lord's day. But I wonder what Robert does all day out in that little cabin all by himself.

One glimpse of Robert out a window and he stays on my mind all day. Sometimes it doesn't even require the glimpse.

It all made Anna's heart beat faster, too, feeling Cathy's emotions and letting them carry her back to her youth, to first crushes and first kisses and first love. Was anything in the world ever as poignant as that brand new, blossoming passion?

And then she turned the page and things began to get *really* good.

It's Saturday, and despite Daddy's insistence on keeping me away from Robert, I got to sit next to him in our old farm truck, all the way into town and back. Daddy and Robert were heading to the hardware store on town square for some new garden tools, and Mother insisted Daddy take me along to buy some sewing notions she needed. I wore my yellow gingham—it's pretty and bright, without making me feel I looked like I was trying too hard.

The truck's seat is awfully wide but the gear-shift in the center of the floor made it necessary to

> *put my legs on Robert's side, nearly touching his.*
> *And the truck rides rough, and sometimes when*
> *we hit bumps it jostled us closer to one another.*
> *I whispered, "Sorry" every time I'd bounce into*
> *him, our shoulders or our legs connecting, but I*
> *really wasn't sorry at all.*

Within a few more pages, Anna realized that the summer between Cathy's junior and senior years had already come and gone, and that school had started back. And it seemed that Cathy's father had loosened up a bit by then, enough that Robert was permitted to drive her to school if an errand sent him in that direction, and more than once he picked her up at the end of the school day as well.

> *We had a real conversation today. He asked how*
> *my day was and then gave me the most melt-*
> *ing grin to ask if I'd caused any trouble in class.*
> *"Me?" I said. "What kind of trouble do you think*
> *I would cause?" He said he bet boys were falling*
> *all over themselves to get near me, probably start-*
> *ing fistfights with each other over me. I blushed*
> *and told a fib, saying, "Maybe a few. But can I*
> *help it if they like me?" He said it sounded to*
> *him like they had good taste. And so I smiled and*
> *thanked him and said he must have good taste,*
> *too.*

Turning pages, totally absorbed, Anna learned that from there, their conversations deepened. At first, they discussed simple things like music and books. Cathy told Robert her favorite novel so far was *The Phantom of the Opera*, which she'd read while staying with her cousins for a week last summer, because it was about people who weren't afraid of their passions.

But soon Robert opened up to Cathy. Although he'd

seemed hesitant to discuss it, when Cathy had asked about his past, he'd told her a heartbreaking story. His mother had died, and his father had remarried a woman who took an instant disliking to him, so much that his always stern father had soon seemed to feel the same way.

> *Robert had a little sister named Peggy who his stepmother fawned over, but it seemed the woman just didn't want a son in the bargain. Before long, Robert had been hired out as a farmhand on a large farm fifty miles from his home in Iowa, all the money he made going to his family. And so he finally just ran away. And in the few years since, he's wandered from place to place, town to town, picking up whatever work he can.*
>
> *But the really amazing thing is that he isn't bitter. He isn't filled with hate, or sadness, or anything you might expect. Instead he told me he chooses to see it all as a big adventure, and he said one day maybe he'd even write a book about it all. And then he said the most amazing thing. He said that this chapter was his favorite so far, and it would be all about the pretty girl named Cathy who made him smile every time she came to mind.*

Things continued like this for a few more pages—until finally Anna reached the inevitable moment she'd known would come.

> *Last night at dusk I snuck out of the house and went for a walk in the woods. I knew Daddy would kill me if he found out—but something was burning inside me, and I just had to.*
> *I knew where I was going, of course, but I never*

even made it to the cabin—Robert had heard me
coming and met me halfway. He said animals
moved quieter and quicker than I was and he'd
just had a feeling it was me. I got a little nervous
then—Lord help me—and then I heard myself
babbling, telling him how I'd just felt like saying
hi, and how I'd missed talking to him because
other than a few glimpses out the window, I
hadn't seen him in a week. He said he was glad I
came, and that he missed me, too—and after that,
we just talked, about everything and nothing. I
told him Daddy didn't like me being around him.
And he said I should probably get back to the
house before I was missed.

So we said goodbye, and I turned to go—and
then the most wonderful moment of my life hap-
pened. He grabbed my hand, pulled me back
toward him, and when I spun to face him, he
kissed me.

It was simple at first—just a firm, still kiss on
my lips. And it tingled all through my body like
someone had lit a Fourth of July sparkler inside
me. But when I just stood there after that, frozen
in the shock of it, he kissed me again. He lifted
both his hands to my face and gave me a slow,
deep kiss just like in the movies. I almost didn't
believe kissing like that was real—it seemed too
passionate to be true. But now I know it is.

After the kiss, he said, "Sweet dreams, Cathy,"
just before I scurried back through the forest
toward home. When I got there, I realized I was
touching my lips, that I'd lifted my fingers there
at some point without even realizing—maybe in
some effort to keep on feeling it. Or maybe . . . to
protect it and keep it safe.

Duke sat on a fallen log next to the lake watching the last remnants of the sunset streak the Ohio sky with vibrant pink light, and wishing like hell he could get Anna Romo off his mind. For a while she'd been nice to think about—damn nice. But now . . . it was too much.

Though admittedly it was mostly the sex on his mind. How the hell did a man stop thinking about sex like that?

When he'd woken up next to her it had been like . . . waking from a dream. A dream too damn good to be true. And pure impulse, some urge toward self preservation, had propelled him to quietly get up, go downstairs, put on his clothes, and leave. Because it had been one thing to give in to his lust in the moment—but hell, who could say how she saw things, or what regrets she might have? And he supposed he'd just wanted to get the hell out of there, bring it to an end, before he could find out the hard way. Maybe he hadn't wanted to risk her waking up, glancing over at him, and looking horrified by what she'd done. Or, more specifically, who she'd done it with.

When she'd looked so freaked out finding him at the front steps the next morning, he'd wondered if it was about his scar. If it was more noticeable in the morning sunlight than it had been in the late day shadows. If seeing him the morning after had made her second guess the decision.

After all, she was probably lonely, same as him. She was probably hungry for a little human affection, also the same as him. He didn't expect it to mean anything, and he didn't need for it to. He didn't need to start caring about her, not in that way.

And hell, he'd taken Lucky's sister to bed, something he hoped Lucky would never find out about. Funny—he'd never kept much from his best friend, but lately he'd run into more than one thing he didn't care to share, even with Lucky, and now he'd created another. Some things were sacred, and a guy's sister seemed like something you didn't mess with.

All things considered, it had just seemed best to keep it

simple, not treat it like a big, serious thing. Women always wanted to do that, but sometimes sex was just sex, just two people making each other feel good.

Mostly, that was what sex had been for Duke, his whole life. He'd had the occasional girlfriend, but mostly that led to jealousy and trouble. And as for being in love . . . Hell, he saw all kinds of people fall in love—he'd seen Lucky fall two summers ago—but he'd never experienced that himself and he didn't understand exactly what it was. He knew about physical attraction to a woman, and even something visceral that grew from that into attachment, but he didn't know much about romance, and that all just seemed like one more reason not to make this into something it wasn't.

Even if the way he'd wanted her had gone beyond his understanding, or past experience. Even if he'd felt a real connection with her while they were doing it, something he'd seldom experienced before—if ever. Even if he'd felt somehow safer talking to her in bed in between the two rounds of sex than he had felt anywhere in a very long time.

It's just because you thought you'd never have a pretty woman's affection again, that's all. It had just been . . . relief. Nothing more.

And maybe they'd even do it again.

But probably not. Because in retrospect, he could see how complicated it could get. Again, she was Lucky's little sister. And regardless of who she was, he couldn't really just walk away from her right now—well, not without it being a major life change when he was already in a pretty rotten place to begin with.

It doesn't feel so awful with her.

He wasn't sure where the words came from, only that he heard them in his head. And he couldn't deny the truth in them. A life that had felt empty and broken before he'd run into her in the woods that day now felt a little better, and when he was in her presence even better still.

That seemed important. But he wasn't going to let himself

dwell on it and try to figure out what it meant. In fact, he was giving this far too much thought anyway. *Quit thinking so damn much. Or think about something else.*

But suddenly Duke couldn't quite remember what he used to think about before Anna had come tripping her way into his little world in the woods here. What had filled his head then?

He thought back and found the answers. Mostly bad stuff. Anger. Painful memories. Helplessness. Emptiness. And he'd calmed himself by trying his damnedest to focus on anything else. Birds in the trees. Fishing. The smell of honeysuckle. One day he'd even taken a honeysuckle blossom and popped the liquid inside into his mouth the way his grandmother had taught him when he was little, the sweet-tasting burst on his tongue taking him back to a time and place when he'd felt loved, and safe. But it had only been a moment. One moment in time in the midst of what otherwise was mostly dark, black, ugly.

Until Anna had come along and filled his head with something better. Even when he'd been annoyed by her, she'd been a hell of a lot more pleasant to think about than other things. But maybe he could only admit that to himself now that some time had passed.

He thought about what to do now that it was dark out. He'd mostly found it easy to go to bed early here, and to rise with the sun—but he wasn't sleepy yet.

And the truth was—he knew what he wanted to do. What he was *itching* to do.

The truth was—every time he'd seen her since they'd had sex on her couch and then in her bed, it had been all he could do not to grab her and kiss her and hope it would happen again.

But he hadn't. For all the reasons he'd just thought through. She was his best friend's sister. He didn't need this kind of complication in his life, especially right now. And even if she'd seemed totally into him when they were doing it—hell, she'd even started it—he still wasn't sure what that meant, what she saw in him, or how she viewed him. And frankly, he still wasn't sure he wanted to find out. He knew he was no good for her, not in any way that went beyond sex—surely she knew it, too.

So given all those good reasons for him to just head back to the cabin and call it a day, it was beyond his understanding when his feet began to lead him through the woods toward the big Victorian house.

"I Only Have Eyes for You" by the Flamingos echoed through the house. And mmm, what a sexy song—Anna had never quite noticed that until she sat there, caught up in the magic of Cathy and Robert's first kiss. Her skin tingled just thinking about it, imagining how it must have been. She only now realized that at some point, it had gotten dark outside and the house was dark as well, except for the room she sat in.

When she sensed movement, she looked up—to see Duke filling the doorway. She hadn't heard the screen door. She hadn't heard anything. Only the sultry, seductive music.

It was a small room, so it took him only two silent steps to reach her. After which he bent slightly toward the easy chair where she sat, then lifted his hand to skim his knuckles delicately down her arm, from shoulder to elbow. The touch fluttered through her, all the way to her panties.

She wasn't sure exactly when their gazes had locked, only that she felt captive within his. She tried to say something—anything. "I . . ."

But when she trailed off, he stopped any further useless attempt with a gentle "Shhh . . ." Then he said, "Spread your legs."

Whoa. The command at once caught her off guard and turned her on. And she thought of protesting. Because if this was still only sex, if that was all he wanted, she had to say no. She had to. She'd just get hurt further if she didn't. And she again began to speak, only without being sure what she was going to say. "But . . ."

His words came soft but certain. "Just do what I said, Anna."

Anna. Had he ever called her that before? Other than when they'd first met and he was proving he knew who she was, she didn't think he had, and it touched her—even if it was jarring to feel something tender in the midst of such thick heat. Despite the cool night air wafting lightly through the window, she'd begun to sweat.

And now she didn't hesitate—she spread her legs. Because even if she knew she should say no, she also knew she wouldn't. That she, in fact, couldn't.

She knew, plain and simple, that fast, that she wanted him too much to resist, her heart be damned.

" . . . he was shy and dared not confess his love, even to himself."

Gaston Leroux, *The Phantom of the Opera*

Ten

There was something new here, something different. As Duke pressed his palms to her silky inner thighs—God, he loved those little rolled up jean shorts—it sizzled through him like sparks about to burst into flame. But it was a heat that was about more than sex. It was . . . something he'd never felt before.

He'd never made love to a woman so beautiful—but the newness here wasn't about that. And he wasn't sure any one woman had ever aroused him so thoroughly, filled him with such need—but it wasn't about that, either. Hell, he didn't know *what* the hell it was that seemed to permeate his skin—his very soul—right now, he only knew that everything around him felt like *more*. Every color in the room felt richer, more saturated; every texture around them, in the curtains, the chair where she sat, the denim of her shorts, seemed somehow deeper, more touchable. The light in her eyes was more luminous, her skin tanner, smoother, softer.

The isolation he'd come to Half Moon Hill for was suddenly . . . a thing that felt all the more precious for being able to *share* it with her in this moment. He liked knowing they were the only two people anywhere near; he liked knowing they could take their time soaking in every nuance of what they were about to do together. And as for time—for Duke it stood still; there was nothing but this moment. No past with its bad memories and losses, no future wrought with uncertainties or loneliness—there was only now, a moment that felt like it might just last forever if he wanted it to.

He had no plan, no particular ideas of exactly how he wanted this to go—he'd come here on pure instinct and that's what he was still running on when he leaned in to lower a kiss to her perfect inner thigh. And when she shivered a little in response, he did, too—and the want between them was so thick and heavy that he didn't care if she saw. He'd left her the first time they'd had sex because it had seemed like the safe thing to do, and he'd been denying himself any of her since, trying to convince himself it hadn't mattered, that it had been two bodies moving together, two people making each other feel good, nothing more. But the truth he found himself facing as he rained still more gentle kisses on her tender flesh was that the pull between him and Anna Romo was something more than that.

And he still didn't understand what it was, and he remained entirely uncertain if this was wise—but he'd just stopped caring about that. He'd quit asking himself questions and instead gave himself over to seeking, getting what he needed. And from her response so far, she needed it, too. Which he'd pretty much sensed already, but seeing it, feeling it, only amped up the almost brutal chemistry between them.

What did she see when she looked at him? A monster? Something or someone she wanted to keep hidden away up here where no one else could see? But even those last, hard questions fell away, too, as he rose upright on his knees, slid his hands up her outer thighs and onto her hips, and pressed inward to kiss her.

He sank deep into the kissing upon contact, pressing his tongue into her mouth, letting himself get lost in her. And before he knew it, he'd angled her supple body back and across the chair and had climbed up onto it with her, planting his knees in the soft cushion, pressing his erection between her legs as they made out.

There were moments between kisses when he looked at her and knew she felt it, too, whatever this thing was, this stark need that drove him. So strange to feel something so intense with someone he didn't know well—but on the other hand, maybe he knew her better than he wanted to admit to himself. They'd shared some things; they'd worked together for a while now; she'd even cut his hair and shaved his face. So . . . maybe the only strange thing here was the feeling itself—the fact that he'd never known this kind of desire.

Stop thinking, damn it—just stop. And enjoy this. Feel this. Be in this—all the way.

And so that's when Duke finally did all those things—he forgot who he was, he forgot how he looked now, he forgot anything except sinking all the more fully into the moment, the only sound the sexy old song playing in another room.

Soon his palms drifted over her full breasts—producing another shiver, again first in her and then in him—before he moved his fingers to the button on her shorts. She let out a hot gasp of excitement as he popped the button, pulled on the zipper. And then she was biting her lush lower lip, her eyes shaded with lust, and her hands were working at his belt, getting it undone, getting *everything* down there undone.

As she pushed at the waistband of his jeans, he murmured, "Lift up," and they proceeded to shove each other's pants and underwear down.

Even as they continued struggling out of them using legs

and feet, Duke pushed up her tank top and she lifted her arms to let him take it off. When it was gone, he removed his T-shirt over his head and flung it aside as well. "Bra. Take it off," he said. He might sound like a caveman, but he could scarcely form thoughts at this point, let alone sentences, and the bra was the last thing left and he wanted her completely naked.

She didn't hesitate, reaching behind her back to unhook it, and a few glorious seconds later, the hot pink bra was being tossed away and her gorgeous breasts were bared plumply before him.

"Aw God," he murmured at the sight, his longing heightened just when he'd thought there was nowhere higher for it to go—and then he sank his mouth onto one tantalizingly taut nipple. He pulled it between his lips, hard and sweet and feminine, the sexy little cry she released fueling him. As she arched for him, he could almost feel the way he suckled her stretching all through her.

She moved against him, her body grinding rhythmically beneath him—and maybe he should have just let her keep going, but they were so close already that he couldn't resist the urge to lift slightly, readjust, and push his way inside her ripe body.

She cried out again at the firm, smooth entry—and God, she was wet and warm. Never had it been so obvious to him that their bodies had been made to fit together perfectly.

And then he was moving in her, thrusting, driving, and she was panting, moaning, their gazes unabashedly locked, and Duke knew a downright primal connection with her. Damn, all along, he'd thought he'd been having good sex with women—hell, he'd *known* it—but this . . . this eclipsed anything he'd ever experienced.

Soon he yearned to see her towering over him, riding him as she'd done once before on the couch in the front room—he wanted to make her come. Planting his hands solidly on her ass, he said, "Hold on to me tight," and when she locked her arms around his neck and her legs around his hips, he turned them over in the chair until she straddled him.

"Oh God," she breathed. "I feel you so much more this way."

He liked that. Enough to thrust up into her, wanting to make her feel him even deeper, and loving the stark, high-pitched sigh that echoed from her. Their eyes met, her look wild, and he said, "Ride me, baby."

Anna couldn't quite believe this had happened—when she'd least expected it. And if she'd let herself examine it very closely, she'd have felt weak for giving in so easily when she feared it could only lead to heartache.

But that was why she didn't let herself examine it. That was why she just reveled in it, soaking up the pleasure Duke delivered for all it was worth. If this was all she could have of him—his body, sex—well, looked like she'd decided she would take it. And at least in the moment, it felt far, far better than denying herself.

Her body was in control of her now, anyway—she'd succumbed completely to Duke Dawson's charms. Even if *charms* seemed . . . an unlikely word to use in relation to her biker in the woods, he definitely possessed them. In a hard, sexy sort of way.

As she moved on him, the pleasure inside her mounted, rising higher and higher—and when he leaned in to take the peak of one breast back into his mouth, oh God. Sweet release was only a few heartbeats away and she didn't try to hide it. Her breath grew more shallow, her eyes fell half shut, her passion overrode anything happening in her brain. She was lost to sensation, her body filled with it, her senses overcome with it—and then she toppled headlong into the oblivion of orgasm. Her cries of ecstasy filled the room, briefly drowning out the record that still played nearby.

Oh God, I thought I'd never get to feel this with him again. And that somehow made it still sweeter, hotter. And yet . . . she didn't know if there would be a next time, either—and that simple knowledge made her ride out the climax with even more indulgence, made her wring every conceivable ounce of pleasure from it she could.

And as she met his gaze in that moment, she wondered if he could see what she felt—*I just gave all of myself to you.* Never before had she realized that . . . maybe up to now, she'd never really done that with a guy. Even guys she'd been crazy about. Even Bryant, her college boyfriend and the only guy she'd ever really loved. Maybe before this moment, even in the heat of sex, she'd still been concerned about . . . confidence, control. Maybe she'd never let herself go so completely before, even in the midst of orgasm. God. Wow.

She'd never felt so . . . vulnerable. Or so very . . . open.

Trust. Just like she was learning to feel for her brothers and her friends, she'd given that to Duke tonight without even weighing it.

And, not quite ready to keep facing that scary reality, she collapsed softly against him, letting her head come to rest on his shoulder. Her eyes fixed on the soft skin of his neck, like once before. *We all have soft spots. Each and every one of us. Whether figuratively or literally. Even Duke Dawson. Even me.*

They stayed still and silent for a moment, their bodies still connected, until finally Duke leaned slightly to rasp in her ear, "I love watching you come."

She sucked in her breath. Whether or not he'd seen how truly wide she'd opened herself to him, he'd liked what she'd given him. And that drove her to kiss him, hard and passionate—and then he was kissing her back, just as wildly, and then they were moving together again, hard and insistent, his hands on her hips, pushing her down, down, down onto him, forcing small shrieks of pleasure from her throat.

Until finally he surprised her by then lifting her up, off him, until they were no longer joined—and she'd never felt more empty, meeting his gaze with shock to say, "Wh-why?"

His eyes still dripped with heat, want, as he soothed her

with a "Shhh," then lifted her off him further and maneuvered around her to get to his feet.

She instinctively started to turn toward him, her knees still planted in the easy chair, but he said, "No, Daisy—stay like you are."

And as his hands came back to her hips from behind her, she understood they were only changing positions—and that was when he thrust smoothly back into her waiting body, and it was like getting back something she'd lost, something she couldn't do without, like being made whole again. She gasped her pleasure as heat infused her cheeks. She could feel him more *this* way, too. She bit her lip and arched her ass toward him, still ready to give of herself to him like never before.

After that, it was utter abandon—coming from him as much as from her. He drove into her welcoming flesh again and again, each stroke vibrating through her entire body, the sensations stretching all the way out to her fingers and toes. She cried out at each, still in a state of total surrender to the moment, to the heat, to Duke himself.

Another cool night breeze wafted through the window just behind the chair, lifting the thin curtains she'd hung there, and also lifting her hair as it seemed to kiss her bare skin. As Cathy's old records continued playing in the next room, Anna caught a glimpse of the moon out the window—a perfect half moon glowing in the night and tilted to one side—and she thought she'd never felt so much at once. Or maybe she'd just never *let* herself until now.

Duke's raw warmth and masculinity seemed to shroud her, folding in all around her as she closed her eyes, closed out some of the sensation, to better concentrate on the part that came solely from him. She felt the blood slowly drain from her cheeks, as if the rest of her body needed it more right now, to withstand what he delivered so powerfully—until his grip on both her hips tightened and he murmured, "God, baby—God. Now."

And then his plunges into her grew even rougher, harder, and she clenched her teeth and loved every second of knowing he was coming in her, and that she'd taken him there.

Duke didn't question what would happen next or even consult Anna about it—when they were done, he just took her hand and said, "Come on." Then he led her, both of them still naked, to the stairs that led to her bedroom.

Her pretty giggle trilled in his ear. "What—you're not gonna carry me this time?"

"You're heavy," he said, then tossed her a sideways glance to let her know he was kidding.

She used her free hand to playfully slug him in the arm as they climbed the polished wood steps.

Entering her bedroom at night, then lying down with her there, was different than before. Maybe it just felt more natural to be getting under the covers in the dark with her now—or maybe he'd been envisioning her here at night, taking that beautiful body to bed. A small, dim lamp threw a shadowy light across the room, and he was thankful neither of them had bothered to turn it off—he liked seeing her next to him.

"What do you wear to sleep in?" he asked without weighing it.

"T-shirt and cotton shorts usually," she said. "Or a cami if it's hot."

Beneath the covers, she snuggled against him and it felt good. "No fancy lace nighties?" he asked.

She peered over at him. "No. Why?"

He gave his head a short shake. "I don't know—guess I just thought you seemed like that kind of girl. Or you did last summer anyway."

"I guess I used to be, now that I think about it. I have a lot of that kind of stuff—just haven't worn it in a while." She met his gaze again. "Are you disappointed? That I don't wear lacy stuff every night?"

He shook his head once more. "Nah. I bet you're cute as hell in your T-shirt and shorts. And *hot* as hell in your lace when you decide to wear it. Shit—guess I don't much care *what* you wear 'cause you'd make anything look good."

From the look that passed through her eyes, he thought she liked the compliment. Though a soft grin stole over her. "Then why'd you ask?"

He shrugged against the pillow. "Guess I just wanted to be able to picture you here, what you'd look like going to bed at night."

She bit her lip, appearing somehow both bashful and sexual at the same time, and he thought she'd liked that bit of honesty, too. Leaning her head back slightly, her eyes lit with amusement, she asked, "And what do *you* wear to sleep in, Mr. Dawson?"

"Depends," he said. "Sometimes underwear. And sometimes nothin' at all."

When her cheeks pinkened but her expression appeared more aroused than embarrassed, he gave a small laugh. "You gonna picture that in your head when you lay down to sleep tomorrow night?"

She flashed something between a smirk and a grin. "Maybe." Then they rested in cozy, companionable silence for a moment before she said, "I'm glad you came here."

He thought back to earlier, to the mental meanderings that had led him over tonight. "I . . . wasn't sure it was a good idea. But . . . damn, couldn't get you off my mind."

"That's nice to know," she said with another playful, sexy grin, "but that wasn't what I meant. I meant I was glad you came here, to my woods, to Half Moon Hill. It's made my life . . . richer. And a hell of a lot more interesting than it was before." She finished on a light giggle that somehow produced a soft twinge in his groin.

"How'd *you* end up here again?" he asked. They'd talked about it before, sort of, but he still didn't really feel he knew the answer. It had something to do with getting away from

Mike, but that just didn't seem like enough to make a vibrant girl like Anna come to such a remote spot.

And when she met his gaze and hesitated, he knew she was thinking about giving him a more thorough version of the answer, but he could see the uncertainty in her eyes.

"You can tell me," he said. And then he cracked a small grin. "After all, who am I gonna tell?"

She laughed over that—but then the gravity of the moment returned and she said, quietly, "Finding out you're not who you thought you were, and that your mother definitely isn't who you thought *she* was—" She stopped, sighed. "It's like suddenly belonging . . . nowhere."

"But the Romos love you more than anything. They never stopped loving you."

She nodded, then swallowed visibly, and he sensed what an emotional topic this was for her. "I know, and I love them, too. But they have this whole history together that I don't have *with* them. And to know I was the source of so much pain for them . . . is tough to bear sometimes. Though the hardest part isn't about them."

"What is it then?" he asked.

"It's . . . about my mom—my other mom, the one who abducted me." She stopped then, shook her head. "God, sometimes that still sounds so weird to say. Because I loved her, you know? She had a lot of problems, and that made problems for me, too, but I loved her—and it's difficult to reconcile that the mother who loved me was also someone capable of . . . stealing me. Taking me from the family where I belonged. Uprooting me from all I knew. I'm glad I don't remember much about that time—and I guess I blocked it out—but it's just hard to think of her being willing to put me through that, to take me from people who loved me, who gave birth to me—you know? I've just recently figured out that her lie has made it . . . hard for me to trust in people, hard to let myself count on them. But I'm getting better at that."

Duke only nodded, because there seemed little else to say. After all, what words of comfort existed for such a strange and horrible thing?

Next to him, she sighed, her dark hair fanning across the pillow like silk. Even in sadness, she was possibly the most beautiful woman he'd ever known. "And another hard part is just . . . not really knowing who I am anymore. I mean, maybe that sounds simple—find out you're a Romo, become a Romo. But it's strange to know I'm not the same person I would have been if I'd been raised in Destiny alongside Lucky and Mike. And it's hard to wonder . . . who I was supposed to be. It's hard to know that if I hadn't been abducted I'd probably be someone . . . better."

At this, something inside Duke tightened painfully. "What do you mean, Daisy? That doesn't make any sense."

She swallowed again and he felt her discomfort with the subject. And yet she went on, sharing it with him. "If I'd been raised here and never left I'd be . . . Amy. Or Jenny. Or Sue Ann. I'd wear pretty dresses and bend over backwards helping people out. I'd know how to bake, and maybe even sew. I'd know why my stupid cat follows me around meowing all the time," she said, adding a roll of her eyes to that one. "I'd just be . . . more like what they all expected. And instead, I'm this person they don't really know, this person who doesn't dress the same, or act the same. And I just don't get the cat thing," she said, sounding almost exasperated.

But he had no idea what she was talking about. "The cat thing?"

"Everybody here loves their cats. And their dogs, too, I'm sure—but Amy has foisted cats on everyone and they're all totally into their cats now. Even Mike. Even Lucky."

Duke nodded slightly, head still on a pillow, facing her. "Yeah, now that you mention it, Lucky does seem pretty into that cat. He always tries not to let it show when people are around, especially other bikers, but I know what you're saying."

"So I'm just . . . not necessarily what they want me to be. And the thing is . . . I've always liked myself. I mean, maybe some of my confidence was just about being brave and acting like I had it all under control so I could *have* it all under control—but some of it was real. And now . . . well, maybe I don't always feel quite as good about myself as I used to. I'm not as perfect as everyone else in Destiny. And I never will be."

Duke hated the dejected look on her face and could hardly believe what he was hearing. So he just gave it to her straight. "Daisy, that's the craziest load of crap I've ever heard."

Her jaw went slack, her eyes wide. "Huh?"

He narrowed his gaze on her, trying to think how to explain what he meant. "Look, you're fucking beautiful. And amazing."

She still appeared just as confused. "I am?"

"You're smart, you're sassy, you're funny as hell, you don't let anybody push you around, and you know how to take care of yourself. So who cares if you don't know how to bake a pie? Your cobbler was pretty damn good, though. And who cares if you aren't a carbon copy of every other chick in town? You do your own thing and I dig that, baby. I like that you don't try to be like everybody else. I like pretty much everything about you if you want to know the truth. And you make a pair of cutoff jean shorts damn sexy, by the way."

Next to him, her expression slowly changed, and he saw some light in those gorgeous brown eyes again. And even if he'd said a little more than he'd meant to, he was glad if it made her see that she was incredible just the way she was and that she didn't need to apologize to anyone for it.

She sounded uncharacteristically bashful when she said, "Thank you, Duke. That means a lot to me." But he guessed he was learning there were a lot more sides to Anna Romo than he ever would have suspected.

"Well . . . you're welcome" was all he came up with in reply.

"So anyway," she said, "my big solution to all of this was . . . run away to Half Moon Hill. I didn't know it was running at the time—it seemed like a good idea. And I'm comfortable here. But like I said, you've made it more interesting. And better." The last part came in a shy sort of whisper that kind of turned his heart inside out.

Duke didn't answer—he didn't know what to say. He'd probably already said too much. And after all, an hour ago in the woods, he'd been telling himself all the reasons he couldn't let himself get any closer to her, and just because he'd come here anyway didn't mean he suddenly felt differently about that. He didn't know *how* he felt on that score—it was all too damn complicated.

"Your turn," she said then.

And his gut tightened. "Huh?"

"I still don't really know why you're living like a vagrant in my woods. And in one way, maybe it's none of my business. But in another way, it is. And I just spilled my guts to you, on your request. So what's driven you to such extremes, Duke?"

Duke knew he could just not answer her. And that would probably be wise. After all, one reason he liked the woods was that it got him away from people. People who wanted to ask him stuff, and find out how he was doing, and try to make him feel better. Because it all just made him think about what had happened—and that was what he didn't want to do.

But she'd just bared her soul to him. And the night was quiet—the records downstairs had quit playing at some point and now all that remained was the gentle noise of crickets outside. And they were all alone here, far away from the rest of the world. And though he'd never been the most open guy, if there was ever a time or a place when it felt . . . safe to be open, this was it.

"I've . . . been through some shit, Daisy."

"I know," she told him.

But did she? Could she know? She could only know what

Lucky had probably told her—she couldn't know all of it, or about the hole it had left inside him.

"Lucky ever tell you much about the Devil's Assassins?" he asked.

She shook her head. "Only that it was the biker gang you were in together in California." She lowered her voice. "And that you had to do bad things."

Duke didn't like thinking about those days much, either—he and Lucky had both worked hard to leave that misspent part of their lives far behind—but . . . "At least then, I felt I had some control. Don't get me wrong—we lived on the edge every day, not knowing if we'd make some wrong move that would make it our last. But I still knew that whatever happened to me, I was ultimately responsible for it—I'd made it happen, one way or another.

"And I made some choices I'm not proud of, done things that have made it hard to sleep at night. But I was in survival mode then, and I always did what I had to do to keep myself as safe as possible—and to keep Lucky safe, too."

"He told me you saved his life once."

Duke nodded. "It was a bad night—the night we ran and left the DAs in our dust." Should he tell her what happened? He wasn't sure. It was a big thing—something that could make her see him differently, badly. But it was a part of his life, so . . . shit, he'd just say it. "We didn't have any choice—we had to run after a bar fight where somebody ended up dead." He paused, watched for a reaction on her face, but saw none. Tough cookie, his Daisy. And damn, he liked that. "Lucky suffered over that—but me, I saw it for what it was. You choose to live in an environment like that, you know you might not survive. The guy pulled a blade on Lucky, and I wasn't gonna let *that* shit go down—so I hit him with a bottle. Then he turned on me and this time it was Lucky who hit him, with a big beer stein. We both did what we had to do, looking out for each other—that was all."

Again, he waited for a reaction, and what he got this time

surprised him even more. "You put yourself at risk to save him—thank you for that."

"I'd do it again in a heartbeat," he told her. "And see—to me, it all even made a weird kind of sense. You live by the gun, you die by the gun—and I knew, and the other guy knew, that any given day could end the way that one did. It was an ugly way to live, but at least I understood the rules. And then . . ."

His voice trailed off because his chest went tight. Hell, this still wasn't easy. He shut his eyes. Kept them shut. Wished maybe she'd just forget the conversation and let them both fall asleep now.

But when he opened them a minute later, there she was, still waiting patiently for him to go on.

So he took a deep breath and tried to find the courage to face the one thing in the world that really scared him. And that had really *scarred* him, too. Not only on the outside, but on the inside.

He told her, "Then I let a friend die while I stood there and watched."

" . . . death was all around him . . ."

Gaston Leroux, *The Phantom of the Opera*

Eleven

$\mathcal{I}$t was hard to meet her gaze after that, but he dug deep and found a little more courage and did it anyway. Though he wished they'd turned off that damn lamp now. This would be easier in the dark. Like in the woods. In the dark no one could see you.

When she spoke, her voice came soft, tentative—she clearly already understood the weight this held for him. "Lucky told me a little . . . about what happened to your friend. But . . . I don't know much."

Duke swallowed anxiously, hating his weakness. He hadn't known he had that inside him—weakness—until the day Denny Bodkins had died.

"Denny was older than me—in his fifties. He had a big gray beard and the beginnings of a beer belly. He rode a Harley flathead that Lucky painted for him last year." Lucky ran a thriving business painting motorcycles for a living. "Denny had Lucky airbrush a pair of dice on his gas tank— said he'd rolled the dice and come out on the winning side. Across the bar one night he told me he'd been into some bad shit when he was younger, but then he met Linda, his wife, and she turned that all around."

Duke had been a little envious when Denny had told him the story—he couldn't quite imagine how a woman's love could have as big an impact as the one Denny had described, and though he'd never wanted to be tied down, he couldn't deny that Denny was one of the happiest guys he knew.

"He and Linda didn't meet until their forties, and to be honest, I'll be damned if I could see what he saw in her. Don't get me wrong—she's a nice enough lady . . . but I just never saw what was . . . special about her. All I know is that when she'd walk into Gravediggers and Denny was already there, her smile lit him up like nothing I'd ever seen. Once he told me that she made everything right in his world."

The corners of Anna's mouth turned up slightly, and her eyes took on a soft, dreamy quality. "That's sweet," she said.

And yeah, it *had* been. But Duke couldn't smile about it. Because he knew the rest of the story.

He took a deep breath before trying to finish it. "A bunch of us were on a big ride on a Sunday afternoon. It was the dead of winter, but it was one of those warm, sunny days that come out of nowhere, and it seemed too good to waste, so a bunch of us bikers called each other up, and we met at Gravediggers at noon that day. We headed down across the river at Portsmouth into Kentucky, then rode all the way to Cave Run Lake."

It made Duke's heart hurt now to recall what a great day it had been. Sunny and nearly sixty degrees—rare warmth in this part of the country in January—and it had been good to take to the road with some of the friends who hung out at his bar. There had been about a dozen of them—two couples and the rest lone riders. But now came the bad part, the part he knew would give him nightmares the rest of his life.

"We were riding too fast coming back. You know how early it gets dark that time of year and we were racing the daylight." He stopped, shook his head. "I'm not sure whose fault that was—I just remember saying we'd have to haul ass getting home, but that it didn't seem like a big deal."

"Maybe it was *nobody's* fault," Anna suggested. And when he stayed quiet, digesting that, she added, "Sometimes no one is to blame, even when bad things happen. Sometimes things just . . . are. That's something I've come to believe myself anyway."

Because it was easier than hating the woman who stole her? Duke wondered, but he kept the thought to himself. He could see the point of not blaming when it wouldn't fix anything—but he'd found that concept harder to embrace when some of the blame lay with *him*.

So he just said, "Maybe," and went on. "But it was me leading the pack, going too damn fast, when we topped a rise on 23 and there'd been a wreck on the other side." Just remembering it almost stole his breath. And he suffered the sudden urge to be back in the cabin in the woods, by himself—but he knew he couldn't run away from this moment the way he'd run away from everything else, and that he had to keep going.

Though he could no longer meet her eyes. He guessed he just didn't want to see the horror—or pity, or any other reaction that would show up there. He still wasn't used to the shame the memory heaped upon him.

"A Camaro and a heavy-duty pickup had collided just a couple minutes before. The passengers were out of the vehicles, safe and standing off to the side, but the cops hadn't even shown up yet and the left lane was blocked." Duke's breath grew shallow then—it was like his lungs had suddenly stopped working right, like there just wasn't enough air. But he made himself go on. Because he still felt like he owed it to her somehow. Or . . . maybe making himself say it was just one more way of punishing himself.

"I managed to veer into the slow lane, but I skidded into the guardrail. And everybody else with us managed to dodge the wreck one way or another, too. Except for Denny." Breathing became harder and harder. "He slammed on his brakes and slid sideways—his bike went down on its side. Linda hit the pavement and came off the bike. But Denny stayed on it." He could still see the scene in his mind, unfolding in what had felt like slow motion. Yet . . . in another way, it had all happened so damn fast. "The bike kept sliding—right up under the pickup. And then the truck burst into flames, just like that." He snapped his fingers, because truly, that was how quickly it had taken place. "And Denny was under it— trapped on the bike, pinned there."

"But . . . that wasn't your fault, Duke. None of it." Beneath the covers, she touched his arm.

She hadn't heard the rest yet, though. And he glanced at her only briefly before drawing his gaze back down. "I was stopped way closer than anybody else, even closer than Linda. And I was running toward the accident when the gas tank blew." His voice went quieter then—not on purpose. "I saw him, Anna. I saw him in the flames. And he must have seen me, too, because I heard him screaming my name. And Linda was yelling, 'Help him! Help him!' And I kept thinking that if I could just get a hand on him that maybe I could get him outta there. But I just stood there. I just stood there and watched him burn alive."

She stayed silent for a moment, absorbing it, he supposed. And his gut burned—the same way it had for weeks afterward, giving him the sensation that he was disintegrating from the inside out, being eaten up by tiny embers just like a piece of paper that never really catches fire but slowly crumples to black ashes anyway.

And when finally she said, "That's a terrible thing to have gone through, Duke, but you're not to blame. You couldn't have—" he stopped her by gently lifting two fingers to her lips.

"Stop," he said.

"Why? It's the truth. You yourself told me he was pinned."

But Duke shook his head. "I *think* he was—I'm not sure. And I could have *tried*, *should* have tried. But I didn't do *anything*."

He was glad when Anna stayed quiet longer this time—he didn't want her trying to absolve him; that wasn't why he'd told her. "I know what you're thinking," he went on. "That I wasn't the only one there, that I didn't cause the accident, that I'm no more at fault than anyone else."

"Right," she said.

"But I was the driver in the lead, going too fast. And I was the only one close enough to try to get to him in the end. And I didn't because . . . I felt the heat from the flames. And I was . . . afraid."

"A healthy fear," she countered. "You'd have died, too."

"Maybe that would have been better," he told her. "If I could have saved him first. Because I don't have anybody to miss me when I'm gone—but Denny had Linda, and now she's alone, and none of it makes any sense to me. And . . . I don't know when the hell I became afraid—of anything. I thought after the Devil's Assassins nothing could scare me. I thought I'd run the gauntlet, gotten through the bad part, and the rest would be easy now. And then when I least expect it, life suddenly doesn't make a damn bit of sense anymore."

"But—"

"Shhh," he told her quickly. "I appreciate you trying to make me feel better, baby—but you can do that all day and I'll still know inside that I was a coward.

"And so now you know," he concluded quickly, more quietly.

But even now his Daisy kept coming at him. "Not all of it. I don't know . . . how you got hurt."

Duke sucked in his breath—and *felt* the scar on his face.

He saw it like . . . his own version of the scarlet letter, or that he'd been branded by fate—it was the constant physical reminder of what had happened that night, the thing that would never let him begin to forget it. Maybe that had been one more reason to live in the woods. The beard, the lack of mirrors—he hadn't had to look at it. But coming out of the woods to be with Anna changed that, made him face that reminder on his cheek, like it or not.

"Yeah . . . forgot that part," he said quietly. And he supposed that, somehow, it just hadn't seemed important compared to Denny's death. "Like I said, I slid into the guardrail—had to slam on my brakes. My bike's mirror ended up cutting my face. I didn't even know it at the time—didn't know it until after Denny had died and the EMTs showed up."

She nodded, a guarded sort of sympathy in her brown eyes, and he suffered the familiar sting of feeling . . . broken. In a way the whole world could see. And, of course, right now, only Anna could see—but that was more than enough.

"I still don't really get why you're living in that shack, though," she told him then. "Or why you sold the bar. And Lucky thinks you're with your family in Indiana."

Yet one more small sting shot through him. God, she was full of questions.

Another uneasy swallow before he said, "I sold the bar because I couldn't face Linda or anybody else who knew and loved Denny. I couldn't just . . . live life like it was normal again. It *wasn't* normal. Pouring drinks for people seemed . . . fucking meaningless when Denny was in the grave and Linda could barely even make it to the funeral. I just didn't want to do it anymore."

"What about your family? Did you go to Indiana?"

At this, everything inside him stiffened. "That didn't work out."

"And then . . . ?"

"Then I just started riding. With no real idea where I was headed. And I ended up back in Destiny—I guess the bike knew the way. But since I'd lived in the apartment above Gravediggers, I didn't really have any place to go when I got here." Aw shit, that sounded pathetic.

"You could have called Lucky," she suggested timidly.

Yet he only shook his head. "I was too raw inside—couldn't deal with seeing *anybody*." And that fresh rawness had come from what had happened in Indiana—but he'd said too much already and he just wasn't gonna go there, so he moved on. "Then I remembered Lucky once telling me there was an old cabin in the woods here—said he'd hung out there with friends, drinking, when he was a teenager. When I found it, I figured it was a good enough place to stay for the night. And when I woke up the next day, I . . . guess I liked how quiet it was. And I kept planning to leave, but . . . one day turned into another, and another. Guess I was just too beat down inside to keep trying." His heart felt tired, remembering those first few days here. Denny's death, his visit to Indiana, the way he looked now—it had all added up to make him feel like some kind of monster. And that had been pretty damn immobilizing.

She stayed quiet and so did he, and he realized the whole story—even without the part about going home—embarrassed him a little. Now *she* knew he was weak, too. "I hope you don't have any more questions, Daisy, because I'm about spent here."

"I do have one more."

Shit. Couldn't she take a hint? When he lifted his gaze back to hers, it was to flash a look of warning.

Which didn't work.

"What's your real name?" she asked.

"Huh?" The question caught him off guard, seemed out of the blue.

"I'm pretty sure your mom didn't hold you in her arms when you were born and say, 'I think we'll call him Duke.' So what's your real name?"

He hesitated. He didn't particularly want to tell her; he

couldn't remember the last time he'd told *anyone*. There was nothing wrong with his name—he just . . . didn't feel like that person anymore.

When he didn't reply, she said, "Well then, where did the name Duke come from?"

This one was easier to answer. "When I was in high school, I got into it with a teacher who said I acted entitled. I didn't even know what that meant—and mostly, I was just being a troublemaker. Anyway, the guy started calling me 'the duke'—and I guess it stuck."

"Makes sense," she said easily. "But you still haven't told me your name."

Shit, why was it so hard for him to say? Maybe because it had been a long time since he'd been that kid. That kid who'd had normal hopes and dreams and . . . a more tender heart. That kid who'd felt loved.

But finally he whispered, "David. My name is David."

He met her eyes once more, long enough to see the light in them. "David," she repeated. "I like it."

He said nothing—he didn't know what to say. And he wasn't sure what had happened to the little boy once named David Dawson.

"So when I wake up in the morning, David," she whispered, "am I going to be alone?"

"Do you want to be?"

She drew her chin down slightly, appearing at once vulnerable and confident. "Not really. But I wouldn't try to make you stay if you'd rather go. What would be the point?"

He nodded, thought about it, and said, "You won't be alone, Daisy."

And if he wasn't mistaken, a look of contentment came over her just before she said, "Goodnight, David." Then she closed her eyes.

And Duke lay there watching her like that, realizing with a soft, muted sort of amazement that she hadn't thought he was horrible, and that somehow, despite his protests, her simple understanding had made him feel a little less awful. And that was the last thing he'd expected.

"One more thing," she said, eyes still shut.

"What's that, Daisy?"

"You were wrong when you said no one would miss you if you were gone. Lucky would miss you. And I would miss you, too. A lot."

Duke felt a little weird sitting at Anna's kitchen table the following morning as she served up pancakes, scooping them from the griddle onto his plate with a wide metal spatula. "I'm good at pancakes," she told him happily. "So at least that's the beginning of a breakfast menu for the bed-and-breakfast."

"Thanks for making them," he told her after a short hesitation.

She met his gaze. "It's nice to have a reason to. Cooking for two seems a lot more worthwhile than cooking for one."

"I used to cook for myself," he told her, not necessarily agreeing with her thinking. "In my apartment above the bar."

After putting a couple pancakes on her own plate, she cast a grin. "Oh yeah? What did you cook?"

He shrugged. "I make a mean burger. And in winter I can cook up a pretty good pot of chili. Nothing fancy—just stuff like that."

She nodded, now lowering the empty griddle back to the stove before joining him at the table. "Maybe we can grill hamburgers some night. I bought a gas grill on sale last fall—you've probably noticed it in the garage."

"Sure," he said, giving a quick nod of his own. He wasn't sure he wanted to promise—or get too cozy playing house here—but the idea didn't sound bad to him. Then, almost thinking aloud, he said, "Actually, guess I still do cook for myself. Out in the woods."

She stopped in the midst of pouring syrup on her pancakes, eyes widening on him. "Oh?"

"Fish," he said, answering her unasked question. "I catch fish from the lake and fry them in an old pan I found, over an open fire. Bass and bluegill mostly."

"I like fish," she said with just a trace of a smile, clearly hinting.

And thinking her cute as hell, he supposed he didn't mind saying, "Maybe I'll make you some sometime."

"So I was thinking," she began—and he cut her off by saying, "Uh-oh. That's scary, Daisy."

But his sarcasm didn't daunt her. "I was thinking maybe we could go see Lucky together. Let him know you're here. I know he'd want to know. He misses you."

He and Lucky weren't the kind of guys who ever talked much about missing each other, but the truth was—seeing Lucky sounded . . . good. Well, sort of. Part of him wanted to just keep on doing what he'd been doing—keeping to himself, working on Anna's house. He'd gotten used to living a solitary life. And somehow . . . the more people he dealt with, the more he would be forced to deal with what had happened to Denny. He still wasn't quite sure how to function normally again, and staying in the woods sounded easier.

And then there was the part about Anna.

"You mean, like, letting him know you and I have been . . ." He raised his eyebrows at her across the table, skeptical.

"Well, I hadn't thought that far ahead, but . . . yeah, now that you mention it. I mean, I don't see any reason to keep it from him."

"But . . . you're his sister."

"And . . . ?"

"Well, I'm not sure . . . He might not want me to—" He stopped, sighed. "And besides, either way, I don't know if it's a good idea in general. I mean, there's a reason I've been living where I'm living. Because I like being alone right now, ya know?"

"But you've also started spending time with *me*. So maybe

you don't like being alone as much as you think." Now she was looking all sassy again, in a slightly superior way. And he probably wouldn't have liked it on another woman, but on her, he did.

Even so, though . . . "No matter how you slice it, Daisy, not sure he'd like finding out I'm gettin' it on with his little sister, or that he'd . . . get where I'm at right now. So, uh, maybe this isn't a very good idea."

"Duke, Lucky loves you," she said.

And hell—despite himself, the words struck him hard. Because that was one more thing he and Lucky didn't sit around saying to each other—most guys didn't—so maybe he'd never really thought of it exactly that way in his head. Or maybe he'd forgotten *anyone* loved him. But maybe she was right. Maybe what he had with Lucky was strong enough, sturdy enough, that he would understand what had driven Duke away, and that he'd be okay with Duke seeing his sister. Maybe.

So that's what he told her, keeping it plain and simple. "Maybe."

"No, Lucky definitely loves you, trust me on this."

He just rolled his eyes. "No, Daisy—I meant maybe we'll go see him. But just maybe. So don't go calling him up on the phone and setting a dinner date, okay?"

She smiled. "Okay." Yet she clearly knew she'd won.

And Duke wasn't in the habit of letting women make decisions for him or coerce him into anything he didn't want to do. But with Anna . . . damn, maybe sometimes she knew what he wanted better than he did. Or maybe he needed to be pushed and she knew just the right ways.

Yet after he stood up and carried his plate to the sink a few minutes later, then walked to the bathroom down the hall, he glanced in the mirror and saw . . . his scar. The jagged line that cut its way down his face now. And he realized that for a little while anyway, he'd forgotten about it. With her. Even if usually, when he was with her, the knowledge of it was always floating there in the back of his mind. Or the front of it. But she'd made him forget about it last night   until they'd started talking about the accident—and he'd actually forgotten about it again this morning, until just now.

Damn, how had that happened?

And for the first time, he began to wonder if it was actually maybe even possible for her to forget about it, too.

"Gradually, I gave him such confidence that he ventured to take me walking . . ."

Gaston Leroux, The Phantom of the Opera

Twelve

In the week that followed, they had sex twice more, both times amazing. Sometimes they talked after, other times they stayed quieter—but they didn't speak further of the accident that had Duke living in the woods. It wasn't that Anna didn't want to know more, and maybe find some way to help him deal with it—she did, and in fact, she had attempted to bring it up again, but he'd quieted her by flashing a look of annoyance and then saying, "Maybe this will shut you up, Daisy," just before he kissed her. And if he insisted on shutting her up, she at least liked the method he chose.

The truth was, the things he'd told her about the accident scared her a little. Sure, she'd known she was dealing with a very troubled man in Duke, but . . . somehow finding out why, with all the details, made it more real. Duke had seen and experienced horrible things, and he was holding himself responsible for them. She wasn't sure how a person dealt with that—or if Duke ever would. And though she knew she would be there for him in any way he needed her to be, she also kept reminding herself that this was a good reason not to get too serious about him, or too attached. She had enough troubles of her own without trying to take on those of someone with even more wounds inside that hadn't yet begun to heal—and again, who knew if they ever would?

They also continued to work on the house, and the progress being made began to excite Anna. For so long now, since last summer, the idea of her bed-and-breakfast had been just that, an idea. But with Duke's hard work speeding things along, she could envision opening by autumn.

On the nights that found them in Anna's bed, Duke stayed over. But on other nights he still made his way back to the old shack. An idea that bothered Anna now, but she sensed that he still liked the solitude he found there—so she didn't argue when he went tromping off toward the forest, even as absurd as it seemed to her that he continued living in dilapidated surroundings, fishing for his dinner, and washing up in water from the stream.

And though sometimes they exchanged easy conversation, often they would spend hours working on the house side by side, barely exchanging a word. Duke's choice. She always tried to make conversation, but if all she got back was the occasional "Yeah," "No," and "Uh-huh," she understood that he just wasn't in the mood to chitchat. And she'd decided that was okay.

Because while she continued to develop feelings for him and thought of him as more than a casual lover, she wasn't sure he felt the same. And she wasn't inclined to press the subject. And again, maybe that was best—maybe it was wise to keep this a casual liaison like he'd told her from the start. And the one thing she knew for sure was that Duke Dawson wasn't suddenly her boyfriend—because boyfriends didn't go off and sleep in the woods when you had a perfectly nice house to offer them.

All in all, she wasn't sure what their relationship was or what she wanted it to be. But for now, she was just trying to be cool about it, take it day by day, enjoy it for what it was, and not let her feelings for her outlaw biker get out of control.

Even if she thought of him almost constantly. Even if she'd been so open and honest with him in a way you couldn't take back.

And she'd also been so bold as to take the initiative to help him move forward, at least a little, doing something he'd expressly told her not to. She'd broken the news to him yesterday while they'd been standing side by side, painting porch rails with a coat of primer—as he lectured her on needing to pick her color scheme so he could start on the biggest part of the rehab, the clapboard siding she'd decided to use.

"Relax," she'd told him. "I promise I'll make a decision over the next couple of days."

"So you keep saying," he groused, swishing a small paintbrush up and down one of the new spindles he'd outfitted the whole porch with. Then he narrowed his critical gaze on her work. "Slightly thicker coat, Daisy. Don't skimp so much."

"So . . ." she began, seeing an opening, "I ran into Tessa at Home Depot when I was picking up the primer yesterday."

He answered offhandedly, having refocused on his own work. "Yeah? She doing good?"

Anna nodded. "She was getting some paint chips. Now that she's doing interiors full time, her business is booming even more."

"Good."

"And when she asked how work on the house was going, I . . . admitted to her that I have a helper. And that it's you."

Duke stopped painting and just gave her a look.

"Don't be mad," she said quickly.

"Don't you think I should have been in on that decision?"

She blinked, a bit nervously, half agreeing with him but half not. "Maybe, but I'm not sure you ever would have made it. And Tessa was thrilled to hear you're back in the area. She said Lucky misses you like crazy."

He lowered his chin dubiously. "He told her that, did he?"

"Of course not. She said ever since you left he sits around and sulks, and she knows that's why." And when he didn't respond to that, she decided she should go on. "So Tessa suggested you come over one night. With me, too, if that's okay."

He looked disgruntled. "So did you tell her what we've been up to? Besides fixing up the house, I mean."

She shook her head. "No. That I kept to myself."

"Funny how when it's *your* business, Daisy," he groused, "you don't go telling people so fast."

"Are you mad?" But she rushed ahead before he could answer. "Because you shouldn't be. Because, again, he's going to be thrilled to see you. And I explained that you'd been . . . keeping to yourself, and she said she wouldn't tell Lucky yet. She thought it would be nice to surprise him. Thursday night. She wants us to come over and grill out with them."

Anna waited for an answer and didn't get one—so she finally went back to painting, deciding that apparently this was a bad idea and that Duke just wasn't ready for it yet.

Until, a few minutes later, he stopped priming to refill the paint tray they both shared, and as he poured the white primer, he said quietly, "I guess I can go to Lucky and Tessa's place with you on Thursday." He didn't look up as he spoke.

Even so, Anna glanced away slightly to hide her smile, lest he think she was making too much of it. She only said, "Good. I'll let her know."

And her heart fairly sang with the knowledge that she was bringing Duke and her brother back together this way, at the time when Duke surely needed a friend more than ever.

But then, just like every time she felt that happy little *zing* over anything concerning Duke, she reminded herself: *Don't get attached. Don't get serious. You two are so different. And God knows the man has some problems. And besides, he's not the settling down type. And you're not, either—or at least you haven't been so far. So stop feeling the* zing*!*

But as usual, the *zing* kept coming—especially when she finally let herself peek over and watch as Duke began to paint again. Because he peeked over at her at the same time. And their eyes met—just for a brief moment before they both darted their gazes away like a pair of shy teenagers.

And she couldn't deny that, boyfriend or not, she cared more for Duke Dawson each and every day.

Of course, in addition to working with Duke on the house, Anna was still getting comfortable in her job at the bookstore. At first, dealing with the customers had held some challenges, emotionally. People couldn't help themselves from noting that Anna Romo was actually out and about in the community again.

"I haven't seen you since last summer when you first came home," Rose Marie Keckley had said. "Where on earth have you been hiding yourself?"

Lettie Hart had told her, "I thought maybe you moved back to . . . wherever it was you were for all that time. But it's nice that you didn't."

And indeed, all their comments were kind ones, albeit still fraught with some of the curiosity people had indulged in last year—but she found that the more she *was* out in the community, the less of an oddity she became.

Today was her first day working in Under the Covers on her own—Amy was taking her beloved cat Mr. Knightley to the vet for a flea treatment and some shots and, expecting it to be traumatic, had informed Anna that she'd probably be by herself all day.

"Seriously?" Anna had asked, a bit taken aback. Not by the idea of manning the bookstore alone, but that a cat's vet visit required such drama.

"Maybe even longer," Amy had informed her. "In fact, it's very possible you won't see me for several days. That's why I scheduled you with so many hours the rest of the week. Mr. Knightley takes these things very badly. I hope you don't mind."

Anna had shaken her head. She'd noticed the excessive hours, but . . . well, she knew Duke didn't mind the alone time working on the house, so he'd just have more of it the next few days.

Fortunately, the work at the bookshop was easy, and people in Destiny were nice, and she was learning to appreciate the fact that they cared about her. And it was a beautiful June day—temperatures topping out in the high seventies—so she propped open the front door, using as a doorstop a small, portable, wooden bookshelf on wheels that Amy often used to display sale books outside. She'd been instructed to call Tessa if she had any questions. And though she still thought it beyond extreme that Amy would be totally incommunicado based on a visit to the vet for her cat, she decided it only meant that Amy was perhaps a little more eccentric than Anna had yet realized.

The day passed easily, with quite a bit of store traffic. But things had slowed when, only a few minutes before closing time, a pretty young blonde walked in. Anna greeted her with a smile and a hello. "Anything I can help you find? Or just browsing?"

The girl forced a smile, but she appeared troubled underneath. "Actually, I'm looking for Amy Bright. Is she here?"

Anna tilted her head, sorry to disappoint the girl, who looked to be in her early twenties. "I'm afraid Amy's not working today. And she might be out for the next few days. Is there a message I can give her?"

The girl shook her head, visibly let down. "No, I'm just an old friend and I was hoping to talk with her." She attempted the smile again, but it still didn't make it to her eyes. "I don't know how well you know Amy, but . . . she's a good listener, and such a nice person." Then she sighed, no longer hiding her sadness.

Anna felt a little like she had when she'd stumbled upon Jenny Brody's private duress. But she followed her instincts. "I've just gotten to know Amy recently, but she's great." Then she proceeded cautiously to add, "Is there anything *I* can do? I'm happy to help if I can."

That's when the girl seemed to realize she'd been letting her emotions show—and pulled herself together, suddenly looking more confident. "That's awfully nice of you, but no worries." Then she held out her hand. "You must be new to Destiny since I moved away. I'm Christy Knight."

Even as Anna took Christy Knight's hand, she knew her eyes had widened. Because she knew who Christy Knight was. Her parents had died in a fire that had traumatized Logan last summer. And she felt an instant kinship with her, much as she had with Duke. This girl knew about loss, too. "I'm . . . Anna Romo," she replied softly, wondering if Christy would know her name, as well.

"Oh. Wow," Christy said, giving Anna her answer.

And the two of them stood there looking at each other for a moment, until Christy said, "I know who you are," at the exact same time Anna said, "I know what you've been through."

They both laughed then, a bit nervously perhaps, until Christy went on. "I was already back in Cincinnati, living with friends, by the time you came home last summer. But I heard about it, and I remember thinking how hard that must be." Then she gave Anna a quick once-over, appearing almost incredulous. "Though . . . you look like you're doing great!"

Anna offered a soft smile. "It's been . . . a process," she explained. "One that's still ongoing. But yeah, all in all, things are getting better all the time."

"That's wonderful," Christy said, though in addition to the sincerity in her voice, Anna also heard a little sadness.

"Are you back in Destiny to stay?" Anna asked, curious.

But Christy was quick to shake her head. "Oh—no. I'm just here for a garden party over the weekend at Miss Ellie's—do you know her?"

Anna nodded. Miss Ellie was the town's elderly unofficial matriarch, and her home on Blue Valley Lake, Anna had been told, was the site of lots of outdoor get-togethers. She'd received an invitation to this weekend's party, too, and hadn't yet decided whether to go. "Yes. I've met her a time or two."

"For some reason, it seemed important to Amy and Logan that I come. Both of them called me about it, and Amy e-mailed me a couple of times, too. I guess they're just trying to make sure I feel included or something—which is nice. And I came a few days early, just to tie up some loose ends."

When that same tinge of sadness returned to her voice for the last part, it compelled Anna to ask, "And you? How are *you* doing?"

It tightened Anna's chest to see poor Christy still trying to smile, though it was clearly a strain. "It's . . . a difficult time."

Given that she'd lost her parents over a year ago, it worried Anna to think she was still suffering so much that it showed. "I . . . know I'm not Amy," she said, "but I'm willing to listen. I feel like you and I . . . understand each other, given that we've both lost a lot."

At this, Christy boldly raised her eyes to Anna's, almost as if searching them. "How did you do it? How did you deal with everything so well? I mean, you seem . . . so together."

"Well, first of all, I might not be quite as together as you think—but I find that sometimes acting the part sort of . . . helps it become real. And second, when you feel like you've lost everything, you just . . . go on. Somehow. You just do it. Because that's all there is to do. You figure out what works for you, what keeps you functioning, how you can best get through it. And you just . . . know there's sunshine beyond the clouds."

When the hint of a smile formed on Christy's face, Anna laughed at herself. "Oh God, that last part was corny, I know."

Yet Christy shook her head. "No—I kind of liked it. It's a nice idea. And maybe up to now I've just been sort of . . . wallowing. In my sadness. In my fear. In my lack of direction. But . . . I'm going to try to do what you said—figure out what works for me. And concentrate on moving toward the sun. So thank you."

Anna shook her head. "I didn't do anything really."

"Yes you did," Christy informed her. "You said just the right thing when I most needed it. You know, I love Amy to death, but . . . maybe I'm glad you were here today instead."

Duke wasn't particularly comfortable with where he was. Geographically or otherwise.

Why again had he agreed to go to Lucky's house when he wasn't at all sure he was ready to explain all this or see anyone? He should have said exactly what he would have said before the accident—something like, *Gonna have to cancel that, babe, 'cause I'm not up for it.* Since when did he let anyone make his decisions for him?

And why had he agreed to meet Anna at the bookstore right on the town square? Yeah, it would have been out of her way to come back home when she got off work, but so what? She was the one who had organized this little party, so why was he catering to her? She'd gotten pretty damn pushy—aw hell, she'd been pretty damn pushy all along— and it would have served her right if he'd not shown up.

But he *had* shown up, and as he walked toward Under the Covers—a pale green building decked out in flower boxes and looking just a little too damn cheerful for his liking—he tried to keep a low profile. He kept his hands tucked in the front pockets of his jeans, his eyes to the sidewalk before him. He wished he were back at the house installing the new windows he'd started working on a couple of days ago. It was damn hard work to do by himself with that many windows—but easier than this, being in the middle of Destiny when he didn't want to be. Shit, he hoped nobody would see him. And though he'd probably grow his goatee back at some point, it made him kind of glad he'd stayed clean-shaven for now and that his haircut was so different than before. Since he didn't know most people in Destiny that well, he figured it made him all the less recognizable.

As he ambled toward the bookstore from the spot where he'd parked his bike in front of the bank, he found himself thinking back over his past—his romantic past. The truth was—he hadn't had a lot of romance in his life. Women, yes. Sex, plenty. But romance—who had the time for it, and who wanted to be tied down by it? He seldom had. And he'd not missed it.

Even when Lucky had fallen for Tessa, even when they'd been drinking beer one night last summer out at Lucky's place just before his wedding, and he'd asked Duke if he'd ever been in love.

Duke had just looked at him. "Nope, and can't say that I care to be if it makes you start asking dopey questions like that."

"You *think* you don't want it," Lucky had said, "and God knows I never thought I did, either. I mean, I just never thought much about it. But when it happens, man—when you go there—" He'd stopped, shook his head. "You just can't even imagine what it feels like."

"A trap?" Duke had been quick to sarcastically reply.

Lucky had taken another drink from his longneck and said, "Best damn trap in the world then, dude."

They'd been on Lucky's deck, woods all around them, crickets chirping, the steady sound of Whisper Falls in the distance, and for a brief moment, Duke had actually been jealous.

But he'd gotten over it, fast. Lucky might need that kind of tie, that kind of bond with somebody—but Duke didn't.

Only now . . . he couldn't keep from asking himself—was he falling in love with Anna Romo? He instinctively shook his head at the mere thought as he walked—but that didn't take away the question.

No other woman had ever made him feel . . . so powerful and so weak at the same time. No other woman had ever made him just . . . want to spend time with her, whether it was in bed or out. And he might try to deny it, to himself, to her, to anyone else who would ask, but everything about her fascinated him. The way her mind worked. The way she had so many different sides to her. The way she faced her troubles head on—she didn't give up on things and go running away somewhere. Maybe she had run to Half Moon Hill, but at least she'd done it with a plan, some ambition. Sure, she drove him a little crazy on occasion, but the more time went on, the more he realized that he thought the world of her.

And hell, if he was in love with her, well, maybe that explained why he'd agreed to see Lucky and Tessa tonight, ready or not. And though the idea of loving her scared him to death . . . well, he could see an upside. He could see what Lucky meant about it being a good sort of trap—even if the very idea of staying trapped went against his grain.

Or . . . maybe this wasn't love at all. Maybe he was jumping the gun on that. Maybe it was best to just . . . ride this out, see where it led.

But love or not, the one thing he knew for sure was that she was different from anyone he'd ever known, and she . . . inspired him. To be better. To face things. To come out of the woods—even if he wasn't ready to stay out for good, even if something kept drawing him back there, at least for now.

It wasn't yet six, closing time for the bookshop, so he slid onto a bench just outside to wait. It was a beautiful day out, the kind when even he had to admit he was glad to be alive. *And that doesn't have any damn thing to do with Daisy, either.* Even if he'd almost found himself wishing she was at home today, helping him, when he'd stood outside nailing the first double window into the front of the house, then shimming and insulating it. Even if he was looking forward to showing it to her tomorrow, since they'd probably get home after dark tonight.

That was when he tuned into voices, coming from inside the bookstore. Anna and another woman talking. He had no idea who the other woman was or what she had been through—he only knew he heard Anna saying encouraging things, about pushing on, and functioning, and sunshine.

And damn, he had to admire her. He just had to. Because she'd been through shit just as bad as anybody else. Worse maybe, because a situation like hers—well, he imagined it had to screw with your head, that there was probably a lot of temptation for anger and "what if"-ing the situation to death. He knew about playing the "what if?" game—and he'd learned it was useless and only made you focus on everything that had gone wrong instead of what had gone right, even if there was very little of that second part sometimes. But Anna—she was just . . . out there, living, being, doing. She was rebuilding her life, piece by piece, just as he was helping rebuild her home.

And so, in that moment, he tried to . . . take her words to heart. He tried to think forward to a time when things might feel a little normal again. He tried to remember that guy he used to be—that guy who had his shit together and didn't let anything get in his way or knock him down. And then, just for a few seconds, he tried to think about who he might be able to become.

He knew from Lucky that not everyone in town had instantly warmed to Anna—he supposed last summer she hadn't exactly been as warm and fuzzy as most people in Destiny. But he couldn't help thinking maybe they'd all forgotten what she'd been through just because they hadn't been there for it. He knew what it was like to have heavy baggage no one else understood. And he thought she carried hers damn well.

A few minutes later, a young blonde exited the store and all went quiet inside. And he thought about going in but decided to just wait outside, keep soaking up the day, and let Anna have a little alone time in case she needed it the same way he still did.

When she came out, she looked . . . drop-dead gorgeous in a black belted tank and a long animal-print skirt, more like the kind of clothes he'd seen her in last summer. Spotting him on the bench, she smiled. "Hey. Been here long?"

He shook his head, and despite not wanting to look too excited to see her, he had a hard time not smiling back.

"Figured we'd take my car to Lucky and Tessa's, and pick your bike up here on the way back home."

Home, she'd said. Like she thought of it as his home now, too. But he only replied, "Sounds fine." Then added, "About time I got a ride in that Mustang, girl."

"Come on—I'm parked in Amy's spot in back," she told him, still all smiles, and he was more than happy to duck out of sight with her as they walked around behind the building.

"You'll be happy to know," she went on, "that I used my time between customers today to decide on a siding color."

"And?" he asked as they headed toward the vintage car, its top already down.

"Well, I kept thinking blue, blue, blue. Because it's warm. And cozy. But then I kept coming back to yellow—you know, the buttery shade we looked at. Imagine that with white trim, but also a little peach mixed in for some of the gingerbread. That just feels happy and cheerful and inviting to me. And I think people want that, don't you? Just to feel happy. And welcomed."

They'd both gotten in the car now, and he was about to reply—when she kept right on talking. "And I also sort of imagined a sign out front with a golden half moon on it. I'm not sure yet what the rest of the sign would look like, but I just thought the moon would feel like . . . a beacon or something." Finally, she stopped talking and gave her head a short shake. "God, wait—I know that sounded corny. Why am I so corny today? Anyway, the yellow—I've decided on the yellow. What do you think?"

And Duke barely knew *what* to think. Except that she still looked so damn pretty he wanted to kiss her. But he didn't. Because maybe he didn't want to seem so damn caught up in her, right here and now, for no particular reason. And besides, maybe he still wanted to be irritated with her for shoving him into tonight. Though it was getting harder and harder when she was so happy. "I think it's a good choice, Daisy," he said. "It'll look great."

And when her eyes lit joyfully, it stunned him to think she valued his approval that much. An idea that caused a twinge in his gut. And another in his groin.

"I'm glad you think so, because it's been a tough choice, and you know the house nearly as well as I do now, so your opinion is important to me."

"I don't think I've ever seen you so excited," he told her, because she sounded downright exuberant at the moment.

She tilted her head, flashed a look that said: *Oh, come on.* So he corrected himself. "Well, okay—I've never seen you so . . . chatty." Then he tried, just a little, to be annoyed again. "Could barely get a word in edgewise if I wanted to."

But she just rolled her eyes and laughed. "Guess seeing the outside repairs is just finally making it seem real to me. And I *am* getting excited. In a chatty way," she added with a wink and another giggle.

And how on earth could he combat that gorgeous laugh?

So he just gave up and laughed along with her, and as she pulled out from behind the building and onto the street, late day sun shining down on them, he realized that, suddenly, going to see Lucky and Tessa didn't sound so bad. And in fact—hell—to his complete surprise, he was even looking forward to it.

" . . . we will save you in spite of yourself."

Gaston Leroux, *The Phantom of the Opera*

Thirteen

Duke had been to Lucky's house on more occasions than he could count, but this time was different. When Anna pulled her Mustang into the driveway, both Lucky and Tessa came out to greet her, but Duke could immediately see Lucky squinting, trying to figure out who was with her. It was jarring to feel like a stranger here, even for a minute. *But that's the road you paved. You chose to go away, distance yourself from people, even your best friend.* And in that moment he realized, with regret, that he envied Lucky the life he'd built even more now than he had before. Funny how they'd once been at exactly the same starting point but had ended up at such different destinations.

Even as he slammed the door to the convertible and took a few steps toward his old friend, Lucky still didn't seem to recognize him. Then it hit him that Lucky had never seen him without a goatee, or with such short hair. And then there was the scar, too—which Lucky had seen before, but not since it had healed.

"It's me, brother," he said. He'd always called Lucky that—he wasn't sure how it had started, but Lucky was the only person who'd ever earned that endearment from him.

Lucky flinched, drew back slightly. "Duke?"

"In the flesh."

But he, understandably, looked no less confused. "What the hell?" Then he looked toward Anna, now rounding the car's candy apple red fender, and back toward Duke. "What are you doing here, man? And where's your beard? And—" Once more he glanced at Anna and then back again. "What are you doing with my sister?" He didn't look angry about the last part, but damn curious, that was for sure.

Duke barely knew how to begin. So he went with "Long story."

Lucky's brow knit. "Good thing we got some time then." After which he shook his head, as if trying to wrap his brain around the fact that Duke was really standing in his front yard—before saying, "Damn, bro—come here." Then he pulled Duke into a quick but hard guy hug, slapping him on the back.

And though Duke had never been one to do much hugging on other guys, even guys that meant the world to him like Lucky, he couldn't deny that it felt good. That someone wanted to hug him because he missed him, valued him.

"It's damn good to see you, brother," he heard himself say without even planning it.

"You too." Then Lucky looked to Tessa and Anna—before shifting his eyes back to Duke once more. "Why don't we take a walk."

Tessa quickly said, "Yeah, you guys take some time getting caught up. Anna and I can fire up the grill and get the steaks going."

Duke found himself tossing a glance of thanks in their direction—then he and Lucky headed around the house, past the deck, and toward the woods.

"I don't know how to begin," Duke said, "so guess I'll just spit it all out and see where that leaves us."

Lucky gave a short nod as they stepped into the dark shade of the trees on the path that led to Whisper Falls.

Funny how, even here, it felt like a safe place to Duke, safer than being out in the open, like shelter, a refuge. It seemed a fitting setting for what he had to say. "I had a hard time after Denny died."

"I know, man—you sold Gravediggers and went home to Indiana. How could I forget?"

Yeah, maybe that hadn't needed to be said. But he wasn't good at this—even after having recently told Anna, this was still hard. Maybe it was hard to let his best friend know how weak he'd become—Lucky was tough, but in ways, Duke had always been the stronger one. He'd always known how to keep feelings from getting in the way of what you had to do to get by sometimes—like that night they'd left the Devil's Assassins. But then, somewhere along the way, he'd lost that strength.

"Things," he began, "were maybe even worse than I let on."

Lucky stopped walking then, looked at him. "How could they be any worse?"

Duke swallowed back what little remained of his pride and said, "I didn't end up in Indiana. I ended up staying in that old shack you once told me about in the woods beside your sister's house."

Lucky just stared at him, mouth slightly ajar.

But Duke simply went on. "I can't explain it except to say I just needed to . . . be alone. I was . . . having trouble facing people. Or maybe I was having trouble facing *myself*. Either way, it was just easier being someplace where it felt like . . . I didn't exist."

Lucky still appeared dumbfounded. And Duke felt like

he'd somehow let Lucky down—he wasn't the strong one anymore. "How the hell did you survive out there?" Lucky asked. "I mean, that place was in bad shape when I was a teenager—it's gotta be worse now. Can't be fit to live in."

Duke shrugged. "Fish in the pond. Some good camping equipment. An occasional trip into town for supplies. I don't need much to get by."

"Don't?" Lucky asked. "As in you're still living there?"

Another shrug. "Mostly."

And again Lucky raised his eyebrows. And Duke realized he'd just stuck his foot into an area where he'd only planned to tiptoe lightly.

Though now he had no choice but to go there. Damn, he wished he'd thought more about what to say. "Some nights I stay at Anna's place."

Lucky stayed quiet a moment before speaking. "So you're saying you and Anna . . ."

It was hard to meet his friend's eyes in that moment—but he tried. "She's been . . . good to me. Good *for* me. I never planned . . . I just started helping her work on the house and . . . it happened." And when Lucky only remained silent, casting a steely glare Duke's way, he decided he'd better keep going. "Look, I know you know how I've been with women . . . in the past. But I need you to know I respect the hell out of her, Lucky. In fact, I think she's pretty fucking amazing. And she and I . . . I don't know where we're going, and the truth is, I don't know if either one of us are ready for anything big . . . but, like I said, she's been great to me, and I appreciate that. And I hope you don't think I'm a prick for getting involved with her."

He watched then as Lucky let out a heavy breath, and the air instantly seemed lighter around them. "Dude, you can relax. I'm not Mike. I'm not gonna try to pry into Anna's life and tell her who she can or can't see."

It was like Duke could breathe again, too. "Well, that's a relief," he murmured. "I mean, her name's on your chest, brother." Duke had been right there watching as Lucky had had his missing little sister's name etched permanently into his skin, over his heart, back in California during their gang days.

"And I love her," Lucky said. "But the fact is, despite that I know everything you've ever done and that it should probably scare me for you to be with my sister, it doesn't. You know everything I've ever done, too, and I'm still good for Tessa. And there's nobody I trust more than you, even if you're with Anna." Then he cracked half a grin. "Even if it caught me off guard at first. About like your chin did. Where the hell's your goat, man?"

Duke laughed. Thank God Lucky was being so cool about this. It was only then that Duke realized he'd been far more nervous telling him about Anna than telling him about living in the woods. "Anna made me shave it off."

At this, Lucky condemningly arched one brow. As if to imply his little sister had Duke whipped that fast.

"Because I'd let it and my hair grow and I looked like a fucking caveman is all. She wanted me to look less scary if I was gonna work on the house. And I guess I don't much blame her."

Lucky tilted his head. "Why are you working on her house?"

Duke offered up yet another shrug. "Something to do, I guess. Forgot how much I like that kinda work, actually."

From there, they talked more about Duke's choice to retreat to the woods—and he tried to play it off, but he knew it worried Lucky—and he supposed he could understand why. "Just a thing I had to do," he said.

"A thing you're about done with?" Lucky suggested.

Duke thought about the question. "Getting there, I guess. But gotta do it my way, in my own time."

At this Lucky just nodded acceptedly, and Duke was glad his friend wasn't going to push him on this.

"Truth is, Anna had to twist my arm to come here tonight. I'm just . . . not used to being around people anymore, man."

"But this is me. And Tessa. We love you."

Just as Anna had promised him. And he didn't know when Lucky had gone all soft to start saying stuff like that—he still had the long hair and the tattoos, but Duke decided the sweet people of Destiny must be having an effect on him. Regardless, though, it was good to hear. Hell, he must be going soft, too.

"I know, brother. But after being alone for so long . . . it's just a little strange is all." They resumed walking and shared a companionable silence as they approached the falls. And when they both stood looking out over the top, the water flowing calm and serene toward the drop-off, Duke said, "Glad I came, though. Damn glad."

The four of them sat at a round table on the deck eating dinner as the sun dipped behind the trees, ushering in cooler evening air. Conversation flowed easily, and even if Duke wasn't as talkative as the rest of them, Anna thought he looked . . . comfortable. And it made her feel happy inside. To have pushed him a little. And just to be there with him—and with her brother and Tessa, too.

"Seems like you're settling in at the bookstore," Tessa said to Anna. And she couldn't deny to herself that maybe Amy's big plan was working—maybe spending time at Under the Covers was bringing Anna the rest of the way back out of her shell and making her appreciate socializing again.

She nodded, smiled. "I guess I am. It was a good decision, so I'm glad Amy prodded me into it."

"Sometimes Amy's proddings," Tessa said with a tilt of her head, "lead to good things. She pushed me toward Lucky very early in our relationship. And she definitely pushed Rachel toward Mike."

Though Amy had told Anna she'd given up being the town matchmaker once she'd found Logan, Anna found herself wondering what Amy would think of her and Duke together, or if she'd have any insights to impart.

"Speaking of Rachel and Mike," Lucky said, shaking his head incredulously, "I still can't believe they're having a baby."

Duke blinked, the news drawing him from his silence. "Mike is gonna be a father? Damn, that poor kid!" And they all laughed.

"Like I said that night after the ball game," Anna announced, "if it's a girl, it's going to be Aunt Anna to the rescue, for sure."

"But at least maybe this will give him something to do besides monitoring *your* every move," Tessa suggested with a playful raise of her eyebrows.

"Well, that *would* be a perk," Anna agreed. Then she gave her head a tilt, thinking of another of their friends. And looking to Tessa, she said, "I don't know if I should say this, but . . . I'm worried that Jenny isn't doing well with the news. Given that she's been trying to get pregnant and can't."

Tessa sighed. "Yeah, I don't think so, either. It's a tough situation. And tough for Rachel, too —just in a different way. I can scarcely imagine two people less emotionally prepared to have a baby than her and Mike right now. It'll change their whole lives. And I know they were using birth control, so I understand why they were so surprised."

After that, Lucky caught them up on his son from a previous relationship, Johnny, who was now twelve—going on sixteen suddenly, according to his father. "Starting to worry me," he said, " 'cause I don't want him turning out like me."

But Tessa shushed him. "You mean you don't want him going down the wrong paths the way you did. Otherwise, though, I hope he turns out *exactly* like you."

"Probably need to get him interested in something where you can keep an eye on him," Duke said, surprising Anna by adding to the conversation. "If somebody'd done that for me when I was a kid—really showed an interest—might've made a difference."

"I was thinking the same thing," Lucky said, "so I've got

him helping me fix up an old clunker I bought from Willie Hargis—a beat-up old Skylark I'm gonna run in the demo derby the last weekend in July."

"Demo derby?" Anna asked. "What's that?"

"A demolition derby," Tessa answered for her husband, instantly looking more irritated than happy. "It's being held in Creekside Park—the first time Destiny has ever had one, but they're hoping to make it an annual event." Finished eating now, Anna's sister-in-law crossed her arms and rolled her eyes. "Lucky just *has* to be in it. Even though he knows I don't like it."

"Look, honey," he said, "the fact is, riding around on a motorcycle is probably way more dangerous than driving a car in a demo derby." But then he stopped and glanced toward Duke, clearly remembering what he'd recently been through. "Sorry, buddy—that was thoughtless of me."

But Duke gave his head a short shake. "Nah, it's just the truth." His eyes went a little vacant at the reminder, though, and Anna wished it hadn't happened probably as much as Lucky did. The two of them exchanged looks, and she wondered if her brother could see in her eyes how much she hated Duke's pain, how she wished she could take it away.

Then Lucky switched his gaze back to Duke. "You oughta come around some at night—help me work on it. Almost got it running—but trying to teach Johnny about engines at the same time is slowing me down some. Could use the help."

Duke was slow in answering. "I don't know," he murmured, shaking his head softly.

Lucky offered a gentle nod in reply.

And it seemed like time for a change in subject, but Anna couldn't think of one. So she was glad when Tessa said to her across the table, "You're coming to Miss Ellie's this weekend, right?"

Even if she didn't really have an answer. "Um . . . I barely know the woman."

"Well, I'm sure you knew her when you were a little girl.

And despite what you might expect, her parties are always fun—and sometimes interesting things happen there."

"That's right," Lucky said.

And Anna blinked. "Even *you* go to these events?"

"Yeah, brother—seriously?" Duke chided him.

Lucky looked only slightly embarrassed as he said, "I know it doesn't seem like my kinda thing, but I went for Tessa the first time—and it was okay. And it's where the entire town accidentally found out about her tattoo." Which Anna knew was a chain of daisies around her ankle.

And she had to admit, "Well, that does sound sort of interesting."

"And rumor has it," Tessa leaned a bit closer to say, "that there's going to be some big surprise at this particular soiree. So I wouldn't miss it for the world. And you shouldn't, either."

Anna turned the idea over in her head. Given her recent appreciation of being more social again, the idea almost appealed now. And though it wouldn't be fun to be the proverbial third wheel attending with a bunch of couples like Lucky and Tessa—who knew, maybe she could talk Duke into going, too. But for now, she just said, "Maybe. We'll see."

Tessa's eyes brightened. "Good. I'll definitely talk you into it before the weekend." Then she smiled. "It really is good to be seeing more of you out and about, Anna. I'm glad you came tonight. I know I've seen you some at the bookstore lately, and the night you went to the ball game with us, but after spending time with you decorating your house last winter, I've missed you." Which warmed Anna's heart almost more than she could fathom. She was still absorbing the sentiment when Tessa looked to Duke. "And it's so good to see you, too, Duke—even if I barely recognize you." She ended with a wink.

It surprised Anna when his reply was a rare, sheepish one. "Yeah, I'm thinking I should grow a beard again, cover this thing up." He pointed to his scar—and Anna's heart broke a little more for him.

But Tessa's answer was perfect. "I don't know, I think it's kinda sexy. Dangerous. Like bikers are *supposed* to be."

"Hey now," Lucky said on a laugh, "the only biker you better be thinking's sexy is me."

Anna watched then as Tessa and Lucky exchanged a look she envied, a look of sureness, of knowing, of . . . slow, enduring passion. "Don't worry, my big bad biker—you know my heart belongs to you."

And yet it was Anna's heart that suddenly beat harder— from a sense of jealousy she never would have expected, from wishing what she and Duke had was . . . more.

A few minutes later as the two couples still sat talking, Lucky tilted his head to say, "One thing—you never said why you didn't go to Indiana like you planned, to your family."

Anna saw Duke's scar twitch, watched his eyes drift to someplace distant again—before he said, "Just didn't work out that way."

It wasn't much of an answer, but Lucky let it drop. So Anna didn't pursue it, either—though it was the first time the question had crossed her mind. She'd known from Lucky that had been Duke's general plan, but when Duke had turned up in her woods, she'd had far more urgent questions for him.

"You know what we should do?" Tessa said out of the blue.

"What's that, babe?" Lucky asked.

"Let's go to the Dew Drop for a little while."

The Dew Drop Inn was Destiny's only watering hole, and Anna had been there a few times last summer. "Sounds good to me," she said—right as Duke answered, "Um, I'll pass."

Tessa let out a disappointed sigh—as Anna tried to hold hers inside. "Come on," Tessa said. "I'm in the mood to have a little fun."

"Fact is, dude," Lucky added, "it'll be quiet there tonight. Big softball tournament going on—most people'll be at the park."

And in one way Anna hated to prod him—she'd already prodded him in so many ways, and maybe he would lose his tolerance if she kept it up—but she still heard herself quietly saying, "Come on, let's go—just for a little while. It'll be nice." And she nudged his ankle through his jeans with her flip-flop-clad foot under the table for good measure—surprised that even such small contact reminded her how good it felt when their bodies touched.

Duke looked over at her and their eyes met. And even now, even sitting with her brother and his wife, she felt it in her gut, and below. That connection—it was more than just physical. Way more than just physical. And in that moment she understood that it was even way more than just powerful chemistry. It had grown. It had . . . bloomed, like a flower, like a bud opening and expanding into something far greater and more complex and beautiful than she ever could have foreseen when this had first started.

She was . . . in love with him.

"Well?" she heard herself whisper. And for some reason, her skin tingled and her stomach churned while she waited for his answer.

Until he said quietly, "Sure, Daisy—you want to go, we'll go."

"Tonight I gave you my soul . . ."

Gaston Leroux, *The Phantom of the Opera*

Fourteen

"*B*ut only for a few minutes," he added.

"Okay," she murmured in reply, dumbfounded. By what she'd just realized.

I love him. I'm in love with him.

It was scary. Far more scary than just sleeping with an ex-outlaw-gang member. Because now . . . now she was in it, deep, in a way she knew she couldn't pull out of. And once you loved somebody—oh boy, it opened you up for . . . everything. Hurt, heartbreak, neglect. What if he never felt the same way? What if he never got past the wounds still festering inside him? What if he never opened up to her completely? What if he just kept retreating to the woods, running from everything, including her?

Or what if he stopped running, faced life head-on—but still didn't want her in the way she now wanted him? What if he just never loved her back? Because he didn't have the capacity to? Or—maybe even worse—because once he got himself back together he decided he just wasn't that into her?

He leaned slightly forward then. "Are you okay? You look weird."

"Thanks a lot," she said, trying to laugh it off as she realized that all three of her companions now watched her, appearing slightly concerned. "I'm . . . fine. Just can't believe you actually agreed to do something so crazy as have a little fun is all. That's not like you."

And as Tessa and Lucky laughed at her teasing sarcasm, Duke said low, too low for the other two to hear, "Come on now, Daisy—you and me have had enough fun together that you know better."

And she surged with moisture between her legs. And almost couldn't breathe for a few seconds. Their gazes stayed locked.

It all boiled down to one horrible fear: *What if he doesn't love me back?*

Only then another question came to mind. *But . . . what if he does?*

And she knew she should probably keep right on being scared to death of what she'd just figured out—but a funny thing she suddenly remembered about being in love: It made it easy to push sensible fears aside and just bask in it, just live in it, just appreciate it—at least for a while.

So in that moment she began to bask, and to appreciate. This was where she was in life and there was nothing to do but experience it, come what may. *Trust.* That's what it all came down to—even if with Duke it felt like a far more dangerous risk than with anyone else she knew.

And maybe . . . maybe he would feel it, too. Maybe he would see in her the same impossible magic, the same magnificent light, she saw in him. Maybe.

Duke Dawson, it seemed, was reminding her more and more all the time what it was to be brave.

And so she simply stood up, reached down to take his hand, and said, "I'm ready—let's go."

Duke really didn't want to go to the Dew Drop Inn. But as Anna pulled the Mustang into the parking lot, Lucky's Jeep behind them, and he saw that only a few cars and trucks sprinkled the gravel lot, a strange wave of relief swept over him. Strange because—when had he become this guy who was afraid of people? *You can ride with a badass biker gang, break laws, run your own biker bar, and kick more than a few asses that needed it—but you can't walk into the mild little Dew Drop Inn without your stomach churning?*

It almost made him laugh, and even more so when he noticed some of the changes bar owner Anita Garey had made to the place since she'd bought it a few years ago. The flat, gray, cinder-block building had somewhere along the way gotten a coat of beige paint with dark brown trim, and a new neon sign above the door spelling out the bar's name in electric blue cursive. Neon beer signs and strings of mini-lights still glowed through the windows, but underneath them neatly tended flowers grew: red impatiens. His mother had loved impatiens.

As promised, it was as quiet inside as the parking lot indicated. Anita, an attractive woman in her fifties, stood behind the bar, wiping it down, her sparkly top glittering in the dim lighting. He'd met Anita on enough occasions—like Romo family weddings—that at first he worried she'd recognize him and tell everyone in town he was back. But when she merely tossed a casual wave at the group, he remembered he looked different now and that she probably assumed Anna had brought in someone she didn't know.

They took a table, and Lucky went to the bar, returning a few minutes later with three longnecks and a glass of wine for Tessa. They made easy small talk after that, more discussion about the car Lucky was fixing up for the derby—and Tessa talked more to Anna about that party this coming weekend. Duke drank his beer—the third he'd consumed in the last couple of hours—and didn't mind that he was feeling this one a little. He'd never sought comfort in a bottle, but at the moment, maybe a little intoxication made it easier to be here, and to quit thinking about it.

Only a few other tables were occupied, and when an older couple got up to dance near the jukebox, most eyes fell on them. They looked to be in their sixties and Duke found them easy to watch. They looked happy. Not bubbly happy, but . . . comfortable, content, pleased with life. They made him think of Denny and Linda in a way, but he pushed aside the pang of guilt that came and just tried to feel . . . glad for them. Everybody couldn't be happy, but at least some people were, and he guessed maybe that was what kept the world turning, kept life moving forward.

When the song ended, the man walked to the jukebox and inserted some coins, pressed some buttons. Duke didn't recognize the music they danced to, but it reminded him of some of the old stuff Anna played around the house most days.

Soon, a middle-aged couple got up and joined the older folks, and though they didn't look as skilled at the dance moves—which he though looked something like the jitterbug—they laughed and had fun with it.

"Woohoo—go Caroline!" Tessa called out, and the woman looked over, eyes wide, but then covered her smile with her hand, as if embarrassed.

"That's my friend Caroline Meeks, and Dan Lindley, Sue Ann's boss at Destiny Properties. Amy fixed them up last summer."

"How's little Amy doing?" Duke heard himself ask without quite planning it. Once upon a time he'd indulged in a little harmless flirting with her, thinking she was cute.

Tessa smiled. "Doing great."

"She ever marry that Logan guy?" He'd been present for the proposal last year at Lucky and Tessa's wedding reception.

"Not yet, but they keep saying they're going to set a date for this fall."

He nodded, glad to know Amy had that . . . that thing . . . that happiness he'd seen in Denny and Linda, and again just now on the dance floor.

That was when the songs switched and more new-but-old-sounding music filled the room. Anna's eyes went bright and wide as she said, "Oh, it's JD McPherson—I love this song!" Then she turned to Duke. "Dance with me!"

"What?" he groused instinctively, pulling back slightly—yet his Daisy, never easily deterred, ignored his response, grabbed his hand, and yanked him to his feet before he could protest.

Drawing him onto the floor with the other two couples, she took both his hands and began swinging them back and forth to the rhythm as she started dancing. Duke didn't dance. Period. And yet . . . he found himself beginning to move, his body falling with surprising ease into mimicking what Anna did. Sort of, anyway.

"I don't know how to do this," he said to her, loud enough to be heard over the music.

Her eyes sparkled as she laughed. "Me neither—but we'll learn together." As if to emphasize the idea, she released one of his hands, then spun her way into his arms and back out. After which she raised her eyebrows at him as if to say: *See, we can do this.*

Though he thought they probably looked ridiculous. "I think you're drunk, Daisy," he told her with a smile. Even being ridiculous—even making *him* ridiculous—she made him feel good inside.

"Who cares?" she said, eyes still alight, both of them still moving sloppily to the song about a north side gal. "Come on. Dance with me."

And so he did, feeling all the while how bad they were at it, but still . . . somehow having fun. Feeling almost . . . easy inside. Like maybe his life wasn't so bad.

Mainly, he liked making her happy. He liked . . . how little it took, how simple it was. And it was hard to believe how much she'd been through and that something as small as a song, and a bad dance, could make that pretty trill of laughter echo from her. In those moments, her brown-sugar eyes, her soft rosy blush, her dark hair flowing all around her, was all he could see.

And he wasn't sure how long he'd been giving her a look that surely told her everything he was feeling—he only understood how transparent he'd become when he realized she was *returning* that look. Her smile faded, slowly being replaced by a smoldering desire.

It was when the song ended, even as another started to play, that she stopped dancing, stepped near him, and said, "We should get out of here."

Despite himself, he felt a little playful. "Why? Because I'm such a bad dancer or because you're . . . warm for my form?" He raised his eyebrows teasingly.

And a loud peal of feminine laughter tore from her throat.

But then, letting her eyes fall half shut as she cast a sexy smile, she leaned closer, her breath as soft as silk on his skin as she whispered in his ear, "The second one."

They didn't talk much as they drove back toward town, but Duke gently, gingerly ran his fingertips in a circle over the top of Anna's thigh through her skirt. The sensation almost made it difficult to drive, but she couldn't bear the idea of asking him to stop.

When they pulled onto the town square and Duke got out to ride his bike back to the house, she felt a little abandoned without him. And she probably drove a little too fast to get home. But she liked knowing the lone headlight behind her was his, and that he was as eager to get there as she was.

"Hey," she said softly as she got out of the car after pulling into the driveway.

"Hey," he returned, his voice gravelly with the heat she always felt moving so potently between them.

She'd had such a good time with him tonight—talking,

laughing, even dancing—but now she wanted to have a different kind of fun.

Only it wouldn't be just fun now. And maybe it never *had* been just fun. From the first time they'd touched, she couldn't help thinking, feeling, that she and Duke shared a real connection. And now, now that she knew she'd fallen in love with him, she just wanted to celebrate that, relish that, in the most intimate way possible.

She loved having his hand at the small of her back as she unlocked the front door. Even just that tiny touch echoed all through her. And she just wasn't sure when the last time was that she'd felt this happy. *So don't think too far ahead, and don't worry about anything—just be in this moment and let it be beautiful.*

The first thing she saw when she stepped inside and turned on a light was Erik, sitting on the sofa table in the foyer like a furry black statue. Duke noticed, too, saying, "There's your fur ball."

"Meow," the cat said.

"Hi," she greeted him softly, then stepped over to pet him.

"You're not usually so nice to the cat," Duke observed. "What's that about?"

Anna bit her lip. Wow, this love thing was having a serious effect on her already. "Maybe I'm just . . . happy." And after lowering her purse to the table next to the kitty, she turned back toward Duke and let her cheerfulness give way to the full-on passion swirling inside her. All smiles gone now, her voice came out in a mere rasp. "Maybe I want to make you happy, too. David."

She could see a familiar desire lurking in his gaze as well, even as he cast her a teasing, chiding look. "Don't call me that, Daisy."

"Then don't call me Daisy."

When he said nothing in reply, but their eyes stayed locked, she said, "Besides, I like David. David suits you."

He gave a short shake of his head, eyes half shut as they

stayed on her. "No it doesn't," he said quietly. "David was somebody else. I don't know that kid anymore."

She tilted her head, gently but boldly arguing the point. "Your mother thought it suited you. I bet *she* doesn't call you Duke, does she?"

He hesitated. Then he said, "My mother's dead."

Oh Lord, big mistake. And talk about a mood killer. She'd been trying to make him feel good about himself, see him the way *she* did. Now she wished she could call back the words. "I'm sorry—I didn't know."

"It's okay," he told her.

But Anna couldn't help being shocked. She wasn't sure why—people died, her own "other mother" had died—but she'd just thought when Lucky had talked about Duke going home to his family that he'd mentioned, in passing, Duke's mother.

"When did she die?" she heard herself ask. *But shut up, why are you making him dwell on this?* And yet, she just . . . wanted to know things about him. She wanted to understand him.

It took him a moment to answer. "Um . . . about six months ago. Right after I saw her at Christmas. Heart attack."

"I'm sorry," she said again. And then she thought about the timing of it. And maybe she should be quiet, or change the subject, or just kiss him or something—but instead she wondered aloud, "Was that before or after the accident?"

His voice stayed quiet. "Before. By just a couple of weeks."

Only . . . Anna felt confused the more she thought about this. "But Lucky never mentioned . . ." She stopped, shook her head lightly. "He never said anything about you going to a funeral." It just seemed odd that she wouldn't have heard about it given that her brother and Duke had kept in close touch up until these past few months.

Duke wasn't sure how much to say, or how much he *wanted* to say. There was something easy about talking to Anna, even easy about being open with her—but this was one more thing he didn't want to think about, one more thing he shoved away whenever it came to mind. And he wasn't even sure how they'd gotten from the subject of her cat to his mother in just a few short seconds of conversation, but he wasn't prepared for this. He would probably *never* be prepared for this.

A big part of him just wanted to turn around and walk away. Wanted to get back on his bike and ride through the night. Wanted to go stalking back through the woods in the dark to the cabin. Every instinct urged him to run, shut it down, get away from it. It seemed like the only way to . . . stay safe. From . . . something. From . . . the truth about his life, he guessed.

And yet . . . they'd had such a nice night. He'd felt so good inside—almost normal. He'd danced, for God's sake—a definite first for him. And they'd been just about to go to bed together, and underneath it all, he still ached with desire.

What it came down to mostly was that . . . he owed her more. Than to run. Running was easy. But it would be the wrong thing to do. Because he cared about her. And maybe . . . maybe this meant he'd started caring about her even more than he knew, but whatever the reason, he just couldn't quite make himself walk out on her right now.

So instead he forced himself to tell her. About what she'd asked, about his mother's funeral. "I didn't go," he said, his own voice sounding hollow to him, like something coming from far away. And then came the worst part, the reason why. "They . . . no one let me know. That she died."

It was hard to look at her after that—hell, it was hard to just be here, still in her house, his feet on her polished hardwood floor, everything around him seeming . . . too good, too nice, for him. But he forced himself to keep his eyes on her, as much as possible, watching as she blinked, still clearly confused, not quite getting it. "I don't understand."

He worked to swallow back the large lump that had risen in his throat, aware of the sheen of sweat gathering on his skin despite the pleasant night air wafting through the screen door and open windows. There was nothing left to do but say it. "They just . . . didn't bother telling me. I . . . only found out when I went home, after the accident."

He couldn't quite focus on her anymore—he couldn't focus on anything—but he was vaguely aware of her shaking her head some more, obviously still confused. "Why wouldn't they . . . ?"

Duke looked away then, toward the nearest window, curtains blowing around it from the breeze, thinking of the woods, feeling the trees almost calling to him, reaching out to him. He should be there right now, blending into them, being invisible, like he'd grown accustomed to. But all he could really see in his mind was his father's craggy, unsmiling face. And because the only other choice remained to run away, he swung his gaze back to her and spewed out, "My dad always hated me and I always knew it. It's why I left." And then he slowed down a little, spoke more quietly, trying to stay calm, not scare her. "My granddad died when I was sixteen and he . . . he'd kept things sane for me. But after that, working with my dad and his brothers in their construction business . . . wasn't good. And the work was all I had, all I knew how to do."

He stopped then, trying to think how to go on, how to explain a lifetime of trouble in the shortest possible way.

"My mom . . . was hurt by the things I did, the bad stuff I got into after I left home. But when I got out of that, when I cleaned up my life, she took me back. Into *her* life. They all did . . . my dad, my sister, my uncles."

His eyes had dropped at some point—he realized he was staring at their feet: his work boots, her dressy flipflops woven of red and brown leather and matching the red paint on her toenails. He struggled to make himself keep talking. "That's what I thought anyway," he told her. "But when I went back to the farm a few months ago and found out she'd died and that they hadn't even fucking let me know—"

He stopped then, realized his hands had clenched into fists

and that his eyes felt wet—he shut them tight for a minute, willing that part away. *You're almost there, almost done— just get the last part out and then it'll be over.* "When I went back after the accident, my father told me he didn't want anything to do with me. Said I was a piece of shit who'd never been any good to anybody and never would be."

Anna's skin crawled with horror as she stood before him listening, all the blood draining from her face. To know any father would ever say this to a son who needed him. To know Duke had heard this when he'd been in such a bad place. To think he'd gone home to his mother only to find out she wasn't there anymore—and to be kicked in the teeth with such coldness. Oh God. She'd thought she'd understood what he'd been through, what he was dealing with. But this . . . this, it turned out, had to be his deepest wound of all— and he'd been hiding it still, from her, from Lucky.

"That's when I came here. To the woods," he went on, sounding calmer now, but also maybe . . . sadder. "I guess, added to everything else, finding out he thought I was worthless just made it . . . hard to go on. And easy to stay someplace that felt . . . safe."

Anna was overcome with the need to fix this somehow. If only she could, if only she had that power. She knew she didn't—but she still had to try. She peered up at him and spoke from the bottom of her heart. "You have to know how wrong he was, Duke—you have to."

She watched the man she loved as he stood there clearly trying to get hold of himself. He took a deep breath, eyes downcast, blinking—until he found whatever it took to meet her gaze once more. He looked so tired that she just wanted to hug him. "Sometimes I do," he said, "but other times, Anna . . ."

And in that moment Anna wasn't sure such outrage had ever gripped her body. She could barely breathe beneath the weight of his sorrow and thought she'd never been more livid at another human being than she felt toward Duke's father right now. Even her "other mother," when she'd learned the truth. A crime committed in love just wasn't as ugly as one committed in hate. Her anger spilled over as she said, "You listen to me, Duke Dawson. You *are* good. You're plenty good!"

She stopped then, took a breath, felt something softer welling inside her then. "You're good . . . to me. David. You're . . . the best thing that's happened to me in a long time. In fact, I think you're incredible."

She watched as Duke's eyes filled with disbelief, maybe doubt, maybe wonder—she couldn't tell. And she didn't want any confusion about what she felt, about how she saw him. So she followed the stark, desperate urge to lift her hands to his cheeks and kiss him with all the love and need inside her.

"Please," she heard herself murmur against his mouth between kisses. "*Please.*" At some point, Duke's arms had closed around her, at once quenching and fueling her intense thirst for him.

When the kissing stopped, he whispered, "Please what, Anna?"

And it was only then that she realized she'd said it loud enough to be heard. The word had seeped from her lips unbidden, and the truth was—she didn't even know what she'd been asking him for. *Please let me love you. Please let me be there for you. Please be there for me.*

And then—oh! She understood.

She was asking him for . . . everything.

But you can't tell him that. You can't put it into those kinds of words when he's shaken up, vulnerable. And maybe the words didn't need to be said anyway. Maybe she could just show him.

So instead she said, "Please . . . take me. I need you inside me right now more than I think I've ever needed anything in my life."

Oh God, those were pretty freaking intense words, too—

which had come out sounding a lot less controlled than she'd planned. But they were just as true, she realized, as the other thoughts in her head. And they were out there now—she couldn't take them back. So she looked longingly up into his warm gray eyes and, one more time, said, "Please."

"Your fear, your terror, all of that is just love and love of the most exquisite kind, the kind which people do not even admit to themselves."

Gaston Leroux, *The Phantom of the Opera*

Fifteen

After that, things turned urgent, fast. He worked at the hook and zipper on her skirt—she struggled to get his blue jeans open. Both rushed to yank their shirts off over their heads, and Duke's gaze dropped briefly, wildly, to her red bra, before he reached for the straps, looping his thumbs inside, shoving them from her shoulders. She pushed his jeans down as he grabbed on to her undone skirt, tugging it and her panties to her thighs.

When finally they were naked, she reached for him again—but he clamped on to her shoulders, turned her around, and propelled her toward the staircase. She thought he wanted to go upstairs, to her bed—and though she personally didn't want to wait even that long, she also wasn't in the mood to argue, so she started up them.

"No," he said quickly, halting her. "On your knees."

Oh. Okay. He didn't want to wait, either. Good.

Now it was pure lust and need that had all the blood draining from her face, every part of her body tingling as well, as she dropped to her knees on the second step, then leaned forward, planting her hands on a higher step and arching her back. His strong hands closed over both sides of her ass, making the heated anticipation all the sweeter, and she heard yet one more unplanned plea leave her lips. "Oh God—please." And this time, she knew exactly what she was begging for.

He answered by plunging that hardest part of him into her softest. She cried out as the rough entry rocked her body from head to toe—perfectly. And it *was* perfect, because as much as she loved moments when Duke was tender with her, right now she wanted to feel him everywhere, in every molecule of her being, and this was the kind of sex she craved.

He drove into her hard, hard, hard, his strokes relentless. She bit her lip, shrieked her pleasure with each thrust, and just as she'd resolved to do with her emotions earlier, she basked in it.

For a while, she closed her eyes, simply drinking in every hot impact. But then she opened them, looking to the steps directly in front of her. She wanted to feel where she was, the urgency of it, the rawness. She became more aware of her palms and knees pressed into the polished wood, of the songs of crickets and tree frogs bringing the summer night in through the windows, along with a soft breeze. All her senses became engaged, somehow succeeding in helping her feel Duke even more.

All except one. Taste. And she wanted it all in that moment with him—again, she wanted *everything*. And she wanted to give him as much as she took. Maybe even more. She just wanted to love him in every way.

And so she heard herself saying, "Wait. Duke. Stop."

He went still in her, his hands molding to her hips, the

sounds of their labored breath louder to her now than the night sounds. "Wh-what?" he managed to rasp. "Did I hurt you?"

"No," she breathed. "Just . . ," She looked over her shoulder at him. "I . . . I . . ."

Finally, he eased out of her, and the loss was almost painful, but she still wanted what she wanted. And so she turned over to sit on one of the steps and looked up into his eyes. "I want . . . to taste you."

He appeared a little overcome, unsteady, at the words. His jaw went slack, the scar on his cheek seeming to relax along with it. His eyes clouded with lust. And she could have sworn his mouth trembled just slightly as he said very quietly, "Okay."

Anna didn't do this with just every guy—and as she reached out, taking the stone column of his erection into her hand, it dawned on her that this might be the first time in her life that this particular act had been her idea. *It's a lot better that way.* She already knew that, instinctively.

Gingerly, she leaned in, ran her tongue up his hard length. And the pleasure of tasting made what she was sharing with him right now complete. It also multiplied her desire, along with her boldness.

And so then she parted her lips and took him between them. His low groan warmed her soul. Had she ever felt closer to another person than she felt to Duke right now? She didn't think so. And maybe that was dangerous. *But no, no—stop. Bask in it. Be here, right now. Believe in this. Don't be afraid.*

So she made love to him with her mouth, her lips, her hand. His fingers threaded lightly through her hair. He whispered things. "So good, baby, so good." "Just like that." But mostly, he stayed quiet other than the heated sighs and moans that sounded, to her, like the sweetest music.

After a while, she drew back, released him, looked up at him. Wondered if he could see the love in her eyes —or if maybe he'd felt it in her ministrations. And she whispered, "Back in me, please."

"Anything you want, honey," he told her. And then he knelt onto the step below the one where she sat, eased his arms around her waiting body, and entered her once more.

She gasped at the gloriously welcome intrusion, her arms curling around his neck. It was the first time she'd gotten to do that tonight, wrap around him at all, and it felt good to hold him, to cling to him a little. *I love you.* Oh God, she wanted to say it so bad—*but don't. Not now. Too soon. Just too soon.*

And so she just continued to hold him as he moved in her, to kiss him as he rocked her body. Now his strokes were slower and more rhythmic. And Anna couldn't imagine a pleasure more complete.

Until he said, "Aw—aw baby, I'm gonna come. You're making me come."

And it was only afterward, as he whispered in her ear, "Sorry, Daisy," and she said, "For what?" that she realized she hadn't had an orgasm this time.

"I, uh, didn't mean to finish yet. And you didn't . . . get to."

But Anna didn't really care. Sometimes sex was about coming—yet sometimes it actually wasn't, and this was one of those times. Still, of course, she wouldn't turn down an orgasm. So she just laughed, feeling giddy, fulfilled in a way that went far beyond what a climax could bring, and glanced toward an antique clock on a table next to the front door to say, "It's early yet. And I have faith in you."

Duke set the old wooden level he'd found in the garage on the sill of the window he was installing in the room Anna liked to call the library. Morning sun shone in through the brand new glass. Since the window was straight, he began to nail it in place.

Last night . . . God, he still couldn't believe last night. He'd been mentally prepared to go over to Lucky's, to tell

Lucky what had been going on with him, so even though it hadn't been easy, it had been fine. But coming back to Anna's and spilling his guts about his mother's death and his father making him feel more like shit than he already had . . . that he hadn't planned on.

Even now, it was easy to let himself be a little embarrassed about how emotional he'd gotten. And about the fact that she knew now. About his dad. That his dad didn't want him around. That his dad didn't want him . . . period. Hell, just remembering it all again in this moment had his chest tightening, his throat thickening. He hammered a nail in place a little harder than he needed to, felt the strain of the muscles in his arm.

Calm down. It's over.

But it was still a lot to deal with. His greatest shame— the part that had felt even more unspeakable than what happened to Denny. Shit, he hadn't even managed to get it out when he was talking to Lucky, the friend he'd come through hell with—and yet he'd told Anna?

And then she'd said he was incredible.

When he really thought *she* was the incredible one.

But then she'd even made him *feel* incredible—like . . . like the king of the fucking world. Had anyone ever made him feel that good before, that special? Duke had gone through most of his life feeling *un*special, *un*important— somewhere along the way he'd decided life was just a thing you had to get through, as best you could, and that if you were lucky you might find some fun or happiness along the way, but that mostly it was just . . . a stretch of time to be handled. But last night, there for a little while on the stairs in the foyer, that had changed. He'd been special. And he'd found something miraculous, some*one* miraculous, someone he couldn't possibly deserve.

As usual for them, they'd moved to her bed after the steps. And they'd done it twice more. He'd made her come each time, remembering that she had faith in him. Liking it. He'd known she was joking in a way, but he also liked showing her that he wanted to make her feel good, too. Duke had always been an equal opportunity lover—if he was gonna be with somebody, he wanted her to have as good a time as he did. But this, last night, went way beyond that. His desire to bring her pleasure last night had risen from somewhere way deeper.

And that part was difficult for him, too. Because he didn't know where it had come from, or what it was about. He only knew that he was getting in too deep here, feeling too much. That had seemed dangerous enough a couple of weeks ago, but now . . . it seemed far worse. He didn't know how to do this, how to be like this with someone. He wasn't the kind of guy she needed, the kind of guy she deserved. Sure, he was feeling better at times, starting to come back to life—it was like she'd helped him start breathing again. But just because he was more functional than he'd been when they'd met in the woods, it didn't mean his father was wrong about him. It didn't mean he knew how to change himself into a better man. It was all just so . . . heavy. And he had enough heavy stuff in his life already.

So maybe he should just back off, like he had before. Not to hurt her, but . . . well, just to keep a handle on the situation.

"Hey, I'm off to the bookstore."

He could hear the smile in her voice even before he looked up to see her standing in the doorway. Damn, she looked beautiful in another flowy skirt, this one stopping above her knees and giving him a view of the long, tan legs below and the stylish strappy shoes that showed off her pretty feet. Oh shit, when had he started thinking she had pretty feet? He raised his gaze back to her eyes and simply said, "Okay."

"Sorry I slept in and we didn't do breakfast—you wore me out last night." She winked then, and he felt it in his groin. Along with her happy sense of trust, trust that everything was great between them.

"No problem," he told her, his words coming out stiff.

That was how he started backing away—he could feel him-self putting up that wall this very second, the wall that kept him from being too relaxed around her, too open, too easy. He wondered if she was beginning to notice yet.

That was when she closed the remaining space between them, slid her slender arms confidently around his neck, and kissed him. Okay, she hadn't noticed. And he kissed her back. Because he couldn't not. In fact, the tape measure he held in one hand dropped to the rug beneath their feet with a soft *plunk* because he needed his hands—he needed to slip them around her waist and pull her closer. And by the time she eased her tongue into his mouth, he was lost to kissing her completely.

When the kisses ended, she let out a soft, pleasured sigh that seemed to move all through him. And then she tilted her head, cast a speculative smile, and said, "I'm probably work-ing all day again at the store, unless Amy suddenly shows up. Think you'll still be here when I get home?"

Say something doubtful. Or vague. Tell her you're not sure. "Do you want me to be?" he asked instead.

She nodded. "Very much."

"Okay. Then I will be."

"Good," she said shortly, clearly pleased—and then she turned around and left.

Duke stood there listening as her heels clicked lightly on the hardwood, moving away from him, and exiting through the front door. A moment later he heard the sound of the Mustang starting, and then accelerating away.

What the hell had he just done? What had happened to backing off?

Despite what you just told her, tonight would be a good time to get your ass back to the cabin. Even if it hurt her to come home and find the house empty, that would be best. For both of them. And right now the solitude definitely appealed.

But . . . maybe seeing Anna tonight appealed more.

Shit. Backing off wasn't gonna be so easy this time.

True to her prediction, Amy didn't show up at Under the Covers for the rest of the week. More than once, Anna envisioned her out at the cottage she now shared with Logan on Blue Valley Lake, comforting Mr. Knightley, whom she imagined stretched out on a couch with a thermometer in his mouth and a hot water bottle on his head.

It was Friday night and Anna was unwinding by sitting on the screened back porch with Cathy's diary. And as another vision of the very spoiled Mr. Knightley came to mind, she realized her own kitty was stretched out alongside her thigh on the wicker sofa. She glanced down at him. "Don't let this go to your head, but I think you're tougher than Mr. K. And that's good, because if you ever need to go to the vet, I'm not shutting down my whole life on your behalf for three days—got it?"

"Meow," the cat said.

Anna took it as acceptance and gave a short, quick nod. "Good kitty."

The sound of a hammer echoed from the side of the house where Duke was finishing the last of the many windows. Knowing they were both thoroughly tired from a long week of work—even if very different kinds—not to mention more mind-blowing sex, Anna had brought home a pizza. After eating, Duke had wanted to finish the last window before dark, so Anna had decided it was a good time to catch up with Cathy.

She opened the leather-bound diary to the bookmarked page.

> *When Robert didn't come to work at the house yesterday, I knew something was wrong. Daddy, on the other hand, didn't even worry—he just said Robert was probably being lazy. Then, "Or for all we know, he's run off. People like him,*

*you never know what to expect or how long you
can count on them." I thought it was harsh given
that Robert has been as dependable as the day is
long, and I'd actually thought Daddy had taken a
liking to him in the recent weeks, especially since
he'd trusted him enough to drive me to and from
school sometimes.*

*And of course I was worried about Robert, so
after supper I said I was going to go butterfly
hunting in the meadow over the hill, but instead I
snuck through the woods and to the cabin.*

*I knocked and, getting no answer, I let myself
inside. I found Robert lying in his bed asleep,
but I could tell he wasn't well. It was strange to
watch him sleeping—and it made me think how
. . . innocent a person is when they're asleep. Or
maybe the word I'm looking for is vulnerable.
Anyway, I confess to sitting in a small chair and
just watching him, thinking of him almost like a
little boy in those moments. And I felt bad that he
had no mother to take care of him when he was
sick the way I do—because is there any better
comfort than that?*

*After a bit, he woke up and was, naturally,
surprised to see me. He tried to smile, but when
he couldn't quite muster it, that's when I understood how sick he must be. He said he thought he
had a fever, and he joked to ask me if I was real
or if he'd just hallucinated that the prettiest girl in
the world was sitting next to his bed. I wanted to
kiss him again that very moment, believe me, but I
kept myself from it.*

Cathy went on to write that she'd returned home by dark,
but later, after her parents were asleep, she'd gathered pro-
visions for Robert and snuck back out. She took a thermom-

eter, half a bottle of antibiotics her father hadn't finished
after a bout of bronchitis last winter, and a thermos of the
chicken soup her mother had made the previous day.

> *His temperature was 101.5, so I wet a washcloth
> in his sink and laid it across his forehead the
> way Mother does for me when I'm feverish. And I
> poured some soup in the thermos lid. I ran a glass
> of water and watched him take one of the pills.
> Then he fell asleep, but not before thanking me
> and giving me one of his handsome Robert smiles.*
>
> *It was only then that I realized how strange it
> was to be in the cabin with him, to be where he
> lived. So different from my house, or anyone's
> house who I know. He has so little—and yet he's
> never bitter. Whereas my father has so much
> and seldom seems truly happy. And even though
> Robert's belongings are few, and my father has
> provided him with such sparse living quarters
> and furniture, I felt . . . good there. Because I felt
> him there. And I'm not yet completely certain, but
> sitting there watching him sleep again made me
> think that I might perhaps be in love with him.*

At the end of that paragraph, Cathy had drawn a heart
reminiscent of ones you'd find on a schoolgirl's notebook,
and it made Anna smile. First love—it was so magical,
so innocent. But then, *any* time you were in love it was
magical—being with Duke was reminding her of that. He
was so different from anyone she ever would have pictured
herself with, but she wouldn't have changed a thing about
him. Even his wounds. Even his scar. Yes, she hated that
he'd been hurt so badly in so many ways, yet his history
made him into this man she'd come to love when she'd least
expected it, and it had in fact brought him to her, so how
could she want to take that away?

Anna read onward, learning that Cathy had returned to the cabin the following two nights, seeing Robert's condition improve greatly. They'd spent more time talking, and Robert told her how much it meant to him that she'd risked her father's wrath to care for him.

> *I'd always thought of Robert as so strong until*
> *then. But now I understand that everyone needs*
> *to be taken care of sometimes.*

Anna stopped and read that line again. She let it settle deep in her bones. Cathy had been wise beyond her years.

The diary went on from there, sometimes about Robert and their continuing encounters, including two more kisses that had clearly rocked Cathy's world—and Anna's, too, in a way—and other times she resumed writing about family matters or school. But Anna could see in the words—could feel—Cathy growing, trading in her innocence for love and courage and confidence and wisdom. *I want to be Cathy when I grow up.*

About a week later in the diary, Cathy came home from church with her parents to find a book lying on her bed— and Anna knew even before reading the words that it was *The Phantom of the Opera.*

On Saturday, when Amy was still absent, Anna worked at Under the Covers until two, then closed up shop. Upon arriving that morning, she'd found a message from Amy on the store's answering machine thanking her for working all week, then practically insisting she close early today and come out to Miss Ellie's. "Logan and I will be there and it will be a good chance for you to fill me in on anything I've missed."

And though Anna didn't really feel Amy had missed anything so important that it required getting together outside of work, she would have felt bad to ignore the message. And she'd gotten a call from Tessa that morning reminding her about the garden party as well. And so she'd decided maybe it would be nice.

But as the day had gone on, she'd decided it would be even *nicer* if Duke went to the party *with* her. She'd mentioned it last evening and not gotten much of a response—but by the time she was locking the shop's front door, she decided to drive home and try to persuade him.

When she pulled in, she found him standing on an easel ladder installing a new light fixture above the garage door.

"That looks great," she said, getting out of the car. The fixture matched the ones he'd soon be putting on both sides of the front door.

"Thanks," he said, eyes still on his work.

"Almost done?"

He stopped twisting the screwdriver in his hand to glance down, his look teasing her. "Yep, boss—you got something else urgent lined up for me to do?"

And she smiled up at him. "Actually—yes, I do. Go to Miss Ellie's garden party with me."

He arched one eyebrow at her, his smile fading. "No thanks, Daisy—I'm fine here. You go and have fun. I've got more light fixtures to put in."

Anna shifted her weight from one foot to the other, not ready to give up on this yet. "You'd be doing me a bigger favor by going with me. I've practically promised I would now, but I don't want to go alone. I mean, you know how that is." She'd decided she was not above playing on his sympathy—since she thought his going would do him just as much good as it would her, if not more.

"Guess you shouldn't have promised then," he told her, after which he continued twisting a screw into place.

She sighed, disappointed. "I really can't change your mind? I drove all the way home just hoping you'd go."

He kept working. "Sorry, babe, but no." Then he stopped and looked down at her. "I had a nice time at Lucky's the other night. And the Dew Drop afterward wasn't bad. But a big party with a lot of people?" He shook his head. "Not up for it."

Anna knew he had already conceded to her a lot on this stuff. But she also couldn't help thinking he sounded as stubborn as the man she'd first encountered in the woods. And she didn't want pure stubbornness to be the reason he didn't go. "Duke, I know it's not easy, but they're nice people. And you probably think you don't have anything in common with them, but you don't have much in common with me, either, and still we—"

"Look, woman," he interrupted her. "Are you trying to drive me insane?"

She stopped, took a deep breath, pursed her lips. "No," she said calmly.

"Then get this through your head. *I'm. Not. Going.* Got it?"

And though the last words had been a question, he'd definitely asked it in a very final sort of way. So that she had no choice but to give up and quietly say, "Got it."

Then she took the few steps back to her car and got inside. When she looked back to Duke, his eyes were on his work again. She regretted being so pushy now, but . . . he wasn't even going to say goodbye?

As she started the car and began to back out, she kept waiting, thinking he'd glance back up, say something, maybe wave—and when none of that happened . . . well, perhaps it was silly, but her chest tightened and she experienced her first real pang of worry about having given her heart to Duke Dawson.

Walking into Miss Ellie's party alone was as awkward as Anna had feared. She stepped through a white latticed archway into a lovely English garden to immediately realize two things: She didn't see anyone she knew, and everyone else had brought a covered dish. *If I'd known, I could have made a blackberry cobbler.*

The spat with Duke didn't add to her confidence level, either. She knew she'd been pushy; she knew his refusal had nothing to do with her. And yet the memory of him snapping at her stung more than it would have just a week ago. She felt so much closer to him now. *But it's okay—everything's fine. Just do this. Put on your best confident face, your best confident self—then in a couple of hours you can make your excuses and go home to Duke and everything will be good.*

Taking a look around the garden, Anna was struck by the beauty of it. A few small white wooden café tables with matching chairs dotted the open spaces, but the real centerpiece was the white gazebo. And inside sat Miss Ellie herself, looking as pleased as punch for no particular reason Anna could discern. She couldn't help thinking it would be a real gift to be so content at that age.

Since she still saw no familiar faces, she decided to go greet the elderly woman. Stepping up into the shady gazebo, she smiled down and said, "Hello, Miss Ellie—I'm Anna Romo. Do you remember me?"

The old woman's eyes widened with delight as she peered upward. "Why, you're the little Romo girl who was away for so long," she said. And Anna rather liked the way she'd put that—there was nothing about having been "missing" or "taken" or "lost," and the idea of just having been "away" was much nicer.

"Yes. I just wanted to say hi and tell you how lovely your flowers are."

"Oh, I don't believe there are any showers in the forecast today, dear."

It took Anna a moment to realize Miss Ellie had just misunderstood her, leaving her stuck for a reply.

But Miss Ellie went on. "I understand you bought that big old house up on Half Moon Hill."

Anna nodded, glad for a new topic. "I'm planning to open it as a bed-and-breakfast," she said.

"Well, it's much too late in the day for breakfast, but there's plenty else to eat." She motioned toward the food tables. "And if you need to lie down, just go on inside."

Anna began to nod uncertainly—and just then an arm

hooked through hers and she found that Jenny Brody had stepped up to join them. "Miss Ellie is hard of hearing," she said to Anna, "so you kind of have to yell. And then just roll with whatever she says."

"Ah," Anna said, tipping her head back.

Then Jenny peered down at the elderly woman, speaking loudly. "I'm going to steal Anna away, introduce her to some people."

"All right, Jenny, you do that," Miss Ellie said. "Maybe that handsome young war hero. They'd make a fine couple."

And at this, Anna glanced over to Jenny, who now looked just as confused as Anna, though she said to Miss Ellie, "All right then—I'll be back over a little later."

As the two exited the gazebo, Jenny shook her head. "Miss Ellie's been my nearest neighbor for most of my life, and she's usually sharp as a tack other than the hearing issue, so even I'm stumped on that one."

"Thanks for the help anyway," Anna said. "Tessa and Amy talked me into coming today, but so far, you're the first person I've seen who I know."

As promised, Jenny led Anna around to make the acquaintance of a few Destiny-ites she hadn't yet met, including Caroline Meeks, whom they'd watched dancing at the Dew Drop Inn. But when, a little while later, they found themselves alone again, Anna couldn't help asking . . . "If this is a bad topic, feel free to tell me to shut up—but how are you doing? I mean, the last time we talked . . ."

Anna trailed off, deciding too late that she shouldn't have brought this up, but Jenny shook her head and said, "No, it's fine. It's nice of you to ask." Yet she looked troubled. "And I wish I could say I feel better, but . . . I'm still not pregnant. And Rachel *is*. And—" She stopped, letting out a frustrated sigh. "She doesn't even appreciate it, Anna."

"I knew it upset you when she and Mike announced it at the Whippy Dip."

Jenny nodded, still looking sad—and then guilty. "But oh God, I'm sorry—Mike is your brother. You're going to be their baby's aunt. So forget I said anything. That was wrong of me."

Yet now it was Anna who looped her arm around Jenny's, feeling the need to comfort her. "It's okay—I'm sure anyone would react the same way in the same situation."

Though Jenny looked doubtful. "Would they? Because I feel terrible about it."

"You feel what you feel—you can't help it," Anna told her. *If feelings were easy to turn off and on, after all, life would be simple. Duke wouldn't have hidden himself away in the woods. I wouldn't have retreated to Half Moon Hill. I wouldn't be so attached to Duke already that his cross words from earlier still sting.*

When Jenny merely nodded but looked unconvinced, Anna dared to ask, "Can I give you some unsolicited advice?"

"Sure," Jenny said.

"With Rachel, just . . . lay low, and try not to think too much about her having the thing you want. Instead, just try to keep believing you'll have what you want, too, and maybe good things will happen." Then she scrunched up her nose. "Does that sound too hokey?"

Jenny shook her head, clearly working to summon a smile. "No, actually it sounds . . . pretty wise."

Anna shrugged. "Don't know if I'd go that far. And I'm not sure I always do a good job of living that way myself. But sometimes there's just not much to do but keep your head down, barrel through, and know there has to be something good waiting on the other side."

Jenny and Anna had been walking as they talked, and just then the stone path they'd been following led past a white lattice trellis draped with pink roses, and beyond it stood a small crowd—and finally some people she knew. Namely Tessa and Lucky, Mike and Rachel, Sue Ann and her boyfriend Adam, and Tessa's parents. They were all smiling, talking, laughing, so much that Anna and Jenny exchanged a look. "What on earth are we missing back here?" Anna asked her companion.

But then Jenny pulled up short, spoke quietly. "Maybe they're talking about the baby." And it was clear that if so, Jenny didn't want to hear the conversation.

That was when Tessa spotted them, though, turning to face them—and it struck Anna that other than on her wedding day, she didn't think she'd ever seen Tessa look happier. She practically glowed. "Oh, Anna's here! Anna and Jenny, I'm so glad to see you guys! Come here—there's someone I want you to say hello to."

Jenny cast a cautious smile. "Who on earth is it?"

And Tessa exclaimed, "My brother! Isn't it amazing? We didn't even know! He didn't even tell us! He just showed up at my parents' house first thing this morning—home from Afghanistan, safe and sound!"

"Miss Ellie's war hero," Jenny murmured just loud enough for Anna to hear.

But Anna didn't have a chance to respond before Tessa took her arm, pulling her into the small crowd to say, "Anna Romo, meet my brother the hero, Jeremy Sheridan!" And when she least expected it, Anna found herself face-to-face with possibly the most handsome man she'd ever seen.

" . . . he was a charming fellow and showed that he was not lacking in intelligence."

Gaston Leroux, *The Phantom of the Opera*

Sixteen

"Um, hi," Anna said, extending her hand when he reached out to take it.

He was tall, lean, with light brown hair, a strong jawline, and the most smoldering eyes she could have imagined. And when he smiled, it practically lit up the entire garden. "You're even prettier than everyone said."

She blinked, a little unnerved. Who was everyone? And they'd said she was pretty? And he thought so, too? How had she suddenly found herself feeling quite wooed by a guy she'd never seen before, and with all these eyes upon her? "Um, thanks." Though when he squeezed her hand in an almost intimate way, she decided it was probably a good time to take it back.

"I'm really happy to meet you, Anna," he said with

smooth confidence as she withdrew her hand. He wasn't shy, or subtle.

Just then, Rachel's grandma, Edna Farris, rounded the trellis. "I hear little Jeremy Sheridan's home and that he's some kinda big war hero, so I came to see with my own two eyes." And when Jeremy shifted his gaze from Anna to Edna, the older woman grinned. "Sakes alive. Ain't so little anymore, though, are ya? Come 'ere and give me a hug."

Anna watched as he turned to scoop Edna into a big bear hug, and when it ended, Edna said in her direction, "This one used to help me with my fall apple harvest when he was just a young'un in high school." And then she looked back at handsome Jeremy. "So what's this about you savin' a bunch o' fellas' lives over there in Afghanistan?"

"Wasn't that big of a deal," Jeremy said, giving his head a modest shake while still casting a grin. "Was just in the right place at the right time and did what I'd been trained to do." And then he explained about thwarting an ambush just before a large convoy of U.S. troops had passed through.

Anna thought she sensed just a hint of seriousness behind his smile as he told the story, but by the end, Edna was saying, "Well, I'll be a monkey's uncle—ain't that somethin'," and his father was slapping him on the back, and he was all humble, handsome smiles again.

And a moment later, Jeremy was shaking Lucky's hand, saying, "About time I got home to celebrate my sister getting married. Gotta admit, surprised me to hear who she was marrying, but I can tell already how happy you make her."

More than once after that, Jeremy found his way back over to Anna, making a point of expressing his interest in her. "So I hear you're opening a bed-and-breakfast? What's a pretty girl like you want to hide herself away up on that hill for?" he'd inquired with a wink. "I hear you grew up in Indy. What made you choose small town life over the city?" "Looks like you're fitting back into Destiny life just fine—

maybe you can give a few tips to a guy who's been away awhile, too?"

Time and again, though, he was pulled away by one person or another, especially as more people arrived at the party. He politely excused himself every time, and Anna now had plenty of other people to talk to—but she noticed that he repeatedly worked his way back to her. He was charming, and every bit as handsome as she'd thought upon first seeing him. And she couldn't deny being flattered by how taken with her he seemed.

And if she hadn't already fallen in love with Duke, she might well have been taken with Jeremy Sheridan in return. But she *had* fallen for Duke. So even as she enjoyed chatting with the war hero returned home, she knew that was all it was—chatting.

At one point in the afternoon as she stood catching up with Rachel and Mike, Mike said, "Now, Jeremy Sheridan—that would be a good guy for you, Anna."

"Mike," Rachel lectured him at the same time Anna flashed him a look.

He threw his hands up lightly in his defense. "I'm just pointing it out, that's all."

Anna narrowed her gaze on him. "Don't you have enough to worry about in your own life at the moment without butting back into mine—Daddy?" She raised her eyebrows.

And his shoulders slumped as he let out a tired sigh. "Oh God, I keep forgetting that." Then he shook his head helplessly. "How on earth did that happen?"

Rachel, too, looked wearied by the subject, almost making Anna feel bad for bringing it up. "Do you know how many people have congratulated us today? And how hard it is to smile? Because . . ." She sighed as well. "I know babies are precious and all, but we're still pretty stressed out about this."

Just then, Anna caught sight of someone waving at her from across the way and realized it was the young woman she'd met at Under the Covers a couple of days ago, Christy

Knight. She excused herself from Rachel and Mike and made her way over to Christy—who seemed in better spirits today than when they'd met.

And as they stood talking a few minutes later, she realized just how glad she was she'd come. She really *was* getting to know people here. And she was also getting to like them. She was no longer the long-lost Anna Romo, no longer the town curiosity. That honor now belonged to Jeremy Sheridan, who handled it with far more grace than she had. But then, it was probably easier coming home as a war hero than someone who had been abducted. She almost laughed at the absurdity of the thought—and realized she was actually seeing a bit of humor in something she'd never dreamed she could. She was becoming part of this idyllic little town, relaxing into it, carving out a role for herself here at last.

And if that wasn't amazing enough—she was in love. And even if Duke wasn't ready to embrace Destiny along with her just yet, that was okay. *Everything in its own time.* She had faith in him—when she'd said that the other night, it had been about far more than orgasm—and she felt better in this moment than she had in a very long while.

She still stood making small talk with Christy Knight five minutes later when a woman named Mary Katherine, who had been introduced to Anna as Miss Ellie's daughter, began tapping a fork on a wineglass to get everyone's attention.

When finally everyone in the garden went quiet, looking her way, she said, "I know a rumor has gone around Destiny that there would be a big surprise at today's party—and I'm pleased to tell you that it wasn't just a rumor. I'm very happy to introduce to you all, for the first time, Mr. and Mrs. Logan Whitaker!"

The entire crowd gasped aloud, Anna and Christy along with them, as Amy and Logan came whisking through the white latticed archway that led into the garden, hand in hand. Amy looked radiant and glowing in a flowy white sundress, a yellow flower tucked behind one ear. Logan appeared as handsome as ever in crisp khaki cargo pants and a blue polo shirt. Amy was smiling, laughing, looking absolutely joyful in a way Anna felt all the way to her toes as applause broke out.

Anna happened to be standing closer to the couple than most of their friends, and when Amy spotted her, she smiled and waved. Then called to her, "Mr. Knightley didn't really get a flea treatment or shots!" Then she held up her left hand, flashing a diamond ring. "We eloped to Las Vegas!"

It was late in the afternoon that Rachel found herself alone with just her girlfriends. She sat at a large, white wrought iron table outside the garden under a billowing maple tree with Tessa, Amy, Jenny, and Sue Ann. Maybe most people wouldn't consider a crowd that size private, or "alone," but after a few hours in the crowd at Miss Ellie's, still just on the other side of the rose of Sharon bushes in the distance, being in a circle of only her close friends made her feel more relaxed than she had all day. She loved Mike with all her heart, but since coming home to Destiny a few years ago, her friends had been her safety net, her safe place.

"Where's Anna?" Jenny asked. "We should invite her to join us."

"Being monopolized by my brother probably," Tessa replied on a laugh. "I was going to tell her we were sneaking out for a little girl talk, but I didn't see her anywhere."

"It's so great that Jeremy's home," Amy said. "What a surprise, huh?"

And they all just looked at her. Sue Ann said, "Look who's talking about surprises! What on earth got into you, eloping?"

Rachel remained just as stunned as everyone else, and was eager to hear Amy's reply.

Blushing prettily, Amy said, "We just decided we didn't want to wait—and that we wanted to do something adventurous. I mean, do you guys realize how little of the world I've seen beyond Destiny? And it just made sense that if I'm going to start having more adventures that I do it with my soulmate, right?"

Rachel smiled and tried to ignore the current queasiness in her stomach, something she still hadn't quite shaken, glad to let Amy's exciting news distract her. "You deserve grand adventures, Ames!" she said.

"So—tell us everything," Tessa prodded.

And Amy gave them all the fun details from start to finish, about the beautiful ceremony in the garden at the Bellagio, about the gorgeous white dress she'd bought in a boutique in the hotel, about the honeymoon suite complete with rose petals on the bed. "And Logan was so romantic every step of the way." She sighed happily, and Rachel couldn't have been more pleased for her sweet friend.

Only then Amy's happy smile faded as she looked in Rachel's direction. "You got cheated, though. Out of being maid of honor." The agreement Rachel, Amy, and Tessa had embarked upon had put Rachel in line to be Amy's.

Yet she shook her head, eager to let Amy know it was okay. "Your happiness and adventures are way more important to me than being a maid of honor—I promise." And then another wave of nausea struck and she made a face, pressing her palm to her belly. "Ugh. Seems I have other things to worry about these days anyway."

"Still sick, huh?" Sue Ann asked, her expression filling with sympathy.

"Yep."

"That's definitely the worst part of being pregnant for sure." And as the only mother in their group of friends, Rachel figured Sue Ann was qualified to know. "You know," Sue Ann went on, "I don't want to pick on you, Rachel, but . . . you really didn't have any clue you were pregnant?"

"Hey, it's not as obvious as you might think when your birth control pill makes it so you only have four periods a year," she pointed out. "And . . . I'm sure I was in denial, too. I mean, if the signs were there, I guess I subconsciously chose not to see them." She released a heavy sigh, feeling tired. "I still can't quite wrap my head around this. Is that awful?"

And that's when Jenny said, *"Yes!"* and the whole group went quiet.

Rachel met Jenny's gaze across the table, stunned. "Huh?" she murmured.

"Yes, it *is* awful," Jenny said in a snappish tone Rachel had never heard from her, ever, in their whole lives. "I'd give anything to be pregnant right now, Rachel, and all you can do is complain about it and act like it's a burden. Well, that's not right. It's a baby, Rachel—you're having a child! You're bringing a new life into the world! That's amazing! It's a miracle! But to you and Mike, it's just an annoyance."

When she finished, everyone stayed silent.

And Rachel felt like she'd been slapped. She knew Jenny was trying to get pregnant, but . . .

"Look, Jenny," she said, "I'm truly sorry you haven't been able to conceive yet. And I'm sure as time passes, Mike and I will adjust to this—but right now, it's something we didn't choose and we're not sure we're cut out for. So you're not the only one going through something. It's not my fault you and Mick are having trouble getting pregnant. And . . . I don't think you're being a very good friend to me right now."

In response, Jenny appeared as affronted as Rachel felt. "Well, I don't think you're being a very good friend to me, either."

Rachel sat staring at Jenny, her dear girlfriend since they were little, unable to believe they were having this conversation. Occasionally she and her friends had disagreements or momentary squabbles, but nothing like this.

It broke her heart.

But she believed in her right to feel the way she felt, that her feelings were valid and just as important as Jenny's.

"I'm . . . going to go," Jenny said, brow knit, looking close to tears.

Then she stood up and began walking toward Blue Valley

Road. The little yellow cottage she shared with Mick was the next house up, within sight through the empty meadow that separated the two homes.

"Um, I'll go after her," Sue Ann volunteered a moment later.

And after she was gone, Rachel said to Tessa and Amy, "What was *that*? Am I really so horrible?"

Amy reached over and took her hand. "Of course not. Jenny's just . . . in a bad place right now."

Rachel let out what she knew was an immature *harrumph*—because you could do that with friends. Or you *should* be able to anyway. "Well, I'm not in a great place myself." She looked back and forth between Amy and Tessa. "Do you know that I've been so up in arms over this that I forgot to feed the cat yesterday. You guys—what if I forget to feed the baby?"

They both made comforting sounds and Tessa said, "Well, for one thing, it will cry and let you know. And for another, you won't forget. You just won't."

"I really do worry," she confided in them, "about Mike and me as parents. Some people are cut out for that and some aren't. And we've both always been in agreement that we fall into the *aren't* category, at least so far."

Now Amy was patting her hand. "Well, you'll just change categories, that's all. Don't worry—everything will be fine. And with Jenny, too."

Rachel blinked, still in shock. "I don't see how. I mean, we've been friends our whole lives and this feels . . . big. What if we don't forgive each other? What if we can't? And what if I have this baby and she can't handle being around it—or me?"

Duke washed his hands in Anna's downstairs bathroom sink, same as he did every day when he finished work on the house. Then he looked in the mirror. At his scar.

Anna had accepted him with it—hell, more than accepted him. She'd made him feel human again. And Lucky hadn't blinked—though he'd seen it right after the accident, too.

Tessa had even gone so far as to make light of it. And no one at the Dew Drop had seemed to notice.

But how would people react if he walked into some fancy party at that old lady's house on Blue Valley Lake? Wouldn't that be different? A dark bar was one thing—but wouldn't a guy with a jagged scar on his face stand out a lot more, be a lot more out of place among the fine folks of Destiny, on a bright summer afternoon, all of them drinking their punch and eating their deviled eggs and apple pie?

Funny, he'd gone to more than one event last summer related to Lucky's wedding, and he'd gone to Mike's wedding, too—and he hadn't given a damn what anyone thought of him. Even then, before the scar, he'd known he'd probably stand out in the crowd, but he'd been good with who he was and he'd figured if anybody had a problem with him, they could fuck off.

So what's it mean if you're so damn concerned with what they think of you now?

That you don't like who you are anymore?

He took a deep breath, let it back out. *You hit the nail on the head.*

Not that it was a surprise. A guy doesn't take the steps he'd taken if he had his shit together. But maybe he'd thought he was doing better—*getting* better—until Anna had tried to press him into going to that party this afternoon and he'd acted pissy about it.

Now he felt bad. She was so brave, and so good to him in so many ways. He was sorry he'd been snotty to her. Even if she was pushy as hell sometimes, she didn't deserve that. What she deserved was a stand-up guy.

Looking back to the mirror, he took another deep breath. And he wished he had a decent shirt to put on, but most of his stuff was in a storage locker in Crestview, so a clean gray T-shirt would have to do. He was thankful he'd been washing some stuff in Anna's laundry room and wouldn't smell like lake water.

Twenty minutes later he'd taken a shower and put on clean clothes.

One last look in the mirror. *It's not a big deal—it'll be fine. Do this for Anna.*

Walking out the door, he got on his bike and took the curvy roads down to Blue Valley Lake. Fifteen minutes later he'd wound his way there; it was easy to spot the house where the party took place due to the cars lining each side of the country road.

It was *less* easy to stop and park, but he did. And his stomach went hollow as he put down the kickstand, but he didn't hesitate—he got off the bike and walked up in front of the cute little house and made his way around to the side where he could hear people talking and laughing.

One more deep breath—he'd just walk in and find her. And Lucky and Tessa. And it would be as easy as she'd said. And even if it wasn't . . . well, it felt like the right thing to do. Because he was pretty sure it would make her happy to see him there.

He approached the white archway that appeared to lead into the party, then paused to steal a glimpse inside. Just to get the lay of the land.

And what he saw nearly made his heart stop.

Anna stood talking with some tall, clean-cut, good-looking guy—who looked way more like someone she should be with than he did. She was smiling up into his eyes and he was leaning close, saying something near her ear that made her laugh. Duke's gut pinched tight.

"Did you see Jeremy Sheridan?" he heard a young girl's voice say nearby—then he glanced to his right to see two teenagers talking. They hadn't noticed him. "He's home from Afghanistan and he's standing right there talking to Anna Romo. She's so lucky! My mom said he's some kind of hero, that he saved a bunch of people's lives or something. And OMG, he's sooo cute!"

As he shifted his gaze back to Anna and the "war hero,"

Duke's stomach sank. He'd been right the first time. He didn't belong here and it had been stupid to come.

Maybe he'd been stupid about a lot of things, in fact.

Glad no one had seen him yet, he turned around, crossed the yard to where he'd parked his bike, and started back toward Half Moon Hill.

"May one at least ask to what darkness you are returning?"

Gaston Leroux, *The Phantom of the Opera*

Seventeen

*H*e was probably riding too fast, but he didn't care. The curves in the road, the wind on his face—they were good distractions. Not that he wasn't thinking about what he'd just seen. The image had burned itself into his brain.

He wasn't angry. Just . . . well, maybe the right word was *hurt*. Disappointed. He and Anna had no ties, no commitment—she was free to do what she wanted, the same as him—but he just hadn't expected this. He'd just thought things were good between them. Good enough that he'd spilled his guts to her, told her everything. Good enough that . . . well, he'd just thought maybe it was something a little . . . special. And that it would last longer. Hell, the truth was, even if he'd beat himself up for letting himself feel so close to her, maybe somehow he'd also started believing that he could learn to be a better man for her.

Damn, he'd been foolish. Foolish to let himself get emotionally involved. Foolish to think he'd ever stood a real chance at that anyway. And he didn't blame her—he knew she wouldn't intentionally do anything to hurt him—but hell, how could he ever compete with a guy like the one she'd been standing there with?

They were only standing. They weren't making out or anything. Only standing. Talking.

But that didn't matter. It had been easy to see romance brewing, easy to see that the war hero was into her and that she looked pretty into him in return.

Jeremy Sheridan. He knew the name. It was Tessa's brother.

And hell—didn't that make it all just perfect? For Lucky's sister to end up with Tessa's brother? Sounded like one big happy family. And a guy like that . . . it made sense in other ways, too. He was more what Anna deserved, more the kind of guy she fit with. He would be good for her—way better than Duke could ever be. They'd looked . . . perfect together. Perfect gorgeous woman with the perfect handsome guy. One who didn't have calluses on his hands or darkness in his heart or a jagged scar on his face.

And even as he pulled into the driveway, his tires flinging a little gravel, he knew maybe he was blowing this out of proportion. *Way* out of proportion. But this had been a wake-up call.

You and Anna—it's easy while you're up here alone, nobody else around, in your own private little world with her. But in the real world, the two of them together just didn't make sense.

So it was best to just back away now, while he still could, before the pain of it got any worse.

Anna's day had turned out far better than expected.

As she drove toward home, the warm night wind in her hair, she smiled thinking of Amy's big surprise. And also appreciating how full of simple wisdom Amy sometimes was, especially for someone who hadn't spent much time outside the small town of Destiny.

Wow. The people of Destiny really were enriching her life. There'd been a time when she couldn't quite have imagined that. *Funny how things can change.*

She also thought about Jeremy Sheridan. The truth was, he was just her type. And he seemed like a great guy. But the further truth was, she was in love with another man and she hoped that man would be waiting for her with open arms when she reached the big Victorian house that had really begun to feel like home now. *Just since Duke?* Was sharing the house with someone making it that way? She wasn't sure and decided not to examine that too closely. She simply looked forward to being with him.

It caught her off guard to see the house completely dark when she pulled in the driveway. She'd expected lights on, a friendly, welcoming glow through the windows. That's when she realized his motorcycle was no longer parked behind the bushes next to the garage where it had sat unmoved for days, ever since their visit to Lucky's house and then the Dew Drop. Her stomach sank.

Still, she approached the house with . . . hope. Or confidence. There would be some explanation inside—a note saying where he'd gone. Or . . . maybe he was just asleep. It was early for that—not yet ten—but he'd been working awfully hard lately, so maybe it had caught up with him and he was just tired. And he'd moved the bike somewhere . . . for some reason.

Stepping inside the quiet house, she flipped on a lamp in the foyer, then made her way to the kitchen, turning on lights along the way and keeping an eye out for a note or anything else that might explain where he was. Finding none, though, she then climbed the same stairs they'd recently made love on, and headed to her bedroom. Her cat followed her the whole way, meowing his head off, but she ignored him.

Her bed lay empty, untouched.

As did every bed in the house, she discovered as she checked each guest room.

Stepping back out into the shadowy hallway after looking in the last, she drew in her breath, let it back out, tried not to feel abandoned, or panicky. Though she knew then where he must be. He must have gone back to the cabin.

So she would go there, too.

She took a flashlight to help her find the way—and keep her from tripping over anything or spraining an ankle. The woods felt eerie in the dark—every sound made her uncomfortable, and she worried about things she couldn't see.

But she also thought of Cathy following this same trail through the darkness to take care of Robert when he was sick. And wasn't this the same in a way? Duke wasn't ill, but if he felt the need to come back out here when he'd said he'd be at home waiting for her, he was obviously troubled.

Seeing the dim glow of the lamp she'd spotted next to his sleeping bag when she'd been here before somehow heartened her. *At least he's not gone, at least he didn't just disappear from your life.* She didn't realize until that moment that she'd actually harbored that worry, and something in it was deeply frightening. *It would be that easy. He has nothing to hold him here. You could just wake up one morning to discover he'd cleared out completely and you'd never see him again.*

Her first fears had been right, valid—it was dangerous to love someone. It gave them so much power over your heart. And it was even more dangerous to love a loner like Duke Dawson. David Dawson. Whoever he was. In certain, special moments, she thought she knew—she thought she understood him completely. But right now, she didn't feel like she knew him at all.

Don't think that way. It's fine. He'll be glad to see you. And whatever brought him back out here will be . . . will be . . . Well, he'll explain it away. Somehow.

Her movements suddenly seemed loud to her, and remembering Duke's comment about that once upon a time made her think—know—surely he heard her coming. But no movement stirred around the cabin; no one opened the door to greet her.

So she knocked on it. Then said, "Hello?" trying her best to sound cheerful. Pressing on the door where the handle had once been, she tentatively pushed it open.

Duke sat at the table in the dim lighting sharpening a knife on a whetstone. Anna couldn't help thinking how ominous a sight it made, and that if she'd found him like this when they'd first met, she'd be terrified. Now, she figured it was probably a knife he used for scaling fish or something—but seeing him like that reminded her, grimly, of who he was. There was an undeniable darkness within him. And she'd thought maybe it was leaving him—she'd been so arrogant as to think she might even be the one conquering it—but she knew now, instinctively, that she'd been too optimistic.

"Duke?" she ventured when he still didn't look up.

Even now he only deigned to toss a quick glance her way before returning his attention to the knife. "What are you doing out here, Daisy?"

"That's what I was going to ask *you*." She feared her voice came out timid, just like in the beginning with him. Another thing she'd thought was long gone.

The quick shake of his head was barely perceptible. "Just felt like getting some fresh air, that's all."

But she wasn't going to be timid with him—not anymore, not after everything they'd shared. "You could open the windows at my house the way we do most nights."

He still didn't look at her as he spoke. "Just felt like sleeping out here and . . . spending a little time on my own. Don't make such a big thing of it."

She drew in her breath at the accusation. She hadn't made a big thing of it—but it *was* a big thing. "I'm not—but it's just . . . not how things have been lately."

Now he finally turned a steely gray gaze on her. "Look, Daisy, I just wanna be alone tonight if that's all right with you. So just go back to the house, go to sleep, and I'll see you in the morning. Okay?"

His tone, everything about the moment, sent a chill through her despite the warmth of the night. "Okay," she replied softly.

And then she stood there, thinking there would be more. *Because there* should *be more. There just* should. *A goodnight. An apology. A reminder to be careful. Something—anything—softer.*

But as painful, awkward seconds passed, she realized nothing else was coming. That was it. Just the cold dismissal.

She felt as if she were moving in a haze, like a mere shadow of herself, as she finally turned and walked back out the door, pulling it shut behind her.

Anna barely slept. Not only because the bed now felt so empty but because the last week or two began to feel like a mere dream. Had she imagined the closeness that had grown between them? Had she made it all up? No. No, she knew she hadn't. *But if one of you is suddenly acting like it never happened, does that make it not real?*

Stop thinking so much. Things will be better today. That was what she told herself as she got up early, took a shower, got dressed. *He said he'd see you in the morning, he said it wasn't a big thing. It will all be fine.*

As she hit the stairs in bare feet, ready to go down and think about breakfast—lately, they'd eaten together, eggs or pancakes or something, and she wasn't sure what to expect today—she heard movement and realized Duke was here.

She walked into the kitchen to find him closing the refrigerator door, a bottle of water in his hand. She'd given him a key long ago, to make things easier, but he looked up as if she might think he didn't belong here. "Just getting some water before I get started. Clapboard's being delivered tomorrow, and Lucky's cleared his schedule to come help me for a few days, but I've got plenty to get finished before then."

Something in Anna froze up at his all-business tone—and the fact that he sounded almost angry underneath it. Nothing was better today. She barely knew how to respond. Like last night, she heard herself murmur, "Okay."

And then he stumbled slightly and a cat's shriek filled the air—"Mrow!"—and Duke found his footing as he looked down to snap, "Get outta my damn way, cat."

Anna's back went ramrod straight. "Maybe *you* should get out of *his* damn way."

Duke flashed a challenging look at her that might have frightened her in earlier days with him. Then he said, "I'll be outside."

She tried to be nicer, smooth things over. "You don't want anything to eat?" Not that *he'd* been remotely nice.

"No," he practically growled, then started toward the back door.

"Duke, what's wrong?" she asked. She didn't want to play games here, act like this was normal—she wanted to get to the bottom of it, now.

But he only said, "I need to get to work," as he continued toward the door. "If you're ever gonna get this place open, I need to get stuff done."

"Well, I don't have a specific date in mind to open," she replied, "and . . . maybe I think there are *some* things more important than that."

He'd stopped moving now, his hand resting on the doorknob, but his gaze lay on something outside, through the window, as he said, "Well, I won't be around forever. So if you wanna get this place in shape while you've still got my help, I need to work. Understand?"

What she understood was that he was shutting her out, shutting her down. That simple. No conversation with anyone had ever left her feeling so dejected. "Yeah, sure," she said. "I understand."

And as she watched Duke walk out the door, across the screened-in porch, and then outside, it was like . . . he was walking away from her in a much bigger way. And she feared he wasn't coming back. His words echoed in her brain. *I won't be around forever.*

Did I think he would be?

Maybe I did.

But of course it made sense that he wouldn't. God knew he'd never made her any promises, never said anything about caring for her—and Lord, she'd found him living in the woods! Clearly the man didn't know what one day to the next held for him; clearly he was just finding his way, moment by moment.

That all seemed startlingly clear right now. As clear as it had when she'd first found him outside the cabin.

She supposed she should have remembered all that before she'd let herself start caring about him so deeply, before she'd surrendered to falling completely, helplessly in love.

"Can I help?"

Duke looked up at the sound of Anna's voice. Damn, why couldn't she just get the message? He'd been hoping she'd stay inside, find other stuff to do. Maybe he'd poured it on too thick about so much work remaining—he'd just been trying to get away from her. He'd been trying to stop feeling . . . anything.

The second he caught a glimpse of her—in cute shorts and a little summer top as usual—he had to draw his eyes away, back to the piles of pale yellow siding before him. "No work at the bookstore today?"

From the corner of his eye, he saw her shake her head. "No."

Damn.

The truth was, he could use the help. In between bigger projects, he'd continued working on trim repairs and had just had some additional wood delivered on Friday. There were

miniature spindles that could be sanded and—now that they'd
selected a color scheme—painted, while he kept plugging
away at some final repairs around the porch and steps. But he
still didn't look at her. Because that only made him hurt. And
he just had to shut out all those feelings for her. Somehow.
"Okay then—yeah," he admitted, "you can help."

"Just tell me what to do," she said quietly, and on the inside
he felt like what she'd thought he was in the beginning—
some kind of monster.

But stop feeling that. Stop feeling anything. Stop thinking.
Just focus on the work at hand.

He'd retreated to the woods to forget about Denny, and
about his father's rejection, and his mother's death. But he
wasn't sure where to go to forget about Anna given that she
lived here. He'd gone back out to the cabin last night, but
she'd just followed him there. So for as long as he was working on the house, he supposed there was no getting away
from her.

You could just quit on the house. You've done plenty
already. She could hire someone to do the rest—she might
not like that idea, but it wouldn't be the end of the world if
she had to.

Still, he didn't think he could do that. And he wasn't even
sure why. Maybe because he'd agreed to help her. And he
took satisfaction in the work. And he'd left enough behind
lately already—somehow, despite everything, he didn't want
to leave *this* behind, undone, too. Maybe it was a point of
pride—though it was surprising to find he had any left.

"See those little spindles and trim pieces?" he said, pointing. He'd separated the various pieces of wood into piles
yesterday morning before installing the new light fixtures.
"Those all need to be sanded." She'd helped him sand the
shutters a few weeks ago, so he knew she didn't need any
further instruction on that.

"All right," she said—and the gentle tone of her voice
still made him feel like an ogre. But he just ignored it, just

propped up that invisible wall that kept him from responding to it.

From there, he simply focused on what he had to do. Measuring, sawing, hammering. He worked in a different area than she did whenever possible, and when they were near each other he simply acted as if . . . they weren't. Though at times the silence between them seemed so loud that he wished she'd put on some of those old records before coming outside. And he even considered suggesting it—but didn't. Being so quiet with her was awkward, but better to be awkward than to open any kind of door that might let emotions back in.

A couple of hours into the day's work, he knelt on the porch, hammering freshly cut boards into place. And he realized that, long after he'd drained the bottle of water he'd helped himself to this morning, Anna now appeared at his side offering him another.

He looked up, took it from her hand, said a short "Thanks." Then tried not to feel the fact that their fingers had touched, or that he'd looked into her eyes for a second, or that he wanted to tell her to be sure she drank plenty, too, because it was getting hot out here.

Uncapping the bottle, he took a long, thirsty swallow, and only as he lowered it from his mouth and began to screw the lid back on did he realize she still stood there beside him, staring down at him.

He let out a breath, tried to will her away. *I can do this if she keeps her distance, if she just lets this go. But not if I have to keep looking at her, feeling her. Shit, Daisy, why can't you just make this easier on both of us?*

Finally, he felt he had no choice but to glance up at her. But he didn't meet her eyes. He tried not to really see her. "What is it? Done sanding?"

She shook her head—and shit, even if he didn't really peer into those brown eyes, he could still feel the pain there, the confusion. But it didn't change anything. It didn't make him any better of a man, it didn't make him any less scarred, it didn't make him into the kind of guy Tessa's brother was—the kind of guy she deserved.

"No," she said, and he saw her swallow nervously and hated that he was making her feel that way. "I just . . . wondered if I'd done something wrong."

Aw hell. Keep it simple. "No."

"Then . . . then why do you seem mad?"

"I'm not mad. I'm just working."

He lowered his gaze from her face, but he still saw the tender, hurt way she bit her lower lip before she asked, "Are we not . . . anymore?"

The question nearly stole Duke's breath. Because it sounded so painfully . . . final. And he . . . just hadn't thought that far ahead and didn't particularly want to. But . . . maybe she didn't have a choice on that, either, if she was putting it to him this way. So he said what he had to, the only reply that made any sense to him, that allowed him to walk away from her the easiest and would hopefully allow her to do that, too.

"Look, we've had some good times together . . . but it's not like it was anything serious. We barely know each other, after all." His stomach knotted even as the words left him, but it still seemed like the wisest way to go.

"Well, I feel like we *got* to know each other," she insisted. "I mean, we shared things."

God, why on earth had he expected Daisy to be any less tenacious about *this* than anything else? As usual, he'd underestimated her.

And she was making this hard—harder than it needed to be. Which forced him to do the same thing.

So he just shrugged. And pretended it had been nothing. "Heat of the moment, I guess." And hell, it was impossible to keep looking at her—at all—so he dropped his gaze to the peeling paint on the wooden boards before him, which he and Lucky would cover with fresh new clapboard tomorrow. "It's nothing personal, Anna—I'm just not into anything serious, ya know? Got enough shit on my plate as it is, so figured we should cool things down." And when she still stood there, now saying nothing, he even felt forced to add, "Make sense?"

And finally, her tone becoming a bit less delicate and a bit more clipped, she said, "Sure. Makes *perfect* sense."

So now she was mad. And he should just let her be. But he wanted to make her understand. "We can still work on the house together. I'll stay until it's finished. But after that, I should probably move on, ya know?"

Anna thought about asking him exactly where it was he'd decided to move on to, exactly where it was he thought he'd be so much happier. But she held her tongue. If he could throw away what they'd had so easily, so coldly, what did she care where he went? Or why he didn't want to be with her anymore?

So even as her heart broke inside her chest, she kept wearing the stronger face she'd finally managed to put on and again said, "Sure. Whatever you say."

Just then, the trill of the old-fashioned rotary phone in the kitchen rang through the open front windows. And part of Anna wanted to just keep standing there, trying to somehow hold him accountable, somehow make him understand that he owed her more than this now—but another part of her saw the ringing phone as God's way of telling her to walk away now and quit acting so needy. *He never promised you anything. Never. So stop trying to squeeze from him something he obviously doesn't want to give. Stop being weak.*

"I'll . . . go answer that." She pointed vaguely toward the sound, and then she turned and walked away. Trying her damnedest to look confident, feel confident, like always. To put back on that bit of armor. And yet somehow it suddenly didn't come to her as effortlessly as it always had. It was as if Duke Dawson had somehow torn down everything she'd ever used to protect herself, all in just a few short weeks.

As she headed for the phone, letting the screen door slam behind her, she lectured herself. *Why did you do that? Why did you stand there interrogating him? Why did you embarrass yourself that way?*

But she knew the answer. It came to her as easily as breathing. *I thought we had more. I thought it mattered. I was sure of it. So sure. And I still can't believe he's making it so much less than it was.* He was belittling every moment they'd spent together, devaluing her love for him. He was making it all . . . nothing.

Picking up the phone, she shoved it to her ear and said, "Hello?" probably a bit too harshly.

"Oh, you're there. I almost hung up." It was Tessa.

She tried to soften her voice. "Sorry—was outside." *Getting my heart ripped to shreds.*

"Working on the house with Duke?"

Something in the simple question made her want to cry. *It's because Tessa assumes everything is still good between us—and I don't know why it isn't.* "Um . . . yeah."

"So . . . I have a weird question to ask you," Tessa began then, sounding tentative.

And Anna wanted to hang up the phone. She'd had enough weird today to last her whole life and it wasn't even lunchtime yet.

"The summer carnival starts on Wednesday," Tessa went on, "and I wondered if you'd want to go with a big group of us."

Anna was confused. "That's a weird question?"

"Well, the weird part is . . . Jeremy wanted me to ask you. And I don't know how serious you and Duke are. Like, if you two are way into each other and it's all hot and heavy, totally feel free to say no—no problem. The thing is—I couldn't really tell Jeremy you were seeing somebody because of Duke not wanting anyone to know he's in town yet. So I told him I'd ask. And I thought I should. Just in case. Because he's totally smitten with you, Anna. And don't get me wrong—I love Duke—but . . . well, I couldn't help thinking how fun it would be if you and Jeremy hit it off, too."

Anna just stood there listening to Tessa rattle on, clearly uncomfortable with the situation. And when she finally finished, Anna was stunned. She'd known Jeremy was taken with her yesterday, but she hadn't thought any farther ahead than that. She'd mainly been thinking about getting home to her man. The one who didn't want her anymore.

She asked a necessary question. "Does Lucky know?"

"He noticed Jeremy was into you. How could he not have? And he just said it looked like Duke had some competition. He's not a buttinski like Mike. Even if Duke *is* his best friend. So I think . . . whatever you want to do would be fine with him."

Anna quickly weighed her options. Duke didn't want her. Jeremy did.

The answer seemed pretty simple.

So, raising her voice enough that Duke might hear it through the open windows, she said, "Well then, yeah, I'd love to come. Tell Jeremy I'm glad he asked you to invite me and I'll look forward to seeing him."

"Are people so unhappy when they love?"

Gaston Leroux, *The Phantom of the Opera*

Eighteen

"So what's up between you and my sister?" Lucky asked the next day as he held a plank of pale yellow clapboard while Duke nailed it in place. Anna had just left for a shift at the bookstore, and he supposed Lucky had saved the question until she was gone.

Duke kept his eyes on what he was doing as he said, "Less than was up before. Why?"

"Just wondered. Since she's going to the summer carnival with Tessa's brother on Wednesday."

"Hmm," Duke replied. He'd pretty much figured that out from overhearing Anna's phone call yesterday, and he knew he had no one to blame but himself. But on the other hand, he saw it as just saving himself from getting any further into . . . caring about her. Being attached to her. He'd found it strangely easy to be attached to Anna Romo.

But now it stopped.

And she could move on to somebody who made sense for her, somebody the whole town of Destiny would approve of. Hell, probably even Lucky would think it was a better idea.

"You okay with that?" he asked Lucky as they reached for the next board.

"With her and Jeremy? If that's what she wants, sure. He's a great guy. Big hero."

"That's what I hear," Duke murmured under his breath.

Which is when he caught Lucky arching one eyebrow in his direction. "You jealous?"

Duke met Lucky's gaze for a second, then lowered his eyes to the clapboard as they lifted it into place. "No, brother, can't say that I am." *Liar.* The word echoed in his mind. Where had that come from?

"Mind if I ask what happened between you and her? I mean, you two seemed . . . good together when you came over last week." Then Lucky pinned him with a hard look. "You danced with her, dude."

Again Duke gave his friend a quick glance, but drew it away to reach for the hammer in his tool belt. He knew exactly what Lucky was getting at—for Duke Dawson to dance with a girl, *that* kind of dancing, to fast music . . . well, to someone who knew him well, it probably seemed like one step below a marriage proposal. But he decided to play it off light. "Guess I was a little drunk. And I didn't want to hurt her feelings, that's all."

"That's all my ass," Lucky accused.

Duke narrowed his gaze on his friend and reiterated, "*That's all.*"

"Okay, okay. If you say it's fine with you for her to go out with Jeremy, then guess I'll believe you. Just seems . . . weird to me. Like I'm not getting the whole picture. And for what it's worth, it's not that I'm concerned only for Anna's sake. I'm concerned for yours, too."

"Well," Duke said, hammering a nail, "you don't have

to worry about *me*, brother. It was my idea to slow things down."

At this, Lucky just gave a short nod.

And Duke added, "It's okay if you're relieved. That I'm not gonna corrupt your sister any more than I already have, I mean."

Lucky burst out laughing—and Duke even joined in a little.

But then a moment later, as they continued working, Lucky said, "Truth is, I was kinda surprised about you and Anna at first, but . . . then I liked the idea. Too bad it didn't work out."

When Anna had come to the Destiny summer carnival last year, she'd met up with Logan, dragged him onto the ferris wheel, and kissed him. All in all, it hadn't gone well and she'd felt silly. This year, she felt like a different person. And she was thankful that Amy and Logan seemed to have forgotten the whole thing, both of them giving her a friendly wave as they climbed onto the ferris wheel themselves.

"Wanna ride?" Jeremy asked her, pointing toward it.

It seemed like a bad idea—like she had bad ferris wheel vibes now. "How about a different ride?" she suggested. "Tilt-A-Whirl? Scrambler?"

He grinned. "Ferris wheel's too tame for you, huh? You're a girl who needs more action?" He added a wink.

And she said, "Something like that, I suppose," just to keep things simple.

Even though, in some ways, she felt more "tamed" and appreciative of gentle things than ever in her life. Destiny was quieting her soul, and she thought that was a good thing. In fact, she thought she could be on the verge of a real, lasting happiness if . . .

Well, the *if* didn't matter. Her love affair with Duke was done, whether she liked it or not. It was time to move on. Time to give Jeremy Sheridan a chance to steal her heart.

She glanced absently toward a star-filled sky as they walked along. *Please, please, let him steal it. Let him make me forget all about Duke. Let him make the whole Duke thing seem like nothing more than just . . . some good times,* like Duke had called it. Her heart ached at the memory.

"You okay?" Jeremy asked.

"Sure—why?"

"Just looked like you didn't feel well there for a minute. Sure the Tilt-A-Whirl's a good idea?"

She nodded. "I'm fine." She was determined to have a good time tonight if it killed her.

So they rode a few rides. And Jeremy bought her cotton candy, which they shared. Sometimes they hung with Amy and Logan. Other times they walked around with Tessa and Lucky—who, she noticed, said nothing to her about Duke, even when she quietly thanked her brother for helping with the clapboard siding these past few days.

"Finished it up late this afternoon," he said. She and Amy had gone straight from a shift at the bookstore to meet the rest of them at the Whippy Dip before heading to the park, so this was news to her.

And since Lucky and Duke had been working their way around the house, starting on one side, wrapping around to the back and other side, leaving the front for last, it excited her to think the next time she saw her house, the front would look so different. "I can't wait to see."

"It looks good," he told her with a matter-of-fact nod as they stood talking in the midway—and, foolishly, she almost wanted to ask him about Duke. *Has Duke said anything about me? Do you know what happened between us? Is there any way to fix it?* But then she got hold of herself, remembering: *Why would I want a guy who doesn't want me?* And she remembered she'd come here with Jeremy— who was a *great* guy, a handsome guy, a sweet guy, and that it would make much more sense to focus her attention on him.

So instead she just confirmed with Lucky that he hadn't mentioned working on the house to Mike, now not only because of the hovering factor but because of keeping Duke's presence just between them.

"Don't worry," Lucky said. "He's so freaked out about this baby thing that the last thing I want to do is give him something else to grumble about."

She turned then to see Jeremy surrounded by a small crowd of people, all of them smiling, clearly glad to have the hometown boy back in the fold. Time and again tonight they'd been stopped by various Destiny-ites, not to fawn over the long-lost Anna Romo for a change, but over Jeremy Sheridan.

What was it like to have that many people care about you, to have a long, special history with them, to be such a valued part of a community? When she'd come here, the idea of that had overwhelmed her—there'd been too many people and too *much* care, and it had felt almost artificial in a way because none of them had really known her; they'd only known the little girl she'd been before she'd gone away. And so she'd retreated to Half Moon Hill—just like Duke had, even if for very different reasons. But now they had come to know her, and she to know them, and she began to like the idea of . . . more than just fitting here, and being able to function here— but the idea of really being a part of it, building memories with the people here, having what Jeremy had.

"Sorry about that," he said with a smile when he rejoined her. "My old basketball coach from high school and his wife wanted to say hello—and then some of my parents' friends."

She shook her head. "Nothing to be sorry for—it's nice."

He tilted his head and gave her a speculative grin. "You probably got a lot of that when you first came home, too, didn't you?"

She tried to go with a light version of the truth. "Kind of. Though I didn't really know anyone, so it was a little different for me."

He nodded as if he realized how unusual her own return to Destiny had been. Maybe Tessa had filled him in. "But things are easier now, right?"

She nodded. "Getting that way."

"Good," he said. "You're a nice person and you've been through a lot, so you deserve things to be easy now." And then he kissed her. Right there in the middle of the midway between the swirling lights of the rides, the bells and whistles of games, and various and sundry residents of Destiny strolling leisurely past.

It wasn't a long, passionate kiss, but it wasn't just short and sweet, either. His hand was on her cheek and his mouth was firm yet gentle on hers. It was . . . a nice kiss.

And when it was done, Jeremy cast her a slightly embarrassed smile—though his eyes shone a glassy blue beneath the lights and she could tell he felt something, that he wanted her. "Sorry about that, too," he said. "But I can't blame that one on anybody else but me. I don't usually go kissing girls I barely know in the middle of a crowd, but guess I was just . . . swept up in the moment."

Anna could barely nod—because it had surprised her so much that she was still trying to process it. And that's when a group of guys around their age approached, one of them saying, "Hey Sheridan, heard you were back in town!" just as another said, "JerSher, back in the house!"

Jeremy looked up with a laugh and she could tell he was glad to see them—probably old high school buddies. She watched as a bunch of "guy hugs" and backslapping ensued—and just then a hand touched her arm and she turned to see Mike.

"Hey," she said with a smile.

He returned it. "So . . . you and Jeremy Sheridan, huh?"

And like an old habit, her defenses went up. "You have a problem with *that* now?"

But he actually laughed as he gave his head an easy shake. "Relax, because no, I still think he's a great guy. And who you're seeing is none of my business anyway, right?" He sounded surprisingly self-deprecating for Mike. "But I figure if you're actually seeing a guy I approve of, I may as well not keep it a secret."

Well, what a relief. And a pleasant surprise. Even her over-protective big brother liked her seeing Jeremy. It was easy to tell, in fact, that *everyone* who'd seen them together tonight liked the idea of her and Jeremy. Destiny's favorite-son-turned-war-hero with Destiny's long-lost-child-princess—it probably seemed like . . . a fairy tale. One she could actually buy into. It would be nice to be "his girl." He would treat her like a queen; she already knew that. On his arm, she'd become as deeply embedded into the community as he was. She had come to love the people of Destiny—and if she was with Jeremy, she'd naturally become someone they would love in return. And they wouldn't love just the memory of her as a little girl, or the idea of who they wanted her to be—they would really love *her*. And it would be the perfect happy ending to the tragic nightmare that had started when she was taken all those years ago as a child of five.

It sounded pretty great to her.

She only wished his kiss had made her feel the same *zing* she experienced just by catching a glimpse of Duke walk past her window.

She only wished the very thought of her wildman didn't make her long to be back in his arms without a thought for who loved her or why. She'd felt so safe there. She'd felt appreciated and desired for exactly who she was at her very core, no trying necessary, no particular memory or image she was trying to live up to.

But the same thing she'd had to keep reminding herself for the past few days came back to her now, too. *Duke doesn't want you anymore. And he obviously never cared as much as you did. So no matter how it seemed, you have to let go of that—you have to move on.*

"Fun house?"

She looked up to find Jeremy back at her side. And Lord, he was handsome. Tawny-haired, blue-eyed, lean but muscular body, perfect smile. But what seemed most important at the moment was—he appreciated her. He wanted her in his life. So she smiled back at him and said, "Sure."

The rest of the night was a whirlwind for Anna. So much going on, so many people, so much fun. And it really *was* fun—once she let herself go, once she stopped thinking about Duke.

Of course, there were more serious moments—like when the group of them ran into Jenny Brody and her husband, Mick. While Mick talked to Lucky and the rest of them, Anna asked Jenny how things were going, and Jenny said, "Did you hear about what happened between me and Rachel at the party?"

Anna hadn't, and according to Jenny, "I said horrible things to her. About her not wanting to be pregnant. And the worst part is, I meant them. I didn't *want* to mean them, but . . . it was just hard to hear her complaining about it. And then I stomped off in a huff, like . . . a baby." She stopped, sighing at the irony. "I'm afraid I've ruined our friendship forever."

"You can't help how you felt in the moment," Anna told her. "And you can't take back how you reacted. But just give it a little time . . . and maybe it'll work itself out."

Jenny was hard to convince, though. "I was really horrible, Anna. I mean, I might be entitled to my feelings, but . . . ugh, jealousy is such a horrible thing. I can't believe I was so ugly about it."

"Well, maybe Rachel would love to just let it go, too," she suggested.

But Jenny still shook her head. "I saw her tonight, a little while ago. I tried to smile at her and she looked away. *Just plain looked away.* It was awful."

The truth was—hearing about Jenny's problems at least

helped distract Anna from her own. Though she wished she'd felt she'd helped Jenny more, in the end just advising her to be patient and not beat herself up over it. "We're all human," Anna reminded her. "We all make mistakes." God knew she'd made a few. And she'd probably make a few more. But she was doing her best and she'd come to the conclusion that most people *were*.

It was later, when Jeremy suggested the ferris wheel again and Anna agreed this time, that he kissed her some more. Longer this time. And it was . . . romantic. Warm summer night. Charming, handsome man. It was the kind of moment young girls dreamed of and old women remembered with wistful sighs.

Only it's with the wrong guy.

When the pesky thought entered her head, she ignored it and kept kissing him. She shut it out. She didn't want to ruin it. She wanted to one day be the old woman looking back on this with a wistful sigh.

I can have it all. I can have the perfect Destiny romance with the perfect Destiny guy. I can make Mike happy—I can make the whole town happy. Oh God, her parents in Florida—wait until they heard, because she already felt pretty darn confident that they'd love her being with Jeremy Sheridan, too.

When finally the kisses ended, Jeremy gave her a sexy, dreamy sort of look, his eyes falling half shut, to say, "I knew coming home was gonna be good, but I didn't know it was gonna be *this* good. I'm so glad you're here, Anna."

She tried to relax, told herself to feel happy.

She heard herself force out some words. "Me too."

But as she stepped off the ferris wheel hand in hand with her brand new war hero a few minutes later, she realized it was the first time she'd ever missed being called Daisy.

When she got home that night, the house lay still and dark. She'd almost gotten used to that again—to the emptiness, to knowing Duke would rather sleep in the woods than with her.

They'd worked hard to keep their distance from each other ever since that last heartbreaking conversation—and it had helped that she'd been scheduled to work at Under the Covers every day since and that Lucky had come over bright and early each day to help turn her house a buttery shade of yellow.

She couldn't see it in the dark, though, unfortunately. *Oh well, I'll see it in the morning.*

As she lay down to sleep, she found herself remembering times she'd spent with Duke—particular moments that had seemed special.

But if they weren't special to him, *why should they be special to* me?

The next morning, she got up determined to feel better—for good, not just for a few distracting minutes here and there. Her life was great, after all. She was financially comfortable, a piece of security not everyone possessed. She had a loving family of her own now. She was forming strong friendships and making a home here. She would soon open her own business. And she could even make a cobbler now!

And she had a handsome hometown boy ready and willing to take a big place in her life—she could feel that. And she'd noticed more than one pair of envious female eyes on her last night.

I have it all. And I'm fine. I'm more than fine. I'm fabulous!

And now I'm going to go outside and see my new clapboard siding.

Rising from the kitchen table, she placed her cereal bowl in the sink and headed for the front door. Descending the steps, she walked out into the yard where she could take in the whole house. And wow—the yellow was all she'd hoped. Sunshiny and happy and cheerful! With freshly painted white shutters already back in place, too, it was the first time she could almost envision what the house was going to look like when it was finally done. Soon she would at last be ready to open her bed-and-breakfast!

It was then that her eyes were drawn to the left—Duke had just come from the woods, ready for another day of work. And he looked so . . . simply sexy in a pair of jeans and a T-shirt, a light, unshaven stubble on his chin, the haircut she'd given him beginning to grow out just a bit. He was starting to look kind of rugged again. In a good way. And she melted a little, all over, at the mere sight of him.

But more than just her physical reaction, seeing him now affected her another way, as well. It hit her that . . . in a sense, he'd always be here. Always. Because he was making her house over, from top to bottom. He was working hard every single day just to turn it from a drab old house into a bright, comfortable, friendly home. And yes, she'd agreed to pay him, but . . . she knew that wasn't why he was doing it; she knew he didn't need the money. And that made him far more than just some hired contractor. His work here, she knew, was a labor of love. Of *some* kind. And no matter how badly he'd hurt her, she'd always have that.

She didn't know if he saw her, but he crossed the driveway in front of the garage and headed toward the back of the house, not acknowledging her.

And without taking the time to weigh it, she called to him, "It looks great!"

He stopped, peered across the yard.

Then after a moment, he changed direction and walked toward her.

As he grew closer, she felt the need to tell him again. "It looks great, Duke. I really love it."

He met her gaze only briefly, then they both glanced back to the house. "Couldn't have done it without Lucky's help," he said quietly.

"I think yellow was the right choice—don't you?"

He gave a short nod. "Yeah, it's nice." From the corner of

her eye, she saw him shift his weight from one work boot to the other before adding, "Lot still left to do, though. Lot more trim to replace and paint. And then the roof. I'll have to get Lucky back over here for that."

"But . . . so far, it's really wonderful," she told him, and for this next part, she looked at him again. Even if seeing his face so close up—the mouth she'd kissed, the eyes she'd looked into, the scar she'd shaved so carefully around—caused fresh emotions to well inside her. "So I wanted to thank you. For all you're doing. I'm really not sure what I would have done without you."

He met her gaze now, too, though she could tell it took some effort and he still didn't smile. "You'd have done okay. You'd have found a way."

She shook her head, entirely unsure if that were true. "I don't know what it would have been."

He gave his head a slight tilt, squinting in the sun. "Come on, Daisy—you're way too feisty to let anything stand in your way for long. You'd have figured it out."

She realized he was giving her a sincere compliment. "Maybe. But I'm glad I didn't have to. You made it . . . easy."

He lowered his eyes, looked . . . almost shockingly bashful. And neither of them said anything else until Duke pointed his thumb vaguely toward the house. "Well, I'm gonna get to work."

She nodded. "Okay. I'll be off to the bookstore soon."

"You have a nice day, Daisy," he said softly, still no hint of a smile.

"Thanks. You too."

She stood in the same spot for a moment more, pretending she still studied the house, but she was really watching Duke walk away. And thinking it was nice to be his Daisy again, even if only for a moment, and even if it didn't change anything.

"They played at hearts as other children might play at ball;
only, as it was really their two hearts that they flung to and
fro, they had to be very, very handy to catch them each
time, without hurting them."

Gaston Leroux, *The Phantom of the Opera*

Nineteen

Anna rang up two romance novels for old Mrs.
Lampley—who tottered along, hunched down over a cane,
and had to be at least eighty. She liked the idea that even
a woman Mrs. Lampley's age still wanted to escape into a
place where passion led to a happily ever after. She wondered vaguely if Mrs. Lampley had had those things in her
life—passion, or happily-ever-after.

Rachel, Tessa, and Amy sat in the overstuffed easy chairs
near the bookstore's door with big, colorful mugs of coffee
in their hands. And though they kept their voices low whenever customers were in the store, she could guess easily
enough what they were talking about: Rachel's pregnancy.

As Mrs. Lampley slowly ambled out, Amy hopped up to get the door for her—and Anna walked around from behind the counter to join the other girls. Not long ago, she wouldn't have—but now she realized the move came naturally and she felt accepted, welcome in their close circle.

"And I'm still so upset about Jenny," Rachel was saying as Anna lowered herself onto the arm of Tessa's chair.

"I'm sure she didn't mean the things she said," Amy quickly chimed in.

"But that's the thing," Rachel said. "I think she did."

"Well, you'll just have to forgive her, that's all," Tessa told her.

Yet Rachel only scrunched up her nose. "I'm not the best at forgiving. Especially when I'm not sure someone even *wants* my forgiveness. She seems to think I'm some kind of ogre or something."

"I'm sure she doesn't," Amy insisted. "It just . . . seemed that way."

"She's really hurting right now, Rach," Tessa reminded her.

And though Anna wasn't sure she should say anything, she decided it was in everyone's best interest, so she tentatively spoke up. "For what it's worth, Jenny's really upset about it, too. She told me at the carnival. She feels awful about what she said and it really hurt her when she smiled and you looked away."

Both Tessa and Amy gasped. "You looked away?" Tessa asked in clear shock.

And Amy scolded her. "Rachel . . ."

Rachel made a pouty face, but also appeared a little ashamed. "Well, I'm mad. And hurt myself. And who are you to talk, Ames—you were downright mean to Anna last summer, in front of everybody."

Anna cringed inwardly at having an unpleasant memory brought up.

But Amy seemed unaffected, saying boldly, "And look

at us now—we're friends and we work together and we've totally let bygones be bygones. Haven't we, Anna?" She flashed a quick look Anna's way.

"Yes," Anna replied quickly. She knew the incident—when Amy had been rude to her at a swim party—had been a result of Amy's frustration, and ultimately Anna had felt they both bore some of the responsibility.

"Just like *you* should, with Jenny," Amy said to Rachel.

Yet Rachel's expression remained resistant. "Well, maybe if I ever feel better," she said, pressing a hand to her belly. "And if I ever decide . . ."

"Decide what?" Tessa asked when Rachel trailed off, looking uncertain—and maybe even a little lost.

She blew out a breath before answering. "You know what the worst part is?" she asked them. "It's that . . . what if she's right? Maybe she is. Because Mike and I are evil, awful people not to be thrilled by this."

And just like with Jenny, Anna was fast to say, "You're entitled to how you feel. Everyone is."

"But maybe I would have been a lot smarter to just keep it to myself. I only thought . . . that I could be honest with my friends. I thought everyone would understand, and be supportive. Like you guys are."

"When all is said and done," Tessa said, "you and Mike will do fine. You know that, right?"

But Rachel, looking unconvinced, let out a sigh. "Let me tell you a story. The other day, we were at Edna's." Anna had grown used to Rachel calling her grandmother by her first name—it was just the nature of their relationship. "And she said she'd seen an antique changing table she wanted to buy for us.

"And so I said, 'What's it change into?' And Edna laughed and said she hoped I was joking. Which is when Mike said, 'But really, what does it change into?' And then she told us what it was, and we looked at each other and he just said, 'This is going to be a disaster.' And I was like, 'You're right.

We're doomed.' And Edna told us we were being a couple
of babies about having a baby. And maybe we are." She
stopped, sighed. "We're . . . just a little scared."

The girls continued to say comforting things to Rachel—
and after a few minutes, talk turned to the newlyweds, Amy
and Logan. "How's married life, Mrs. Whitaker?" Rachel
asked, seeming glad for the change of subject.

And Amy smiled a dreamy smile. "Couldn't be better."

"Any regrets about eloping?" Tessa asked.

To which Amy replied with a quick shake of her head.
"Not a one. I know I always dreamed about a big, traditional
wedding, but . . . I like that we did something *un*traditional.
It makes me feel all . . . devil-may-care."

And Anna had to stifle a laugh. *Devil-may-care is having
a wild affair with an outlaw biker living in a shack in the
woods.*

"And speaking of exciting romantic adventures," Rachel
said, switching her look to Anna, "you and Jeremy, huh?"

Oh crap. She kind of didn't want to think about that right
now. Oddly, thoughts of her hot, risky, painful affair with
Duke felt easier. Even if that didn't make much sense. "Um,
yeah—maybe, I mean. We just met. But . . . so far so good."
She'd added the last part mainly for Tessa's sake, feeling the
need to sound interested so no one would be disappointed.
And she *wanted* to be interested. No, she *was* interested.
She was determined to be as into Jeremy as he was into her.

"Well, Mike is elated," Rachel said.

And Anna replied, "I know—he couldn't resist telling me."
And as they all laughed, she thought how *un*elated Mike
would be if he knew what she'd been doing with Duke—
until recently, anyway. The very thought made her shiver.
And just then she realized—oh God, somewhere along the
way she'd actually started caring a little bit about pleasing
Mike, too. And . . . she wasn't sure if that was a good thing
or a bad one.

"So work on the house is going well?" Amy asked.

And Anna wasn't altogether sure that was a safer topic, but she said, "Um, yes, actually, it's going great."

"And are you and Erik getting adjusted to each other?"

And it hit Anna . . . "I keep meaning to ask you something about him—I can't believe I haven't in all this time."

"What do you need to know?" Amy asked cheerfully.

"Well, he just seems to spend an awful lot of time meowing and following me around. And for the life of me, I don't know why. What does he want? And he's not hungry, I promise—I feed him all the time trying to shut him up."

Amy gave her head a thoughtful tilt and said, "Well, does he do it when you're petting him or snuggling with him?"

Anna thought about it. "No, now that you mention it. But . . . well, I'm on the run a lot, so I guess there hasn't been a whole lot of that."

"Well then . . . he probably just wants a little more attention from you. He probably wants you to make him feel special, like you care about him—that's all."

And Anna felt positively thickheaded. It had been so simple. And it made such easy sense. And it occurred to her now that the nicer she was to him, the less complaining meows she heard. "I, uh, guess I never thought of that."

Though the emotion caught her off guard, it actually touched her to think the cat needed her. Up to now, she'd thought of them as . . . sort of just existing together, like a couple of outcasts who happened to share the same space and tolerate each other. But this . . . well, it changed things. And it made her wish Erik were here to scoop up into her arms right now.

Maybe Amy was right and an inn did need a cat. Maybe Anna needed a cat, too.

It was turning out that Anna needed a lot of things she'd never realized before coming to Destiny.

In the week that followed, life took on a strange sort of normalcy for Anna—or maybe it was more just like a predictable routine that she grew comfortable with. She worked two midday shifts at the bookstore, but mostly she stayed at home. She paid more attention to her cat on a regular basis, and she also spent a lot of time working with Duke on the house. Mostly they didn't talk as they worked, or they spoke only about practical things—like the work itself and how it should be done—but that was okay.

On the second day of this, when she joined him outside, she picked up a paintbrush and asked, "Should I keep putting primer on the rest of the trim pieces or start painting some of what I primed yesterday?"

And Duke looked over from where he stood measuring the door frame that led into the screened porch to say, almost kindly, "You don't have to help, Daisy. You're probably tired from working at the bookshop so much lately."

But she replied, "No, I want to. I want to be able to look at the house and know I did at least a little of it."

"You did the whole inside, though, right?"

"Mostly, yeah—with some help from Sue Ann and Tessa. But this is different. I just . . ." She leaned back to take in a fuller view of the house. "When I pull into the driveway I want to be able to see it and feel . . . connected to it or something." Then she stopped, shook her head. She was saying too much, speaking too openly—an old habit with Duke. Yet it was a habit she needed to officially break. "But forget I said that—probably sounded silly."

Though Duke shook his head then, too, and said, "Nah—I get it." And then he told her to finish priming the trim pieces and spindles before she started painting any. "I've got other stuff to do before I need any, and that way everything has time to dry between coats."

The truth was, though, that in addition to wanting to have a hand in finishing the exterior, she also just liked working alongside him and missed it when she didn't do it. She'd come to find it . . . comforting—on a level she didn't really understand.

Even though they didn't talk much, it was a . . . companionable silence. Not tense like at first after he'd returned to the woods. Or more recently after what she thought of as their "breakup." Though she knew the term wasn't really accurate. You couldn't break up with someone you were never really officially together with. And that was where she'd made her big mistake—thinking they were together, in a way that counted for something.

And a lot of hurt remained inside her. And there were times when she cried over it—though she tried to make sure it was at night, long after he'd left. And preferably in her bed, with the lights out—because if she didn't shine a light on it, that made it seem like less of a big deal. It was easier not to dwell on the emotions if the only part of the day that remained was falling asleep.

But she was steadily letting go of any anger she'd felt toward him. Because she had to remember that he was in a dark place in his life right now and she'd known that going in. Maybe, deep down, she'd thought she could change that. Maybe she'd romanticized it, thinking they were two wounded souls who could heal each other. But what she'd come to understand was . . . she was a lot farther along the road to healing than him. It was that simple.

And while she'd known a lot of loss, while she'd felt her life had been stolen from her, while there'd been a lot to make peace with . . . she'd never felt unloved. She'd never felt responsible for someone's death. And Duke was struggling with both of those things, and now that she'd gained a little perspective, she thought it had been downright arrogant to think she could save him. Maybe no one could. And maybe he even knew that. Maybe that was what had brought him to the woods in the first place.

Duke's suffering made her sad. The fact that Duke had been careless with her emotions hurt. But all she could do was keep pushing forward and try to get over him. And having Jeremy Sheridan come along when he had . . . well, even if she didn't swoon over him, it was a good start. Maybe she'd start swooning *soon*. Even if a mere glance up from her work to where Duke stood hammering a piece of white door frame into place made her heart beat faster.

On Friday afternoon, they both continued painting the recently primed wraparound porch that had begun to seem much larger than ever before. And for some reason, she'd actually found herself making more conversation with him today—being the cool, confident, unaffected chick she'd always been until recently. And though she wasn't sure if it was some act of self-preservation or if it only meant she was getting back into a more upbeat mood, she chose to just appreciate it for what it was and not question it too much.

It was late in the day, and the El Dorados sang "Forever Loving You," the music pouring out the window over them, when she said, "Think I'm gonna go put together a casserole for dinner."

"Sounds good," he said with only a light glance her way.

"I'll let you know a few minutes before it's ready so you can clean up."

He gave a short nod in reply.

That was part of the routine they'd fallen into—they'd continued to eat lunch and dinner together when she was home; since he was there working at mealtimes, it only made sense. The chicken casserole she was about to make was a simple one, the recipe coming from Tessa, who was too busy to cook much more than Anna did. And just like when working together, she and Duke didn't talk much during the meals, but he always thanked her, and even though she knew he was a big boy and could take care of himself, it still made her feel good to know he was eating something he hadn't had to catch in a lake and cook over a campfire.

After a quick shower, Anna threw together the casserole, put it in the oven, and then decided to give herself a treat while it baked. She'd been so busy the last couple of weeks that she'd barely had a chance to read Cathy's diary. And in fact, the last time she'd stopped, she'd finished the first volume, and so now she picked up the second and carried it out onto the screened porch, settling on the wicker sofa to read.

> *Tonight when Mother and Daddy attended evening church services, I stayed home, pretending to be sick. I hate to lie, especially on the Lord's day, but all I know is that it didn't feel wrong. And that I have to follow my heart because it's the heart God gave me, after all.*
>
> *When they were gone, I met Robert in the woods and we walked to the lake and took a ride in the little red rowboat Daddy keeps for fishing but only takes out on the rare occasions when Uncle George comes to visit.*
>
> *I've never cared much for boats, but one ride with Robert changed that. I can honestly say I never realized the lake was so pretty. I never noticed how the willows droop down over the south bank, almost dipping into the water. I never knew the sun setting behind the woods on the far side could make the trees glow orange and pink.*
>
> *When Robert had rowed to the center, he gave me one of his more devilish smiles and asked me what he got for all his hard work. I asked him what he wanted. And he told me a kiss would be nice. I was nervous, just like always so far, but at the same time it felt like the colors from that bright, glowy sunset were somehow running through my veins. And so I leaned over to kiss him, feeling ever so brave, ever so ready. But then I lost my balance and slipped off the wooden seat and ended up on my knees on the floor of the boat—and in Robert's arms, because he caught me when I fell forward.*

*My face was so close to his. And the closeness
was maybe the most amazing thing I've ever felt.
Embarrassed, I whispered that I hadn't done
that on purpose. And he grinned and teased me,
saying, "Sure you didn't." And then we kissed for
a very long while, so long that I got lost in it—
and never wanted to be found.*

*Last year in school we had to write an essay
about the most wonderful place we'd ever been.
I chose the city of Cincinnati because we go
there every December to see the skyscrapers all
lit up, and the toy train display, and the department store windows all decorated with sparkly
immitation snow and reindeer whose heads move
mechanically.*

*But if I had to write that essay now . . . and,
well, if I could be honest about it . . . I would
write about floating in a rowboat across the lake
hidden in our woods with Robert. I would write
about kissing him there, surrounded by the tall
summer trees and the calls of tree frogs and hoot
owls. I would write that being on that lake in
Robert's arms is definitely the most wonderful,
beautiful, heart-thrilling place I could ever be.*

Turning the diary facedown on her lap, Anna sighed. And
felt at once how wondrous life and love were, and also how
fleeting. *If only we could freeze such perfect moments in
time and just stay there, just keep them. What would my
perfect moments be?*

She sucked in her breath as the answer came. Because
they were all about Duke. Making love to him on the stair-
case, and in her bed. Dancing with him at the Dew Drop Inn.
Driving along, the wind in her hair, stars twinkling above,
with the gentle caress of his hand on her thigh.

And the truth was, even earlier moments—being carried

by him through the woods, feeling captured in his arms when she'd backed down the ladder—held a certain magic. Because she hadn't known exactly what was happening— only that *something* was. She wished now that she'd realized those moments were important so she could have appreciated them more, savored them somehow.

But then she bit her lip. *Aren't you supposed to be concentrating on Jeremy Sheridan now? Didn't you decide that was the smart thing to do?*

She just let out a sigh, though, and faced the truth. *I love Duke.*

And he might not love me back, and he might not be in my life for longer than it will take him to finish the house, but I love him anyway. And I'll move on—maybe with Jeremy— but for this moment, right now, I'm just going to own my feelings and not deny them. I'm in love with Duke Dawson whether I like it or not. Or . . . maybe she was in love with David. Maybe David was the guy who'd danced with her even though he didn't know how, the guy who'd opened up to her about his family, and his past. And maybe Duke was the one who'd run away from all that when it had . . . gotten too heavy for him or something.

Picking Cathy's diary back up, Anna continued reading. As usual, some of it was about everyday life in Destiny, but more and more of what she wrote focused on Robert. There were more clandestine dates—more boat rides on the lake, walks in the woods, picnics in the meadow filled with wild-flowers.

> *He tucked a daisy behind my ear. And then he made a chain of small purple flowers—statice, I think—and put them around my shoulders like a necklace.*

On another Sunday evening when Cathy feigned a head-ache, Robert pushed her in the swing hanging from the big

maple tree, and Anna couldn't help thinking how far Cathy
had come from the days when she'd been so lonely that she'd
counted butterflies as her friends.

And on another voyage across the lake, Cathy brought her
father's camera.

> *I took a picture of Robert across from me, and*
> *he took one of me, as well. Then we put our faces*
> *close together and Robert held the camera as far*
> *away as he could and took one of us together. His*
> *birthday is soon and so I'm going to secretly get*
> *the photos developed at the drugstore in town and*
> *frame them for him.*

And then Anna reached an even more stirring part of the
diary.

> *We lay on the blanket kissing beneath the sun,*
> *and to feel his body against mine gave me almost*
> *a sense of . . . drowning. But in a good way, if*
> *that makes any sense. And when his hands drifted*
> *onto my breasts, I didn't move them. I couldn't.*
> *God help me, I had longed for his touch there,*
> *and when it came, it felt like being touched every-*
> *where.*
>
> *When he unbuttoned my blouse, I let him. Nei-*
> *ther of us spoke. I remember hearing grasshop-*
> *pers chirping, and the song of a bird somewhere. I*
> *ached to give myself to him. And I have wondered*
> *and worried if that's wrong, and I always come*
> *back to the same answer—following the heart*
> *God put inside me.*
>
> *And so when he undid my blouse and then even*
> *my bra, I didn't protest. I even—heavens above—*
> *found myself arching, somehow trying to push my*
> *breasts more thoroughly into his hands.*

*His touch made my whole body feel . . . liquid
and melty, that's the only way I can describe it.
And when he kissed me there . . . I couldn't have
imagined such pleasure.*

*He told me he'd fallen in love with me. I con-
fessed that I loved him, too.*

*And I would have denied him nothing in that
moment, I'm quite sure—but he stopped there,
telling me it was best, reminding me how young
I am. I pointed out that I'm sixteen, and that his
being eighteen doesn't make him so awfully much
older. He said he thought I was a young sixteen
and he was an old eighteen.*

*Something in that stung, made me feel silly and
naive. And I asked him what he was saying. Was
he saying he loved me and then getting ready to
break my heart all on one hot September day?*

*But then he said he just thought it was best
to go slow, that he didn't want me to do anything I might regret later. And it's very good of
him, I think, to care enough to show that sort
of restraint. And yet . . . I fear I want him to be
unable to show restraint. I want him to be mad
with desire for me. Because then I would know we
both feel exactly the same way, and after that . . .
well, nothing could happen that I would ever
regret.*

Slipping the ribbon she'd been using as a bookmark in
between the diary's pages, Anna snapped the book shut. She
could smell her casserole and knew it was probably ready,
and she hadn't even warned Duke to give him time to clean
up. She'd been too swept up in Cathy's first love. She knew
those feelings, that desire. And she wondered desperately
what would happen next, how Cathy's love affair with her
Robert would end up.

But at the same time, maybe she didn't *want* to know. Because if Robert ended up breaking Cathy's heart . . . well, she thought she was dealing very maturely and capably with her own broken heart at the moment, but if Cathy's heart got broken on top of that, she feared it might just make her crumble to pieces and decide there was no such thing as real, lasting love and that she'd be afraid to ever risk her heart again.

But . . . maybe Robert won't break her heart at all. Maybe they'll find a way to be happy. Maybe Cathy's father will come to accept him. Maybe I'll discover they got married and lived for many happy years together in this house before he died and she ended up here alone.

But either way, Anna thought it seemed like high time to set the diary aside and go take her casserole out of the oven. Then she'd have another quiet meal with her heartbreaker, waiting to see what tomorrow would bring.

Duke was almost sorry to find out the next morning that Anna wasn't working at the bookstore today and didn't have any plans. It was a Saturday and he'd figured she'd be gone for at least part of the day.

The truth was that she'd been a pretty big help lately. And that there were times he was finding it nicer to work with somebody than to work alone. Which told him that his self-imposed isolation wouldn't last forever. Spending time with Anna, and then Lucky, as well as the one night out he'd had with them and Tessa, had shown him that maybe he really *was* starting to miss being with people. And maybe he didn't want to be quite so invisible anymore. Maybe he was done with trying not to exist. It sure as hell hadn't worked anyway.

But he also continued to value some alone time.

And more than that, the longer he was around Anna, and the nicer she was to him . . . the harder it got. Not to want her.

Well, he'd *never* stopped wanting her, but it was getting harder to push those hellaciously strong urges aside.

When he'd seen her with Tessa's brother, it had been like a light bulb going on over his head: *You're not right for her. You're not good for her. You'd better realize that and stop with all the damn talking and sharing. In fact, you should get out now, before this gets any heavier.* He still wasn't sure even now how the hell he'd ended up in such heavy places with her. Since when did he go baring his damn soul to people anyway? *You'd think living in the woods alone for a couple of months would have made you better at shutting the hell up and keeping stuff to yourself.*

But damn, the fact was . . . he still wanted her. If he was honest with himself, he fucking ached for her. It was hard to work with her, even in silence, and not be agonizingly aware of her body. Her boobs filled out the little tank tops she wore all too well and it was no secret, to him or to her, that he'd had a thing for those short denim shorts from day one. He wondered if she had any idea that there were times when he was working with a hard-on, when he was hammering a nail but instead thinking how much he wanted to nail her to the new yellow siding or the newly repaired porch.

And he was beginning to wonder . . . if he didn't let shit get heavy between them again, if they just kept it all light, and hot, about fun and sex, if they could get back to that.

Nah, would never work. Once you've gone there, you can't back away from it.

But as he looked over at her where she stood painting the new porch rail, he wanted her so much that his fingers itched with yearning to touch her, and his cock twitched with the rough need to plunge back into her tight warmth. Damn, they were good together in bed. And on the couch. And on the stairs. And right now, if he could, he'd happily take her right here on the front porch in broad daylight.

But then he remembered—Tessa's brother.

Maybe Anna had already fallen for *him*. Yeah, she'd seemed pretty broken up over Duke backing off with her, but she seemed a lot better with it all now, so maybe things with the war hero had really taken off. Maybe she'd want nothing to do with Duke if he made a move on her anyway.

"Since I Don't Have You" by the Skylines echoed through the window—in recent days Anna had resumed playing the old records she'd found in the attic and he liked that it filled the quiet space between them. So it came as a surprise to him—probably as much as to her—when he suddenly decided not to be silent anymore.

"Heard you're seeing Tessa's brother." He tossed a quick glance her way, but by the time she looked over, he'd returned his gaze to the paintbrush he swept back and forth over new wood already primed in white.

"Any reason I shouldn't be?" she asked.

Feeling her pointed look, he just said, "No," as casually as he could. Then he dipped his brush in the paint tray and smoothed more white paint onto the porch.

A few minutes passed—he didn't know how long. The harmonizing voices of the El Dorados spilled through the window to his left. Then he heard himself ask her what he really wanted to know. "Is it serious? With that guy?"

Now it was she who kept her eyes on her work as she answered, her tone much more easygoing than before. Maybe even kind of . . . aloof. "I just met him."

Yeah, well, you'd just met me, too, when things started up and they still seemed pretty damn serious—no matter what I said about it. "Is that a yes or a no?"

"No, actually," she said, now seeming almost haughty about it. "At least not yet. Why?"

He gave his head a short shake, tried to sound unconcerned. "Just wondering." But . . . shit—he was happy and sad at the same time. If she'd said it was serious, it would have made it a whole lot easier to just leave the idea—of being with her again—alone. Which sounded smart, and . . . safe. But at the same time, he couldn't deny a sense of relief that she wasn't head over heels with the dude.

But you still can't make a move.

No matter how good she looks, no matter how good she'd feel.

No matter how much you still sense that weird electricity between the two of you that started this whole thing.

So he wouldn't. He'd just put it out of his head and keep working on the house. And ignoring his urges as best he could.

Even if a mere glance just then tightened his groin.

It's okay. Just keep working. You've done it all this time— just keep on doing it.

Anna bided her time, focused on her work, and then— eventually—dared sneak a surreptitious glance in Duke's direction. What was with him and all the questions? It was one of the longest conversations they'd had since . . . since things were good between them. And the nerve of him to even ask! Seriously! *He dumps me and then interrogates me about seeing another guy? Who* did *that?*

But maybe he's glad—like relieved—that I'm seeing someone else. Maybe he just wants to make himself feel better, like he didn't abandon me. Whatever. Jerk.

She looked back to her paintbrush, concentrated on covering a deep nick in the wood.

And then she let herself peek back over at him again. Who had told him about Jeremy? Lucky? Had to be.

And why did he have to look so hot, damn it? Why did he have to be so darn muscular? She'd personally never been much of a tattoo-loving girl, but somewhere along the way, the inked motorcycle on his arm had begun to appeal. *Vroom, vroom.*

Crap. Stop lusting over what you can't have and get back to work.

As Anna continued painting, she was almost angry at Duke for even starting that kind of discussion with her, for making her think he might care, for reminding her—even if not directly—that she and he had so recently had a closer relationship. But that they weren't close anymore.

And right when she'd been doing so well, too. Or . . . sort

of, anyway. Right when she'd come to appreciate just spending time with him, even if silently, but convincing herself there would never be any more than that. It wasn't as if she'd ever quit wanting him, feeling that gut-deep tug between them, that powerful chemistry. But she'd at least managed to make some peace with it and accept that the good part—the amazing part—of their relationship was over.

Well, it is. Just get that through your head. He's made it more than perfectly clear, after all.

And I wouldn't want him now anyway. Not after the way he just pulled the rug out from under me emotionally. Chemistry or not.

Seeing that the paint tray resting on the porch between them was nearly empty, Anna lowered her brush to the edge, then stood to go get the paint can and refill it. She started past Duke—when his hand shot out to close firm around her ankle.

She flinched, going still. "What is it?" she asked, thinking something was wrong.

She peered down at his handsome face—just as his grip softened, and he grazed his work-roughened palm up her leg, over her knee, and onto her inner thigh.

She sucked in her breath, feeling the touch in her panties as she read the pure lust in his eyes.

Oh boy. Now she knew why he'd asked.

"I thought it was an aberration of my senses, a mad dream."

Gaston Leroux, *The Phantom of the Opera*

Twenty

"Duke," she said, her voice coming out too whispery, and trying like hell not to feel what she felt, "what are you doing?"

"Touching you." And oh God, those gray eyes of his had never looked warmer, or more seductive.

"But, um—" She stopped, swallowed. *Get hold of yourself. Push his hand away. Tell him he's crazy if he thinks you'd let anything like that happen now.* Yet she couldn't quite manage those things, it seemed. Maybe she'd forgotten exactly how good he had the power to make her feel. With just one little touch. And that, she was forced to remember, was nothing compared to the promises that touch held. "I thought we, um . . . didn't do that anymore."

"Touch?" he rasped.

And something in the mere word, combined with his hand still on her thigh, nearly buried her.

But be strong here. "Yes, touch," she said. "Or anything else. Like . . . kiss. Or have sex." *Crap, it would really help if I stopped sounding so . . . breathy. Like a woman on the verge of being seduced. And it would help if I didn't feel like one, either.* "It's . . . it's not fair to me," she managed to say. "On again, off again—and you get to make all the decisions about that?"

"I . . . I guess I was thinking," he began—and then his fingertips were moving, beginning to caress, and she was trying to hide how thready it suddenly turned her breath. "I was thinking we could maybe . . . do what we talked about in the beginning. Just . . . keep it light."

She blew out a breath, the spot between her legs tingling wildly.

Part of her couldn't believe this was happening, that it was even real. Talk about out of the blue. And another part of her was remembering what she'd just told herself, that there was no way she'd ever let anything more happen between them after the way he'd hurt her. Yet then there was this whole *other* part—and it was mostly the part that pulsed with desire. Need. Hunger. And *that* part . . . well, that part seemed willing to be swayed. Chemistry could be a very powerful thing.

"The thing is . . ." she began—but it was hard to think straight the way he touched her.

"The thing is that . . . it's just not the right time for me to get into a big, heavy relationship—you know that. We talked about that. But that doesn't mean we can't still have a good time together."

She sucked in her breath. She appreciated what he was saying, that he was at least trying to explain, but . . . "Duke, I . . . I don't know . . ."

"Yes you do," he murmured deeply. "You know you want this as bad as I do." And then he slid his hand higher, higher, to the edge of her shorts, his fingers flirting with the edges, then slipping just inside.

To her near shame, she let out a small gasp. Was he worth it? Worth knowing he didn't feel what she did? Worth going down that emotionally rocky road again? Part of her wanted to just push him away and say no. But their eyes had stayed locked the whole time and she knew hers gave her away—so maybe a mere gasp didn't matter.

That's when he pushed to his feet as well. And then he was taking the paint tray from her grasp, lowering it to the porch. And then his hands were on her hips and his body pressed to hers and he said, their mouths less than an inch apart, "I want you so fucking bad, Daisy. Don't make either one of us suffer."

And then he kissed her. And she had a split second to make a decision—at least about the kiss. And she kissed him back. Because it was too delicious. And his hands on her were too warm and sure. And she loved him too much to push him away.

She knew she probably shouldn't let this happen, that she'd only get hurt even worse in the end, but . . . at least if she was going in with her eyes wide open, it meant she was making an informed decision. And he was telling her right up front this time that he didn't want this to go anywhere, so wouldn't knowing that from the start help her handle it better? And besides . . . how could she resist the man she'd fallen in love with?

Next, Duke was moving them, maneuvering her body back against one of the thick, round posts that held up the porch's awning. And she was unwittingly curling one leg around his, locking their pelvises together, because he was as hard as a rock against the crux of her thighs, and it was the best thing she'd felt since the last time they'd been together, and she wanted more.

Her body simply took over when Duke's hands dropped to her ass and he hoisted her upward, murmuring, "Wrap your legs around my waist," against her lips. She did as he said, fully supported by him now, her back still against the post.

And then she was moving against him, grinding hotly, too
excited to stop, her breath heavy, quick. They'd ceased kissing at some point and her eyes had fallen shut, but she felt
every inch of where their bodies connected. She drank in
the heady, musky, still-woodsy scent of him, and when he
said, "Come for me, Anna," the words trickled down her
spine the same as if his fingers skimmed along her back—
and she exploded in pleasure in his arms. She didn't hold
back because she couldn't—and Duke had seen her every
intimate response and behavior already anyway, so there
was no *urge* to hold back with him. She cried out her climax
on the front porch just before noon as vigorously as she ever
had in her bedroom in the dark.

The next thing she knew, he was kissing her some more,
and carrying her—down the wooden steps and into the cool
green grass beneath the maple tree where Robert had once
pushed Cathy in a swing. He laid her down, undressed her,
the carpet of grass soft against her back. She worked at his
zipper, pushed at his T-shirt until it came off over his head.
It was a good time not to have neighbors—and the tree trunk
was thick enough to block them from view should any rare
traffic pass by.

She parted her legs beneath him willingly, lovingly, ready
to welcome him. And he pushed his stiffened length inside
her, filling her up, making her feel whole again. They both
let out soft noises at the entry, and she could hear them
breathing. Fats Domino sang "I Want to Walk You Home"
somewhere in the distance.

Without meaning to, Anna clawed her fingernails into
his shoulders as he suckled her breast. She arched against
him. She never wanted it to end. She tried to just be in the
moment, appreciate it for what it was, and not think of later,
when it might hurt to remember he didn't want this to mean
anything. *Just enjoy this now—that's all there is.*

At some point, the music stopped playing—clearly the last
record in the stack had dropped. A warm summer breeze

sifting through the leaves above them was the only sound other than their gentle moans.

And it made her sad in a way when he eventually rasped, "Baby, I'm coming—I'm coming," because the end meant facing her fears, her emotions.

Shut them out. Be the confident girl, the cool girl. She knew how—or at least she always had, before Duke. And there was a lot of self-protection in that, and that seemed like a good idea right now. *Be the old you, the you who could handle stuff, let it roll off your back and not let it weigh you down.*

And so as he slumped gently against her, she hugged him to her, felt his heartbeat against hers, and affectionately kissed his neck—but then she did what she had to do, she threw back on an invisible coat of armor and pretended this was casual.

A moment later, he was smiling sexily down into her eyes. "Mmm, Daisy, that was great."

And she tried her armor on for size, testing it out by smiling back and simply saying, "Yeah—it was."

Still on top of her, he pulled back slightly, squinting a bit, looking more speculative. "So . . . you're okay with what I said? That we just . . . keep it light."

I'm not sure how to. But she shut that voice out and again said, "Yeah." Though she needed to say more. To convince them both that she meant it. "I know your future is . . . uncertain. So we'll just . . . enjoy each other for now—with no promises." Yeah, that sounded good. And confident Anna could almost even really go there. There was nothing wrong with a relationship like that if both people were in sync on it and felt the same way. *I can feel that way. I will feel that way. I do feel that way. Because he's just too damn good to pass up.*

"Good," he said, dropping a playful kiss on the ridge of her breast. Then he rolled gently off her to lie beside her in the grass, looking down at her, head propped on one elbow.

It surprised her when he even let out a small laugh. "Can you imagine," he asked, "if Mike knew what you and I have been doing together?"

A worry she'd harbored before. But she realized that now, despite earlier hopes . . . "Well, I'm sure he'd go ballistic, but since it's just temporary, we'll probably never have to worry about that."

After that, working with Duke was easier, and a lot more fun. Because things quickly got . . . normal again. He started talking to her again. There was more laughter, and teasing. And though he didn't stay the night that first night, he did the next. It was just easier, he said.

"But no heavy stuff, Daisy, okay?" he'd asked.

She'd been in the bathroom connected to her bedroom, brushing her teeth, when he'd said that from the bed. After rinsing, she'd come out in the cami and panties she'd put on after sex, holding up her hands in playful defense. "I haven't said one heavy word. And for what it's worth," she told him, sliding into bed next to him, "I never set out to make things heavy before. I was just . . . interested in you. I mean, you find a guy living in your woods, you just kinda want to know why. Ya know?"

He let out a soft laugh and she noticed how it made his scar crinkle, even through the light, sexy, unshaven scruff on his jaws. "I guess I can get that. Just didn't at the time, that's all."

"But now . . . well, now I know all the answers. So no more questions. No more pressure to get back out in the world if you don't want to—it's none of my business. From now on I'm just . . . enjoying the ride."

"I'll take ya for a ride, all right," he said, his eyes going all smoldery and seductive in a heartbeat as he slid one hand over her hip.

"You already did," she reminded him happily.

And as she rolled over to go to sleep a few minutes later,

he curled around her. Just like old times. *But these are new times—don't forget that. This is temporary. And that's okay. Because he rocks your world and your world needs to be rocked some more. And you can be perfectly happy taking from him whatever he chooses to give.*

And as she drifted off in Duke's strong arms, she finally believed that. It had taken over a day of internal pep talks, but she really felt it now—she was living in the moment, back to having a fun, wild, casual affair with no big worries or commitments. She was confident, cool Anna again. And it felt damn good.

Duke woke in the night, aware that she lay in his arms. He looked down at her, the room dimly illuminated by moonlight, and thought how amazing she was, and how beautiful, and the mere knowledge of those things stretched all through him, through his muscles and all the way down into his bones, and made him want to hold her tighter.

Until he remembered to follow his own rules and not feel those things. Even though it was hard not to. Even though he knew it hadn't been very fair of him to start this up again between them with no warning, telling her it had to be this way—no big deal, just casual.

During the day, and even the evenings, it was easy—just spending time together, just having fun in bed. But waking up in the middle of the night, when he wasn't quite as in control of his mind, it came harder. *It's still best, though.* It was still the only way he could do this, the only way he could be with her without letting the weight of it crush him. And whatever that weight was about—well, he chose not to think about it and to follow the instinct to just push it up off him, one way or another. So that was what he was doing. Making this situation workable for now. And keeping himself safe. And keeping her safe, too—because one of these days she'd figure out what he already knew: that she deserved a better guy than him.

All in all, he thought it was going pretty well. Most of the time.

So that was what he focused on. The times when it felt good, and simple, and easy. And as for how it felt right now . . . well, he'd just fall back asleep and push it away again.

A few days later, Anna returned home from Under the Covers in the early evening to find a note from Duke on the kitchen counter:

> *Gone fishing. Be back by dark. Took a sandwich, so don't need dinner tonight.*

And she couldn't help smiling. It was like . . . he was normal. Like they were in a normal relationship.

But wait, don't fool yourself, Anna. It's not a real relationship—or at least not a committed one. And she'd fully adjusted to that idea now. Yet she still thought it was nice that when he'd needed some alone time, he'd let her know he was taking it. And he'd told her he was coming back.

So Anna took a shower, put on a T-shirt and cotton shorts—pajamas for her—and after eating part of a leftover salad she and Duke had made the night before, she curled up with Cathy's diary again. A cool evening breeze floated into the screened porch.

And finally, finally came the part that Anna had known surely would, but reading it gave her chills anyway.

> *This is surely the most amazing day of my life. I feel . . . whole. Like there was a part of me missing all this time but I just didn't know it. And now I will always want that wholeness. Always.*
>
> *After school I told Mother I was taking a walk because the fall colors are so pretty just now— and I took the pictures in the little black frames I bought out to the cabin to give to Robert for*

*his birthday, along with a cupcake I purposely
brought home from the Sunday school party at
church yesterday, just to save for him.*

*I could tell he was very moved, and I realized
that probably not many people had done many
things to make him feel special in his life. I was
glad I had.*

*But that's not the amazing part. No, that part
came when he asked me to sit down on his little
bed with him and he began to kiss me. His kisses
are like heaven to me, and I'd been craving them
since the last time we met. And soon enough we
were lying down on the bed together, all our limbs
mingling like wild growing vines.*

*Just like that day in the meadow, Robert began
to undress me, but this time he didn't stop. And I
didn't ask him to. I did tell him at one point that I
felt a little shy, and so we got under a blanket and
that took it away. He was very sweet the whole
time, and he asked me more than once if I was
sure. I told him I'd never been surer of anything.*

*He said he loved me and I returned it again.
The words fall from my lips so easily now—
they're almost the only thought in my head at any
given moment when I'm with him. Or even now
that I'm away from him. I love you I love you I
love you*

*I am a woman now, as they say. And I do
indeed feel older, wiser—as I said before, more
whole. But I don't feel . . . womanly. I am a girl in
love with a boy. And I am a girl in love with life.
I never knew it could be so sweet and joyful until
Robert.*

*It hurt at first, but he warned me it would, and
he kissed the pain away. And after that, there was
simply . . . how can I describe it? A connection*

*like no other. It was our two bodies joining, but
also our souls. I had no idea. Just no idea.*

*Leaving him was difficult. But sleep will be
sweet.*

I love you I love you I love you

When the back screen door opened, Anna looked up, tears
in her eyes.

Duke said, "I caught enough bluegill to grill up for dinner
tomorrow night if you want." And then he realized she was
crying and looked alarmed. "Geez, Daisy, I left you a note—
said I'd be back."

And she let out a laugh through her tears, reaching her fingers up to wipe them away. "I know that and that's not why
I'm crying, silly," she told him. Then she sniffed, and tried
to be her slightly more sophisticated self. "Besides, we're
casual, remember? I appreciated the note, but I'm cool with
the 'no promises' thing—really."

He lowered his chin, looking wary. "Then what are you
crying about?"

She gave her head a quick shake. "Just something I read."

"What?"

She supposed there was no harm in telling him, so she
held up the diary. "This belonged to the girl who lived here
back in the fifties," she said.

"The one who left the records and other stuff you told me
about."

She nodded. "This is Cathy's diary and . . ." *Okay, don't
ruin things by talking about mushy stuff like first love.* "And
it just makes me emotional sometimes."

"Bad stuff happen to her?" His brow knit.

Though she was still getting over feeling weepy, she
smiled. "No, good stuff mostly. It just makes me realize
how . . . fleeting life can be. How quickly it all passes by. And
it's strange to read something written by someone whose life
was really just beginning then but who's dead now."

He nodded, looking like he was taking that in. But then he said, "That's kinda deep, Daisy."

She laughed, rolled her eyes. "Well, you asked. So if that's too deep for you, tell me about your fish."

"Well, they were small and blue and I feel emotional because their lives were really just starting but they're dead now."

Anna gasped at his humor, then set the diary aside, hopped to her feet, and ran over to smack him on the arm for making fun of her. But soon enough his arms were around her and they were kissing—and then running hand in hand for the bedroom.

Anna was working at Under the Covers by herself when the door opened and Jeremy Sheridan walked in. Did he look even more handsome than she remembered? But even if he did, she cringed inside— because she'd sort of forgotten he existed—that quick.

"Hey, beautiful," he said, flashing a winning smile.

"Um, hey." She smiled back, but feared it appeared wooden.

"Sorry I haven't been around lately—my folks prodded me into a last minute trip to Florida to visit your parents."

She flinched. Her mother had left a message on her answering machine to call, but they'd been playing phone tag since then. "Why?" she blurted.

And Jeremy laughed. "Nothing to panic about, Anna. My parents and yours are friends—in fact, there are a few other Destiny transplants in the area where they live, too. You should get down there sometime—your mom mentioned you haven't come to visit yet."

Anna nodded. "I know. I keep saying I'll come, but remodeling the inn has kept me from making the time."

"Cute little beach town," he said. She'd seen pictures and it looked wonderful. And his tan explained the more-handsome-than-she-remembered part. "It was good to unwind and relax for a few days. But I'm glad to be home—

and I'm hoping you'll go with me to the big Fourth of July picnic out at Ed and Betty's farm."

Anna went numb. Other than meeting Betty on her first day working here, she barely even knew the Fishers, but she'd gone to their place for this same event last summer—because everyone did. And now Jeremy was asking her to go again—tomorrow. The bookstore had been quiet lately, and she hadn't seen Tessa and Lucky, or she probably would have heard about Jeremy's trip—and also been reminded about the Fourth of July picnic. But since she hadn't, the whole thing caught her off guard.

"Um, wow," she said, at a loss. Because the Duke thing was temporary, right? And before the Duke thing had started back up, she'd been determined to like Jeremy. Because he was a great guy. And it made all kinds of sense. And even if she didn't want to think about it, Duke would be gone one of these days—whether from her life altogether or just from her bed—and what then? "I, um . . ." But crap, she still didn't know what to say.

Jeremy laughed good-naturedly. Which she thought was kind, under the circumstances—he'd asked her on a date and she was acting like a dope. "Tell you what," he said. "Sounds like maybe your plans are up in the air, so how about this? You can call me tomorrow if you decide you'd like to go. Or just meet me there. I'm a flexible guy. How's that sound?"

Too, too nice. He was *such* a good guy. "That sounds great," she said. "And sorry I'm so . . . up in the air, as you said."

"Not a problem, Anna," he replied with another gorgeous smile.

And after he walked back out, the little bell on the door jingling up above his head, she couldn't help asking herself a question. *Am I being smart or crazy?* Jeremy was a sure thing—for right now anyway. While Duke was a wild card. And she knew that, in the end, she had little chance of winning the game they were playing. He held all the cards, after all.

As she drove home a little later, she continued thinking it through. *You know he's going to leave you again. Whether it's tomorrow or next week or next month. And it's all pretty perfect right now.* And even the fact that they worked so hard at keeping things light was fine, truly fine. She liked light and fun as much as anyone, and frankly, light and fun was easy now because she felt as if they'd already waded together through all the hard parts. *But he's still going to leave you. Because he's a troubled man. And you can't fix somebody, or heal somebody. You can be there for them, you can contribute to their happiness— but you can't fix them inside; Duke has to do that himself.* And no matter how good things seemed right now, Anna just didn't know that he would. Because his troubles ran deep.

How much of yourself are you willing to give to a man so wounded? How much of yourself are you willing to sacrifice? And no matter how cool and confident you are, no matter how light and fun things feel right now, how much of your heart will he take with him when he goes?

So don't be foolish. You owe him nothing. In fact, going to the picnic and fireworks with Jeremy tomorrow night would probably be a good break, and a good reminder that there was life beyond Duke Dawson. *It's really not healthy for you to spend so much time alone with him anymore anyway. You'll be attached to him when he leaves. But if you get out some, if you keep your options open, then it'll be a lot easier when you wake up one morning to find the bed empty or come home one night to find the house dark.*

Anna approached Half Moon Hill deciding that she would call Jeremy and tell him she'd love to go to Ed and Betty's with him tomorrow night.

And then she pulled in the driveway and glanced over to see Duke standing beneath the maple tree smiling at her. Next to Cathy's old swing, which he'd apparently found in the attic and just hung up.

"And I waited and lived on in a sort of ecstatic dream."

Gaston Leroux, *The Phantom of the Opera*

Twenty-one

Anna felt as if she were in a sun-drenched haze as she crossed the yard in a summery dress and sandals to greet him.

"What do you think?" he asked, still grinning. And oh Lord, the man was sexy without even trying.

"I . . . think it's amazing."

This made him balk slightly. "I wouldn't go *that* far. Just slapped a coat of paint on it and put on some sturdy new rope is all."

How could she explain? "It's . . . Cathy's," she said. "The girl who lived here. She wrote about it in her diary."

Duke's jaw dropped and she could see that even he was a bit affected by this news. "I found it in the attic when I was up there working on the windows, but . . . never thought about where it had come from. So it's that old, huh? Been here since the fifties?"

She nodded. "Her boyfriend pushed her on it. It hung from this very tree."

They both looked up into the thick green leaves. "Probably from this same branch," he speculated.

And she nodded. "That's always how I pictured it. Hanging exactly like this."

Anna stood on one side of the swing, Duke on the other, and they looked at each other between the two thick twists of rope. And she knew that Duke felt the same magic in the coincidence that she did. The wonder of it passed between them wordlessly as her skin tingled.

"Thank you," she said. And then she leaned over the swing and kissed him. "For hanging it. It's the perfect touch for the yard."

Their eyes met again amid the fresh connection this brought them. And it was like when they'd made love in the yard, almost in this very spot—she didn't quite want the moment to end. Because as Cathy had shown her—it was all so fleeting.

And then Duke said, "Take a seat, Daisy," and pointed to the swing below them.

She said nothing—just turned around and sat down on Cathy's swing. Then she lifted her feet up and Duke began to push her. And the evening air smelled sweet with the scent of the roses by the house as a golden butterfly fluttered past beneath the tree. And Duke's hands, each time they touched her back, felt sturdy and strong. And Anna imagined the joy Cathy had experienced in this very spot all those years ago while the boy she loved stood behind her, lifting her higher and higher.

Life was fleeting, but maybe there were some things that didn't change much.

The following day, they worked together putting up the new trim pieces Anna had so diligently painted. She let Erik out—and tried to be responsive to his affectionate meowing by occasionally reaching down to pet him between carrying pieces of trim to Duke. Though at one point when she almost tripped over the cat, she looked down to say, "I've come to like you a lot, but seriously, you're so needy. You could stand to work on that."

It was the kind of day Anna liked best—hot and sunny and blue-skied, but dotted with enough puffy white clouds that whenever she started to think it might be getting *too* hot, a cloud floated in front of the sun to deliver some shade. More of Cathy's records played inside, and music spilled through the open windows while they worked.

Later, as the sun began to dip toward the tree line, Duke grilled hamburgers from the freezer while Anna tried her hand at baked beans, and she also made deviled eggs. They cut up a watermelon she'd bought at a roadside stand a couple of days ago and soon sat on a blanket in the backyard eating their summertime feast.

They took their time, going back for more watermelon and some cookies Anna had gotten from the bakery in town, and quickly found themselves in that ethereal space where darkness was falling but you could still see everything around you. The light chirps of crickets filled the air, and lightning bugs began to blink in the distance.

She'd bought the gas grill thinking it would be a nice option for her B&B guests, but—thinking of the meal she'd just finished—Anna found herself deciding it seemed silly to offer a grill without a picnic table or two at which to eat. "I should pick up some lawn furniture," she mused, looking around the large but mostly empty backyard. "Tables and chairs, maybe a lounge chair or two. Bet I can get it cheap when fall comes. Just like the grill last year."

"Yeah, probably can, but . . ." Duke cast her a look she couldn't quite interpret as he took the last juicy bite of a watermelon slice, then dropped the green rind on his plate and set it aside.

"You don't think I should?"

In response, he gave his head an undeniably sexy tilt. "Nah, it's not that. Guess I was just thinking . . . the blanket is nice for now." And with that, he playfully pushed her to her back, met her gaze with those seductive gray eyes, then kissed her.

Okay, he was definitely right—the blanket had its merits.

She began sinking into his sweet, hot kisses, her arms twining around his neck, when booming sounds in the distance interrupted them, made them sit up—in time to see a bright burst of pink and green fireworks in the distance.

And she gasped lightly—remembering Jeremy. And that she'd never called him. Or even thought about going tonight. The truth was—the moment she'd seen Cathy's swing yesterday, she'd forgotten all about the picnic invitation, as well as the man who'd so kindly issued it.

As more fireworks lit the sky miles away, Duke said, "Must be from that farm everybody goes to on the Fourth of July."

"Betty and Ed's," she murmured. "I'd almost forgotten what day it was." She and Duke had cooked out, made a picnic of their own, but they'd never once talked about it being a holiday.

"Surprised you aren't down there at the big celebration," he said.

"I was invited." She still felt rather dazed by the realization.

"Why didn't you go?"

They'd both continued watching the fireworks, but now Anna glanced over at her lover, feeling sheepish inside. "I forgot."

The man next to her raised his eyebrows, his expression teasing her. "Forgot?"

So then she admitted the truth—to both of them. "Guess I had better things to do."

"Hanging out here with me?"

She nodded. "Is that okay?" Then she turned her eyes

back to the neon-lit sky. "Or is that too deep for you, Mr. Dawson?"

Next to her, she sensed more than saw his shrug as he said, "Nah, it's okay, Daisy." Then he reached over to hold her hand. "It's nice."

And as she sat there soaking up the moment, she couldn't deny knowing that fireworks from a distance with Duke thrilled her way more than they would close-up with Jeremy. Her heart be damned.

Anna manned the bookstore one afternoon a few days later when Amy and Tessa came in talking about the Fourth of July picnic. And Amy yelled to Anna, who was shelving new mystery novels out of her sight, "Where were *you* that day? I just assumed you'd be there or I'd have checked to make sure someone invited you."

And before Anna could even answer, Tessa chimed in from one of the easy chairs, where she sat with coffee and a book on parenting she'd bought to give Rachel. "Oh, don't worry, I *know* someone invited her—my brother."

"Oh!" Amy said happily. Yet then she must have remembered again that Anna hadn't come. "But then . . ."

Anna briefly shut her eyes, feeling like a horrible person—before exiting from between the two tall shelves. She looked to Tessa. "I'm so sorry if I let Jeremy down. I meant to get in touch with him. I just . . ."

Amy and Tessa both looked at her—not with any sort of accusation in their eyes, but she still felt a bit on the spot.

"I fell asleep."

Amy balked. "That early? On the Fourth of July?" Though she went on, letting Anna off the hook. "But between here and your house, you work so much, so I guess it's understandable."

Just then, the bookstore door opened, admitting Cara Collins, a teenage girl Amy was friendly with, so she turned her attention to her. "Cara—hi! The books you ordered came in yesterday—let me get them for you." And as Amy and Cara stood chatting near the counter, it gave Anna a chance to speak with Tessa privately.

She lowered her voice to say, "Again, I'm so sorry, and . . . I didn't really fall asleep. It was . . . Duke. We're back on again, I guess you could say. At least for now."

And to her surprise, Tessa smiled and shook her head. "That's okay. Jeremy's a big boy, and though I do like the idea of you two together . . . when I saw you with Duke the night you came over, well . . ."

Anna let her eyes open a bit wider. "Well what?"

Tessa's face took on a dreamy, romantic look. "I just thought I saw something special there, that's all. So maybe it's meant to be. You know, destiny in Destiny."

And Anna didn't know whether to be happy or sad. She wanted Duke to be her destiny—but she knew he didn't feel the same way, or that he wouldn't let himself.

Or . . . would he?

Because weren't things getting better between them all the time? And wasn't he seeming more like a man in control of himself, a man who was beating his demons?

Anna tried not to think too hard about any of this—all the time—because she didn't want to get hurt again. But for just this one moment, she let Tessa's words lift her heart and she allowed herself to believe: *Maybe he'll love me back.*

That night on the way home, she stopped to pick up ingredients to make a pizza, thinking it would be a fun twist on dinner for her and Duke. When she arrived home, she found another note on the counter about fishing, though, and figured dinner could wait. It was a wonderfully mild summer evening, so she decided to change into shorts and join Duke by the lake. Maybe she could even learn to fish. Not that she had much interest in fishing, but she was sure if she was doing it with Duke, she'd end up enjoying it.

Duke had mentioned that the path he took to the lake led

directly from the cabin, so she followed the same old trail there through the woods, enjoying the walk—the sights, the smells. The woods themselves felt so different to her than on the first day she'd met Duke—like a friendlier place, a place she'd truly connected with. Because of him.

Reaching the cabin, she knocked—just to make sure he wasn't inside. No answer, as she'd expected. But the last time she'd been here it had been dark, and she'd been upset—and now, she felt the urge to go back inside. Maybe it was because of Cathy and Robert—being in the very spot where they'd made love would make her feel more connected to them, as well. Just like the other night on the swing. Or maybe it was about Duke, too. Maybe she wanted to see again where he'd chosen to live for a while.

Pushing the thick door open, she stepped into the dim interior, took in the scent of old wood, looked around and tried to imagine actually living here. Duke kept it tidy—his sleeping bag was neatly arranged, his few dishes clean and resting on a small dish towel beside the chipped white porcelain sink.

That was when she spotted the picture on the wall—the same faded one she'd seen while letting Duke take care of her twisted ankle nearly two months ago. But now it held much more interest for her, so she made a beeline toward it.

And as she looked closely and understood what it was, she gasped. Robert.

Just as Cathy had described, he sat in a small boat, billowing trees behind him. And though time had badly damaged the photo, she could make out medium hair, confident eyes, and a smile that held a hint of vulnerability. His shirt was open at the neck, his hair slightly longer than she'd have expected for the era. And she could see instantly how Cathy had fallen in love with him. She even found herself reaching out her hand to touch the glass overtop the picture—some effort to be closer to them still.

Then she noticed something she hadn't on her first visit.

Two more nails, set at the right height and an even distance, making her think all three pictures Cathy had given him had once hung here. But the other two were gone. And this one had been left behind? Something about it made her stomach pinch.

Just then, the cabin's door opened and she looked up to see Duke step in.

"Whoa—Daisy," he said, clearly taken aback.

She still touched the picture frame even as she looked at him. "I'm sorry—I came out to see you and . . ."

"Whatcha lookin' at—that old picture? I've wondered about that guy."

"I—I can tell you about him," she said, still overcome with emotion.

Which was when he noticed that part. "You okay, baby?"

She nodded. But then sat down in one of the old kitchen chairs. He pulled the other one out and joined her. And then she told him all about Cathy and Robert—everything she could remember from Cathy's diary.

She concluded by saying, "And I don't know how it ends up yet. And I could rush ahead and read the rest, sure, but . . . there's something that makes me want to stretch it out and just sort of . . . enjoy that time along with her, make it last. In case it doesn't." Then she stopped, shook her head. She probably seemed silly. "How crazy is that, to be worried for someone who . . . who already found out the answer a long time ago and isn't even alive anymore?"

"It's not crazy," he said. "Exactly." He gave her a grin, a quick wink.

"I just . . . want to find out she had a happy life, that's all."

But then Duke reacted as . . . well, as she would expect *most* people to. "You shouldn't let it get to you so much, though. It's just an old diary—whatever happened then doesn't matter anymore."

The assumption made her open her eyes a little wider. "Doesn't it? I mean . . . a life is a life. No matter when it happened—it still matters. To me anyway." She stopped, sighed. "You think I'm a goofball."

"No, I actually think it's . . . a real nice quality about you."

She blinked. "That I'm a goofball?"

He let out a laugh. "No—that you . . . you have this ability to . . . what's the word—empathize? You empathize with people. You get what they're going through better than most people, I think. And that's nice."

She peeked up at him from beneath softly lowered eyelids, both shocked and pleased to learn he saw that in her.

"Now what'd you come out here for?" he asked her then. "I missed that part."

"Oh—I was just going to . . . watch you fish or something. Since it's such a nice night." She gave her head a gentle, self-deprecating shake. Suddenly, she felt as vulnerable as Robert's smile looked in the picture.

"Well, I'm done already and just carried my gear back up. Caught a few, too. And it's getting dark anyway." She nodded and he asked, "You ready to head back to the house?"

And she smiled. Just to be reminded that Duke was staying with her at the house again. And . . . maybe he would for a long while yet. Tessa's words echoed in her ear. *I thought I saw something special there.*

Though Duke carried a string of four fish in one hand, he held Anna's hand with the other as they walked. Maybe she was still emotional about seeing Robert's picture or something, but she found herself savoring every moment, every step. It struck her that—whether or not your time with someone was limited, you should do that—soak it up, enjoy it for all it was worth, every day, every hour. And so she focused on little things like the warmth of his hand in hers. And the way she simply liked feeling him next to her as they decided to make the pizza tonight and grill the fish tomorrow. And how the walk through the lush, dark green forest as night fell was sweeter because she was sharing it with him.

And when they were about halfway up the path, Anna

experienced the powerful compulsion to kiss him. So she stopped walking, released his hand, curled her fingers into his shoulders, and lifted her mouth passionately to his.

And there was no talking, from either of them—just heat.

At some point, Duke dropped the fish he carried. And then his hands were on her ass, through her shorts—and then *inside* the shorts. And all she knew was that she needed him in her, the same way his tongue was inside her mouth at the moment. She wanted it to make her forget every worry, every fear—for anyone. She wanted it to take away anything and everything but that moment.

They struggled out of their clothes, the noise of their labored breath adding to the cacophony of night sounds building around them. Darkness descended rapidly, but a sliver of moonlight angled through the trees to help her see his beautiful, hard-muscled body. She ran her palms down his chest, stomach—then took that hardest part of him into her hand.

A groan left him, but he tried to bury it at the nape of her neck, where he kissed her. And then his mouth was on her breast—kissing, sucking—and then he was lowering her to the ground with him.

Despite her past life as a city girl, Anna didn't spare even a thought for what might be beneath her or around her in the dark as Duke parted her legs with his strong hands and lowered an openmouthed tongue kiss directly between her thighs. As the pleasure assaulted her, she closed her eyes, let her body move in the rhythm it wanted to, and felt like some kind of wild beast in the woods. Just as she'd once thought him.

But then she opened her eyes, caught sight of the moon up through the branches, then lowered her gaze to the man who was making her feel so good. She whispered his name—his *real* name. "David . . . oh God, David." It was the first time she'd dared to call him that since they'd gotten back together and it hadn't been a conscious decision; it had just happened.

In response, he looked up at her, and though it was hard to see each other's eyes in the darkness, she felt the connection. Felt his fingers dig into her ass a little deeper, felt his ministrations go deeper as well. She cried out and gave herself over to the sensations completely—and the next thing she knew, she was whimpering and sobbing as a powerful orgasm rocked her from head to toe.

As he eased up over her body, kissing her breast, her neck, her mouth, this time she tasted the remnants of his affection on his lips, and she thrust her fingers into his hair and kissed him back for all she was worth. He made her feel wild, and free, and hungry for every adventure.

And then he was turning her body over, murmuring, "On your hands and knees, Daisy," and she was happy to oblige, her knees digging into hard dirt for the best possible reason she could imagine.

"I'm gonna take you hard," he rasped then, his hands exploring her back, hips, rear, all from behind.

"Please," she managed to say through the harsh need spreading even more frantically through her now. "Please—hurry."

The words extracted a low groan from him—just before he thrust his perfect erection inside her. Another cry escaped her throat as well. And as he moved in her that way, she thought it was the closest she'd ever come to experiencing heaven. The night was glorious, the air was sweet, the forest seemed to hold them, cradle them, surround them. And the man was . . . perfect. She never would have dreamed Duke Dawson could be her perfect man, but as she'd already learned so many times, life held a lot of surprises, and thank God this was one of the good ones.

When he came in her, she realized that—no, *that* was heaven. The sharing of that moment with him, of knowing she'd taken him there. As they gently collapsed to the forest floor, his arms closed around her waist and his kiss came on her shoulder.

She wanted to tell him she loved him; she almost needed for him to know. But even now she understood it was the sort of thing that might send Duke running, and . . . well, it just wasn't the right time. She wasn't sure when the right time would *be*, but it wasn't now. Now was just about the heaven of it all.

As they put their clothes back on, she heard a distant noise, the shushing of a bush or tree branches. And she assumed it was a deer until she was zipping her shorts and Duke said, "Shhh—hear that?" The sound came again. Something large in the woods. And closer now than before.

They stayed still, frozen in place—and then the beam of a flashlight moved past them, and she heard the voice of her oldest brother. "Somebody back here?"

Trying to hold in her gasp, she looked to Duke and whispered, "Mike!"

"Shit," he murmured. Then his breath was on her ear, his voice barely audible. "You don't want him to find out about us, right?"

Anna's heart beat a mile a minute. She knew Duke still wanted his presence here to be a secret. And if Mike *were* to find out about them, this wouldn't be the ideal way. "Not like this," she replied.

Then he wrapped her hand in his and said, "Come on— let's get outta here, Daisy." And they took off running through the woods in the dark, and Anna had no idea where they were going, but she didn't even care.

"We must make ourselves as invisible as possible."

Gaston Leroux, *The Phantom of the Opera*

Twenty-two

Duke led Anna toward the only place he could think of to get away from her brother right now—they ran hand in hand toward the edge of the lake. As they burst from the trees into the clearing on the bank, he flipped over the old rowboat that rested on the grass facedown and pushed it into the water.

"Um, are you sure this thing is seaworthy?" she asked, voice low.

"Yep, been in it a time or two," he said, stepping down inside, then reaching a hand up to her. "Come on, Daisy."

The boat wobbled as she entered, but she quickly sat down, allowing Duke to begin rowing away from shore. And he said what he thought she was probably thinking. "This can't be the same one from your diary. It's old, but not *that* old."

"And it's aluminum," Anna said. "Cathy and Robert's was wooden."

"There was even an old tarp covering this when I first found it. Your Cathy must have bought a new one at some point."

He was surprised the speculation made Anna smile. "Maybe that means she wasn't alone in the house, that Robert was with her and they shared the boat."

He simply smiled. Just like his Daisy to get all caught up in somebody else's adventure.

But then it was she who laughed a little—and then covered her mouth, clearly worried the noise would carry.

"What's so funny?" he asked.

"That was kind of . . . fun," she said. "Racing away through the woods. I feel bad in a way, of course—he's my brother and all. But it felt . . . exciting. And kind of forbidden."

Duke couldn't deny feeling the same way. Maybe not as much as Anna, but it struck him that of all the times he'd been on the run from somebody, this was probably the only such occurrence in his life that had been . . . fun, like she'd said. And so he gave her a grin and told her, "Yeah—it did."

Then, all caught up in the night, he tilted his head, stopped rowing—because they were already far enough away now, and had gone around a little bend that would keep them out of sight even if Mike came to the shore—and said, "Anything else excite you tonight, Daisy?"

The soft moonlight allowed him to see the sexy look in her eyes as she said, breathily, "What we did in the woods."

Duke still felt that, too, and the memory made his groin tighten again slightly. "That was hot, wasn't it?" And actually, it had been more than hot—but he didn't want to think about the *more* part now, or have to start labeling it, so he just left it at that.

"Probably the hottest sex of my life," she said. Then added, "Except maybe for . . . other times with you. With you it's just . . . always hot."

Which was when Duke abandoned the oars altogether and leaned over to kiss her. And he'd always liked kissing Anna, but something about it right now felt different. More powerful, intense. And before he knew it, he'd laid her down in the boat, both of them stretched out side by side, just continuing to kiss that way.

As they made out, Anna's hands roamed his arms, his chest, his face. And then he felt one fingertip very deliberately tracing the jagged scar on his cheek.

It caught him off guard. She'd never done that before. And yet something in the touch was so . . . tender. It made him stop kissing her and their eyes met, and she did it again—she traced his scar, slowly, from top to bottom.

"Does it bother you?" he heard himself ask. "It's okay if it does—you can be honest. I know it's . . . ugly."

And the look in her eyes was like . . . damn—even in the dark of night, it felt like the warmth of the sun. "God, no," she whispered. "It's just . . . you. Part of you. I don't even think about it or really see it anymore. I just felt it beneath my fingertips is all. And found myself wishing I could take away the reason you have it . . . so that you could be happier."

"Maybe . . . maybe I'm getting that way," he told her.

And as they floated along beneath the half moon shining down on them, they simply kissed, and kissed, and kissed.

About an hour after leaving, Duke rowed them back to shore and listened to make sure all was quiet in the woods, soon deciding Mike had long since given up and headed home.

He walked Anna to the house, where he got a flashlight before heading back out to look for the fish he'd dropped. Animals had probably taken them by now, but he'd had the luck of catching three big bass and a bluegill and decided it was worth it to check. He'd gone fishing with his grandpa a lot as a boy, and catching big bass in the pond on his grandfather's farm was one of his better childhood memories—

along with watching his grandma fry them up in a skillet for dinner.

He shone the light on the path and to either side as he walked, but had no luck. Damn. And before he knew it, he'd arrived back at the cabin.

He was about to start back when he thought of the picture of the boy in the rowboat inside. He wondered if maybe Anna would like to have it since it seemed to mean so much to her. Maybe she'd like to keep it with the diaries and other belongings of the girl.

He opened the door, using the flashlight to show him the way—when another bright beam lit on his face, practically blinding him. "Hold it right there," Mike Romo said.

Well, shit. Duke held still, as commanded.

"I'm a police officer," Mike said, "and this is private property, so I'm gonna have to ask what you're doing here."

Duke still couldn't see a damn thing, even now holding his arm in front of him to try to blot out the harsh light. "Damn it, Mike, it's me," he said. "Duke Dawson."

He sensed Mike's flinch. "Duke?" Then he could make out Mike shaking his head. "You don't look like yourself, man."

"Got a haircut. Shaved my beard." *And got a bad scar now.* But if Anna didn't see it, if she really didn't . . . well, maybe it didn't matter as much as he'd thought.

Mike looked closer, but when Duke said, "You mind getting that light out of my eyes?" Mike lowered the flashlight—allowing Duke to walk over to his propane lamp and turn it on so that a low glow lit the space. There, that was better.

He turned back to find Mike seated comfortably at his kitchen table in his police uniform, where he must have been waiting quietly all this time. Talk about tenacious.

Now for the tricky part.

"So what are you doing out here in the woods, Duke?"

That was a damn good question. As good as it had been when Anna had first asked him—only he knew Mike wouldn't let him off without giving a real answer. He and

Mike shared a quiet respect for each other, and they'd even gone through a pretty tight scrape together a couple of years ago involving Lucky—but that didn't mean Mike trusted him or would cut him any slack.

"I've been staying out here."

"I saw the bike outside." Damn, he'd forgotten about that—he'd recently parked it behind the cabin like he used to—just to get it away from Anna's house. The road didn't get much traffic, but it had just seemed like a good idea. "Thought you went to Indiana."

Like when Lucky had asked, Duke just said, "Didn't work out. So I came back."

Mike raised his eyebrows, his expression rife with doubt. "And decided to live in a ramshackle old place in the middle of nowhere?"

"Needed some breathing room," Duke told him. "Some fresh air."

"There's not even running water," Mike pointed out.

"I'm not picky."

"Did you know this place is on private property?"

Duke noticed Mike didn't point out that it was *Anna's* property. Probably didn't want Duke to know that if he didn't already. In case Duke got in the mood to go raping and pillaging, he guessed. "No," he said. Since he actually *hadn't* when he first picked the place—he hadn't been in a state of mind to even wonder about it back then.

"Neighbor reported somebody lurking around out here," Mike explained.

"Didn't know there were any neighbors that close." Which was one reason he'd thought he'd have privacy here in the first place. But then, Anna had proved him wrong on that a couple of months ago.

"An older lady up the road. Likes to take walks in the woods occasionally, do some bird watching."

Duke said nothing in response, only nodded.

"Who were you with earlier?"

Duke flinched slightly, but hoped he could play it off. "Nobody out here but me and the birds. Why?"

"When I first got up here about an hour and a half ago, coulda sworn I heard voices. Who were you talking to?"

"Like I said, nobody."

Mike just sat there staring him down, obviously not believing him. But he wasn't gonna give Anna away. Mike would surely freak out if he knew Anna was seeing Duke—but it would be even worse if he found out they were running around the woods together in the dark, and he figured it was possible Mike had heard them having sex, too.

Finally Mike said, "You doing anything out here you shouldn't be, Duke?"

Duke cocked his head sideways. "Like what?"

"I don't know—a man with your background could be into about anything. Running drugs, or guns maybe?"

Despite himself, it pissed Duke off. Given their mutual respect, not to mention his connection to Lucky, it surprised him that Mike would bring up Duke's long-ago past and use it this way. "You see any guns? Any drugs?" Duke held up his hands to motion around him. "Feel free to search the place if you haven't already."

"I have," Mike confirmed. "And I didn't find anything—but I still don't quite know what you're up to out here."

"Fishing and sleeping mostly," he said, though he knew his expression had likely hardened at Mike's accusation.

Finally, Mike stood up, clearly preparing to go. About damn time. "I guess you're off the hook for now, and I won't make you clear out just yet, but fair warning—*whatever* you're doing out here, you oughta think about moving on."

Duke stood waiting for Mike to go, glad when the door finally shut behind him.

Damn. Mike knew he was in town now—which meant it was no longer a secret. And Mike would probably be keeping a tight watch around here after this, especially given how close the cabin was to Anna's house. *Man, if you only*

knew *how close I am to your sister. You'd probably have me
arrested.* Suddenly his place to hide himself away—not only
the cabin, but Anna's place—felt a lot less private.

Turning off the lamp, he stepped back out into the night,
closed the door behind him, and leaned back against it until
he heard the slam of a car door from the direction of the
road, then listened as Mike drove away.

Up until now, he'd been . . . floating. Just like earlier with
Anna in the boat. Floating, letting time pass, seeing where
the floating led him. It had, somewhere along the way,
become the easiest he'd felt in a long while. He'd quit worrying so much—about anything. He'd quit hurting quite so
much inside. Oh, it was all still in there—Denny's death,
Linda's loss, his father's rejection—but it had just started
seeming . . . farther away. He'd quit feeling it all so intensely,
day and night. He supposed his Daisy had given him a lot
of better things to think about—working on her house by
day, working on her body by night. He'd have never dreamed
upon first colliding with her in the woods that she'd end up
making such a difference in his life.

But now . . . now it wouldn't be so easy to float. And as he
started up the path toward Anna's house, flashlight in hand,
Duke knew he had some serious thinking to do about what
came next.

As Anna sat with Duke eating pizza on the sofa where
they'd first made love, he told her everything Mike had said
to him in the woods. Damn—she couldn't believe Mike had
sat waiting for someone to come back to the cabin all that
time. It rather took the luster off the sense of giddiness she'd
experienced coming home afterward. Maybe it was silly,
but she'd somehow felt as if she'd stepped into the pages of
Cathy's diary to be sneaking around in the dark with Duke,
then making out with him in a rowboat on the lake. But
now that it came with consequences, it didn't seem quite
as magical.

"I appreciate you keeping me out of it," she said, "but you could have told him."

"But I thought you didn't want him to—"

"That was before he was accusing you of selling drugs." She glanced vaguely in the direction of the old rotary phone in the kitchen. "I have half a mind to call him and tell him you were with *me*. Then everything would be fine."

But Duke appeared doubtful. "Would it, Daisy?"

She blinked, a little confused. "What do you mean?"

Next to her, he lowered his plate to the coffee table, looked her in the eye. "There's a good reason neither one of us wants Mike to find out about us."

"Which is?"

"He won't think I'm good enough for you, and he'd make both our lives hell for it."

She sighed. "But wouldn't that be better than having him think you're doing something illegal? And . . . maybe it's time to quit hiding, Duke. For me, at least, anyway."

"Best I can tell, honey, you haven't been hiding from anybody lately."

"In ways, no. But if I'm still hiding a big secret from Mike . . . well, the old me wouldn't have done that. It's just a habit I fell into after moving up here—keeping to myself, keeping my life more private. But the old me wouldn't have kept you a secret from Mike—the old me would have just told him to deal with it and move on with his life. And maybe that's a part of myself it's time to get back."

Yet now it was Duke who let out a long, tired sort of sigh. And Anna could pretty much read his thoughts. Just because *she* was ready to be completely out in the open now didn't mean *he* was. "Truth is, Daisy, I'm not sure *I'm* up to dealing with Mike on this. I like your brother, but you know he can be a hard-ass, and . . ."

"And it's safe to say he'd be that way about the idea of me and you," she finished for him.

But it made her sad. To think that, even now, she wasn't

worth enough to Duke for him to stand up to her brother.

And yet . . . he'd never made her even one single promise. Technically speaking, their relationship was still "light and fun." She'd just *told* herself things were changing. She'd foolishly let herself believe that—again. *What an idiot you are.*

Just then, though, Duke playfully brought a hand down on her knee in a light slap to say, "Tell you what, Daisy. How about we just let this go for now? How about we sleep on it for a night or two? I'm tired and . . . I've had enough heavy shit for today. That okay with you?"

She nodded. And his words instilled in her a cautious sort of hope. He wasn't suddenly closing up, acting distant, "turning off" their relationship. Maybe things would be fine. Maybe he'd wake up in the morning ready to face the "heavy shit."

But stop. Why do you keep trusting? Why do you keep believing?

Though she knew the answer as soon as she asked the questions. Because it made her happier to keep believing, even if it was foolish, than it would to give up on him and decide that she'd been wrong about him all along.

It surprised Anna—happily—when, after that, things were astonishingly normal between them.

Because Lucky ran into a stretch of days when he didn't have any work, they stopped installing the new trim and Lucky and Duke put a new black roof on the house. Anna stayed on the ground, mostly gathering up the old shingles they tossed down.

She found herself looking often toward the road, sure Mike would be patrolling the area now and spot Duke working—but she only caught sight of his cruiser driving past twice. Once in the early morning hours before they were outside, and again one evening near dusk after Lucky had gone and Duke was upstairs taking a shower.

She'd been passing by a window at the time, so she was

inside as well, and she was glad she didn't have to explain to her brother how miraculous her house suddenly looked these days. It was one thing to let the girls at the bookstore believe she was doing all the work herself, but that was probably harder to believe when you actually saw it. She'd have to figure out how to address that—especially if she couldn't talk Duke into letting her tell the truth about them, an idea that appealed to her more all the time.

During a shift at the bookstore, Rachel dropped by to meet Amy for lunch, and she mentioned that Mike had been doing a lot of work at the orchard they ran with Edna— and Anna decided that, between that and the emotional turmoil of finding out he was going to be a father, it probably explained why Mike hadn't been keeping a closer eye on Duke. Then she looked vaguely skyward, giving thanks for that particular timing. It took a lot to throw Mike off his game as a cop, so it seemed almost fated that now was the one time he was too busy and too flustered to keep worrying about a guy living in the woods.

It was on a sunny day nearly a week after the incident with Mike that Duke and Anna returned to installing the home's new trim work. A lot of it was being nailed into high eaves or the edge of the roof, which meant she was mostly on ladder-holding detail. Though Duke teased her about knowing when it was time to move the ladder, reminding her of the day she'd nearly fallen from it and had instead ended up in his arms.

That night they grilled some fish Duke had caught the previous evening—and then they made love in Anna's bed before falling asleep in each other's arms. Life felt good, settled. She was in love. And even though he'd still never said anything more than "light and fun," she knew deep in her heart that he loved her, too.

So it caught her off guard when Duke rolled over beside her in bed the next morning, sun streaming in through the sheer curtains, and said, as if it were no more important than a discussion about the weather, "Not much more to do on the house, Daisy, and when it's done, I'll probably move on. Just so you know."

Anna's throat nearly closed up. And she felt mired in a strange haze. A minute ago, everything had been fine. And now, with no warning, everything had changed.

She heard herself murmur, "Oh."

He still wasn't looking her in the eye when he sat up and said, "Gonna hit the shower if you wanna join me." Then he turned to grin down at her. Like he hadn't just shattered her world. *Oh Lord. He still really thinks we're just light and fun. That's all it is to him, even now.*

"Um, thanks, but no."

He seemed undaunted. "All right, party pooper. After that, gonna head over to Crestview, get more trim nails since we're almost out. You wanna go, or should I take the bike?"

"Uh . . . take the bike. I . . . think I'll sleep in."

"Sleepyhead," he teased her, walking toward the bathroom.

She tried to smile. Then rolled back over in bed. And crushed her eyes shut, refusing to cry. *This shouldn't come as a shock. It's what he said, what he wanted, what you agreed to. You decided it was worth it. You decided you could handle a casual relationship with him.* But it still hurt to know he didn't think she was worth more.

She pretended to be asleep when he came out of the shower, and she waited quietly until he was dressed and gone.

She didn't want to be weak about this. She wanted to be confident, together Anna. *I need something to make me happy right now, something to take me away from this.* And so she thought of Cathy's diary, which she hadn't read since before that last trip to the cabin when she'd seen Robert's picture.

Grabbing a short red robe from a hook on the bathroom door, she threw it on over the cami and panties she'd slept in, then made her way downstairs with her cat underfoot the whole way. "I'm already feeling tense, so this is a bad time for you to bug me," she lectured Erik as they went. But then she stopped, took a deep breath, and bent to scoop her kitty up into her arms.

Picking up the diary from where she kept it in the library, she headed straight to the screened-in porch. A soft morning mist hung about the shrubs and trees in the backyard, making everything suddenly feel mysterious and mystical. Lowering her cat to the sofa beside her, she opened the diary, determined to find out that Cathy had ended up happy with Robert. Even if she and Duke weren't going to end up that way—well, if Cathy had been happy here, maybe it would convince her that she ultimately would, too. Somehow. Someday.

> *I have barely had time to write because life is*
> *so joyous. I am busy with school, but also busy*
> *loving my Robert. We spend every second together*
> *that we can, and lately, it has been easier than*
> *ever. Daddy is working long hours at the bank*
> *and Mother has become involved with the PTA,*
> *taking her away from home on many afternoons.*
> *When I step off the school bus on those days, I*
> *head straight for Robert's kisses. The woods, his*
> *cabin, the lake—they have become like our pri-*
> *vate world. I didn't know such happiness existed.*

Anna turned the page, her heart lifted by the first entry she'd read and eager for more. But it was a mere three pages later that she felt as if someone had reached a fist into her chest to squeeze the life from her heart.

> *I can't believe it. The worst has happened. The*
> *unthinkable.*
> *We grew too careless, I guess. Too carefree. We*
> *forgot about reality, about the world outside the*
> *one we built for ourselves in the woods.*

And it all happened so fast.

I was lying in Robert's arms in his bed; we were kissing. Thank goodness I was fully clothed—but in the end, maybe it doesn't even matter. Daddy came barreling through the cabin door and there was nothing we could do except tell him the truth, that we were in love.

He ordered me back to the house, and Lord, the venom in his eyes—he made me feel so ashamed, though in my heart I know I've done nothing wrong.

And the next thing I know, only a few minutes later when I'd barely gotten home, there was Robert, standing in the front yard, calling my name.

Daddy came in the back door just then and commanded I stay inside, but I raced out the front door and onto the porch before he could stop me. And there stood my Robert on the front walk telling me that Daddy had ordered him off our property. And saying, "Come with me, Cathy."

He held his hand out, reaching for mine. And my heart felt as if it would beat right through my chest.

I was so stunned, confused. How could I have known even an hour earlier that I would suddenly be met with such a request, such a horrible choice. I simply stood there, lost for an answer.

But Robert was patient, understanding. "I know this is huge, Cathy," he said. "But I can take care of you. I can make you happy. If you'll let me."

Daddy was yelling at him through all this, threatening to call the law, to go get his shotgun. And yelling at me, too. But all I could see were Robert's beseeching eyes, and the hand he still held out, just waiting for me to take it.

How could I choose? My heart said to go; my

*head said to stay where I knew it was safe. How
was I supposed to decide? Home and security? Or
passion and adventure?*

*"I have the truck now," he reminded me. He'd
saved up his pay and just last week he bought an
old farm truck from a man in town. It made me
sad to know he thought that would be enough to
convince me. And sad to know that it wasn't.*

*He held out his hand for the longest time, and
I desperately wanted to take it. With every single
beat of my heart.*

*And yet the time came when I suppose we both
knew . . . that I wasn't going to.*

*Oh Lord, the heartbreak in his eyes. How could
he know, after all, what he was asking me to give
up? He'd never really had what I have—a safe
place, a good life. And it was only in that moment
that I was forced to realize just how good my safe
life indeed is. Parents who love me. Plenty to eat,
new school clothes every fall. A big, warm, dry
house that always welcomes me.*

*I almost wished I were so foolish as not to
recognize it all; I wished I were the sort of silly
girl who would always take it for granted. But
I was too smart. Too sensible. Too wary of the
unknown.*

*And so finally came the quiet moment when
Daddy had stopped yelling, when there was no
sound at all, when there was only Robert giving
me one last desperate look, his eyes begging me
to take his hand and run down off the porch and
away with him. To somewhere.*

*But then he finally let his hand drop. And I
swear I felt my heart drop along with it—it was as
if it vacated my very body, leaving only a gaping,
empty space behind.*

> *I stood numb and almost disbelieving as I*
> *watched him climb up in his truck and drive*
> *away. And a large part of me wanted to run then,*
> *run down off the porch and call his name and*
> *make him wait. I could almost feel the joy running*
> *through me as I envisioned it—I saw me climbing*
> *in beside him, us smiling at each other, him prom-*
> *ising me the world, me believing him because I so*
> *badly wanted to.*
>
> > *But that's not what happened. That's not what*
> *happened at all.*

Her breath ragged, hands shaky, Anna turned the page.
But the next one was empty.
As was the one behind that, and behind that.
Oh God, all the remaining pages were blank!
How could that be? That couldn't be the end. It just couldn't be.
Pushing up from the wicker sofa, Anna rushed inside and climbed the stairs. Then she hurriedly lowered the folding stairs to the attic and went up those, as well. She rushed to the trunk, lifted the lid, dropped to her knees, and rifled through everything left inside. No more diaries.
But then she turned to the stacks of letters tied with ribbon. Yanking the ribbons away, she investigated them all, one by one—Erik by her side the entire time, having followed her up—to find they were all letters from Cathy's grandmother and some cousins, and there was nothing about Robert in any of them.
Anna longed, more than ever, to know Cathy had ended up happy. Even if it wasn't with Robert but with some other man. She didn't care exactly how Cathy's happiness came— she just wanted to know she'd gotten over Robert and moved on to a guy it had turned out she was meant to find; or that somehow Robert had come back.
But no matter how many times she looked through the

contents of the trunk, she never found even one more word anywhere about Robert, or any other romance, ever.

She finally plopped to her rear on the wooden attic floor.

Cathy had lost Robert. And she was going to lose Duke. And this big house that had, for a while, been a much-needed refuge for her was now going to be empty and lonely.

"Meow."

She looked down to see Erik rubbing up against her hip. There was something comforting in it, more than she could have imagined a few months ago. She pulled the black kitty into her lap, hugging him to her and realizing that she really had begun to love him. Everybody needed love and he was just more openly pushy in going after it than most. "At least I have *you*," she said. "And you have me. I won't ever leave you, I promise."

And the cat began to purr, snuggling against her.

"I am thinking that we shall not see each other again . . ."

Gaston Leroux, *The Phantom of the Opera*

Twenty-three

Duke knew Anna well enough by now to know she'd been upset this morning. But he'd just tried to play it off, keep things normal, easy. And hopefully by the time he got home, she'd have worked through that and they could continue putting up the trim in peace.

And it wasn't that he wouldn't miss her like crazy—it wasn't that walking away would be easy for him, either. But he'd known none of this would last forever—his retreat to the woods, his work on the house, his affair with Anna. His leaving would be the best thing for her in the long run anyway, whether or not she knew it yet. And that was what made it the smartest thing to do, for both their sakes.

As he was riding back from Crestview and realized Logan Whitaker's car was behind him, he remembered what he knew about Logan, besides the fact that he was Mike Romo's best friend and now married to Amy. He knew from Lucky that Logan had gone through something bad just like he had. On the job as a fireman last spring, he'd felt responsible for the death of two family friends he'd known his whole life.

And it was with the idea of moving on, in more ways than one, that Duke made a split-second decision. He slowed, eased to a stop at the side of the road—then waved to Logan, hoping he'd stop.

He took off his helmet as Logan eased up alongside him and lowered the passenger window of his Charger. "Need something?" he asked, squinting slightly, clearly trying to recognize whoever had flagged him down.

"It's Duke Dawson," he identified himself.

And Logan reacted as most people did, balking slightly. "Damn—wouldn't have known you, Duke."

Duke didn't bother explaining for now, instead just saying, "You mind if I talk to you about something?"

Logan looked a little wary and Duke understood why. He and Logan hadn't ever hit it off. But he was a nice enough guy to say, "Sure," anyway. Then he motioned up ahead. "If you go right on Blue Valley Road, there's a turnoff about half a mile up."

A few minutes later they stood next to each other looking out over Blue Valley Lake, much larger than the lake on the hill. And hell, it seemed like a downer to bring up such an ugly subject on such a pretty summer day, but Duke got down to telling Logan what he wanted to talk about and why, concluding with, "You seem like you got yourself together, like you've got a good life going. So . . . how did you get over something like that?"

Logan didn't answer for a minute, and Duke saw that his eyes had clouded over. He felt the need to say, "Sorry, man— if you'd rather not talk about it, that's cool. I understand."

But Logan shook his head and said, "No, I was just thinking through the answer. But the tricky part is—it's no single thing. Part of it is time, and distance. And part of it is just . . .

learning to let it go, especially the guilt part. And part of it is accepting that things happen the way they're supposed to in life, even if it doesn't make any sense to us. And part of it was . . . well, for me, it was Amy. She just helped pull me out of it, helped me get strong again, in my mind." Logan stuck his hands in his front jean pockets. "Don't suppose you have anybody like that—a girlfriend—to help you . . . focus on better things?"

But Duke nodded. "Actually, I kinda do. She's . . . done more for me than she probably knows."

"That's good," Logan said. "It helps to . . . not be alone with your guilt. And I guess the most important part is having faith that it'll get easier. It never goes away completely, but the time comes when you just feel . . . better. And if you know that's coming and keep focused on it, you'll get there."

As Duke and Logan prepared to part ways a few minutes later, Logan said, "If you ever need to talk about it more, let me know."

And Duke thought that was a hell of a nice offer, for which he thanked Logan. But . . . "I'm leaving town soon."

Logan gave him a short nod. "Well, good luck with it, wherever you end up."

Duke rode away with a sense of . . . hope. He'd been feeling a lot better about Denny for a while now, but hearing Logan say that would keep happening, more and more, lifted his spirits further. And Anna had definitely given him better things to think about. He'd have to thank her for that before he said goodbye.

And why are you saying goodbye again?

He wasn't sure where the question had come from, but what it boiled down to was . . . complications. Commitments. He wasn't sure he was ready for either, and to stay with her after the house was done seemed like it would fill his life with both of those things. And it would just be smarter to get over Anna, get over all this, and get a fresh start someplace new.

He'd come to the stop sign at the end of Blue Valley Road, ready to turn toward Half Moon Hill, when Mike Romo's cruiser went past—and then stopped right in the middle of the damn highway and backed up. In better times, Duke would have been tempted to make a joke about issuing him a citation for that, but as it was, when Mike turned onto Blue Valley Road and pulled up next to him, he just stayed silent.

"Dawson, that you?"

He didn't bother removing his helmet. "Yep."

"Still keeping to yourself up in the woods?"

"Yep." *Except for when I'm with your sister.* "But don't worry—I'll be heading out soon."

Mike gave a short nod, but then glanced up the road. "Mind if I ask what you're doing out here by Blue Valley Lake?"

Duke could have said he was just riding, but opted for the truth instead. He just wasn't in the mood to fake anything right now. "I was talking to your buddy Logan. Thought he might be able to give me some advice."

Mike looked surprised. "On?"

Duke kept his voice steady, strong—but distant. "Uh, I think it's called . . . survivor's guilt."

And that was when he saw Mike's eyes change. As he remembered what Duke had been through, he supposed. Maybe he'd forgotten up to now? Either way, his reply clearly had Mike viewing this whole situation in a new light—that fast. "I'm sorry about what happened, Duke. I know it was bad."

Glad he still wore his helmet and sunglasses so that Mike couldn't see any reaction on his face, he simply said, "Thanks."

"And listen, sorry if I came down on you hard that night in the woods. I guess I didn't stop to think about . . . well, any legitimate reason you might've needed . . . room to breathe."

Duke couldn't help himself from saying, "That's a big

change in attitude, Officer Romo. What'd I do to get on your good side?"

Mike didn't look the least bit pissed, though, as he answered. "Maybe I just remembered you're my brother's best friend for a reason. And that everybody goes through bad stuff from time to time, and that maybe I could stand to be a little more decent to you."

Beneath his helmet, Duke's jaw dropped. But he only said, "I appreciate that, Mike." Then he gave his head a tilt, wondering what he was missing here. "If I didn't know better, I'd think maybe *you* were going through something."

"I am," he admitted. "I'm having a baby in about six months and I'm scared shitless."

"Wow," Duke said. Just that. Though he'd already heard this news, he thought Mike Romo was about as ready to be a father as *he* was—and that wasn't saying much.

"Yeah, wow," Mike repeated.

"I'm sure it'll work out," Duke said. Since he had to say *something.*

Mike nodded, seeming more like his straitlaced cop self than he had there for a minute. "Yeah, it will. 'Cause it has to. Sometimes in life you gotta rise to the occasion, and guess my time's now."

Rachel lay on a table in a doctor's office in Crestview, naked from the waist down under a white paper sheet, wondering where the hell her husband was. Just then, he came through the door—looking drop dead handsome in the same uniform he'd been wearing the day they'd met. "Sorry I'm late."

"This is not the time to stress me out, you know." She could hear the tension in her own voice.

"I know, honey," he said. "I'm sorry." Then he walked over, bent down, and kissed her on the forehead.

And she couldn't recall a time when she'd ever seen Mike Romo act so contrite. "Who are you and what have you done with my husband?"

One corner of his mouth turned up in the semblance of a smile. "Guess I'm just realizing that . . . we need to pull ourselves together about this. We're having a baby and we can handle it. There are people with far worse problems."

Rachel was still trying to figure out where the real Officer Romo was when the door opened again, this time admitting an ultrasound technician. "Are we ready?"

"As we'll ever be," Rachel quipped.

And a moment later, she saw . . . well, the most extraordinary thing—an intricate set of dots on a screen that the female technician informed her was their baby. She looked at it, studied it closely as the other woman talked—pointing out the head and other body parts—and it became more *real* to her, more *alive*, than it had been up to this moment.

And then something *totally* unexpected happened—her heart began to swell.

Because it was their baby. *Their* baby. Hers and Mike's!

And he was holding her hand, squeezing it tight. And breathing became a little difficult as it struck her fully. And she heard herself saying, "Oh my God, Mike, look! Look what we made together! It's . . . a baby." Which she'd known all along, of course, but . . . to see it, even just like this, was different. It was . . . inside her. Moving, becoming, growing. Into a tiny little human being!

A glance up at her handsome husband's face revealed he was undergoing a similar revelation. "God . . . it's amazing, isn't it?" he murmured.

As she swallowed back the lump in her throat, her excitement became mixed with . . . an unexpected sense of peace. It dropped over her like a blanket at the moment when she'd least expected it. And though she'd refocused her attention on their baby on the screen, now she looked back up at Mike and said, "Everything's actually going to be okay, isn't it?"

"More than okay, honey," he said warmly. "I'm starting to think it's gonna be . . . freaking incredible."

Then Rachel laughed. "I just hope you like the baby more than you like the cat."

And Mike said, "As long as the baby stays off the counter and doesn't get hair in my cereal, we'll be okay."

"Aren't you worried about Lucky driving in the demolition derby?" Amy asked Tessa. They sat in the easy chairs at Under the Covers while Anna stood behind the counter.

"Kind of," Tessa said. "But it's hard to imagine anyone more capable than him, so I'm sure it'll be fine." Then she directed her attention toward Anna. "Are you coming to the derby Saturday night to see Lucky drive, Anna?"

Anna glanced up, in a bit of a fog. "Um, I didn't realize it was this Saturday already, but yeah, sure."

Now Amy turned her head toward Anna, too, flashing a look of concern. "Are you okay? You seem . . . sad today. Or something."

"I'm fine," Anna insisted. And she tried to smile. But she could tell it hadn't quite made it to her face.

A few minutes later, as Amy was talking with a customer, Tessa stood up and walked over to her. "What's going on? What has you so down? Something with Duke?"

Anna didn't mind sharing with Tessa, and she'd have been honest with Amy, too, if Amy had known Duke was in town. "He's just . . . well, he's planning on leaving soon. And I kinda didn't see that coming."

Tessa appeared even more shocked by this than Anna had been. "Where's he going?"

Anna shook her head. "Who knows? And it doesn't even matter. The upshot is that he . . . obviously isn't into having anything *real* with me. Whether it's because he's a loner at heart or he just doesn't care enough about me, I don't know—but he's ready to leave. And . . ." Okay, this part suddenly wasn't as easy to share. Especially given that she'd spent most of her life pretending to be strong in order to actually *be* that way. But it seemed that once she'd let down that wall, it wasn't so easy to put it back up. And so she heard herself whispering to Tessa—because she didn't want her voice to crack, "It just . . . really hurts."

Tessa's eyes widened in understanding. "My God, of course it hurts. I'm so sorry you're going through this. And . . ." She gave her head a forlorn shake. "The man can have *you* and he's leaving? I love Duke, but what an idiot."

"Thanks," Anna said softly. And the truth was, she agreed with Tessa. She kind of thought she was a pretty good catch herself—and she knew that when she and Duke were together and he let down all of *his* walls, what they shared was amazing. And special, just like Tessa had said after seeing them together.

"Is there anything I can do?" Tessa asked, reaching out to touch her hand.

But Anna shook her head. "I'll be fine." *Eventually. Somehow.*

Though Tessa didn't look convinced as she said, "Well, come hang out with us all tomorrow night at the derby and it'll at least get your mind off him for a little while."

Anna nodded, but she didn't say any more because just talking about the situation made her feel . . . weak. *That's the problem about letting down your defenses—once they're down, you're vulnerable, naked, and there's no going back.* She supposed there was a reason she'd always been so careful to present the tougher, stronger side of herself in life up to now. It was so much safer.

And yet, would you take back loving him if you could? Would you take back knowing the wonder of that, the giddy joy it brought for a while? Would you take back the closeness you felt opening up to him, and when he opened up to you? They were hard questions, but the truth was—she couldn't be sure she would change anything. Other than the end of the story. Because she knew for a while she'd made him happy, and she'd helped heal his wounds a little—and even now, that felt worth a lot.

When Duke had come home yesterday after his announcement, Anna had been cordial but quiet. Not by design—it was simply the best she could do. He'd remained upbeat, though, at one point even tossing her a wink to say, "Cheer up, Daisy—I'm not that great."

It had surprised her for him to even bring it back up or acknowledge his news might be responsible for her mood. She'd just said, "You're right, you're not. So I'll be fine."

And he'd laughed. But she hadn't actually thought anything was very funny. And whereas working with him before had been fun and even fulfilling—now, every moment, every little piece of gingerbread trim they put in place, was like taking a step closer to his leaving, and it was difficult to escape the heaviness that weighed her down.

She'd also spent time yesterday still trying to find out more about Cathy and Robert—giving up on the attic and moving on to the computer. She Googled Cathy's name but found nothing useful. And she didn't even know Robert's last name, so locating any information about the boy Cathy had loved was impossible.

Just then, a knock came on the bookshop window and they all looked up to see Sue Ann smile and wave as she passed by—she wore a pretty dress of blue polka dots, and Anna suspected she was on her way to work at Destiny Properties, just off the town square.

On a lark, Anna said to Amy and Tessa, "Be right back," then rushed out onto the sidewalk to stop Sue Ann.

"Whoa there, girlfriend, where's the fire?" Sue Ann asked on a laugh as Anna nearly mowed her down.

But Anna felt too tense to even fake a giggle. "I need to ask you something."

Sue Ann's eyebrows rose in pleasant anticipation. "Sure. Fire away."

"It's about Cathy, the woman who used to own my house. What do you know about her? Do you know if she ever married? Or had kids? And if she married, do you know her husband's name? And did he die before her? Was she alone in the house for many years before she passed away?"

When Sue Ann held up her hands and said, "Stop," Anna realized she was rambling, asking too many questions at once. So she went quiet only to hear Sue Ann say, "I don't really know anything about her family, Anna—but who told you she died?"

And Anna flinched, confused. "Huh?"

"She's not dead," Sue Ann said.

Anna's back went ramrod straight. "She's not?"

Sue Ann shook her head. "No. She just moved to an assisted living facility in Crestview. About ten years ago, I believe. She left the house when she couldn't handle the upkeep due to a bad back. But otherwise, as far as I know, she's doing fine."

Anna nearly fainted. All this time, she'd just assumed the home's previous owner had died years ago—due to the place being in such a state of disrepair. And when she'd signed the papers to buy the house, the other signature had belonged to a man she'd been told lived in Florida, so she'd assumed it was some relative of the owner's whom the place had passed down to or who was handling the estate. "But . . . who sold the house to me? At the time, I didn't much care or pay attention, and it all went through so quickly . . ."

"A cousin of hers, I think—he was a real estate attorney, and she sold the house to him when she moved out. He planned to fix it up and resell it, but just never got around to the fixing-it-up part—and then he moved away." Sue Ann stopped then, giving her head a pointed tilt. "But why do you suddenly care so much about this?"

Anna sighed. How could she possibly explain? *Keep it simple.* "I've just . . . found a lot of her old things. And it made me curious about her." She still couldn't believe Cathy was alive! But now that she actually stopped and did the math—oh Lord, it made sense. Cathy was only around seventy. And sure, she could have died from a disease or something, but regardless, she *hadn't* died, and this meant the picture Anna had been carrying around in her head of Cathy growing old in the house wasn't true. "Do you happen to know the name of the facility where she lives?" Anna asked.

"Sure. It's called Shady Acres Village. It's right off Morningview Highway where it leads into Crestview. You've probably driven past it a hundred times."

Anna still couldn't get over it—Cathy had been that close all this time! But the important thing was—she was going to meet her! And she would find out how the story ended.

That night, over a dinner of grilled chicken salad, Anna told Duke that Cathy was alive and well and living in Crestview and that she planned to drive over and visit her in the morning.

"That's amazing, baby," he said, looking as if he really understood what a big deal it was for her. *He's not actually a jerk. He just doesn't love you, that's all. You have to make peace with that and move on with your life.*

"I thought I'd take her the diaries, and a novel Robert gave her, and maybe the picture of him from the cabin."

Duke nodded. "I actually meant to bring you the picture before now. I was gonna get it the night Mike was there—but that sidetracked me. I'll go get it for you after we eat," he offered.

She tried not to let that touch her at all and simply thanked him.

Later that night, after she'd placed the diaries, book, and photo in a small shopping bag on a table by the front door, Duke walked up behind her, eased his hands around her waist, and lowered a kiss to her neck. It felt good—too, too good—so she pulled away.

He said nothing at first and an awkward moment grew between them—until finally he asked, "Should I go sleep in the cabin? If you don't want me here anymore, I understand."

And Anna let out the breath she hadn't quite realized she was holding. Oh God, this was hard. "No, that would be silly. I do want you here. I just . . ." She shook her head, tried to meet his eyes—and couldn't quite do it. "It means something to me—being with you, like that. And since I know you're leaving soon, I just . . . need to protect myself a little, you know?"

She couldn't tell if he really understood or not—especially given the way men could take sex so very casually. She'd thought she could do that, too, with him, but turned out she was wrong. "Okay," he said. "Whatever you want, Daisy." And they slept next to each other, but not touching. Though, in a way, that was just as difficult as the alternative.

The next morning around ten, Anna arrived at the Shady Acres Village, an attractive retirement community that reminded her of a complex of one-story condos. And though it was nice, it was difficult to imagine Cathy someplace so modern—she was so used to thinking of Cathy living her whole life on Half Moon Hill.

After going to the main office, she told the reception-ist, "I'd like to see Cathy Worth—though that may be her maiden name," she added. The woman behind the desk didn't question her further, making a quiet phone call and then showing Anna to a garden area with picnic tables and chairs, along with a shuffleboard court.

She'd seen pictures of Cathy as a girl in the photo albums in the trunk, but she would never have recognized her now. Still, her heart expanded nearly to bursting as the gray-haired lady with a cane ambled into the garden wearing cropped pants and a simple blouse.

She looked understandably wary as Anna stood up to greet her and said, "Cathy?"

"Yes," the older lady replied.

"My name is Anna and I recently moved into the house where you grew up."

At this, Cathy gasped, and from that second on, it was as if having the house in common gave them a bond that made Cathy trust her.

From there, Cathy sat down at a table with her and Anna explained that she'd found her old belongings. "I brought your diaries," she said, pushing the small bag across the table toward her. "I thought you might want them."

"That was thoughtful, dear," Cathy said. "But I left them with the house because . . . I felt they belonged there, if that makes any sense."

Only then she looked inside the bag—and pulled out the picture of Robert. And her eyes changed, softened, as a sigh left her lips. And for a very brief second, Anna saw in her that girl of sixteen. "Where did you find this?"

"In the cabin," Anna said. "The other two pictures were gone—this was the only one left."

Cathy's eyes rose from the frame she held in her hand to Anna's face. "You read the diaries," she said. Her voice held no malice or embarrassment—just the acknowledgment that Anna knew. All of it.

"I did," Anna confirmed. "I didn't mean to trespass. And I had no idea we would ever meet. But then, when I found out just yesterday that you were here . . . I had to come." And when Cathy didn't respond right away, Anna rushed on to say, "The book is there, too, in the bag. *The Phantom of the Opera.*"

Cathy's gaze had fallen back to the faded photo while Anna spoke, but now she reached in the shopping bag and drew out the Leroux novel. "Oh my," she said, her voice gone fluttery. "These things do bring back memories." Studying the cover, she let out another sigh. "You know, the real romance in this book was between Christine and Raoul. But there *is* something . . . sadly gripping about the phantom, about someone who's never known love, isn't there?"

And Anna sucked in her breath, her thoughts flying to Duke. He'd known love—from his mother, from friends like Lucky and Tessa. But there was something different about *romantic* love, about the way *she* loved him, wasn't there? And even if he didn't want that kind of love from *her*, she hoped someday he'd find it somewhere else.

When Cathy's attention then drifted back to the photo, Anna's stomach churned. Had she done the right thing, bringing Cathy's things? "I hope the memories are good ones," she said.

Cathy didn't smile as she kept staring at the picture still in her hand—but finally she replied, "*Very* good ones."

Anna stayed quiet then, letting Cathy absorb it all, until finally the older woman said, "Well, I *will* keep this picture, if you don't mind. But the book and the diaries I'll send back home with you."

Anna nodded. "I'll keep them there always and treasure them." And as she watched Cathy touch Robert's picture with her fingertips, she asked tentatively, "Whatever happened? With Robert? Did he come back?"

Without taking her eyes from the frame, Cathy said wistfully, "No—no, he didn't. I'm afraid I never saw him again."

And Anna's heart nearly broke into pieces in her chest once more. Maybe she'd known the answer already, deep down, but she'd been hoping against hope to find out she was wrong. She swallowed past the lump rising in her throat to ask, "Did . . . did you find someone else then? Later? When you were older?"

Cathy gave her head a thoughtful tilt, then told Anna, "No, I never married."

And Anna wanted to cry. It would be different if she'd thought Cathy had been alone by choice, that she'd found fulfillment in other ways, but she didn't believe that.

Though Cathy spoke clearly, calmly, Anna could hear the sad truth in her voice. "I always thought someone else would come along—but they just didn't. Maybe it was too much to hope for that kind of love twice in a lifetime. Or maybe I made it too hard for love to find me, locking myself away in that old house."

"And you have no idea where Robert ended up?"

"When computers came into style, I looked for him—I found an obituary I believe was his, in Knoxville, Tennessee. It said he died in 1992, of cancer, and that he had one son. That's all I know."

Anna nodded. It all felt so bleak, she didn't know what to say.

And then Cathy told her, "Not leaving with Robert that night is my greatest regret in life. Maybe it would have seemed reckless, crazy—but sometimes you have to take chances. I always wonder what would have happened if I had. Maybe something awful. But maybe something wonderful. And either way, it would have been *living*, and it would have been better than asking myself 'what if?' ever since."

On impulse, Anna reached out and covered Cathy's hand with her own. "Thank you for being so open with me. Reading your stories has meant a lot to me, made me feel connected to both you and the house. I'm fixing it up and planning to open it soon as a bed-and-breakfast," she explained.

The news seemed to lift Cathy's mood, change her focus. "That's nice to hear. It's always been too big a house for the very few people who have lived there. It'll be nice that more people get to enjoy it."

"I'm glad you like the idea."

"Do you think maybe I could come see it sometime?" Cathy asked. "When it's finished? I'd like to see what you've done with the place."

And Anna nodded, deeply pleased. "Absolutely. I'd love for you to be my very first guest."

Then Cathy squinted slightly, her head tilted to one side. "But you didn't do all that work by yourself surely? It's such a large house."

So Anna shook her head. "A couple of friends helped me some on the interior. And I've also had help on the outside. From a guy . . . friend," she concluded, sounding more sheepish than she liked.

Which had clearly given her away, because that's when Cathy said without the slightest hesitation, "More than a friend. You love him. I can see it in your eyes."

Anna just blinked. "It's that obvious?" Then she sighed. "I used to be so much cooler."

But Cathy only laughed. "I'd rather be in love than be cool."

Anna wished she could deny the truth, but her truth had changed somewhere along the way, so she had no choice but to say, "Me too."

"Never before had she confessed that she loved him."

Gaston Leroux, *The Phantom of the Opera*

Twenty-four

*A*nna left Cathy with mixed emotions. She was happy they'd met, happy that she thought she'd added a little unexpected light to Cathy's life. But she couldn't help being sad that Cathy had spent her life alone, it seemed, and not by her choice.

Rather than going straight home, she stopped at Creekside Park—bypassing the ball fields and the area where the carnival was held each year, which was currently being turned into a makeshift arena for the demolition derby. She instead went to the pretty area that ran along Sugar Creek, the paved path lined with wild daisies that led to a little white gazebo much like the one in Miss Ellie's garden. She wanted to do some thinking in a peaceful spot that wasn't on Half Moon Hill.

She understood completely why Cathy, at sixteen, had

made the choice to stay with her family. Robert had truly had nothing to offer her but his love, and who could say if it would have ultimately been enough for a girl who'd lived a comfortable, secure life up to that time? And yet she hated that Cathy harbored regrets about the decision. It seemed to Anna like it had simply been a no-win situation thanks to Cathy's hard-hearted father.

But the things Cathy had said to Anna still echoed in her mind. *You have to take chances. It would have been better than asking myself "what if?" ever since.* "Ever since" was a damn long time.

Yet unfortunately . . . Anna was pretty sure she knew the answer. If Duke loved her, too, he wouldn't be planning to leave.

And still . . . *you've never told him how you feel.*

And she wondered now if she should.

If she should just throw caution to the wind and do it.

And that way, if he still chose to move on . . . well, she'd never have a "what if?" She might end up all the more humiliated and heartbroken by making herself all the more emotionally naked in front of him, but . . . at least she'd never have to wonder if it would have made a difference in some way.

The idea of it, at a time when she already felt heartbroken and fragile and exposed, was scary as hell. It felt almost as if she'd be saying to him: *Go ahead, hurt me a little more, kick me when I'm down.* And maybe it was a terrible idea because maybe she'd end up so broken inside that she'd never be able to put herself out there with a man again.

And that was the question: Was it better to take every chance, play every last card, reach into her chest and put her heart on the table right in front of him? Or was it wiser to accept defeat, cut her losses, lick her wounds, and keep what little remained of her dignity so that she wasn't completely destroyed?

She soaked up the sun, listened to birds sing, watched a

monarch butterfly flutter lazily past, and then she asked God for some guidance. After which she got in her car and drove back to the house—arriving just in time to see Duke backing down a small ladder that leaned against the front porch. And when he turned to her, he wore a big smile that set her heart beating faster.

The very sight inspired her to smile back as she got out and walked over to where he stood. "Why are you smiling?" she asked. *Maybe he's realized he wants to stay. Maybe he's going to open up to me right here and tell me so. Maybe he loves me, too.*

"It's done," he said.

"Huh?"

"The house." He motioned toward it. "A few finishing touches to put in place, but I just nailed in the last piece of trim, Daisy. And it looks pretty damn good if I do say so myself."

Oh Lord. Already? It was done? Completely?

She looked up at her home. And it was . . . beautiful. The soft, buttery yellow seemed as happy as the sun that shone down on it, and the peach and white trim gave it the warm, welcoming storybook feel she'd hoped. It was hard to believe this was the same old house she and Duke had started working on just a few months ago.

"It's perfect," she told him.

The only thing *not* perfect about it was knowing this signaled . . . the end.

That night, one question burned inside her. *When are you leaving?*

But she didn't ask. Because she couldn't bear to.

So instead, when Duke came in after dark—having said only that he was working on some last touches in the garage—she asked him something else. "Would you like to go with me to the demolition derby tomorrow night?"

He stood washing his hands at the first floor bathroom

sink. And when he looked up at her, she knew the answer before he gave it. "Sorry, Daisy, but no way."

She took a deep breath, tried again. "I'm sure Lucky would love to have you there. And . . . and I would, too." And when he said nothing more in reply, just kept washing his hands, she added, "Don't you think it's time you got out in public a little?"

He turned off the faucet, dried his hands on a towel. "No."

"Why not?"

He looked tired, irritated. "Lotta reasons."

"Like?"

"Damn it, woman, you are still sassy as hell sometimes." He just shook his head, as if in disbelief. "But for starters, too many people. Like your other brother, Mike—remember him?"

Anna drew in a deep breath, let it back out. And told Duke something that had hit her all the more fully today in the park. "Maybe I don't care if he knows about us, like I told you before. And maybe you shouldn't care, either. Maybe it's just time to . . . come out of the dark, be real, be honest."

They stood there staring each other down. She was challenging him and he clearly felt it. But finally he said, "I'm *being* honest—with *you*. I'm not going. For a lotta reasons, like I said."

She let out an exasperated huff. "What other reasons?"

And that's when he curled his hands into fists of frustration and his eyes widened. "Jesus, Daisy, think about it! It's a bunch of cars crashing into each other. You think I want to see that? Hear those sounds? You think I want to be reminded of the last time I heard them?"

Oh God. Anna sucked in her breath. She'd never even thought . . .

And now she felt like the most insensitive person alive. She pursed her lips, lifted her eyes back to his. Her voice came out softer than intended. "I'm sorry, Duke—I forgot. That it would be anything like . . . that."

"It's okay," he said quietly, then looked away, his expression dark now, eyes more vacant.

And she wasn't sure it was okay at all. In fact, maybe this was one reason he was ready to leave. Because she was so damn pushy with him and he wasn't a man who liked being pushed. Into going where he didn't want to go. Or . . . feeling something he maybe just didn't want to feel.

Part of her wanted to throw caution to the wind and tell him she loved him right here and now. She wanted to tell him that she loved him enough to take away everything that hurt him, that she loved him enough to make everything okay if he'd only let her.

But she just couldn't. Because what if she was wrong? Because for her love to make everything okay, he'd have to love her in return. And that seemed more doubtful all the time.

Anna spent the bulk of the next day doing things inside the house. Because it would be time to open her business soon. And as she went from room to room, making lists of any remaining items each needed, and then started to organize the first floor room she was turning into an office, she thought of Cathy and hoped she would like what Anna had done with the place.

Duke was working in the garage again, but she didn't know on what. Mainly, she was trying not to think about him. And when that didn't work, she was trying to accept that . . . well, nothing was going to change here. He really was going to leave, possibly any day now. For all she knew, she could come home from the demolition derby tonight to find him gone.

That's what you get for falling in love with an unpredictable man. And one who's been hurt from too many angles to let himself love. And for a while she'd been so bold as to think she could change that—but she'd finally stopped deluding herself.

As the day went on, she heard hammering outside, coming from the front of the house, so she assumed he'd finished up whatever he was doing in the garage and was maybe replacing her mailbox. She'd picked up a new one— a plain, simple one of matte silver metal—a few weeks ago. And if she was right, well . . . she thought it might possibly be the very last task he had to do for her. And her heart broke a little more.

But she tried to push the emotions aside. She tried to, instead, be thankful for all he'd done to help her, and for all the unexpected joy he'd brought into her life at a time when she'd needed it. Yes, that was a far better way to view the whole thing than to concentrate on the fact that he was leaving. And that she would feel empty without him. And that she'd always wonder what could have been if he'd only . . . *Oh, stop it already.*

You're going out tonight. You're going to have fun. Or she would try her best anyway. She just wished she could quit hurting inside. After all, he wasn't even gone yet. If it was this bad now, how awful would she feel once he'd actually departed?

She was almost ready to leave for Creekside Park when Duke came inside and found her in the foyer to say, "Daisy, can you come outside? I've got something to show you."

She looked up from where she stood digging in her purse for her keys. "Is it the mailbox? I thought maybe I heard you hammering a new post into the ground."

If she wasn't mistaken, he was trying to hold in a smile. "Just come outside and see." And he looked incredibly cute wearing that particular expression—but she tried her damnedest not to notice.

He held the front door open for her as she stepped through—and then she drew up short, stopping on the porch, as she took in what she saw next to the driveway. Indeed the new mailbox stood in place of the old one—and above it, on an extended wooden post, hung a sign: *Half Moon Bed & Breakfast.* Below the sign even hung a small placard that said *Vacancy*, with a little removable wooden *No* hanging in front of it. While the thick post was natural wood, both the mailbox and sign had been painted a dark blue color, with golden yellow words, and each was accented with an array of small yellow painted stars and a half moon. The lettering looked professional and stylized. It was like she'd imagined, but so much better.

"I hope you don't hate the blue," Duke said. "I know we don't have any blue in the house, but it just made sense with the moon and stars."

Anna stood there almost speechless, stunned and amazed by how gorgeous it was. But then she managed to find some words. "No. I—I love it. It's perfect."

"Really? Are you sure? Because we could change it."

She turned to look at him on the porch. "Are you kidding? I wouldn't change anything about it. It's amazing."

"Then hopefully that means you'll like this, too."

And when he shifted his gaze back toward the door they'd just walked through, Anna did, as well—to see a smaller sign mounted next to the front door, with the same design and lettering: *Half Moon Bed & Breakfast*. And below that, in smaller print: *Anna Romo, Proprietor*.

It was all she could do not to cry. Because this made it feel so real, and made her realize how far she'd come since buying the old house nearly a year ago. And how far she'd come, as well, since returning home to Destiny—a place that had felt so foreign to her then but came damn close to feeling like home now. And it also touched her more than she could measure to know Duke had done this for her. "I love it," she said, then shifted her gaze to his. "Did you make these yourself?"

He nodded, suddenly looking surprisingly boyish, shy.

"I didn't know you were artistic."

He gave his head a short, self-deprecating shake. "I'm not, really. Used to draw and paint a little when I was a kid, for my mom. But this is the first time I've done anything like this."

She was stunned to discover that such talents lay hidden inside him. But then, there was a lot more to Duke Dawson than met the eye, a lot more layers than he let most people see—and she felt almost honored that he'd chosen to share this one with her. "I love it," she told him. "You have no idea how much."

And it struck her then that she'd have hated if he'd left and she'd never known about this. And it made her begin to wonder what else she would miss out on, what about him she would never know. And something in the thought combined with how moved she was by this gift from him, and she followed the impulse to lift her hands to his face and kiss him with all the love rushing through her veins.

His arms curved around her, his strong hands warmed her back, and his tongue twined with hers, and Anna sank into it all the more deeply for knowing it might very well be the last kiss they shared. Whether because he left tonight without warning or simply because of the way she'd held back with him these last few days in an attempt at self-preservation. And she'd resume that behavior after this—because it was hard to let herself go with him, knowing it didn't mean as much to him as it did to her—but right now, in this moment, she surrendered herself completely.

When the kissing stopped a few minutes later, she could barely breathe. Still caught in his embrace, she peered into his eyes to whisper, "Thank you. For the signs." And then she pulled away. Before she surrendered any *more* of herself. "I . . . have to go. I don't want to be late."

He nodded in understanding and she rushed back into the house to grab her purse from the foyer table. She took a last look in the mirror and straightened her top. She saw that she'd apparently kissed off the lipstick she'd applied only a little while ago, but she could fix that later. She needed to go now—for more reasons than one.

When she came back outside, Duke no longer stood on the porch and was, in fact, nowhere in sight. So she paused to look at the wonderful sign he'd hung next to the door, and as she went to the driveway, she actually walked past her car to study the bigger sign by the road. It was truly perfect— the perfect final touch—and it was hard to look at it without smiling.

At the same time, though, she couldn't help thinking it hinted at Duke's departure in a real, solid way. And that his leaving felt so wrong, at least to her. And that maybe she'd be like Cathy and regret it forever if she didn't do what Cathy said and take a chance.

Because what if he felt the same way she did? Even if it didn't appear that way, or seem likely at this point, what if he did deep down inside? What if he somehow felt the same way but they never told each other and they missed out on an absolutely amazing, ecstatically happy life together?

And as she got in the Mustang and started the engine, she looked up to see Duke walk from the shady darkness of the open garage out into the sunlight just in front of her car. He lifted a hand to wave goodbye to her. Goodbye. What if it really *was* goodbye?

"Duke," she called. And as he walked over to her car door, she had no plan, but three words rang out inside her. *Now or never.*

"Have a good time, Daisy," he said easily.

And she took a deep breath—and just started talking. "The reason I asked you to go with me tonight is because . . . I'd be proud to have all of Destiny see me on your arm. Because I'm in love with you. And I don't want you to leave. Which I'm telling you in case that changes anything.

"Because . . . deep down, I have to believe you care about me, in some way that matters. But that you're just afraid. To trust in it, or to trust in me.

"The thing is, though—it's not easy for me, either, Duke. I lived with a woman who told me the biggest possible lie every day of my life for nearly twenty-five years. And yet, I've put myself out there with you, more than once, because even though I'm scared as hell to trust . . . I guess I think the risk is worth it. And even if this changes nothing . . . well, I still wanted you to know. That I love you like crazy."

And then she put the Mustang in reverse, backed out, and drove away, her heart in her throat.

"You are frightened . . . but do you love me?"

Gaston Leroux, *The Phantom of the Opera*

Twenty-five

The area around the makeshift arena bustled with activity when Anna arrived. Trailers hooked to trucks carried in beat-up old cars with all the glass removed and numbers and sponsor names spray-painted on the sides. She also saw brightly painted riding lawn mowers, some of them looking like they'd been pieced together from a collection of spare parts, and learned—when she ran into Tessa amid all the action—that the first two heats of the derby would actually be lawn mowers instead of cars.

"What?" she asked Tessa, fairly aghast at the absurdity.

Tessa just shook her head and said, "You heard me right—a lawn mower demolition derby. Lucky even bought an old mower from Edna and fixed it up for Johnny to drive."

"You're kidding."

"Don't I wish. I have to say, this demo derby obsession has

gotten a little out of hand in our house. I was half surprised he didn't find a vehicle for the cat to drive."

She and Tessa had been walking as they talked, and now they approached a garish lime green car which Anna recognized as an old Buick Skylark. The number eleven was painted on each side in red, along with *Lucky's Custom Bike Painting*, though done far more stylishly than on the other cars she'd seen—since her brother airbrush-painted motorcycles for a living. And he was bent over the open hood. "Nice numbering, but what's with the lime green?" Anna asked.

He looked up. "I got what was on sale," he said, then dropped his head back down under the hood.

That's when Anna caught sight of the lime green lawn mower nearby—just before Johnny came running up, clearly excited about the night, and giving Anna a chance to greet her nephew and wish him luck.

A few minutes later, as she and Tessa prepared to head to the bleachers, Anna waited while Tessa hugged and kissed Lucky goodbye. And she couldn't help feeling a little wistful—in a way that bordered on envy—imagining her and Duke someday playing out this same scene.

Only she knew that wasn't going to happen.

She hadn't given him much chance to reply to her declaration of love before leaving, but maybe it had been the look in his eyes. There had been something . . . sad there. And she wasn't even sure what specifically he'd been sad about— because he felt sorry for her or because she was making his leaving more awkward?—but it didn't really matter. All she knew was that it had left her certain that what she'd said *didn't* make any difference, and that she'd put herself out there and taken a chance for nothing.

It wasn't nothing. He knows now he's loved. That matters. And now you don't have to be like Cathy and wonder "what if?" Now you know there's nothing more you could have done to make him stay. That was something, at least. Even if it felt like cold comfort at the moment.

As she and Tessa finally headed toward the bleachers, Tessa saw one of her interior design clients and said to Anna, "You go ahead and find Amy. I'll catch up."

And a moment later she caught sight of Jeremy Sheridan standing next to another garishly painted vehicle—yellow and purple, and apparently sponsored by the local hair salon, the Snip and Clip—with a helmet in his hand. And she knew she could keep going—he hadn't even spotted her—but she felt the need to make some amends with him, as well as close that particular door.

"Don't tell me you're as crazy as my brother and driving in this thing, too?" she said, walking up.

He looked over with a smile. "Sure am. And that goes both for the crazy part and the driving-in-this-thing part."

"Tessa didn't mention it."

He raised his eyebrows conspiratorially. "Nobody knows. Just got a call a couple of hours ago from a high school buddy who was set to drive but broke his toe playing basketball this afternoon."

"Jeremy, I, uh . . ." She wasn't any more prepared for this than she'd been for her declaration to Duke a little while ago, but she decided to just speak from the heart. "I wanted to apologize about the Fourth of July. I'm sorry if I left you hanging."

And as usual, Jeremy was easygoing. "No worries—there were plenty of friends there. But I *was* disappointed you weren't one of them. And you can make it up to me some night soon," he added with a wink. "What do you say? Dinner at Dolly's, a cone from the Whippy Dip afterward? Only Destiny's finest for any date of mine."

She had to laugh. And she couldn't help thinking what a nice boyfriend he would be . . . if only she felt those feelings for him. "Thanks, and I wish I could, but . . . I'm kind of seeing somebody, and I just thought I should let you know."

Both of them kept smiling even as he said, "Well, damn—that's definitely my loss."

And, of course, she knew Duke would be leaving soon—and in a way, she figured they were already as good as over—but she had a feeling her wildman in the woods would be on her mind, and in her heart, for a long time to come anyway.

Rachel and Mike parted ways near one end of the arena—he planned to hang out with Logan, who was on duty tonight as one of several firemen on hand with a truck from the DFD in case any of the collisions caused a car to catch fire.

And when Rachel saw Jenny and Sue Ann seated on the front row of the bleachers, she knew this was the chance she'd been waiting for ever since she and Mike had seen their baby on the ultrasound. Jenny looked happy at the moment, too, which could only help. Rachel slid happily into the vacant spot next to her, leaning playfully into her old friend. "Hey," she said, offering a smile.

Jenny looked up, smiling but clearly shocked by the greeting. "Hey," she said in return.

"Where's Mick?" Rachel asked.

"He's driving one of the Dew Drop Inn cars for Anita."

"Ah," Rachel replied, tipping her head back slightly. "I'd heard she was sponsoring two and driving one of them herself, but I didn't know who was driving the other." Though it made sense that it would be Mick, since Jenny's dad had been dating Anita Garey for the last few years.

"So . . ." Jenny began, still looking tentative, "you and I . . . does this mean we're okay again?"

"More than okay," Rachel told her. "If you'll forgive me for being so insensitive."

Jenny nodded, her pretty smile still in place. "I guess we both were. And I'm sorry for the things I said. You're one of my best friends and that was awful of me."

Rachel wasn't one for a lot of mushiness if it could be avoided, so she decided to move right on to what she'd really wanted to tell Jenny—or ask her. "Jen, I was wondering . . . if you'd be my baby's godmother."

Jenny blinked, visibly taken aback. "But . . . what about Tessa or Amy?"

"No one could ever love my baby as much as you would," Rachel told her. And that was the truth. She knew Tessa and Amy would be crazy about her kid, but for Jenny it would be something deeper. "And I want it to be you. If you . . . well, if you don't think it would . . . upset you. But if you'd rather not, that's okay. I just—"

"It wouldn't upset me," Jenny interrupted her. "I would love it! And I'd be honored."

Rachel let her own smile widen as a sense of relief came over her. "That's great," she told Jenny, giving her a hug. Then she rushed ahead, eager to tell Jenny more. "We saw the ultrasound and . . . it just changed everything. And I totally realize how lucky I am. I'm still scared to death, but now in a much happier way."

As the conversation went on, she could tell Jenny was truly happy for her now, too—and she promised to show her the pictures from the ultrasound soon, and before she knew it, they were talking about baby showers and bassinets.

The whole time, though, she couldn't help thinking that Jenny seemed a little too chipper under the circumstances— even given that they'd just made up. And when Rachel tentatively asked how she and Mick were doing, Jenny bit her lip, looked conspiratorially back and forth between Rachel and Sue Ann, then said, "Well, I wasn't going to tell anybody yet, because Mick doesn't even know, but . . ." And then she opened her purse and pulled out a pregnancy test stick— showing a positive result!

Rachel gasped as Sue Ann whispered, "Holy Mother of God."

And then the three of them broke into laughter and hugs— until Rachel spied Caroline Meeks and Dan Lindley, both having clearly noticed their behavior. "Be cool, be cool," Sue Ann said. "Act natural or we'll give ourselves away."

"If anyone asks," Rachel pointed out, "we can just say it's

about me—that I've finally come to my senses about motherhood." But she couldn't help giving Jenny another big smile. "Oh my God—I'm so happy for you, Jen!"

"Me too," she said, looking downright giddy now. After which Jenny pointed out that their babies would grow up together, and Rachel said they'd probably be best friends, and they both agreed how incredible it was all going to be.

"I don't mean to start being the insensitive one," Sue Ann cut in to say then, "but if you two are done jabbering, they're about to start announcing the lawn mower drivers, and I don't want to miss Adam's name."

Rachel scrunched up her nose in surprise. "Adam's in the lawn mower derby?"

"It was my idea," Sue Ann said defensively. "Since he runs a landscaping business, he has a whole fleet of old, worn-out mowers. He can do this every year and I won't have to worry about him driving a car in the *real* derby." Then she cringed slightly, as if she'd said something she shouldn't. "Though I'm sure it's perfectly safe. I'm sure Mick and Lucky and everyone else driving in it will be just fine."

"Well," Rachel said, shifting her attention back to Jenny, "I'm glad *we're* just fine again."

"**N**ow here come the contestants in the Youth Mower Division." The voice of the older man speaking through the microphone came with a distinct country twang. "Young Johnny Romo's drivin' into the arena, and would ya look at that there mower—you can bet his daddy painted that up for him real nice. Gonna be a shame to bang that one up."

Anna sat watching as the event progressed—six mowers that mainly drove in circles around each other, occasionally smashing into each other—and cheering on her nephew with the rest of the crowd. And when Johnny actually won, Tessa went wild.

The Adult Mower Division heat began after that, and Anna made sure to cheer for Sue Ann's boyfriend, Adam, too.

Unfortunately, his mower stalled after just a few minutes, and someone in the stands yelled out, "Don't be bringin' that one to mow my yard next week, Becker!" and everyone shared a laugh.

Following the mowers came a mini-car heat, including the owner of the Dew Drop Inn, Anita Garey, driving a pink Honda Civic. Anna loved Anita's confidence and the whole way she faced life, so she cheered the hardest of all for her.

Throughout it all, though, even as the air filled with dirt and smoke, and the roar of loud engines blared in her ears, she still kept thinking of Duke, wondering where he was right now, if he was packing up his few belongings, if she'd go home and find a quiet, empty house for good this time. Even if she tried her hardest to keep her focus on where she was and the fun friends she was with. *I'll still have all this when he's gone. It won't be the end of the world.* It would just feel that way.

Anita was the second runner-up in her heat, and as a forklift and a tow truck worked to clear the muddy arena of disabled cars that had been beaten into unrecognizable shapes, the announcer hawked concessions over the loud-speaker. "It's gonna take a little while to get these crushed cars outta the way, folks, so ya got lotsa time to come on down to the concession stand. Get your burger, get your fry, get your apple pie—we got it all for ya down here. And for those of ya wonderin'—yes indeed, Edna made the pie and she's down here sellin' it herself, so come say hi and getcha some pie."

But Anna couldn't think about pie, even pie as good as Edna's. Instead, it only made her think about blackberries and the afternoon she'd run into a wildman.

Duke walked around the cabin, packing up the few things he wanted to take with him. He'd accomplished what he'd set out to do, after all—he'd helped Anna finish the place so she could open her inn. And today he'd finished the mailbox and signs he'd been working on in secret and given them to her. So there was no more reason to stay.

Not that he knew where he was going.

Maybe he'd head west on 32 and find a motel for the night once he got closer to Cincinnati, then decide his next move tomorrow morning. Or he could head south down into Kentucky—but he immediately wiped that thought from his head as it would mean traveling the same road on which Denny had died. Maybe he'd just take some back roads, find someplace to camp tonight, and use the time to think more about where he might go.

The problem was . . . he didn't have a fucking clue. He'd traveled the nation from here to the West Coast on his bike, and he'd seen plenty, but he didn't particularly want to see more right now. He felt too tired for long-distance travel anyway. And he couldn't go home to Indiana—he'd been there, done that, and it had only made everything a lot worse. In fact, he guessed there wasn't really a home in Indiana to go to anymore; he had to face that and get past it. And though he had plenty of friends in the biker community, they were all local, and if he was gonna *stay* local . . . well, then why wouldn't he just stay where he already was?

And hell—why, again, was he leaving?

I'm in love with you. I love you like crazy.

He could still hear her saying those words. And in one way, they hadn't come as a surprise. He *knew* she loved him. He'd known it for a while now. But in another way . . . well, to hear her say it had turned him inside out. Never in his life had anything made him feel so good, so special, while scaring him to death at the same time. *That*, he supposed, was why he was leaving. Even before she'd *said* it, it had boiled down to that.

He didn't know how to love a woman. He didn't know how to be the man she needed. And he sure as hell didn't know how to do it when he felt like the town pariah and was already battling a host of demons.

He imagined what was going on right now down in the heart of Destiny at Creekside Park. The fact was, he'd been to a few demolition derbies in his day and he enjoyed them. He just hadn't thought he would enjoy it *now*—in light of the way Denny's accident had affected him. He hoped Anna got that, hoped she understood why he hadn't gone tonight. Besides, he didn't much see the point in facing the whole town—not to mention letting Mike Romo know about their relationship—if he was getting ready to pack up and leave anyway.

And so going ahead, leaving now, just seemed like the thing to do.

Still, it felt strange to get on his Harley, glance over his shoulder at the cabin and know it was the last time. And stranger still to ride out of the woods, catch sight of the sunny yellow house he'd put so much sweat into, and know he wouldn't see *it* again, either. Damn, it wasn't like him to get attached to places. What the hell was *that* about?

But he took one last look, then accelerated and put his focus on the road before him—the only way to leave was to just do it. *Just do it and don't look back.*

Funny thing was, he'd almost reached the center of town before he realized that was the direction he'd ridden in. But . . . maybe he wanted to take one last look at Destiny, too. And hell, he should've said goodbye to Lucky before he left, but he'd call him in a day or two from somewhere, explain why he hadn't—and try to make it sound like it made some sort of sense.

And as he rode on through town, past the square and the high school and the big church where he'd watched Mike Romo get married last year, he felt . . . empty. *Not much has changed in you this summer, has it?* He'd thought it had; he'd thought he'd come pretty damn far since he'd first retreated to Anna's woods. *But you're still running away. Still trying to hide.* Who the fuck had he become since that damn accident?

That's when he came up on Creekside Park on his left. He

could hear the revving of engines even over his own as he passed. And he suffered the strangest stirring inside him. *Your life is over there.* That's what he felt. It wasn't in the woods. It wasn't even at the house. It was . . . the people. Lucky and Tessa were over there. Lucky's boy was over there. All those good people he didn't quite fit in with but still liked—Amy, Logan, Mike—they were over there, too. And Anna. His Daisy in the Daisy Dukes was over there, as well.

And she was wishing he was with her.

The way he *should* be.

The park entrance lay dead ahead and he turned in.

What the hell are you doing?

But he knew.

I'm not running from any damn thing anymore, that's what. I'm taking my fucking life back. I'm gonna be the man I used to be. Or . . . a better man. A braver man. A man who might actually be worthy of her.

Anna really asked pretty damn little of him, and if she wanted him with her tonight—damn it, he should have gone. And he should be there to support Lucky. And if Mike had a problem with seeing Anna with him, hell—he'd deal with it, that simple.

And then it hit him anew. Anna Romo was in love with him. That was a goddamn miracle. And he'd been about to walk away from that? That seemed like the craziest thing of all.

I can do this. I can be the man she deserves. I can trust in this. I can trust in . . . her.

Looked like they were no longer taking admission fees, so Duke rode on in, getting closer to the derby arena, and closer to the sounds. He parked his bike at the end of a row of cars and started walking, but he approached slowly. Bleachers lined two sides of the rectangular arena—from which mud was flying as one car struggled in place, spinning its wheels. Must have lost the transmission.

He'd go find Anna in the crowd soon, but first . . . well,

he just wanted to watch for a minute, get used to being this close to the sounds of cars crashing into each other. He moved toward one end, where only a few spectators stood— and his heart beat faster.

He couldn't identify most of the drivers because they all wore helmets, but he recognized Lucky's motorcycle helmet in—holy crap—a ridiculous bright green monstrosity he'd have to give him hell about later. The car—which he now saw bore the name of Lucky's business—was located at the same end of the arena where Duke stood and, traveling in reverse, it slammed into the fender of an old-as-the-hills Impala that he guessed was sponsored by the Whippy Dip judging from the number of badly spray-painted ice cream cones all over the sides.

The collision was close enough to make Duke flinch, make his breath catch. *Shit. But it's all right. It's fine. It's just a demo derby. Calm the hell down.*

The derby went on, a dozen or so cars smashing and bashing into each other, and the fact was—it bothered him. It kept his nerves on edge, his chest tight. *But you'll deal with it. And you'll get past it.*

When an old station wagon complete with panel sides backed hard into a Chrysler at the opposite end, it couldn't pull away—their bumpers had gotten attached in the impact. Duke had to laugh watching the two cars pull each other back and forth trying to get apart, and soon a whistle sounded, signaling the drivers to stop, and a guy with a country twang announced, "We're gonna give the fellers who done been eliminated a chance to get outta their cars. Meanwhile, Larry, walk up there and see if ya can't get those two unhooked."

When the action started up again a minute later—the two cars free from each other thanks to Larry, who looked to be the closest thing they had to a referee—Duke decided to go find his girl. Examining the crowd, he thought he located Tessa and Amy—which would make the dark-haired beauty

with them his Daisy. Starting to walk that way, he grew
eager to see the expression on her beautiful face when she
realized he'd come.

But the gasp of the crowd halted his steps, and a glance
back revealed a heavy plume of gray smoke billowing up
from the engine of the Chrysler at the far end of the arena.
The fire truck sat at that end, too, and he watched as Logan
Whitaker, in full gear, along with two other firemen, ran out
to the Chrysler, fire hose in hand. Someone near him said it
was the car Jeremy Sheridan was driving.

And that was when a bright flash to his left drew his gaze
to Lucky's lime green car. Fire under the engine, coming out
the bottom. Where no one up in the stands or announcer's
box could see it yet. Shit.

Working on pure instinct, Duke leapt the concrete barrier
separating him from the field and ran toward the car, yelling,
"Lucky, fire! Get out of the car! Fire under the car! Get out!"

Lucky looked up at him, and though Duke couldn't see
his face through the helmet, he seemed to understand and
reached for his seat belt. Only—he wasn't getting out. Why
not? *Get the hell out, man.* But then Duke realized—Lucky's
seat belt was stuck and he was fighting with it.

Smoke poured from under the hood now—and then orange
flames shot from each side of the hood as well. As people
in the crowd began to react, Duke heard Tessa screaming,
"Lucky! *Lucky!*"

And he sensed the firemen on their way, but he wasn't waiting on them—he couldn't. Lucky continued to fight with the
belt as Duke ran to the car, yanked the door open, wrapped
both fists around the base of the seat belt, and ripped it clean
out of the dilapidated old floor. Then he grabbed Lucky by
the shirt and hauled him from the car so violently that they
both hit the ground a few feet away—at the very moment
flames came from under the dashboard to engulf the front
seat.

The two of them pushed themselves up and got farther

away—just as the firemen arrived to hose the Skylark down. It took only a minute for the flames to be extinguished, and though Duke was braced for an explosion, it never came.

The next thing he knew, Tessa and Anna were both leaping over the concrete partitions and barreling through the thick, damp dirt toward them. Lucky's helmet was off by the time Tessa arrived with tears streaming down her face, throwing her arms around him. And then he caught a glimpse of little Johnny running toward his dad, too.

Just as he realized Anna was running toward *him*.

For some reason, he'd thought it was Lucky she was coming for, but then he remembered—*she loves me*—about the time she connected with him so hard that they both fell down into the mud. "Duke, my God! Thank God you're okay! And thank God you got Lucky out! Thank God you were here!"

Then she pulled back just slightly, lying on top of him, to say, "You're here. You came." As if that part had just hit her.

He nodded. "Because I love you, too."

She blinked prettily, her eyes round with shock. "You what?"

"I love you, too, Daisy. I'd have been a fool to leave you. I mean . . . what the hell am I looking for when I've got everything a man could want right here?"

Anna just lay there, blinking, trying to understand what was happening. Smoke, fire, mud, danger, Duke, and her dreams coming true all in the space of about thirty seconds was a lot to grasp. "My God," she heard herself murmur—and then she kissed him, right there in front of all of Destiny.

Though whether anyone noticed or not, given all the hubbub, was difficult to say. The firemen were yelling to each other, and more people came barreling into the arena to make sure everyone was okay.

As she and Duke got to their feet, she caught sight of Mike pulling Lucky into a hard hug. A few seconds after that, Lucky was grabbing on to Duke's arm to say, "Second time, man. Second time." She knew he meant it was the second time Duke had saved his life.

"Just happy I was here, brother," Duke told him.

And Tessa, her face still tearstained but smiling, said, "Let's just hope the second time's the charm in this case." Then she smacked Lucky's chest, even as she hugged him with her other arm, adding, "And that you quit getting yourself into dangerous situations."

And that was when Anna heard Mike's voice. "You two? Together? Really?"

She turned to find him staring, of course, at her and Duke. And as much as she'd come to appreciate him, she was definitely in no mood for his meddling, so she pointed a menacing finger in his direction and said, "Listen, don't even think about having a problem with this because—"

"Stop," he said, holding out both hands in a calming gesture. "I'm shocked as hell, but I'm not mad."

Okay, things were getting downright surreal now. Her jaw dropped as she murmured, "Huh?"

"Shit, he just saved Lucky's life—again. He can freaking marry you if he wants to."

Oh God—did he really just say that? Heat climbed her cheeks as she rushed to reply. "Uh, you might be rushing things a little there. Don't scare him off."

But then Duke winked at her. "I'm not scared, Daisy," he told her. "I'm not scared of anything."

And Anna decided it was time to get back to business. Lucky was safe, Mike was uncharacteristically acceptant, all was well with her family—so she took the opportunity to press her hands to Duke's chest and push him gently back a few steps, away from the crowd and the burnt-out car.

She looked up into his eyes and said, "So . . . what does this mean? I mean, are you . . . really not leaving?"

"I'm really not. I . . . wanna be with you. I wanna take care of the house with you. I wanna make you happy, Anna. If I can."

Her heart felt like a flower blossoming in her chest, like it was stretching, opening wide. "You just did."

He gave her the sexy grin she loved—and she realized she even loved his scar now because it was part of the man she adored. "Well, I don't know about you, but . . . I've already had enough socializing for the night—I'll give that another shot another time. Right now, I just wanna go home and . . . push you in that swing, and eat your blackberry cobbler, and trip over your damn cat, and . . . make love to you under the stars."

Anna just blinked. Okay, who *was* this masked man? "I've never heard you call it making love before."

He skimmed his knuckles down her arm. "Guess you . . . soften my rough edges a little, Daisy."

"You've softened me, too . . . David. Let's go start on that list you just gave me. I want to do the last one first."

" . . . and now I want to live like everybody else."

Gaston Leroux, *The Phantom of the Opera*

Epilogue

*A*nna took her latest blackberry cobbler out of the oven, pleased with the purply, hot bubbles erupting through the top. It would be the perfect dessert for a crisp fall day.

As she lowered the dish to one of the gingham potholders from Amy, she heard a car door and knew they were here. Walking to the front door with Erik on her heels, she saw Duke helping Cathy out of the Mustang—then watched as the older woman beamed at the house. "Oh, it's wonderful, just wonderful," Anna heard her say.

She bent to scoop her loving kitty up into her arms, then stepped out onto the front porch. But Cathy didn't see her yet, because Duke was busy showing her some of the details. "I made this sign, and painted the mailbox." Then he pointed toward the maple tree, a bright, vibrant orange at the moment. "And that's your old swing hanging there," he said.

Cathy's eyes lit with delight and Anna could almost see the older woman reliving certain treasured memories. It still made her sad to think of all Cathy had lost, but she was thankful she'd taken her advice, and also pleased that she could bring a little more happiness into Cathy's life through their burgeoning friendship and now by having her over as her first official guest.

Next week, the Half Moon Bed & Breakfast would open for business. She'd taken out an ad in the *Destiny Gazette*, and her parents would be visiting from Florida, having insisted on being her first paying customers. Duke had suggested they throw a big picnic while her mom and dad were here, and he'd surprised her with beautiful new lawn furniture for the backyard—which he'd built himself in the garage!

Now Amy and Logan, as well as Jenny and Mick, had put in orders for lawn sets of their own. And Rachel had asked him if he could make a crib. And Amy had commissioned a hand-painted sign for the door of the bookshop. And though Duke had told Anna he'd like to start a business rehabbing old homes, after he'd hung up the phone with Mick yesterday, he'd turned to her and said, "But guess I'm a furniture-and-sign maker for now."

Anna loved seeing Duke eager to put his talents to use and couldn't believe he'd kept them hidden for so long. And though when he'd first decided to stay she'd thought he might want to look into buying back Gravediggers, or maybe open a new bar closer to home, he said, "Nah, Daisy—turns out a quieter life suits me just fine."

Anna and Duke no longer felt like outcasts in Destiny— but Anna knew the fact that they both once *had* been outsiders had played a big role in bringing them together, helping them to trust one another, even if Duke's trust in love had been a little slower in coming. "Men," she murmured to herself, smiling.

But ultimately, they'd both learned to be brave and had

taken steps to move on from the past. And they'd learned that sometimes you had to take chances and just . . . believe.

And Anna couldn't think of a nicer place for both her and Duke to have landed than the little town of Destiny—a place so welcoming that even two outcasts from opposite ends of the spectrum could find a home here at the very same time they were busy finding each other.

Just then, Erik meowed. And Anna looked down at him. "Don't worry, just because I'm not fawning over you every second, I still know you're there." Erik had just wanted to belong somewhere, too. He just hadn't been as cautious about expressing it as she and Duke had.

Duke had led Cathy over to the swing now, and Anna had to giggle to herself over how outgoing he'd become lately. They'd head inside eventually, she supposed, but for now, she was content to just bask in the splendor of the moment.

Walking down into the yard, the kitty still curled in her arms, leaves of orange and gold swirling about her feet, Anna stood back and looked at the grand old house that had brought her and Duke together, and thought about how the house was a lot like *them*: It had been in a sad state of disrepair but now had been made into something new.

Then, glancing around, it hit her. She peered down at the cat and said, "I don't quite know how it happened, Erik, but I have it all. An amazing home, a new business, dear friends, a loving family—and a hot, sexy man who adores me."

In response, the black cat meowed as if he were protesting, making her laugh.

"Yes," she told him. "I know. And I have a sweet and wonderful kitty who I love very much, too."

Anna's Blackberry Cobbler*

½ cup (1 stick) butter
2 cups self-rising flour
2 cups white sugar
2 cups milk
4–5 cups blackberries (enough to fill pan to brim)

Preheat oven to 350°F. Once oven temperature is reached, melt butter in a 9"x13" pan.

In a medium-sized bowl, stir together the flour, sugar, and milk (2% milk is best). The batter will be slightly lumpy. Pour mixture on top of melted butter in baking pan. Do not mix butter and batter together.

Drop blackberries into batter (if more crust is desired, add less blackberries). (Yes, the batter goes in first, then the berries. Don't worry, when you take the cobbler out of the oven, the berries will be on the bottom and the batter will have formed a crust on the top.)

Bake in preheated oven for one hour or until golden brown.

*Thank you to Amanda Beverly of Joseph-Beth Bookseller in Lexington, Kentucky, for allowing me to use her recipe.

Did you fall in love with Toni Blake's
Half Moon Hill?

Then you won't want to miss out on the
rest of her new series set in a beautiful
small town with a lot of heart—and
unforgettable people.

Keep reading and fall in love all over again.

Welcome to Destiny . . .

One Reckless Summer

Jenny Tolliver's been the good girl all her life, and now that her marriage has been busted up by her cheating ex, she's decided it's time to figure out what life holds in store for her next. She never dreamed the answer would be Mick Brody, Destiny's number one hell-raiser. He's exactly the kind of guy Jenny's always kept her distance from . . . but soon the good girl and the bad boy are caught in a raw heat that's out of control.

*F*or God's sake—he'd really just had sex with her. With Jenny Tolliver.

He'd known her name *then,* and he knew it now, too. He wasn't sure why, either time, he'd acted like it was such a mystery. He just hadn't wanted her to know, he guessed, that he'd even realized she existed. That he'd seen her, when they were teenagers, cheering at high school basketball games in that little red-and-white skirt. *Go Bulldogs—ruff, ruff, ruff!* That he'd seen her back then hanging out at the Whippy Dip, with guys who were much cleaner-cut than him but who were still probably talking her out of her panties on hot summer nights.

He blinked, still shocked to remember that *he'd* just talked her out of her panties. Well, not talked—no, not that at all. But the result was the same, and something he would never forget. The police chief's daughter, who had provided him with more than a few teenage fantasies, who he'd been certain would never look twice at him, had just done it with him in the woods.

The wonder of that—and the horror of it—made him drop to his knees on the forest floor and close his eyes. He ran his hands back through his hair, frustrated.

She couldn't possibly understand what was at stake here, why what he'd just done could possibly be the biggest mistake of his life—and he'd already made more than his fair share. And—realistically—she probably couldn't be trusted not to tell people she'd seen him, not to tell her father. Mick emitted a huge groan of defeat at the very thought.

Then again, maybe she *wouldn't* tell her dad. To tell him the whole story would mean admitting to having sex with Mick without having hardly exchanged a word. And why that had happened—why she had let it—he'd never know.

He'd never consciously made the decision to start kissing her, touching her—it had just happened when she'd tried to get past him. It hadn't resulted from thought—but mere instinct.

He truly hadn't recognized her at first, but once he'd figured out who she was, something about her had brought out the animal inside him. And there'd been moments when he'd been sure she'd stop him, and other moments when he'd been much more sure she wouldn't—but he still couldn't believe the latter had turned out to be true.

Although even if she didn't tell her dad, she'd surely tell *someone*. She just didn't have any reason not to.

And then word would get around. And *then* her father would find out. And then everything Mick was trying to do here would fall apart. And he might go to prison, for all he knew—something he should have thought about before he'd agreed to this, but he hadn't. He might go to prison, and that was only *one* lousy aspect of being found here.

I shouldn't have let myself be talked into this. I should be at home in Cincinnati, having a beer at Skully's on the corner, or watching a little TV before bed.

But it was too late for the shoulda-coulda-woulda thing.

He supposed he should get back to the house. He'd only intended to take a short walk, get some air, clear his head from the troubles between those walls. And then he'd seen someone on the property and his body had gone on red alert—he'd closed the short distance between them without even thinking about consequences, his only thought that whoever it was couldn't be here. And the truth was, he hadn't been overreacting. The last thing he needed was a woman trotting around the woods with a telescope that could just as easily be pointed in a window as at the sky.

Which was when he realized the big clear plastic bag she'd been carrying lay right next to him on the ground—she'd been so pissed at him that she'd walked off without it.

And that gave him an idea.

Since he didn't think Jenny Tolliver could be trusted to keep his presence a secret . . . well, it might be wise to pay her a visit, remind her that he was deadly serious about the promise she'd made.

And in the meantime, maybe he'd sleep worse than usual in that hot little house tonight, because he had brand new problems to worry about.

Or . . . maybe he'd sleep better, because he'd be taking even hotter memories back inside with him.

Sugar Creek

Rachel Farris returned to her childhood home with one mission in mind: get Mike Romo, the local police officer, out of her family's apple orchard business and out of their lives. However, neither the hunky cop nor the sexy prodigal hometown girl can anticipate the electricity that heats things up whenever they're together.

Rachel sighed audibly. He was back to being his jerky self, that fast. "No, as a matter of fact, I'm *not* happy. I'm freaking *miserable*, actually."

"Well, it's your own damn fault," he complained.

And that was *it*. She stared boldly up into those dark brown eyes of his, thoroughly disgusted. She'd had it with his rude behavior. She'd had it with . . . everything. "Look, I didn't want to come here tonight. I did it as a favor for a friend. I don't even want to be in this stupid town, but here I am, trying to help out my grandma. And now I've got *you*, giving me ridiculously expensive tickets and acting like I'm a terrible person every time I see you. Well, I'm not that terrible, Romo. So why don't you just take your attitude and your blame and your self-righteousness and shove it up your—"

"Stop!" he said then, reaching up, closing his hands tight on her upper arms. "Be quiet! Be quiet."

At first, she thought maybe he'd heard something outside and wanted to listen. But that's when she realized he was staring at her lips. And that somewhere during her diatribe his eyes had drifted half shut, while his mouth now fell slightly open. He still had that light, stubbly beard going, and being right next to him like this, she could smell that musky scent again—in fact, it was permeating her senses. He stood so close, just a few inches away. How had she not noticed that until now?

As she'd spoken, her adrenaline had risen, and peering up at him, she heard herself breathing—and *he* suddenly seemed to be breathing pretty heavily, too.

"Maybe we should just do this, get it over with, get it out of our systems," he said.

She blinked up at him. "Do what?"

And then he kissed her—hard.

His mouth sank over hers with such power that she had to lean into him just to keep from collapsing.

"Oh. That," she breathed when the kiss ended.

Then she instinctively kissed him again, pressing her hands to his chest. She was a little shocked—by his actions, by hers—but mostly just . . . pleasured.

"Yeah. That," he said, voice ragged with passion.

After which their mouths came back together, kissing feverishly, and Rachel followed the urge to ease back against his sturdy body, now feeling his kiss . . . everywhere.

Whisper Falls

After a failed big-city career, Tessa Sheridan has returned to Destiny to pick up the pieces. The last thing she expected was to fall for the biker next door! They say that former teen rebel Lucky Romo has a dark, secret past—that he's trouble with a capital T. But when Lucky invites her into his world, she can't ignore the sparks igniting between them.

*H*oly crap.

She'd been right. This was Lucky Romo! In the flesh! It was a miracle!

Because his family hadn't heard from him in so long they'd actually feared he was dead. Which was because— uh-oh, she just remembered—they'd also gotten word at some point that he'd joined an outlaw biker gang out west.

Oh boy. Bikers were one thing—*outlaw* bikers were another. Did she have some vile and dangerous criminal helping her look for Amy's cat? Should she just forget Mr. Knightley and run? Maybe the sense of danger that hung around her neighbor was what had kept her from giving him her name. And if she *didn't* run, should she tell him she knew who he was?

Before she could think further, the door on the white house opened and Lucky Romo came walking back out—carrying a small bowl of milk in one large hand. Huh.

He said nothing as he rejoined her in the yard, so she cleverly remarked, "Milk." Then cringed. *Stop with the brilliant comments already!* Lucky Romo lowered the dish to the grass halfway between Tessa and the woods, then stepped back beside her. And that's when she realized what Mr. K. had wanted when he'd been meowing at her. Amy gave him a saucer of milk every night with dinner—and Tessa had forgotten. Stubborn, spoiled cat.

"Is that him?" Lucky asked.

Tessa's heart rose to her throat when she followed his pointing finger toward the edge of the yard, where the forest met the lawn—Mr. Knightley crouched there in the taller grass, peering at the milk as if it were prey. "Uh-huh," she whispered.

Both of them stayed quiet as Knightley slowly, silently inched toward the milk, his movements implying he thought he was being very sneaky about the whole thing. Once he started lapping at it, Tessa gingerly moved in to kneel beside him. He didn't flinch when she reached to stroke his fur, too caught up in the milk, and she sighed, "Thank God," giving the spotted cat an affectionate squeeze. For the first time since Knightley's escape, Tessa felt like she could breathe again. She hadn't lost Amy's cat. Life would go on.

But then she remembered the weirder part: Lucky Romo, of all people in the world, had helped her find him. She still couldn't fathom that this big, tough guy was him. He'd left town at eighteen, which was—she did the math—sixteen years ago now. But this *had* to be him. The whole motorcycle thing fit. As did the name on the back of his shirt. Sure, it *could* be somebody else's business, but he looked so much like Mike with that thick, dark hair and olive complexion.

So this was him. Lucky Romo. Home at last.

But . . . if he wasn't here to reconcile with his family, why was he in Destiny?

The second Mr. Knightley reached the bottom of the shallow bowl, Tessa anchored one arm snugly around him and pushed to her feet. "Thanks," she said. Although peering back up into that tough-guy face and those captivating eyes made her a little dizzy. She'd never known a guy with muscles like this. With long hair. With so many tattoos.

"No problem." He was still Mr. Unemotional, though, his voice flat and detached.

"You saved my life," she felt the need to add.

He gave his head a pointed tilt. "I wouldn't go *that* far."

His words made her remember the whole outlaw rumor. Maybe an outlaw biker dude took that kind of statement a lot more literally than she did. And did this mean she should be scared? She'd been a *little* scared even *before* remembering that part.

And yet . . . even as her muscles stayed tensed, she felt a response to him in other places, too. In her breasts. Between her thighs. Good Lord—what was *that* about? Or—wait. Maybe it was all just nerves, her whole body getting into the act because he was so freaking intimidating. Hopefully. She couldn't tell.

So she dropped her gaze briefly and bit her lip, her heart still pounding too hard, before forcing her eyes back to his one last time. "Well, I better get him into the house before he tries to make another break for it."

Mr. Unresponsive didn't reply, so with cat in hand, she turned to go.

That's when he said, "See ya later . . . hot stuff."

The last words halted Tessa in place. What had he just called her? Looking over her shoulder, she raised her gaze back to his—to find another tiny hint of amusement there as he said, "Your shirt."

Glancing down, Tessa wanted to die. She'd completely forgotten she wore a snug white tank with the words *Hot*

Stuff written in script across it, actually half of a pajama set Rachel had given her for her birthday; the matching pants had little smiling hot peppers all over them. But the worst part was—she wasn't wearing a bra, a fact that was scandalously apparent. She even caught a hint of color through the thin cotton. Dear God in heaven.

Holly Lane

A weekend in a cabin near Destiny seems like the perfect Christmas gift to Sue Ann Simpkins—until her ex's best friend, Adam Becker, shows up at the door, claiming the cabin is his! But when a sudden snowstorm strands them together in very close quarters, Adam realizes that what he really wants for Christmas is a second chance at love. Now all he has to do is convince Sue Ann . . .

"What, um, are we doing?" she whispered in the still air.

"I don't know," he whispered back, sounding earnest and yet . . . maybe a little needful.

And then she lifted her gaze to his and their eyes met and she had the feeling she was looking at him like she wanted him to kiss her.

And she must have been right about that, too, because that was when he leaned slowly, tentatively forward and brushed his lips ever-so-gently across hers. She let out a little gasp as the pleasure it delivered cascaded through her deprived body. Oh boy. Oh wow. Oh Lord.

When their eyes met again, she noticed how blue his sparkled in the firelight and that her chest now heaved a little.

And she said, dumbly, "I have a plate in my hand." Because it seemed like it was going to be hard to kiss him that way.

But he never acted like it was dumb at all—instead he just rushed to take the plate and set it on the coffee table with his—and then he took her back into his arms, pulled her close enough that there was no mistaking the hard bulge in his pants, and lowered his mouth to hers in the most power-ful kiss she'd ever received.

Whoa.

She wasn't usually thankful for blizzards, but suddenly, all she could think was—let it snow!

If that last kiss had been filled with power, the ones that followed were stunningly . . . smooth, controlled, and skilled. Wow. Adam definitely knew how to kiss a woman. As his hands skimmed her curves—one roaming her back, the other drifting seductively up her side toward her breast—it all left her breathless, the pleasures at once simple yet pro-found. The lack of urgency in his kisses combined with the confident way he delivered them gave the impression that he wasn't racing toward some better end—but that he was completely and wholly satisfied by the moment, that he was enjoying the passion passing between them just as much as she was.

She found herself shocked by how easy it was to stand there and kiss him, how her body seemed to take over, instantly comfortable moving against his. Since that's what was happening now, very naturally—her breasts shifted sensually against his chest, her fingers twined in his thick, mussed hair. His hands had eased onto her ass now, which, of course, meant that in front she was grinding against him where he was hard and thick—and wow, talk about being breathless.

This should be more awkward. But instead, it was just . . . pleasure, plain and simple.

Willow Springs

Despite being the town matchmaker, Amy Bright is desperately shy when it comes to her own love life—and helpless when it comes to firefighter Logan Whitaker, with whom she's head-over-heels in love. One smoking-hot kiss could change everything for them . . . but will it ruin a one-of-a-kind friendship, or show Logan and Amy that they've already found everything they need, right here in Destiny?

Finally, after a long moment, she said something so honest to Tessa that it was the first time she'd ever realized how true it was. "I used to think that. But I'm just not sure I believe it anymore. I'm not sure I'm meant to have that kind of happiness."

Tessa's face fell as she instantly knelt next to Amy's chair. "Of course you are, Ames. Everyone is. I went through a long drought myself if you recall, and felt pretty undateable. But then Lucky came along and all that changed in the blink of an eye." Then she shook her head, obviously befuddled by Amy's attitude. "What on earth brought this on?"

Amy tried to swallow back all the emotion that rushed

through her in response to the question even as she heard herself admit, "Something happened."

"Something happened?" Tessa asked.

"With Logan," Amy told her.

Tessa's eyebrows shot up as she moved smoothly into the overstuffed chair across from Amy's and leaned forward, her gaze wide. "Start talking."

So Amy took a deep breath, and then she talked. She told Tessa the whole story of how Logan had kissed her but then afterward acted like she had the plague or something. Only Tessa didn't seem to hear the part about the plague. Instead, she seemed . . . unaccountably overjoyed. "Oh my God, this is so great! I mean, could it be any greater?"

Now it was Amy who blinked her astonishment. "Um, yes. Yes, it could be."

"Because you and Logan know each other so well! You've already got all of that behind you! You know each other's families and backgrounds, you know who the other is deep inside, you know the kind of life each other has lived and wants to live in the future. I mean, Lucky and I had problems with some of that stuff—and it counts for a lot. All you and Logan have to do is get past the awkward friends-to-lovers transition and then you'll have it made."

Amy just stared at her friend, feeling like they'd done a role reversal. It was usually Amy who saw everyone's relationships through rose-colored glasses, refusing to acknowledge the difficult parts. But now she was viewing things from the other side. "Except for one fairly important thing," she told Tessa. "He doesn't want to go from friends to lovers. Because he doesn't see me as a lover—only as a friend."

"But he didn't kiss you like a friend, right?"

"No." He'd kissed her like . . . like she'd always dreamed of being kissed. "But he also said he must have thought I was someone else. I think he sees me as . . . more of a sister."

At this, however, Tessa just made a face. "I think he said that just to cover up because it caught him off guard. And

I'm sure you're exaggerating the part about him acting like you had the plague." Then she gave her head an inquisitive tilt. "But before we go any further, let's back up a minute and answer the most important question here. How do *you* feel about *him?*"

Amy expelled a sigh and let everything she'd thought and felt since that kiss play back through her head. Reliving it quickly made her heart beat too hard and her palms sweaty. Her skin got hotter, too, and she soon noticed that, at the moment, it wasn't particularly easy to breathe. And she still suffered that same mix of happy-sad-confused that had been making her feel a little crazy ever since the kiss. And she realized that even though she knew he didn't want her, would surely *never* want her, and that this whole thing was very likely going to ruin their lifelong friendship, she still felt weirdly happy and giddy inside when she pictured his handsome face in her mind.

And then, *then,* she had no choice but to face the truth, the truth which she suddenly understood had probably been festering inside her for a while now but she'd just been too in denial to admit to herself. It seemed useless to *keep on* denying it now, though, so she finally said to Tessa, "I think I'm in love with him."